$\mathcal{K}$ell opened the door for her, then stepped aside to allow her to enter. . . .

He'd watched Raven during the entire evening as she'd danced and charmed her way through her critical crowd of judges. She was all laughter and wit and vivacious beauty, demonstrating how she'd drawn half the population of London under her spell during her Season.

He himself had felt an unreasonable spark of jealousy.

She was a temptress, pulsing with life and sensuality.

And she was now his wife. . . .

Kell felt every muscle in his body tighten at her disturbing nearness, his instinct for danger warring with the powerful need to take her in his arms. He knew better than to touch her, and yet . . . the impulse was unconquerable. Gently grasping her shoulders, he drew her against him. . . .

By Nicole Jordan
Published by Ivy Books:

THE SEDUCTION
THE PASSION
DESIRE
ECSTASY

ECSTASY

NICOLE JORDAN

IVY BOOKS • NEW YORK

This book contains an excerpt from the forthcoming paperback edition of *Pleasure* by Nicole Jordan. This excerpt has been set for this edition only and may not reflect the final content of the forthcoming edition.

An Ivy Book
Published by The Ballantine Publishing Group
Copyright © 2002 by Anne Bushyhead
Excerpt from *Pleasure* by Nicole Jordan copyright © 2002 by Anne Bushyhead

All rights reserved under International and Pan-American Copyright Conventions. Published in the United States by The Ballantine Publishing Group, a division of Random House, Inc., New York, and simultaneously in Canada by Random House of Canada Limited, Toronto.

Ivy Books and colophon are trademarks of Random House, Inc.

www.ballantinebooks.com

ISBN 0-8041-1979-1

Manufactured in the United States of America

First Mass Market Edition: October 2002

10 9 8 7 6 5 4 3 2 1

To my most favorite bookseller ever—
Gail Stordahl-Brown,
with thanks

Chapter
One

He rose naked from the surf, his wet, sleekly muscled body glistening in the Caribbean sun. Framed against the brilliant turquoise sea, he looked like some pagan god. Yet he was no god. He was the pirate who had stolen her virtue and then her heart.

Heat and vitality and danger throbbed from him as he stood spread-legged on the crystalline white beach, commander of all he surveyed. His engorged male flesh clearly proclaimed his arousal and made her breath falter.

As if he heard her soft gasp, his dark gaze riveted on her. She felt ravished each time he looked at her, even though she couldn't make out his features. She could never see his face, only his dark eyes that were intense and burning.

He came to her then, purpose defined in every lithe stride. The sand was warm at her back as he bore her down, his hungry mouth hot as it claimed hers.

His kiss was ravaging, not in force but in effect; his touch dangerously, wildly sensual as his hands roamed over her at will.

He drank of her mouth, then shifted his caresses lower,

1

gentle and ruthless at once. Pressing her head back, he kissed the arch of her throat, her collarbone, her naked breasts. . . . His lips felt hotter than the sun on her bare skin, the blistering heat searing her flesh. He captured a nipple and suckled hard, shooting arrows of pleasure downward to her moist, feminine center.

She whimpered and parted her legs for him, sighing as he nestled his swollen sex against her softness, the throbbing ache between her thighs soothed and aroused at once.

"Please . . ." she pleaded.

Understanding her urgent need, he slid himself relentlessly within her, his huge shaft filling her, making her want to weep with ecstasy.

But then he went still, denying her the release she craved. The hot darkness of his gaze pinned her as surely as his pulsing masculine flesh impaled her.

"How can you wed him?" he demanded roughly. "How can you think to give yourself to him?"

"I must. I have no choice. I swore a solemn promise."

His intense gaze burned into hers. "Your duke is cold, passionless. He cannot make you feel what I do. He cannot make your blood run hot as I can."

She turned her head aside, knowing all he said was true. She felt a sense of desperation at the thought of her impending marriage. She wanted to forget . . . and yet her pirate would not allow her.

His hand clenched in her hair, his teeth bared in savage insistence. "You belong to me, only to me. You are mine, do you heed me? And I am yours. You created me."

His possessiveness thrilled and excited her. "Yes," she said simply.

He withdrew his slick shaft and sank forcefully into her

again, thrusting completely home. "When you go to him, I will be the one you remember. My touch, my taste, my hard flesh driving deep inside you, making you cry out with need."

"Yes. Yes . . . only you."

She pulled his mouth down to hers, needing to taste him, feel him. . . .

The fierce intimacy of his body locked into hers and he began to move again, taking her, claiming her. He wasn't tender, but she wanted no tenderness. Instead she lifted her hips to meet his deep thrusts, answering him with all the vigor in her trembling form.

"More," he urged hoarsely against her mouth. "Give me more. Surrender . . ."

Climax exploded through her in intense, rigid shudders again and again and again before at last he found his own release. Eventually he collapsed upon her, his gasping breath mingling with hers, their fierce hunger momentarily sated.

She lay back, replete, as silken waves came to lap at her, cooling her overheated skin and the blaze of passion between them. . . .

Slowly Raven Kendrick roused from fantasy to awareness, recognizing her bedchamber. The chill light of early morning filtered through the damask curtains as she lay in bed, her body still throbbing with her powerful climax and the memory of her pirate. He was a wild, sweet fire in her blood . . . and he was merely illusion.

With a sigh of unfulfilled longing, Raven rolled over and drew a pillow to her still-tingling breasts. He was all she would ever have of true passion.

Her lover existed only in her imagination, although

sometimes he seemed as real to her as any flesh and blood man. He had no identity, no past other than the one she had attributed to him. He'd come ashore in her dreams one bright Caribbean morning to plunder her body and capture her heart. . . .

Her eyes closed on the memory of their most recent interlude. She was still hot and moist between her legs from his make-believe claiming, but in real life she had never felt the ecstasy of a man's flesh filling her, burning deep inside her.

She could imagine, though. Indeed, she knew things no virgin should ever know. The rare, erotic book her mother had left behind at her death, *A Passion of the Heart,* had been given to Elizabeth Kendrick by the man she'd desperately loved and was forced to relinquish—a parting gift to keep his memory alive.

Penned by an anonymous Frenchwoman, the journal was a true, tragic tale of love and filled with exquisite details of carnal desire. It had provided solace to Raven's mother for years, for although it mirrored her pain, the vividly told story let her relive her own lost passion.

Yet it was a scandalous tome for any young lady of virtue to possess.

Raven frowned defiantly. Perhaps she *was* wicked to foster such vivid illusions of her pirate, but in her fantasies she could be as unconventional and free as she chose. She could satisfy the deep restlessness inside her, indulge her forbidden hunger without the dire consequences of social ruin. Most vitally, she could give herself completely to a lover without fear of losing her heart and soul, the way her mother once had.

Involuntarily Raven clenched her fists as the familiar dread pulsed through her. She would never give her heart to a *real* man. She'd seen how love had destroyed her mother, made her a slave to dimming memory. For years her mother had sobbed into her pillow each night, lamenting the love she'd lost. By day she had pored over her precious journal, memorizing each poignant line.

Reaching into the bedside table drawer, Raven withdrew the jewel-encrusted book, her eyes blurring as she remembered. It had grieved her endlessly to see her mother waste her life away, wishing even on her deathbed for a man she could never have.

The loss of her mother had left Raven achingly bereft yet filled with determination. *She* would never make the same mistake her mother had made, falling victim to a hopeless love. No man would ever own her soul. She alone controlled the shape of her destiny. She might have resolved to marry, but love would form no part of the equation.

A rap on her bedchamber door brought Raven out of her dark reverie. Quickly returning the journal to the drawer, she bid admission, and her personal maid entered, carrying a tray.

"Morning, miss," Nan said in unmistakably excited tones. "I've brought you a fine breakfast since you'll need proper sustenance. 'Twill be many hours before the wedding feast."

Inexplicably Raven's heart sank at the reminder. Her wedding day at last was here.

She sat up slowly in bed and allowed Nan to set the

tray on her lap, even though she suddenly had no appetite.

The maid poured her a cup of chocolate, talking all the while. "Just think, Miss Raven! You'll soon be a *duchess*. 'Tis just like a fairy tale." Nan sighed, her expression filled with reverence before she caught herself. "Beg pardon, miss. I shouldn't let my tongue run away like that. But I've never known a real duchess before."

Raven summoned a smile she didn't feel. "That's quite all right, Nan. I am a bit in awe myself."

Turning to the hearth, the maid built up the dwindling fire to ward off the November chill, then bobbed a curtsy. "Your bathwater is heating, Miss Raven. If you please, I'll return in half an hour to help you bathe and dress."

"Yes, thank you, Nan."

When the servant had left the room, Raven dutifully picked up her fork but set it down again as her stomach recoiled. In a few short hours she would wed the man she had chosen, a prominent nobleman who commanded the respect of the highest echelons of the ton. She had eagerly anticipated this day for months— so why did she now feel as if she were somehow going to her execution?

Bridal nerves. Her anxiety could be attributed merely to that. Every bride had misgivings on her wedding day.

She shook her head, determined to quell the knots in her stomach. It was absurd to be entertaining doubts at this late date about the plan she'd set for her future. Her marriage to the Duke of Halford would not only be the fulfillment of her mother's most fervent wish for her—securing her rightful position among the nobility—but it meant she would no longer be an outsider.

She would at last *belong* somewhere.

As a duchess, she would be accepted by the cream of society . . . the society her mother had been denied after being banished to the West Indies more than twenty years ago by an irate father.

Raven raised her cup of chocolate to her lips, trying to ignore her qualms. Her future husband, the Duke of Halford, might be a proud, stiff-necked aristocrat more than twice her age—one, moreover, who'd had the misfortune to bury two young wives after accidental tragedies. But as his wife, she would no longer be compelled to fight the despairing feelings of aloneness that had haunted her for much of her life.

She was fortunate to have attracted Halford, considering the disadvantages she faced. Although a British citizen, she'd been born in the West Indies and had only come to England for the first time this past spring, a year after her mother's death. Forcibly swallowing her reluctance, she'd reconciled with her estranged family—her ailing viscount grandfather and her dragon of a great-aunt, who had sponsored her London season as a debutante.

Since then, Raven had grown to realize how very much acceptance meant to her, how deeply she cherished the feeling of belonging.

To her relief and gratitude, her first Season had been a triumph. She was sought after by countless admirers and received a half dozen estimable proposals of marriage, along with several unsuitable ones. She'd fooled even the highest sticklers with her efforts at demure deportment. But with a hidden scandal in her past, she could give the ton no reason to challenge her entrée into its select ranks, no matter how much she might like to thumb her nose in their faces. Not if she wanted to become one of them.

Her unconventionality was a definite drawback, Raven was keenly aware. Her upbringing on the Caribbean isle of Montserrat had afforded her a rare freedom, and she'd spent her hoydenish childhood swimming in secluded coves and playing pirate and riding to the wind. Even her name was unorthodox; she'd been named for the color of her hair, a throwback to one of her real father's Spanish ancestors.

But once in England, she had striven to restrain her natural high spirits, repressing any sign of passion in favor of conformity, enduring the stifling rules of proper conduct because she was fiercely determined to be accepted.

One of her few concessions to restlessness was her early morning gallops in the park. And when she craved passion, she turned to her fantasies and her imaginary pirate lover. Though he was only an illusion—one that sometimes left her aching with an unfulfilled longing— she was certain her pirate could satisfy her deepest hungers far more profoundly than her real-life duke ever could or would.

Raven shivered, suddenly feeling the chill of the winter morning. Sternly repressing her apprehension, she set aside her tray and rose from the bed. Were this any other day, she would be riding at this very moment, but she had a wedding to prepare for.

She had just drawn on a woolen wrapper when another knock sounded on her door. To her vast surprise, her great-aunt entered.

Catherine, Lady Dalrymple, was an imposing figure—tall and elegant with handsome features and silver hair that lent her a majestic air.

"Is something amiss?" Raven asked with a frown. Never once in all the months of living with her great-aunt had she been visited like this. Nor did her elderly relative normally rise this early.

Aunt Catherine managed a stiff smile. "Nothing is amiss. I merely brought you a wedding gift." She held out a small satinwood box. "These belonged to your mother. I suspect Elizabeth would wish you to have them."

Raven felt her heart wrench at the mention of her mother. Opening the box with curiosity, she gasped to find a stunning strand of pearls and a pair of pearl-drop earrings, not large but with a lustrous sheen that suggested great value.

Raven gave her great-aunt a questioning glance, wondering what had caused this show of generosity. Lady Dalrymple usually treated her with a frosty reserve bordering on dislike.

"I harbored grave doubts," her aunt answered her unspoken query, "that this day would ever come. But now that your nuptials actually are at hand, I think you are entitled to have these."

"They are beautiful," Raven murmured.

"Elizabeth refused to take them with her when she left," Aunt Catherine observed with obvious disapproval. "Her defiance was imprudent, considering that she could have sold these for a pretty price. But I presumed you would wish to wear them at your wedding."

Surprised but grateful for her aunt's gift, Raven tempered her response. "Yes, thank you. I would like very much to wear them."

Without speaking, Aunt Catherine turned to take her leave, but then turned back, arching one elegant eyebrow. "I confess you have pleasantly surprised me, Raven. I never imagined you would make such an advantageous marriage."

"Why not?" Raven couldn't help asking. "Because you didn't believe I should aim so high, given the illegitimacy of my origins?"

"Few people know the secret of your origins, thank heavens. No, frankly, I didn't believe you would have the good sense to accept Halford for your husband. You had so many suitors. . . . I feared you might choose someone unacceptable just to spite us."

She had indeed had numerous suitors, Raven reflected. In fact, one suitor in particular had hounded her relentlessly even after her betrothal to Halford was announced, nearly embroiling her in scandal. Thankfully her aunt knew nothing of that near disaster.

"I would never have behaved so rashly, Aunt—despite your estimation of me."

"Perhaps not," her aunt replied. "Still, I doubted your betrothal to Halford would last all these months, what with the vast disparity between you." Catherine's mouth twisted in the flicker of a smile. "Even I consider his grace a stuffed shirt. In disposition at least, he doesn't appear at all to be the right match for you."

"He isn't all that bad," Raven said in his defense.

"Halford is reserved and very proper, certainly, but beneath the trappings of his rank, he is actually a very kind man."

"Well, I am glad you don't harbor foolish notions like marrying for love. Love does not ensure happiness, as your mother discovered to her everlasting grief."

Raven felt herself stiffen. "Yes, quite the contrary. Love can bring great misery. I learned that lesson quite well, Aunt Catherine."

"You obviously have more sense than your mother had."

Raven lowered her gaze to hide her anger, deploring this conversation. She had no wish to discuss her mother or to dredge up painful memories.

The elderly lady pursed her lips together. "At least now you will have the future Elizabeth wished for you. A place in society that her folly denied her."

Stung beyond bearing, Raven lifted her chin and looked piercingly at her aunt. "A place she was *denied* when her family cast her out, you mean," she retorted, unable to keep the bitterness from her tone.

Catherine frowned. "We had no choice but to compel Elizabeth to marry. She was facing total ruin. Her behavior was scandalous in the extreme—becoming obsessed with a married man and letting him get her with child."

Raven bristled to hear her mother's sins catalogued so scornfully. "Grandfather did not have to disown her and send her across an ocean!"

"Perhaps not." Catherine's expression grew even frostier. "But Jervis made the correct decision. No one could expect him to tolerate the shame of his daughter bearing a child out of wedlock."

"So he forced her to wed a man she disliked and then banished her from sight?"

"I assure you, Elizabeth understood that marriage was her only salvation. Wedding Kendrick rescued her from disgrace and saved you from being born a bastard!"

Raven winced at the familiar guilt that curled inside her. She well understood the sacrifice her mother had made for her. And that she had caused her mother's downfall by her very existence. But the necessity of the marriage didn't excuse her grandfather or her aunt for being so heartless and unforgiving.

"If my mother had not been forced to live among strangers," Raven said tightly, "if she had been surrounded by family and friends and her familiar life, perhaps she might have been able to overcome her hopeless passion. As it was, she pined her life away, yearning for a love she could never have."

"She had no one to blame but herself for her weakness. And she swiftly came to regret her grievous error in judgment."

"Forgive me if I sound disrespectful, Aunt," Raven replied with sarcasm, "but how could you possibly know?"

"Because she told me so in her letters. Elizabeth wrote to me upon occasion over the years."

Raven found herself staring. "I never realized Mama wrote to you."

"She did indeed." Catherine's gray eyes remained cold. "Her later letters clearly showed she had come to her senses. She bitterly regretted her fall from grace and losing the rank and privilege to which she was raised. She missed the life she could have had and thought you deserved. . . . Which is why she was so determined you should have a different fate."

That much was certainly true, Raven reflected somberly. Her mother had been nearly obsessive about rectifying her mistake. Elizabeth had spent countless hours—every afternoon over tea, in fact—trying to instill the graces of a lady in her daughter so that Raven might eventually take her rightful position in English society. On her very deathbed, she had made Raven swear to marry into the nobility. . . .

"Do you still have any of Mama's letters?" Raven asked, desirous of changing the subject.

"No. I didn't keep them. But I'm certain she would be relieved to know you had landed a duke for your husband."

"She would be relieved," Raven corrected, "to know I needn't worry about being labeled a bastard. She knew how cruel the ton could be, and she wanted me to be protected by rank and wealth, should my past ever be discovered. A duchess won't be as vulnerable to such slights as a mere Miss Kendrick."

"Well, I for one am *relieved* you have done nothing to shame your family, as she did."

Raven curled her hands into fists, striving for control. "If you were so concerned that I would shame you, Aunt, I wonder that you gave me a home and sponsored my Season."

"Because I was determined to keep up appearances, of course. And because your grandfather would hear of nothing else." Catherine gave an elegant sniff. "In my opinion, Jervis has behaved rather foolishly, fawning over you as if you were his prodigal daughter. But when Elizabeth died, he formed the absurd notion that he had been too harsh—"

"Because he *had* been too harsh," Raven interrupted. Her grandfather, Jervis Frome, Viscount Luttrell, had experienced a change of heart upon learning of his daughter's death, regretting never having reconciled. When his health began to fail, he'd invited Raven to England, desirous of meeting his only grandchild and of making amends for his past intransigence and his estrangement from Elizabeth all these years.

Apparently Aunt Catherine had said her piece, though, for she turned away, every inch the imperious dame. "Enough dallying. You had best make haste. It won't do to keep the illustrious duke waiting at the altar."

"No," Raven forced herself to say coolly. "As one of the chief arbiters of society, Aunt, you should know."

When she was alone, Raven glanced down blindly at the pearls, still feeling the sting of her aunt's scorn. Being scorned was a familiar experience to her.

Elizabeth had infuriated her haughty family, imperiling their social standing by developing a passionate love for a married American shipping magnate and conceiving a child out of wedlock. Disaster had been averted only by marrying her off to an impoverished neighbor's younger son—one who held her in complete contempt, and her bastard daughter as well.

Raven cringed inwardly as she remembered the man who was presumed by the world to be her father, Ian Kendrick. For twenty years now, she had been Miss Kendrick in public, but privately he had never accepted her as his child. Never let her forget that she was in truth a bastard.

He had deliberately made her feel tarnished, unworthy . . . somehow to blame for both her mother's weakness and his own misery. The terms of his marriage contract were clear: a small plantation and monthly income in exchange for remaining in the Caribbean with Elizabeth. Yet until the moment of his death in a riding accident eight years ago, Ian Kendrick had railed at his fate—being exiled to a backwater isle with barely the means to support his preferred standard of living—while his wife languished away, torn by unhappiness over her long-lost love. As for their daughter . . .

Raven steeled her shoulders, willing herself to calm. She'd carried the secret shame of her conception since she was old enough to comprehend the word "bastard." And though her fear of discovery might be irrational, it was the chief reason she had favored Halford above all the other candidates who'd courted her so assiduously. And why she had carefully avoided the unsuitable ones. If she married high enough, if she aligned herself with a nobleman of power and consequence, then she would be shielded from her dubious past.

Admittedly she was guilty of deception for concealing her origins from her intended husband. But Halford would be getting exactly the sort of bride he required, Raven thought defiantly. She was virginal, possessed an acceptably winsome appearance, was of good blood and family connections, and had adequate countenance to fill the role of duchess. And she would willingly give Halford the heirs he wanted.

She would be getting precisely what she wanted as

well: acceptance at last by the polite world that had never considered her good enough. And a husband who was *safe*. She would never make her mother's mistake. Better a cold, loveless contract than a blazing passion that could rip her heart to shreds.

She was in no danger of falling in love with her duke, although she had hopes for eventually developing both affection and a satisfying friendship with him. Sometimes she even managed to delve beneath Halford's stiff, straitlaced reserve and make him smile.

But theirs would be a marriage of convenience, nothing more. They would live together in civilized harmony, both understanding exactly what was required of them.

In any case, her imaginary lover would keep her satisfied. And if she had to resort to fantasy in order to feel passion, to experience desire and warmth and fulfillment . . . well then, she would need such an escape if she hoped to endure a lifetime of her illustrious husband's rigid British formality.

Truly, though, her fantasizing wouldn't present any real harm to her husband or to her vows. She would be entirely faithful to Halford . . . except in her mind.

Raven took a deep breath, renewing her resolve as she turned to ring for her maid. She had made her own bed, as the saying went. Her betrothed would soon be awaiting her at the church—St. George's, Hanover Square—along with several hundred of their friends and acquaintances, the very cream of the ton. And she intended to look her best for her special day.

* * *

Two hours later she descended the stairway to the entrance hall where, with the aid of a cane, her grandfather stood alongside his sister Catherine. The elderly viscount stayed here on the rare occasions when he came to town, rather than open his own cavernous mansion.

Lord Luttrell was tall and silver-haired like his sister, though not as handsome. He'd been ill for a long while, suffering from a weak heart.

Tears brimmed in his eyes, Raven saw when she reached him.

"So you approve, do you, Grandfather?" she asked, offering him a smile. She couldn't totally forgive him for repudiating her mother so many years ago, but they had come to terms of sorts during the nearly eight months since her arrival in England.

He took her hand in his own shaky one. "Very much, child. You are exceedingly beautiful."

Raven did think her appearance pleasing. Her empire gown was of pale lemon lustring, with an ivory net overskirt shot with gold threads. And she wore her mother's pearls, while her raven hair was gathered high into an elegant coiffure.

Beside the viscount, her dragon of a great-aunt agreed even while sniffing in disapproval. "She is indeed beautiful, Jervis, but you will turn her head with such flattery. And Raven is not a child in the least. She turned twenty months ago."

As usual, her grandfather ignored his sister's waspish tone and patted Raven's hand. "I have never been so proud of you. You will make a grand duchess."

Raven bit back an instinctive reply. In her grandfather's opinion—along with the much of the world's—a woman's worth was only measured by her husband's position in society. Yet to his credit, Grandfather only wanted her to be well settled in life.

Despite the strain that had marked their early relationship, Lord Luttrell had welcomed her with a touching eagerness, making her feel like a cherished member of his family. And Raven had found herself immensely glad for the connection. He and Lady Dalrymple were the only blood relations she had left, other than an American half brother whom she could never publicly claim. She'd never even known her real father, the wealthy American shipping magnate who had died some years past.

And she knew the viscount truly mourned his late daughter and regretted his intractability.

"I am sorry your mother is not here to see you," her grandfather said now in a trembling voice.

Raven felt her own throat constrict. She, too, wished her mother could be here to witness her triumphant union.

"Jervis, if you are finished wallowing in sentimentality," Aunt Catherine interjected sharply, "we have a ceremony to attend."

"Yes, of course," Luttrell grunted with a quelling look at his sister.

After accepting her cloak from the Dalrymple butler, Raven allowed her grandfather to lead her slowly down the entrance steps of her aunt's residence to where the viscount's grand, crested carriage stood ready to transport them to the church.

To Raven's delight, her long-term groom, Michael O'Malley, waited beside the carriage to see her off.

" 'Tis a grand sight you are, Miss Raven," the Irishman said in his lilting accent, beaming when she reached him. "And a proud day to be sure."

With a brilliant smile of her own, Raven stepped aside to embrace the hulking, gray-haired fellow. "Thank you, O'Malley," she said, her voice husky with emotion.

She kissed his grizzled cheek, ignoring her aunt's sudden stiffening and her grandfather's obvious frown of disapproval. For most of her childhood, O'Malley had been more father than servant to her. And he had accompanied her to England from the West Indies when she'd come to face her haughty, unknown relatives. She was immeasurably grateful to him for standing her friend.

Turning then, Raven allowed O'Malley to take her elbow so he could hand her into the elegant barouche. When she heard a sudden commotion, though, she glanced curiously up the street to see a closed carriage barreling toward them, its windows shuttered, its coachman wearing a hooded cape that made him appear phantomlike.

Strangely, the coach slowed as it passed the barouche, then rumbled to a halt while three armed, masked figures leapt out. To Raven's shock, two of them pointed pistols directly at her, while the third brandished a cudgel.

"Ye're to come with us," one said in gruff voice, gesturing at her.

"Who the devil are you?" Lord Luttrell demanded.

When Raven stood frozen in bewilderment, the leader lunged at her and gripped her arm, dragging her toward the coach.

With a fierce growl, O'Malley made to intervene, but the man with the cudgel moved directly into his path, swinging his weapon viciously, preventing her groom from coming to her aid.

For an instant Raven wondered if she were imagining this nightmare, but the pain in her arm was very real as she was hauled toward the open door of the coach.

"What is the meaning of this outrage?" her aunt exclaimed in her iciest voice. "I demand you unhand my niece at once!"

But Raven's assailant paid no mind to the order. Instead he wrenched her around and snaked a thick arm about her waist from behind, lifting her bodily off her feet.

Gasping in fury, she fought back, struggling to be free of this rough, crude oaf, but her slippered heels made no dent in his beefy shins. When she bent her head in desperation and bit his shoulder through his tweed coat, her defiance earned her a cuff to the temple from his fist, a blow so violent that she saw stars.

Dazed, she glanced back to see the look of horror on her aunt's face, the fear on her grandfather's.

Her own fright grew as she realized the direness of her situation: she was being abducted in broad daylight!

Then she saw O'Malley struck down with the cudgel. Raven gave an anguished cry of protest, a cry that was cut short as she was shoved roughly inside the coach and facedown on the floor. She felt her gown rip at the shoulder as the coach door slammed behind her.

Stunned, the breath knocked from her, she scarcely comprehended the shouts from outside the coach as the vehicle lurched forward and began to move off. Groping the swaying seat to brace herself, Raven dizzily scrambled onto the rear-facing leather cushions.

She was not alone.

"You!" she exclaimed, recognizing the black-haired gentleman who sat opposite her. He was the same obsessive brute she'd barely escaped from once before: an unwanted suitor who'd assaulted her after refusing to accept her rejection. When she last saw him, he had been fighting O'Malley, who had come to her rescue.

Sean Lasseter's savage smile held unmistakable menace, but it was the pistol aimed at her chest that made her heart jump to her throat.

"So you do remember me, Miss Kendrick, after all these months. I am flattered."

"What do you want?" she demanded breathlessly, eyeing the pistol.

"Simple revenge," her abductor replied, his own tone silken.

"Revenge? For what?"

Drawing a flask from his coat pocket, he raised it to his lips and drank deeply. She could smell the strong liquor in the close confines of the coach, could see the alcoholic glaze in his eyes.

"Surely you know," he said, his voice grim.

Suddenly he lifted the butt of the pistol, and Raven

flinched, knowing he meant to strike her. Frantically she raised her arms to protect her face from the threat, but he rammed the butt into the side of her skull, and she saw no more.

Chapter
Two

"Doubtless you have a good reason for summoning me from my fencing match," Kell Lasseter remarked mildly as he reached the second floor of his gaming house.

His beautiful hostess, Emma Walsh, awaited him at the head of the stairs. "A most urgent reason," she replied in obvious agitation. "Your brother . . ."

Kell felt a prick of alarm, his familiar protective feelings suddenly roused. "What's amiss? Has Sean been hurt?"

"No, not hurt. But he brought a lady here, Kell, and I fear he means her harm. He has a whip, and he has bound her to the bed."

Kell's dark eyebrows snapped together, a different kind of alarm coursing through him. His charming rogue of a younger brother could be wild at times, even dangerous when driven to it—yet he'd never known Sean to act with physical violence toward a woman. Still, during these past months Sean's black moods had come more and more frequently. . . .

"Our reputation." Emma shuddered in horror. "If he rapes her . . ."

Emma was as desirous of protecting the club's renown as he was, Kell thought grimly, but she would doubtless feel sympathy for any vulnerable female because of her own harsh past. Yet his own stomach knotted at her talk of rape.

"You must stop him, Kell. Miss Kendrick is well-known in society, and she has powerful connections."

At the notorious name, he felt himself stiffen. Miss Raven Kendrick was the darling of the ton, and for a time last summer, she had turned his brother's life into a living hell—delivering him to the unspeakable brutality of the British navy.

"Where are they?"

"In your bedchamber."

Kell clenched his jaw, striving not to leap to conclusions. Sean had struggled with his inner demons for years, but since his impressment in the navy, he'd been bitter, brooding, vengeful. Had the torture he'd suffered during his enforced service finally driven him over the edge?

Swiftly Kell strode down the corridor to the bedchamber he normally used when staying overnight at his club. The Golden Fleece was an elegant gaming hell, but the gambling took place on the ground floor below, while this floor held only private rooms.

The door to his bedchamber was locked, he discovered. Kell rapped sharply, uttering one terse word. *"Sean."*

When there was no reply, he spun on his heel and made his way to the adjacent study, then crossed to a second door that connected with his bedchamber.

Finding this one unlocked, Kell entered and came up short, taking stock.

On the bed, a disheveled woman lay on her side, her bound hands stretched overhead and tied to the headboard. She wasn't quite naked, but her fine cambric shift was hiked up above her knees, exposing long slender legs, while her ebony hair flowed in wild disarray over her bare shoulders.

Kell felt his heart give an unsteady jolt. So this was Miss Raven Kendrick, the dazzling debutante who commanded the homage of nobles. Their paths had never directly crossed before, probably because he actively shunned her ilk and her elevated social circles—unlike his brother, who'd earnestly aspired to join her elite ranks.

Her eyes were closed, and she didn't stir, yet she was clearly a damsel in distress.

Kell's first urgent impulse was to rescue her from her plight, but he fought down his natural instincts—shock, horror, fury that his brother would treat any woman so cruelly. He had to remember who she was. A deadly temptress with a heart of ice. One who lured impressionable young men to their doom simply for sport. She deserved to be punished in some fashion for the misery and suffering she'd caused his brother—although this was unquestionably too harsh a penance.

Kell's gaze shifted to his brother. Sean sat slumped in a wing chair near the hearth, cradling a whiskey bottle in one hand, a riding whip in the other. Three long scratches scored the left side of his face.

Involuntarily Kell reached up to touch his own cheek and the wicked scar there. But his scar was an old one and no longer painful, unlike the ones his brother bore, both visible and hidden.

Outwardly, though, they were much alike, with jet black hair and athletic builds, although Sean was slighter and not quite as tall, and his eyes were shamrock green, not nearly black like Kell's.

Sean glanced up now, his green eyes bloodshot, as if he was deep in his cups.

Kell clamped down on his churning emotions, knowing he would need to remain calm in order to deal with this volatile situation.

"Would you care to explain why you've barricaded yourself in my bedchamber like this?" he said finally, stepping inside and closing the door.

Sean waved his bottle toward the quiescent beauty on the bed. "Thish is my revenge," he muttered, slurring his words. "I abducted her. Ruined her noble marriagsh. Her curshed duke won't have her now."

"And the whip?" Kell asked.

"Mean to flog her like I was flogged. A whip, not a cat-o'-nine-tails. Won't hurt as much, morsh the pity." Sean made a scoffing sound deep in his throat. "Devil is . . . couldn't do it shober . . . Needed courage . . ." He held up the bottle.

Kell felt a measure of relief that his brother couldn't cold-bloodedly carry out his planned vengeance but needed to work himself into a drunken stupor. Sean was a charming, reckless rogue with the devil's own tongue and a quick, hot temper—no doubt a product of his half-Irish blood—but his darker nature was purely the result of his English ordeals.

And in this case, Sean's bitterness was entirely justified. Last June, the treacherous Miss Kendrick had sent her groom to thrash him for daring to aspire to her hand. Left unconscious on the London streets, Sean had been taken up by an impressment gang and forced to serve in the Royal Navy for four brutal months, an experience that had left livid scars on his back.

Kell couldn't think of that time without dread and guilt. When his brother had suddenly disappeared, he'd searched frantically and finally rescued Sean from the inhumaneness of the British navy. Yet Kell had once more been tormented by self-blame because he hadn't prevented Sean's suffering or shielded the brother he'd vowed to protect.

Tears suddenly filled Sean's green eyes before he lowered his head. "I *loved* her, Kell. Why'd shhhe have to do that? Taunted and teashed me, then spurned me to wed her cursed duke an' dishposed of me like so much offal. Heartless bish."

Kell himself was filled with anger at the vicious seductress who'd so callously orchestrated his brother's impressment. Even so, flogging her now was insupportable.

Crossing to his brother, Kell reached for the whip. "You don't really want to beat her, Sean. No matter her crimes, you can't be reduced to brutalizing women."

When he took the whip away, Sean immediately protested. "Yesh, I can. . . . Sheesh my hostage. Gonna hurt her th' way shhhe hurt me."

Kell tossed the whip on the adjacent table and noted the other weapons his brother had staged there—a pistol and a lethal-looking knife. Sean had obviously come prepared for every eventuality.

Just then the woman on the bed stirred, giving a low moan. Taking up the knife, Kell went to her. Her patrician face was flushed and feverish, but he fought his feelings of sympathy, reminding himself of her treachery as he carefully sliced away her bonds and freed her hands.

For an instant she opened her eyes, looking up at him with a vacant stare, and Kell froze in reaction. Long, sooty black lashes rimmed incredible blue eyes, making him suddenly understand the bewitching effect she'd had on his brother.

From the huge size of her pupils, though, he could clearly see she'd been drugged. Her lashes lowered and fluttered against ivory skin. Then rolling over with a weak groan, she pressed her face into the pillow.

Deliberately he drew the corner of the counterpane over her, as much to shield her near nakedness from his sight as to ensure her warmth. He had no desire to fall victim to her dangerous allure, as his brother had.

"What did you give her, Sean?" he asked over his shoulder.

" 'Phrodisac. Made her drink it. Thash when she scratched me."

"Not cantharides?" Kell said sharply. "Did you give her Spanish fly?"

"No . . . not that. Shomething Oriental. S'posed to work as well. Got it from Madame Fouchet."

Kell felt another twinge of relief. Madame Fouchet was the proprietor of a high-class brothel Sean frequented. She would have knowledge of aphrodisiacs and appropriate doses. More crucially, she would have shunned Spanish fly, which reportedly could be deadly. Even so, it would likely be many hours before this drug wore off. . . .

Kell ran a hand impatiently through his hair, wondering what to do about this damnable situation.

"Why an aphrodisiac?" he asked absently. "Why not simply a sleeping potion if you wanted to render her unable to fight you?"

"To make her want me." Sean flashed a sad, watery smile. "Like she once did. She wanted me, Kell. She was so hot . . . could not get enough of me."

With that, Sean struggled to his feet and moved toward the bed, determination etching his features. "Gonna use her body the way she did mine . . ."

Just as determinedly, Kell stepped in his path.

Sean blinked at him, then frowned. "You mean to stop me?"

"You can't go about ravishing young ladies, no matter how reprehensible they are."

"But sheesh no lady," Sean replied plaintively. "She looks innocent enough, but she gave me her body. An' doan forget, she's Englissh."

The reminder was like twisting a knife inside Kell. Miss Kendrick had reportedly turned down his brother's proposal of marriage not simply because Sean was untitled, but because he was half-Irish.

Kell felt his jaw clench with familiar fury. Undoubtedly the haughty temptress had the same callous contempt for those beneath her social standing that the disdainful English Lasseters had had for his Irish mother. The same contempt that had led to his mother's death and that still made him seethe.

He glanced over his shoulder, torn between his brother's rightful desire for justice and his own reflexive urge to protect the helpless beauty in his bed.

He shook his head at his particular vulnerability—caring too much for the weak and powerless. How could he possibly feel sympathy for a femme fatale who'd so viciously left a trail of broken hearts across half of England? Especially when he'd sworn years ago never to let anyone hurt his brother again?

Yet, still . . . he would be protecting Sean by preventing his vengeance. Sean had evidently planned to seduce and abandon the beautiful Jezebel, but there would be hell to pay as a result.

"You don't honestly want to see her tortured," Kell asserted in a low voice.

"Yesh, I do!"

"What of the club? Do you want my reputation destroyed by a violent assault on a reputed lady?"

Grimacing, Sean brought his bottle to his lips. "Doan care," he muttered.

Kell narrowed his gaze, belatedly wondering why Sean had brought Miss Kendrick here instead of to his own town house. Perhaps deep inside he'd wanted to be prevented from carrying out his planned vengeance. Or perhaps he'd purposely involved Kell in his machinations, bent on another sort of revenge. . . .

Feeling a familiar ache at his brother's festering resentment, Kell put a hand on his arm. "You should go home, Sean. You won't find any further satisfaction by hurting her. Miss Kendrick's reputation is thoroughly ruined now. Adequate enough revenge, wouldn't you say?"

With a snarl, Sean shook off the restraining hand. "No! Not enough."

Kell gave his brother a steady, intent stare. "Sean," he said in a quiet, warning voice.

The younger man ducked his head, suddenly looking as if he might cry. After another glance at the helpless woman on the bed, however, he nodded drunkenly.

Kell led his brother to the main bedchamber door and unlocked it, glad to find Emma waiting anxiously in the corridor.

"Have someone take him home," Kell murmured. "I will deal with him tomorrow when he's in his right mind."

"Yes, of course," Emma said, putting a supporting arm around Sean's waist and urging him toward the far staircase.

After watching them go, Kell shut the door softly, but he took a deep breath before turning to face his dilemma. What in hell's name was he to do with the suffering, senseless woman in his bed?

Most certainly he couldn't return her to her family in this pitiful condition. Indeed, for her own safety, he would have to keep a close eye on her. If the aphrodisiac she'd been given was even half as powerful as cantharides, she would be driven by sheer lust. And if left on her own, she might assault any man she encountered. . . .

No, better to let her sleep off the drug and return her to her family in the morning.

Kell frowned. Raven Kendrick had thrown off the

cover and was thrashing her bare legs feverishly, twisting her head side to side on the pillow. Steeling himself, he approached the bed.

She had turned onto her back, and her gossamer chemise did little to hide her sweet, firm breasts with their rose-hued nipples or the dark thatch of curls between her thighs. But it was the glorious raven tresses framing her heart-shaped face that held him momentarily spellbound—

Suddenly she reached out, her fingers clutching his arm with surprising strength as she gazed up at him, her eyes wide and unfocused. Kell found himself staring into deep pools of blue fringed by heavy lashes.

He cursed, damning the sudden quickening in his loins.

Yet, as if comforted by the sight of him, she abruptly stilled and let her eyes close. "My pirate," she whispered. The faint smile that wreathed her delicate lips held incredible sensuality. . . .

Hell and damnation. It was nearly impossible for him not to soften toward his beautiful, unwanted hostage. But he had to harden his heart if he had any chance of making it through the night unscathed without becoming her victim.

Extricating his arm from her astonishingly strong grasp, Kell went to the washstand to make certain the pitcher and basin held enough water to cool her fevered body. He'd seen the effects of a similar drug before, at a debauched revelry during his wilder days. She would eventually become hot as a volcano, simmering with sexual need, threatening to explode at any moment. Whatever pain she'd endured at his brother's hands would pale in comparison to the torment she would experience from the drug if she didn't find relief. And if he had the least measure of compassion, he would have to provide it for her, would have to help ease her suffering. . . .

He glanced at the windows where a gray winter light still shone, grimly noting that it was late afternoon. Crossing to the fireplace, he stirred the embers and added a scoop of coal to counter the growing chill. He would have Emma bring up supper later.

At the bureau, Kell poured himself a generous glass of whiskey from a crystal decanter. Then gritting his teeth, he sank into the chair to wait, knowing it would doubtless be a long night.

Chapter
Three

Raven arched against her lover's hand, desperately seeking the exquisite relief of his touch. Her senses were painfully acute. Her skin felt too tight, too sensitive, the ache between her legs unbearable.

"Please," she begged, "make it stop." She felt so feverish, so hot, as she wavered between illusion and awareness.

"Steady," he murmured in reply, as if gentling a fractious mare.

His hand slipped inside her bodice and gently stroked the tender flesh of her breasts, playing over her taut nipples. She sighed at the soothing coolness of his palm offering her relief.

Her fantasy had never been so vivid, so intense. She was acutely aware of her pirate lover in a way she'd never experienced. The animal heat radiating from his body. The male musk of his skin. The delicious taste of his mouth. The demanding gentleness of his caresses . . . Nearly shaking with desire, she reached for him, wanting him with a blind, ferocious need.

He wanted her as well, she could tell. He hadn't fully undressed, but beneath his breeches, he was hard, swollen, ready to take her. Yet when she touched his loins, he stiffened and drew back, out of reach.

His hand moved lower, though, down her body, slipping between her thighs, as if he knew exactly what she craved.

"Let me help you. . . ."

She scarcely comprehended the words, but his voice sounded like poetry: dark, sensual, arousing. Whimpering, she lifted her hips to him and dug her fingers into the bedcovers.

His hands were magical against her moist, yearning flesh, assuaging the terrible sweet ache that consumed her. When he relentlessly increased the pressure, inciting a wild throbbing inside her, a cry of longing escaped her.

Still stroking, he bent to her, his lips finding her peaked nipple through her chemise. Wet, white heat scalded her through the thin fabric.

She moaned aloud at the sharpened pleasure, while his fingers continued to work their sorcery, ravishing her with tenderness.

His caresses roused her blood to liquid fire. She was simmering from the molten heat, assaulted by raw, unbridled feeling. She bucked in an effort to escape the intensity of it, but the dark velvet of his voice urged her on.

"That's it, let go. . . ."

Thrashing her head, she strained against his hand, begging him to take her. How she longed to feel him inside her! But still he refused. Yet to her profound relief, he slid his fingers deep within her, penetrating her slick cleft. She felt her pulse racing, her blood pounding at the hot, voluptuous sensation. She was burning, crying out for fulfillment. She writhed with the frenzied need coursing through her, her body shuddering as her hips undulated.

The rush of sensation ruthlessly intensified, and she went wild with excitement. An instant later she screamed as agonizing pleasure tore through her senses, erupting in pulsating waves, her climax so prolonged, she thought she might die of the painful bliss.

For an endless moment, she shook in uncontrollable spasms as he continued to wring every last drop of relentless pleasure from her quivering flesh. Finally she fell back, delicious rapture washing through her exhausted body. Her limbs felt limp and heavy and utterly boneless as the fiery heat cooled. . . .

Turning to him, she nuzzled her face gratefully into the hard wall of his chest and sank into sleep.

Kell bit back a low curse, keenly aware of the effect Raven Kendrick's meagerly clad body had on him. After nearly four hours of attending her, the pain in his loins was excruciating.

He had relieved her suffering as much as was humanly possible, yet he couldn't relieve his own. She was his captive, completely at his mercy. What kind of bounder would take advantage of her drugged state? Even if she *was* burning to have a man between her legs?

Whatever aphrodisiac she had been given was more powerful than any he knew of. It had made her sexually insatiable and frantic for a lover. Despite his skill, manual stimulation wouldn't be enough to satisfy her. She would need more, would *demand* more. . . .

He eased back, away from her warmth, but that slightest bit of distance was scarcely an improvement.

He should have put out the lamp. Her shift was dampened from the many times he had bathed her feverish skin, and the cambric had molded itself in a transparent film to her body. The rigid peaks of her nipples strained against the delicate fabric.

Involuntarily his gaze drifted down her body, over her slender hips and thighs, and lower, where her shift rode up. Those long, naked legs were so slim and lovely. It was too damned easy to imagine them wrapped tightly around his flanks as he took her—

His arousal throbbed sharply in anticipation.

He drew a slow breath, trying to ease the brutal tension in his body. Her condition would likely last for hours, and he had to find the strength to resist her allure.

Averting his gaze from her body, he instead focused on her face. In sleep she didn't resemble a heartless bitch. On the contrary she looked appealingly vulnerable, with her long lashes fanned out against her smooth cheeks.

He'd rarely seen any woman so arrestingly lovely, but hers was an unconventional beauty: fresh, vivid, wholly enchanting. And her mouth . . . that sensual, provocative mouth was parted in sleep. . . .

He had tried to avoid kissing that incredible mouth, but she had clutched at him, raising her face to his, imploring him. And in a lamentable moment of weakness, he'd given in, tasting her warmth.

"Witless fool," Kell muttered accusingly to himself. He hadn't wanted her to taste so sweet and hot.

She moved closer just then, pressing against him, and Kell tensed. He'd removed his boots and coat but left on his other garments as a barrier between them so he wouldn't be tempted by the intimate contact of skin to skin. Yet clothing had proven little protection.

"My splendid pirate . . ." she murmured, curling her fingers on his chest.

Pirate? That was the second time she had called him that. He raised an eyebrow as he caught her hand and urgently removed it from his body. What would a blue-blooded debutante know about pirates? But then she obviously had more depth of experience than any un-wed young lady rightfully should.

In truth, he'd been frankly surprised by her evident carnal knowledge—and by her boldness. He could well understand how she'd teased and tormented his brother into forgetting his own name.

She stirred against him, and Kell knew his temporary reprieve had ended. With a resigned sigh, he reached down to give her what she craved.

His hand claimed the softness of her, and instantly he felt moisture, warm and silky, coat his fingers. When he slid them along her drenched cleft, she whimpered gratefully.

He stroked her for a moment, then penetrated her warmth with his fingers, sliding inside her hot passage. She moaned and twisted under his caresses, clutching at his shoulders as she tried to get even closer.

The movement of her body only sharpened his desire, and Kell clenched his jaw against the pain. She was like live fire to his touch: beautiful, hot, wild.

His own breath was ragged by the time she climaxed for what seemed like the hundredth time tonight. Her cry was sharp and agonized, her body arching and shuddering in his restraining arms.

He held her close until the feverish tempest within her had stilled. As soon as she relaxed, though, he eased away, not knowing how much more torture he could endure.

Taking advantage of the lull, he closed his eyes, needing a moment's rest. What he really should do was stroke himself to assuage the savage ache. . . .

He must have dozed off, for he woke to the most incredible sensations. A dark-haired woman was leaning over him, staging a delectable assault on his helpless body. She had unbuttoned the front flap of his breeches and was trailing her lips over his swollen erection, ravishing him as he slept. . . .

His hand curled in her raven hair, urging her on—

Startled awareness made him go rigid.

Wide awake now, Kell caught her hands and dragged them to her sides. A mistake, he realized, for she only leaned closer, giving him a perfect view of her bare swelling breasts that now spilled over the bodice of her shift. Ripe and rose-hued, they loomed eager for a man's caress . . . his caress.

A lightning stroke of desire surged through him.

Dragging his gaze from her luscious breasts, he found himself staring up into wide sapphire pools that were glazed with passion.

"I will never love him, I swear," she murmured huskily. She bent even closer, her tantalizing mouth hovering over his. "I am yours. Only yours . . ."

"Bloody hell," Kell muttered under his breath. He'd refused to take advantage of Raven Kendrick's slumberous state, but she had done just that to him in her hunger for a man.

And he wasn't a damned saint—far from it. The temptation to take her was so great, he could feel himself yielding.

She kissed him then, her tongue sliding enticingly into his mouth, seeking. In self-defense, he shifted his hands to push her away, but her nipples stabbed his palms.

Kell groaned. When she straddled his hips, he no longer could summon the will to resist. She was feverish with wanting, every flame-hot inch of her ripe for the taking, and he intended to allow her to have what she craved.

He grasped her hips, lifting her slightly and easing her onto his huge erection, drawing a harsh breath at the exquisite feel of her sleek heat. . . .

Suddenly she stiffened. She gave a sharp, twisting movement, trying to impale herself on his rigid shaft, but then she stopped, a look of quivering surprise on her face.

A startled surprise that Kell shared. Shock reverberated through him at her virginal tightness. She was untouched by a man. . . .

Frantically he jerked his hips, withdrawing from her chaste body and holding her away.

She looked down at him in bewilderment, her hair a tangle around her beautiful face, her glazed eyes pleading.

"Please . . ." she whispered.

Without waiting for him, she ground herself against his muscular thigh, her pelvis thrusting wildly against him in an agony of need.

Compassionately he gripped the firm, sweet flesh of

her buttocks and aided her, setting a hard rhythm until she exploded yet again, crying out in rapture and collapsing bonelessly upon him.

Lying there in the painful aftermath, Kell held her exquisite body as if it were fragile glass, as if he were afraid to touch it.

How in hell could she *possibly* still be a virgin? With her courtesan's lashes and sultry mouth and her reputation as a seductress, he'd naturally presumed her carnally experienced. Her desperate lust could be accounted for by the aphrodisiac, of course, but there had been nothing innocent or virginal in her practiced kisses or her bold caresses.

A gamester by profession, he would have wagered half his fortune that she was no virgin. A wager he obviously would have lost.

Devil take it, her eager assault on his manhood suggested clearly that she was no stranger to a man's body. . . .

Yet perhaps she was indeed carnally experienced but had been saving her virginity for her husband. Her *noble* husband. Kell frowned suddenly, recalling that Miss Kendrick was supposed to have wed her duke yesterday. In fact, that celebrated event was what had driven his brother to finally act, to mete out his avowed vengeance.

Kell took a deep, steadying breath, unintentionally inhaling the delicate fragrance of her hair. What had his volatile younger brother gotten him into? And what the devil was he supposed to do with her now?

Just then she gave a sigh and buried her nose in his shoulder, making a mewling sound like a kitten. An odd tenderness flooded Kell—a totally involuntary response that grated on his nerves.

He was still enraged at her for wounding his brother so savagely, yet for the first time, he began to question Sean's veracity. Sean's claim that he'd enjoyed her sexual favors, that she had in fact offered her body, was clearly untrue. Was it also possible that Raven Kendrick wasn't entirely the vicious Jezebel she had been labeled?

Admittedly Sean's feelings toward her had been warped by his recent brutal impressment. Yet his darker side had fomented long before, Kell knew to his sorrow. Worse, his brother still harbored a simmering resentment against *him*, blaming Kell for abandoning him to their uncle's perversions more than a dozen years ago.

Kell squeezed his eyes shut at the familiar anguish. Since their mother's senseless death when he was fifteen, he'd felt responsible for Sean, who was five years his junior—even though their paternal uncle had assumed legal guardianship for them both. But he had failed miserably in his duty to protect his young brother, unwittingly leaving Sean to their uncle's debauchery.

He'd tried desperately to make amends since then. Remembering, Kell raised his fingers to his cheek. His scar had resulted from a violent fight with their uncle, when he'd discovered William Lasseter's sordid crime. He'd wanted to kill the bastard, but instead he'd escaped with Sean to Dublin, vowing to keep him safe.

For a time they'd known no other home but the streets, scrounging for their very existence, struggling to survive. Kell had quickly learned to rely on his exceptional gaming skills to put food in their empty bellies. They'd had only each other, and then their uncle had pursued them to Ireland. . . .

Deliberately Kell crushed the dark memory. Yet he couldn't quell his growing misgivings about his brother, or summarily dismiss Sean's vengeance as focused merely on Raven Kendrick and not on himself as well.

He would have given his life for his brother, if need be. It pained him to think Sean might have deliberately sought to destroy the tenuous reputation he'd fought so hard to build for his gaming house.

But why else would Sean have brought Miss Kendrick here, if not out of vindictiveness?

Reminded of the blue-eyed siren in his arms, Kell winced. Her hair drifted like cool silk against the backs of his hands, her soft breasts and slim thighs scorched him like hot coals, eliciting powerful emotions inside him that he didn't want to feel. . . .

"Bloody hell," he cursed again, damning her and his brother both.

Her, for arousing the most savage lust he'd ever known. And Sean, for inciting this damnable situation.

Chapter
Four

Fighting free of murky unconsciousness, Raven opened her eyes to find herself staring at a warm, crackling fire. She lay still for a moment, letting her gaze drift around the unfamiliar bedchamber. While tastefully rich, there was nothing remotely feminine about the gleaming mahogany furnishings or the burgundy and gold appointments. This was a man's room. Sweet heaven.

Disoriented, she raised a hand to her aching temple as wicked memories of her pirate lover danced in her muddled brain. Where in God's name was she?

"Good, you're awake," a pleasant female voice murmured.

Turning her head sharply, Raven winced at the pain, then froze as she recognized the elegant, golden-haired woman who had risen from a chair and was moving to stand beside the bed.

This woman had tried her help her, she remembered— Dear God, had her nightmare been real?

"I wasn't dreaming, was I?" she managed to ask, her voice a thin rasp.

"No, I am afraid not."

Raven blanched to have her fears confirmed.

"How do you feel?"

She felt miserable. Her groggy head was pounding like carriage wheels on cobblestone, and her mouth tasted as if she had swallowed sawdust. . . . Gingerly Raven felt her scalp and discovered a lump above her left temple. Moreover, her wrists were bruised and scraped from her bonds, and there was a raw tenderness between her legs—

Shying away from that appalling realization, she regarded the woman. "Where . . . am I? How long . . . ?"

"A gaming club on St. James Street. The Golden Fleece. I am Emma Walsh, the hostess here. And you were brought here yesterday."

Memory came flooding back in a vivid rush, making Raven shudder. She had been abducted on her wedding day by a former unwanted suitor who'd struck her viciously. When she regained consciousness to find herself trussed to a bed, Sean Lasseter had forced a vile concoction down her throat. Everything afterward was a blur, but her dreams had been steamy and erotic, filled with exquisite lovemaking by her pirate lover. . . .

Raven squeezed her eyes shut, desperately hoping she was mistaken about the brazen events of last night. Had those too been real? The passion, the warmth, the tender caresses . . . Aghast, she shook her head in denial.

"You're safe now," Emma said reassuringly.

Raven forced herself to open her eyes. "I remember you," she finally said. "You tried to stop him. . . ."

"Yes. But I fear I wasn't very successful." The hostess set her jaw grimly, as if in remembrance. "I had to call Kell."

"Kell?"

"Kell Lasseter. Sean's older brother. He owns the club. He knows how to handle Sean when he gets in one of his dark moods."

"Kell . . . that was who . . . He was with me last night?"

"Yes. If not for him, Sean might have hurt you even more seriously."

Raven looked away, heat searing her cheeks as she recalled the lover who'd shared her bed last night. The wicked things he'd done to her, the liberties he'd taken with her body. And her own wanton response. She had thought he was her pirate. . . . Dear God.

She tried to thrust those memories aside as another realization struck her. "My family . . . do they even know where I am?"

"I don't expect so."

"They must be frantic with worry. My grandfather has a weak heart . . ." Raven drew a sharp breath. "God, what will I tell him?"

"Perhaps you shouldn't fret about that just now. I have brought you some breakfast. Do you think you can eat a bit now? You were in no condition to manage food yesterday."

Forcibly shifting her attention, Raven glanced at the tray on the table, surprised to find herself hungry. "Yes . . . thank you."

"I also brought you a robe. I believe I am taller than you are, but my clothing will do in a pinch." Emma glanced down at Raven's body. "You should permit me to launder your shift."

Raven flinched as she recalled what had happened

to her beautiful wedding gown. Sean Kendrick had cut it off her while she'd struggled with all her might against him and her bonds. And he had ripped her necklace away—

Her hand went to her throat. "My mother's pearls!"

"Don't be alarmed. I have them safe. The clasp is broken but I think it can be repaired."

To her dismay, Raven felt her eyes suddenly burn with tears, and it was all she could do to swallow them.

Giving a sympathetic smile, Emma squeezed her hand. "You will feel better after you refresh yourself. You'll find a chamber pot beneath the washstand and warm water in the pitcher. But I expect you will want a bath. I'll order it for you at once. And I will find you a day gown to wear."

With an appreciative nod, Raven forced herself to sit up. "I am not normally so helpless."

"Of course not. But you have been through an ordeal that would have most young ladies expiring from shock."

She managed a weak smile. "I still might expire from shock."

Emma's gentle laughter was warm. "Well, I'm certain Kell will do what he can to help you and make things right."

Raven groaned inwardly. She couldn't possibly face him. Not after what had occurred between them last night. Apparently he'd been her savior, and yet he had taken advantage of her helpless state—the cad.

When she realized that Emma was holding out the wrapper for her, Raven drew off her shift and slipped on the blue brocade garment, murmuring her thanks.

"You needn't thank me," Emma replied. "Kell instructed me to see to your needs. He wishes to speak to you when you feel up to it."

But I don't wish to speak to him, Raven reflected silently.

When she was alone, she slowly got out of bed. She felt shaky, the remnants of the drug she'd been given still in her body, while a tight, cold knot of panic had settled in her stomach at the thought of her future. She was facing disaster—

Refusing to consider her dire state, she managed her ablutions, then sat in the chair before the hearth and made herself nibble at the breakfast Emma had brought her.

She indeed felt a little better when she'd swallowed a few bites of toast and a soft-boiled egg, but nothing could mute the chaotic pounding of her thoughts. The very act of eating reminded her of the man who had succored her last night, of his tenderness. He had given her lemon-flavored water to cool her parched throat, she remembered. And he had bathed her feverish body over and over. . . .

Raven groaned again at the tormenting memory.

Just then a quiet rap sounded on the bedchamber door behind her. With a start, she glanced over her shoulder, dreading having to respond. Before she could decide whether or not to bid entrance, the door opened and a man stepped inside the room.

Sweet heaven, she hadn't dreamed him. He was tall and athletically built, with ebony hair that was thick and curling. A lock fell carelessly over his strong brow, calling attention to his harshly sculpted features and a mouth that was alarmingly sensual. Yet it was his gaze that disturbed her most. Those intense black eyes fringed by dark lashes were startlingly familiar.

Raven stared. The resemblance to her imaginary lover was uncanny. . . .

Still there were differences. A scar slashed across this man's left cheekbone, making him look more dangerous than her pirate lover ever had in her dreams. And there was no tenderness in the chiseled features of his face.

He shut the door behind him and leaned one shoulder negligently against it, surveying her with a cool, raking glance.

Raven felt herself flush as she saw him take stock of her attire. He must know she was naked beneath her wrapper.

She came to her feet and faced him, clutching the edges of her robe to her throat defensively. Her lover had never made her feel threatened, either.

"What are you doing here?" she demanded, instinctively lashing out, believing anger was better than vulnerability.

"I believe this is my bedchamber." His reply held an edge of wryness.

"A gentleman would not intrude on a lady this way."

Her belligerence sent one jet black brow winging upward. "That presumes I am a gentleman."

He spoke like one, certainly. The timbre of his voice was low and cultured, that same voice that had consoled and cajoled her all night long. He was dressed informally, however, wearing a brown superfine waistcoat over a white shirt and buff buckskin breeches and boots, with no coat or cravat.

Pushing himself away from the door, he moved toward her deliberately. He must be a sportsman to have developed such a lithe, muscular body, Raven reflected absently. And he emanated a raw vitality that buffeted her senses—

Willing away her disturbing awareness, Raven held her ground as he came to stand directly before her. "Must you be here when I am not dressed?"

"It is a bit late to worry about observing proper convention, considering last night. I saw every one of your charms when I was soothing your fever."

"You call what you did 'soothing'?"

"What I *did* was alleviate your suffering, Miss Kendrick. Believe me, you would have been much worse off had I not intervened."

Raven set her teeth at the mocking gleam in his midnight eyes. She had never seen such a darkly, insolently beautiful male . . . except in her fantasies. To her dismay, she felt herself flushing again. "Did I . . . ? Did we . . . ?"

Somehow he understood her stumbling queries. "Yes, you did assault me. It was all I could do to keep you from ravishing me. But no, we did not enjoy sexual congress. You're not entirely unscathed but nevertheless still a virgin."

Under his slow, deliberate stare, her cheeks turned scarlet, and she had to look away.

"Not a very convincing performance, Miss Kendrick."

The edge of contempt in his voice made her chin snap up again. "What do you mean?"

"Your pretense of the affronted victim isn't at all persuasive. You might be virginal, but you are hardly an innocent. You can't expect me to believe you've never lain with a man."

Raven was hard-pressed to answer. She had never lain with a *real* man, of course. Yet doubtless the knowledge she'd gleaned from the journal had made her appear far more practiced than she actually was.

"What you believe," she replied, humiliation making her sound breathless, "is of little consequence. I am not obliged to explain myself to you."

She had to mentally brace herself against the impact of his hard gaze. Suddenly feeling a spell of dizziness, Raven turned and sank into the chair again, letting her head drop into her hands.

Amazingly enough, his tone bore a trace of compassion when he asked if she was all right.

"Oh yes, I am simply thriving," she muttered with no little sarcasm. "I am regularly accustomed to being abducted and beaten and drugged!"

He stepped closer. With a finger under her chin, he turned her face up to his, his piercing, dark-eyed gaze assessing her intently.

"How could I possibly be all right after everything your brother did to me?" Raven demanded, her voice unsteady. "First he struck me with the butt of his pistol and rendered me senseless. Then he tied me up and forced me to drink some foul potion. . . ." She held up her arms, revealing the livid bruises on her wrists. "He *brutalized* me."

A grim frown scored Kell Lasseter's mouth for an instant, but then he visibly repressed it. "I am sorry for what my brother did to you, Miss Kendrick. It was inexcusable. But you are not entirely blameless yourself. Not when you seduce gullible young bucks for sport."

Raven's gaze narrowed with her own frown. "That is a lie! I have never seduced anyone, most especially your brother. The worst I am guilty of is offering him friendship."

"You spurned him because of his Irish blood and his lack of a title—because you considered him beneath your notice."

"I rejected his suit, yes, but when he proposed marriage to me I was already betrothed."

Kell Lasseter's expression only hardened, his stare unwavering, relentless. "But you had him thrashed for daring to raise his eyes to you."

"I certainly did not! Your brother became drunk one evening when I was at Vauxhall Gardens with friends. He accosted me and tore my gown and almost ravished me—"

"So you deny setting your groom upon him?"

"Yes, I deny it!" She shot him a fierce look. "My groom only intervened to protect me, for which I was eminently grateful. As it was, I barely escaped scandal."

"But first you ordered Sean beaten half to death."

"I tell you, that was not what happened. O'Malley struck him, true, but only to make your brother release me."

"Your groom just happened to be strolling through Vauxhall with you, Miss Kendrick?" Lasseter drawled, his tone sardonic.

"No, he was keeping a watchful eye on me in case of trouble! Your brother had been tormenting me for so long, he had become dangerous. During the fireworks he separated me from my party and dragged me into the woods. O'Malley came after us. I'm not certain what happened to your brother after that, since I was rather distraught at the time. To my knowledge, O'Malley left him there to sleep off his inebriation."

A muscle flexed in Kell's jaw. "That is nothing like the story Sean tells."

"If so, then he has been deceiving you—completely distorting the truth."

"The scars on his back are no distortion, Miss Kendrick."

"What scars?"

"From the brutal floggings he endured. Compliments of the British Royal Navy. Sean was taken up by an impressment gang that night and spent four months in hell. Have you any idea of the damage a cat-o'-nine-tails can inflict on a man's flesh? Those scars will be with him till the day he dies."

Raven stared, not knowing what to say.

"Is it any wonder Sean was desirous of revenge after enduring such brutality?" his brother asked grimly.

She swallowed, unaccountably feeling a measure of guilt. "If that's true, then I am sorry. But I swear, it was not deliberate. I had no idea what happened to him. After that night, he never approached me again. Frankly, I was thankful to no longer have him plaguing me. I was at my wits' end. . . . But I never saw him again until yesterday."

Kell regarded her skeptically, studying every emotion that crossed her beautiful face. Her complexion held a delicate pallor from her ordeal, highlighted by hot flags of anger and humiliation burning on her cheeks.

Was it possible that her version of events was the truth? That she wasn't to blame for Sean's impressment? Or was she simply an excellent actress with the skill to dupe him along with every other witless male she encountered? Even if she hadn't deliberately orchestrated Sean's downfall, would she even care if she sent an innocent man to his doom?

"Perhaps you don't know your brother as well as you think you do," she muttered defensively, breaking into his thoughts.

Kell found it difficult to scoff at her observation. Was Sean really the victim in this damnable conflict . . . or was she? Once more Kell felt a surge of anger at them both.

"In any event"—she drew an unsteady breath—"he should be well-satisfied with his revenge, since he has totally ruined me."

Her lower lip suddenly trembled, the first sign he'd seen in her of any frailty. When she blinked back her tears resolutely, Kell felt his heart twist hard. Her vulnerability touched him in a place where he thought he had no real feeling left.

She squared her shoulders, drawing her dignity around her like armor. Her eyes glistening, she held his stare with defiant pride.

Kell swore under his breath at his body's unwilling reaction to her arresting beauty. Those eyes were such a vibrant, startling blue . . . the color of a wild Irish sea. They haunted him almost as much as the memory of her nipples rising eagerly to his mouth last night.

Still half feeling the thrust of her soft hips against his loins, the softness of breasts barely constrained by her shift, Kell clenched his teeth. Lust was hazardous, and so was sympathy.

"Where is your brother?" she suddenly asked.

Her question made Kell frown. "Why does it matter?"

"Because he should be made to face his crimes. What sort of coward is he to behave so viciously and then run away, leaving you to deal with the aftermath?"

"He didn't run. I sent him away."

She closed her hands into fists, obviously working herself into an outrage. "Well, I can assure you, he won't escape punishment. He should be hanged for what he did to me."

Kell felt every muscle in his body go rigid. He'd known the situation would eventually come to this. That Miss Raven Kendrick would likely want retribution. And that if he were honest, she *deserved* retribution. His brother's treatment of her sickened him. Even so, he'd spent much of the night stewing over how to extricate Sean from this debacle.

Even if Raven Kendrick were not as vicious as purported—which was seeming more likely by the moment—the danger to Sean was acute. He might not hang for enacting his revenge, but with her family's powerful connections, he could very well go to prison.

Bloody hell. Sean deserved punishment, certainly, but prison would destroy him.

Kell felt his resolve harden. He couldn't allow his brother to suffer that fate. If Raven Kendrick intended to bring charges . . . well, he would simply have to persuade her to reconsider. And that meant determining what possible recompense he could offer her.

When he remained silent, she eyed him mutinously. "I should like to go home now."

Kell hesitated only an instant. "I'm afraid I cannot allow you to leave just yet."

She stared. "Why not? My family will be worried sick for me."

"I can't return you to your family, looking like something the cat dragged in."

"Your *brother* dragged in, you mean."

"Perhaps, but I'm still not convinced you're the victim in this case."

"Your opinion is entirely beside the point."

"Even so, you'll remain here for the time being."

"Why, so you can molest me again?"

"*Molest* you, Miss Kendrick?" Kell eyed her measuringly. "That is all the gratitude I get for my trouble last night?"

Her cheeks flushed at the reminder. "I hardly think I owe you gratitude."

"No? I seem to recall you begging me to soothe your needs."

"I was clearly not in my right mind."

He flashed her a mocking smile, now intent on drawing her fire. If she was angry at him, she would be less likely to focus her outrage on his brother. "Well, have no fear. I don't mean to touch you again. Does that disappoint you?"

He was deliberately provoking her, and she rose to the bait. Her eyes flashed with revolt. "If I were a man . . ."

Kell raised an eyebrow. "What would you do?"

"I would challenge you on a field of honor."

"You would lose."

She rose to her feet, passionate fury in every line of her body. "You cannot keep me here!"

"I think I can. You obviously need time for your hot temper to cool."

It was a measure of how raw her nerves were that Raven reacted to his arrogant tone as irrationally as she did—drawing back her arm to slap the mockery off his handsome face. He caught her hand before she could do any damage, his grasp a velvet manacle on her wrist.

Raven winced reflexively at the pressure on her bruised flesh. Instantly she saw a softening in the hard intensity of his eyes. She was suddenly aware of a new tension that charged the air. His gaze felt unbearably intimate, while his touch seemed to burn her bare skin.

She drew a sharp breath. How could he remind her so much of her pirate lover? Her gaze dropped to his sensual, hard-looking mouth. How could she be feeling this yearning to have him kiss her again?

Forcibly she dragged her gaze from his mouth. She wanted to hate him, not to feel a powerful surge of desire.

As if he could see the sudden flare of need in her eyes, he released her hand abruptly and turned away.

Without speaking, he went to the side door and locked it, then pocketed the key. Moving to the other door, he paused. "Finish your breakfast and have a bath first. Then we'll talk." When he had let himself from the room, she heard the key turn as he locked that door as well.

Raven stared after him, wanting to scream with frustration while at the same time fighting down rising panic. She was trapped here, at the mercy of a blackguard. Perhaps he *had* saved her from his brother, but there was a very real sense of danger about Kell Lasseter. She didn't believe he would simply release her to return to her family unscathed.

And once she did return?

She raised a hand to her temple as the disastrous events of the past hours struck her anew. Even if her ailing grandfather hadn't expired from shock, the consequences of last night would be unavoidable. She had been thoroughly compromised, her sterling reputation destroyed. Halford would doubtless shun her. Indeed, any chance of marrying well had been totally shattered. Her life was ruined, as were her mother's dreams for her.

Unbidden, a sob rose to her throat. She felt cold, sick inside—

Shaking herself fiercely, Raven lifted her chin and steeled her spine. She couldn't afford to indulge in despair. Her first priority was to escape. She would *not* remain here as Kell Lasseter's prisoner.

She went to one of the windows and peered down. Two stories was not too far a drop if she fashioned a rope out of the bedsheets. But then what? She had no clothing or shoes or money to pay a hackney. And she could hardly traipse through Mayfair dressed as she was and totally defenseless. . . .

Trying desperately to think, Raven turned to pace the room and caught a glimpse of herself in the cheval glass. Merciful heaven. She hardly recognized the woman standing there. She looked wild and wanton, her hair a tousled mane around her shoulders, her cheeks and mouth flushed with color as if she'd just passed a passionate night engaged in lovemaking—as indeed she had. With Kell Lasseter.

She groaned again. No wonder he thought she'd seduced his brother for sport. This brazen creature appeared perfectly capable of such cruelty.

Reminded of Lasseter, Raven gritted her teeth. His behavior had been far from gentlemanly. He'd not only treated her with disdain, but he seemed to be almost deliberately goading her—and enjoying her bristling response. How she would have liked to wipe that mocking smile off his compelling face. But at the moment she was powerless. She glanced around the room. What she needed was protection of some kind, a weapon. . . .

She searched the armoire first and then the bureau drawers. When she encountered a pistol, she almost shouted in triumph. It looked very much like the one Sean had threatened her with yesterday. And it was primed and loaded. A tight smile compressed Raven's mouth. She still might not have the means to return home, but she felt less helpless armed. And now she would have the upper hand with Lasseter. She could force him to accede to her demands.

Buoyed by a surge of hope, Raven grew calmer. By the time two footmen carried in a copper hip bath and numerous pails of hot water, she had her emotions passably under control. Still, it was difficult to remain composed. Although the servants politely averted their gazes, she had to suffer the mortification of being seen in these iniquitous circumstances. And it vexed her when they locked the door behind them upon leaving, calling attention to her imprisonment.

The bath felt soothing to her aches and bruises but stung her various scrapes and raw patches, a fresh reminder of the outrages perpetrated against her yesterday. Beginning to stew again, she gingerly washed her body and then her hair. She spent the next half hour brushing it out and letting it dry before the fire, all the while nursing her anger at Kell Lasseter and his villainous brother. Having a target for her wrath at least kept despair from overwhelming her.

She could find no hairpins, so she plaited her long tresses and fashioned them into a knot at her nape. When she finished, however, there was still no sign of Mr. Lasseter or any clothing for her. Her temper started to simmer. When at last he appeared, she was seated in the chair, facing the door, with the pistol hidden beneath the folds of her robe.

"Finally you deign to show yourself," Raven said with no little asperity. "Perhaps I neglected to inform you, sir, that I don't relish being held prisoner."

"You are not a prisoner, Miss Kendrick. You are availing yourself of my hospitality."

"Indeed?" Her voice dripped with disbelief. "Your hospitality leaves much to be desired. First you lock me in, then you keep me waiting for hours."

"It has been but an hour."

"An hour longer than necessary. And I have nothing to wear. Miss Walsh promised ages ago to find me some decent clothing."

"I told her to delay. I didn't want you disappearing before we had a chance to discuss your situation."

"We have nothing to discuss. I wish to go home immediately."

His midnight eyes regarded her speculatively. "I hoped I could prevail on your better nature."

"At this moment, sir, I have no better nature."

The half smile he gave her held a wry charm that might or might not have been deliberate. "I have a name, Miss Kendrick."

"I don't doubt it. Blackguard, knave, miscreant . . ."

The smile became a wince. "I can understand your sense of ill-usage—"

"Ill-usage! Is that what you call what you and your brother did to me?"

He went on as if she hadn't interrupted. "But you seem intelligent enough. You must comprehend the predicament you are in."

"Oh, I comprehend perfectly." She looked away for a moment, striving for composure. "I am facing catastrophe."

"It would benefit us both if we could come to some mutual agreement. What will it take to have you forget this incident ever occurred?"

Her gaze flew to his. "You think to bribe me to secure my silence?" She gave him a smoldering glance. "If you expect me to let your brother go unpunished, you have taken leave of your senses. Even if I were willing to overlook his transgressions—which I am not—my grandfather will be enraged enough to prosecute. Your scoundrel of a brother will be fortunate if he doesn't spend the rest of his life in prison."

His dark eyes narrowing, Lasseter studied her from beneath heavy black lashes. "Naturally you would wish redress for your grievances. But I'm a gamester. I'd lay odds you would prefer to find a way out of this debacle."

"Of course I would. But there is no possible way to hush up a scandal of this nature."

"You could go abroad till the tempest dies down. I am a wealthy man. I would be willing to fund an extended stay."

Her own smile held scorn. "No amount of wealth or time will salvage my reputation."

He hesitated. "There is always marriage."

Raven stared. "Are you mad?"

"It isn't mad at all. Under the circumstances, it may be your only option."

"And just whom do you propose I marry? What gentleman would be willing to have me now that . . ." Furiously she quelled tears that suddenly threatened. "Now that I am damaged goods."

His expression remained enigmatic. "I imagine some acceptable candidates could be found for a woman of your . . . advantages. Perhaps no one with the title and fortune your duke possessed, but—"

"No, a title is doubtless beyond my reach now," she said bitterly.

Hearing the humiliating tremble in her voice, Raven shook herself, refusing to cry. Instead she rose to her feet, pointing her pistol directly at her nemesis. "I should like to go home now, sir."

Kell Lasseter's eyes suddenly hardened, probing her with an even stare. "I am not a man who likes to be threatened, Miss Kendrick."

"I frankly don't give a fig for what you like. You will do as I say and allow me to leave."

He gave a devilish laugh, blithely ignoring her wrath. "Or what? You will shoot me?"

"Yes, exactly. You will have Emma bring me a gown and then you will provide me with a closed carriage to deliver me home."

"No, I don't think so."

"I am not bluffing, Mr. Lasseter. And I am reckoned a good shot."

He crossed his arms over his chest, his very stance challenging. "You intend to shoot me in cold blood? Somehow I doubt it."

His supreme arrogance spurred her temper, already seething beyond caution. She couldn't remember ever being this angry.

"Go ahead then," he ordered, his own tone mocking. "Do your worst."

Seeing that smirk on his sensual mouth was the culmination of all the past hours of fear and frustration and despair; Raven's wrath boiled over.

Consigning him to perdition, she took careful aim and squeezed the trigger.

Chapter
Five

The explosion was deafening. With a startled grunt of pain, Lasseter doubled over to clench his left thigh. Almost at once a crimson streak spread beneath his fingers to stain his buff-colored breeches.

Aghast, Raven pressed a hand over her mouth, scarcely believing that she had actually shot him. Her gaze flew to his, only to find him skewering her with a menacing stare. With his beautiful, scarred face and coal black eyes, he looked supremely dangerous.

When he moved toward her, she took a defensive step backward. His scar stood out in a livid white line, and for a moment, all she could see was that and the promise of vengeance in his eyes. Yet instead of coming after her, he stumbled over to the bed, where he sat back against the headboard, grimacing in pain.

Blood was already soaking into the tangled sheets, Raven saw with horror as he grabbed a handful of linen to press against the wound.

"Are you badly hurt?" she murmured weakly.

Lasseter shot her a searing look. She had to school herself not to flinch from the smoldering intensity of his eyes.

Wanting to be of help, Raven started toward him, but his eyes flashed a warning and narrowed on the pistol in her hand. "For God's sake, put that damned thing down before you do any more damage."

Just then the door flew open and Emma Walsh stood there, a look of alarm on her beautiful features. "What happened?" she demanded, her gaze flying between Raven and the wounded man on the bed. "I heard a gunshot."

"Miss Kendrick has come to no harm," Lasseter bit out, "if that's what concerns you. Although she has mortally wounded me."

"Merciful heavens," Emma breathed, taking a step toward the bed.

Abruptly he held up a hand to forestall her. "I'll be all right. Just fetch some bandages."

When the hostess had hurried away, Raven spoke in a contrite tone. "Did you mean it? Are you really all right?"

"No, devil take it!" he retorted. "I am certain to be crippled for life."

Remorse filling her, Raven set the pistol down on the table and moved to the bedside. "Let me see."

When he growled a protest and made to rise, she pressed him back down with her palm, finding his chest firmly muscled beneath the crispness of his shirt. Keenly aware of his masculinity, she bent over him and pushed his hand away from his leg so she could inspect the injury. She uncovered a gash perhaps an inch long on the side of his thigh.

"It doesn't look too deep. . . . Certainly not a mortal wound as you claimed."

"I am devastated to disappoint you."

His reply was rough with pain and edged with hostility.

"There is no call for you to be so nasty, Mr. Lasseter. I am sorry I hurt you—"

"Why don't I believe you?"

Her cheeks flushed with hot anger. "I think I was entirely justified in shooting you."

"That is purely a matter of opinion. You could have deprived me of my manhood, if not put a period to my existence."

"It is only a flesh wound," Raven said defensively. "I could have injured you far worse had I wished to."

"Regrettably you will have to be satisfied with my bleeding to death."

Her eyes narrowed on him. "You are trying to make me feel guilty, aren't you?"

"The thought had crossed my mind."

He raised a sardonic smile to her glare, which only increased her vexation. When her fingers curled reflexively on his thigh, he flinched and grasped her hand to hold it away.

Raven abruptly went still. A shimmering awareness of danger of another kind filled the air as she met his glittering gaze.

Kell felt the same danger and cursed silently. His wound was far from lethal but painful enough to aggravate the devil out of him, so how could he possibly be feeling aroused at her mere touch? But there was no question his cock was swelling into an unmistakable erection. His only excuse was that he'd just spent a long, excruciating night of unsated hunger with this blue-eyed spitfire. . . .

Gritting his teeth, he damned her for causing him such pain, equally damning himself for wanting her so much. Intent on driving her away, Kell deliberately reached up and pulled his shirttail from his breeches. To his satisfaction, Raven Kendrick gave a start and jumped back.

"What are you doing?"

"Removing my breeches so I can see to my wound." He sent her a challenging glance. "Don't worry, Miss Kendrick. I don't intend to assault you. I prefer my women warm and willing."

Her chin lifted. "Will you please stop calling me Miss Kendrick in that odious tone?"

"What would you have me call you? Vixen? She-devil?"

When she merely looked daggers at him, he grinned tauntingly. "If you don't want your sensibilities offended, you had best turn your back. But first bring me that basin and pitcher of water."

With unaccustomed meekness, Raven did as she was bid, carrying the basin to the nightstand beside the bed, then fetching the pitcher and a towel. When Lasseter gave her a hard look, she scurried across the room to stand before the hearth, keeping her back to him.

She heard a rustle of clothing, then heard him swear as evidently he peeled the fabric of his breeches and drawers away from the wound.

Raven bit her lower lip. She had not wanted to injure him severely, merely to nick him and bring his level of arrogance down a peg or two. But either her aim had been slightly off, or he had moved at the last instant.

"I truly am sorry," she offered in a small voice after a moment.

"I trust you are." He gave a disgruntled sigh. "But I suppose the fault is as much mine as yours. I should have known better than to provoke an angry female with a gun." To her amazement there was an edge of dark humor in his voice.

His next question surprised her just as much. "Where did you learn to shoot like that?"

"Well . . . my groom taught me. O'Malley instructed me on any number of skills—riding and shooting particularly."

"O'Malley?" The hardness returned to his voice. "The same O'Malley who thrashed my brother and left him for the impressment gang?"

Fortunately she was spared having to reply when Emma Walsh entered, her arms laden with bandages and salves.

Glancing over her shoulder, Raven saw the hostess deposit her supplies on the bed, then inspect the bloody gash on Lasseter's leg. He had removed his breeches and used them to cover his loins, yet seeing the woman's lovely blond head bending over his bare thigh, Raven was startled to feel a prick of jealousy sting her. It shouldn't bother her in the least that they were behaving with the intimacy of lovers. . . .

"The wound doesn't look too severe," Emma said softly. "Do you need help bandaging it, Kell?"

"I can manage," he replied tersely. "You can clean up this bloody mess afterward, if you will." He hesitated, and Raven suddenly felt his gaze bore into her. "And pray do something with Miss Kendrick. Escort

her to your room and dress her. I'll take her home before she has a chance to wreak any more destruction."

Raven gave a slow exhalation of relief, even as she
felt an unexpected sense of regret. By shooting Kell
Lasseter, she had achieved precisely what she wanted.
So why did she feel so little satisfaction at hurting the
insufferable man?

Half an hour later, Raven found herself wearing a
borrowed kerseymere gown that was several inches too
long and a bit large in the bosom. But at least the high
neckline covered her modestly and left little reminder
of the wanton she'd been a short while earlier. More
thankfully, she had tucked her mother's pearls safely in
the pocket of her own cloak, which Emma had also
managed to rescue the previous night.

When a rap sounded on the bedchamber door, the
hostess opened it to reveal her employer. He was limping slightly, Raven saw as he stepped into the room.
Her gaze going to his left thigh, she noted he had
changed into a new pair of breeches; she could barely
see the outline of a bandage beneath the stockinet
fabric.

"The damage doesn't appear to be too extensive,"
she murmured pointedly, "if you can walk without the
aid of a cane."

His mouth curled up at one corner. "I'll survive, my
sweet termagant. But don't make the mistake of thinking I forgive you."

Whatever contrition she had started to feel was instantly dashed. Her irritation was only exacerbated when
he perused her oversized gown, lingering on her breasts

as if he could see beneath the excess fabric. His probing gaze took liberties with her figure no other man
had ever dared, the reprobate.

Pulling the lapels of her cloak closed, Raven raised
her chin defiantly.

Still, it was hard to maintain a semblance of hauteur
when he escorted her along the corridor, for she was
required to hold up her too-long skirts to keep from
tripping. It was even harder to ignore the smarting of
her conscience, for Lasseter's unsteady gait was clearly
unfeigned, and she knew he must be in some pain.

He paused at the end of the hall and startled her by
reaching up to draw her hood around her face. "I don't
expect any guests to be present at this early hour, but I
see no need to advertise your identity."

Raven felt her heart sink at the reminder of her
plight, but she determinedly tried not to think about it.

When they descended the grand staircase, she received a glimpse of the entrance hall and the rooms
beyond. For a gaming hell the decor seemed surprisingly elegant, with the gleam of rich wood and polished silver and sparkling crystal catching her eye. The
huge chandelier in the entryway alone must have cost
a fortune. Clearly the Golden Fleece was a successful
enterprise.

She stole a glance at its enigmatic owner, wondering
how a man who gave every outward appearance of being a gentleman had come to be involved in such a disreputable trade. Lasseter wasn't the devilish scoundrel
she might have expected, given his dangerous aura and
his brother's propensity for violence. Despite his biting
wit, he hadn't strangled her when she'd shot him. And

last night, he had treated her with the tenderness of a lover—

Swiftly Raven crushed the feelings of warmth she'd so briefly entertained. Kell Lasseter didn't deserve her admiration. He was a mere gamester, one who doubtless had rescued her only because he didn't want his brother being thrown in prison for life. And he had held her there against her will. She should despise him for his despicable treatment of her.

A closed carriage awaited them on the street. When asked, Raven gave the coachman her great-aunt's address and allowed Lasseter to hand her inside.

Without speaking, he settled beside her and then remained silent as they got under way. Perversely Raven almost wished Lasseter would talk to her, even if only to harangue her again for shooting him. She needed the distraction. The knots in her stomach had returned with a vengeance, for she recalled just how hopeless her future now was.

Disaster stared her in the face. Her character was in ruins, her dreams shattered. Her grandfather would doubtless disown her the way he had his own daughter. And her mother . . . Mama would have been devastated to see her mired in scandal and disgrace.

Raven shut her eyes, remembering her mother's final moments—her once-beautiful face wasted by fever, her strength drained by the fatal illness. But her grip had been fierce on her daughter's wrist as she had pleaded in a voice hoarse with desperation:

"Promise me, Raven. Swear to me you will wed a nobleman who can protect you from my folly."

"I promise, Mama. Of course I promise."

The pale lips had formed a frail smile of relief. "I can die in peace now."

Oh, Mama.

Tears welled up in the back of Raven's throat at the memory, while the chaos of her emotions threatened to overwhelm her again. Elizabeth Kendrick had lived for the day her daughter could return to England and take her rightful place in society without fear of being branded a bastard. And now that dream lay in ashes.

Pain sliced through Raven, while a sickening sense of inevitability swept her. There was no possible way for her to fulfill her promise now. And she had no one to turn to. She felt desperately alone, bereft of all sense of direction or purpose.

"Here," she heard a low male voice murmur beside her.

She took the handkerchief Lasseter offered her and brutally bit back a sob, cursing herself for being such a weakling. When she felt his penetrating gaze on her, she turned her face away and clenched her jaw till it ached.

Raven had herself under better control when the carriage drew to a halt. But she sat staring out the window a long moment, knowing there was no way to avoid a tempest when she faced her relatives.

"Do you need more time?" Lasseter asked. Amazingly enough, his dark gaze held sympathy.

"Yes, but I suppose it would be pointless, since the outcome wouldn't change." She stiffened her spine. "There is no hope for it. I must brave the dragon."

"Dragon?"

"My great-aunt, Lady Dalrymple. She has been waiting for me to cause a scandal since the day I arrived in England. No doubt she'll derive great satisfaction because I have lived up to her poor opinion of me."

"You think she will hold you to blame for what happened?"

"Absolutely. I'm certain no other young lady of her acquaintance would have managed to be abducted on her wedding day."

His sensual mouth curved in a half smile that strangely was devoid of sarcasm. "You are indeed rather unique in my experience, Miss Kendrick," he remarked, making it sound more a compliment than a slight.

He opened the carriage door and carefully descended, then turned to help Raven down. When he shut the door and made to accompany her, she shot him a quizzical look.

"I intend to see you safely inside," Lasseter said, and Raven didn't argue. She was absurdly glad to have him beside her.

They had started up the flight of steps together when she saw him grimace. Realizing his wound must be paining him, she offered her arm for support. Lasseter gave her a long, measuring glance, but after a moment's hesitation accepted her assistance, draping his arm around her shoulders and allowing her to bear some of his weight.

"You really should have a cane," she murmured, striving to ignore the intimacy of the contact. "My grandfather keeps several here at my aunt's house. I will find one for you."

Thankfully he released her when they reached the

landing. Her stomach churning, Raven pushed open the front door and entered with Lasseter behind her.

For a brief moment she considered taking the coward's way out and simply sneaking up to her rooms. But the two footmen standing at attention in the entrance hall had already spied her. And just then her aunt's butler appeared.

"Miss Raven!" Pleasure and relief wreathed his lined face. "You have returned! Were you harmed?" The aging butler caught himself. "Forgive me, miss. We have been frantic with worry, awaiting word of you."

"Thank you, Broady." Raven managed a smile. "I wasn't seriously harmed. Will you please inform my aunt that I am home?"

"Certainly, miss, and his lordship as well. Your grandfather has taken to his bed, he was so distraught over your disappearance."

Raven felt a renewed surge of guilt. She had been so concerned with her own dire circumstances, she hadn't wanted to think about how her grandfather's health would be affected by her abduction. The shock of her ruination might very well kill him.

Just then her aunt called out from the rear parlor. "Raven, is that you?" The silver-haired dame came into the hall. "In God's name, are you all right?"

"I'm well enough, Aunt."

"What happened? We feared the worst."

"Perhaps we should speak in private," Raven suggested, preferring not to air the shameful details in front of the servants.

It was no doubt a measure of how overset Lady Dalrymple was that she ignored the suggestion. "All we could think of was that someone held a grudge against Jervis . . . or perhaps Halford. Who were those brutes who abducted you?"

Raven gave Lasseter a quick glance. His mouth was set grimly, and she sensed the tension in the muscular lines of his body. He expected her to denounce his brother, she knew, and yet she found herself hesitating.

What point would be served by naming Sean Lasseter as her abductor? Did she truly want to see him in prison? And what of the consequences to Kell? He could very well be implicated in his brother's machinations.

She owed him more than that, Raven realized. He *had* saved her from his brother's violence, after all. And he had behaved honorably last night, after a fashion. He'd succored her in her dire need without taking advantage of her terrible vulnerability. How many other men would have acted with the same nobility? And then she had shot him for his efforts. . . .

Raven took a steadying breath, committing herself. "I'm not certain who they were, Aunt. They wore masks and never showed themselves before they struck me unconscious."

Beside her, she sensed Lasseter's sharp glance. She could feel his gaze boring into her as she went on with her fabricated tale. "Thankfully, this gentleman rescued me. This is Mr. Kell Lasseter, Aunt. Mr. Lasseter, my great-aunt Catherine, Lady Dalrymple."

He gave a brief bow, while the elderly lady stiffened. "Lasseter? Of the Derbyshire Lasseters?"

"The same, my lady," he responded.

"You are Adam Lasseter's eldest son." When he didn't deny it, a mingled look of horror and distaste claimed her haughty features. "I am acquainted with your unsavory reputation, sir! You are a notorious gamester, your mother was an Irish nobody, and it is common knowledge that you murdered your uncle!"

Shocked by the last charge, Raven couldn't help but stare at Lasseter.

The smile he gave was dangerous. "I wonder which you consider my greatest crime, Lady Dalrymple? The fact that I'm a gamester, of Irish blood, or rumored to be a murderer?"

She shuddered, while her hands rose to her cheeks in dismay. "Dear God. I had hoped . . . We are ruined!" She suddenly glowered at her great-niece. "How *could* you, Raven? How could you bring this murderer into our midst?"

"*Murderer?*"

Raven gave a start to hear her grandfather's gruff voice. He had descended the stairs halfway, garbed in his dressing gown, and his face was flushed with outrage.

Holding on to the banister with one shaking hand, Lord Luttrell pointed his cane at Lasseter. "Seize that man!"

For a moment, no one moved. Then the footmen suddenly understood the command and hastened to obey, leaping forward to apprehend Lasseter.

When they tried to grab his arms, however, he fended them off with lightning-quick reflexes—lashing out with his fists and delivering several hard blows to the face and stomach of each footman, felling them both with ease.

Raven gasped to see the two strapping servants lying on the parquet floor, groaning and wheezing for breath.

Even injured, Lasseter had been more than a physical match for them—although now he was gritting his teeth, obviously in pain from the bullet wound in his thigh.

"Damnation, I said seize him!" her grandfather roared.

When the elderly butler moved forward, Raven hastily stepped into his path, holding her arms out wide, shielding Lasseter and determined to protect the aging butler as well. "Broady, stop!"

She cast a frantic glance above her. "Grandfather, you don't know what you are doing."

"I do! I intend to have that scoundrel arrested and thrown in prison!"

"You are gravely mistaken. He is not a scoundrel!"

"If he abducted my granddaughter—"

"But he didn't! Indeed, he rescued me from the brutes who thought to hold me hostage." She hesitated only an instant before embellishing her tale further. "Moreover, he was wounded defending me. Truly, I owe him a debt of gratitude."

"Finally you admit it," she heard Lasseter mutter in a wry undervoice.

Raven gave him a sharp glance over her shoulder, daring him to challenge her lies. She thought she saw a mocking gleam of humor in his dark, penetrating gaze, along with something that appeared almost like admiration as he stood there flexing his bruised knuckles.

Her great-aunt, however, had a look of stark shock on her face to see two of her servants splayed on the floor of her magnificent entrance hall.

"Broady," Raven murmured, "will you please assist them?"

With a brief glance at her ladyship, the butler answered, "Of course, Miss Raven," and hurried to comply.

When he had helped the footmen to their feet and escorted them toward the rear of the house, Lady Dalrymple shook herself from her stupor and resumed her tone of haughty outrage. "What in heaven's name are you thinking, Raven Kendrick?" She glared at Lasseter. "I will not have this . . . *savage* in my house."

His own gaze remained cool, and so did his tone. "It pains me to disoblige you, my lady, but I have no intention of leaving until this situation with your niece is resolved."

Raven intervened hastily. "Mr. Lasseter should be allowed to sit down, for I'm certain his wound is paining him. And Grandfather, you must sit as well. You should never have left your bed."

"Well, you are the reason he was driven to his sickbed!" her aunt retorted caustically.

"Why don't we repair to the parlor to discuss this in a civilized manner?" Raven replied, gritting her teeth.

She led the way into the parlor and was glad when all three followed her. Only her grandfather, however, took a seat. He was clearly making an effort to control his temper, Raven thought, but he didn't look particularly well.

She remained standing, not only because she felt less vulnerable that way, but because she could more easily hide her inner turmoil. The violent fisticuffs just now had shaken her more than she would have expected, but so had her relatives' precipitous anger at her rescuer. It disturbed her to see Lasseter condemned out of hand. The charge of murder was a grave one, certainly, but despite the aura of potential danger that hovered over him, she found it hard to credit that he was actually a murderer. At the very least, she was willing to reserve judgment about his past until she had proof one way or the other.

Yet it was her own future that distressed her most. She could think of no tolerable outcome to this nightmare. And the worst could still happen. Her grandfather's health could prove irrevocably damaged by the shock he'd sustained. Or he could try to throw Lasseter in prison or challenge him to a duel. . . . What a disaster that would be.

She cared about her grandfather—and even her great-aunt—and didn't want them to be hurt further by this debacle. But how could she spare them? She could flee England, as Lasseter had suggested, in an effort to shield her family from disgrace, but where would she go? And her escape would still leave them to bear the brunt of her shame. Unless she could somehow manage to extricate herself from the scandal, she would take them down with her.

Her great-aunt had resumed ranting, Raven realized belatedly, but she had missed most of what had been said.

"Catherine, you will give Raven a chance to explain what happened," Lord Luttrell interjected gruffly.

Raven bestirred herself to respond. "I am sorry, Grandfather, but I have no good explanation for yesterday's events. Believe me, I would have spared you this if I could."

"I take leave to doubt that!" Aunt Catherine asserted. "You have been waiting to humiliate us ever since you arrived."

To Raven's surprise, she felt Lasseter move to her side, as if prepared to defend her, and she was heartened by his unspoken support.

"That is totally untrue," Raven answered her aunt, setting her jaw. "You make it sound as if I chose to be abducted."

"Well, whatever the truth, we are totally ruined now. Several hundred people saw you jilt Halford at the altar. We did our best to hush up the scandal, announcing that you were suddenly taken ill. But no one will believe that flimsy tale for long. Indeed, we are already suspected of prevarication. Halford has been here three times demanding to see you and was furious when we couldn't produce you. The last time he declared he had washed his hands of you and would cut all connection with us. And Lord and Lady Wycliff clearly smelled a lie. . . ."

Raven bit her lip in dismay. Brynn Tremayne, Lady Wycliff, was one of her closest friends. And Brynn's husband, Lucian, had been like a guardian to her when her other dearest friends had left for America last summer. They both would have been gravely concerned for her. In fact, had Lucian known the truth of her abduction, he might very well have invoked all his vast resources at the Foreign Office, where he worked, and turned London upside down searching for her.

"Not to mention the ignominy of your disappearance," her aunt continued scornfully. "You vanish for an entire night and return with this . . . this criminal."

Her nose rising two inches, she looked down it at Lasseter, while disdain dripped from her voice. "No, there is no hope for it. We must find a husband for you at once."

Raven stiffened at the raw nerve her aunt had struck. "I will not allow you to find a husband for me, Aunt Catherine."

"What do you mean, *you won't allow it*? Marriage is the only thing that could possibly save us from utter ruination!"

"Perhaps so, but you won't choose my husband for me."

"You obviously have no conception of the shame you have brought down upon our heads!"

"I understand quite well, Aunt, but I won't meekly permit you to marry me off the way you did my mother."

Lady Dalrymple drew herself up to her full height. "I cannot credit your insolence! This is the gratitude you show me for taking you in? Well, hear me, young lady. You are no longer welcome in my house!"

"That is quite enough, Catherine!" her brother exclaimed.

"No, Grandfather," Raven said tightly. "She is right. It would be best for all of us if I left. I will not remain where I am not wanted."

Defiance blazed in her eyes, and from the sidelines of the battle, Kell watched in fascination. She reminded him of his mother when her Irish temper was riled; Raven Kendrick was scrappy like his mother, certainly. A beautiful spitfire who aroused his own primitive male instincts more keenly than any woman he'd ever met.

Against his will and better judgment, he'd begun to admire her spirit and courage in the face of adversity, not to mention her sharp wit and beauty. A supremely dangerous combination.

Mentally Kell shook his head, realizing how significantly his opinion of her had changed in a few short hours. Until this morning, he'd thought his brother almost justified in wanting revenge against a treacherous temptress who took cruel pleasure in destroying men's lives. Yet now Kell found himself questioning that version of the tale, and worse—struggling against the unwanted feelings of protectiveness Raven Kendrick stirred in him.

She was still a dangerous temptress, he had no doubt, but the vulnerability in her remarkable eyes struck a responsive chord in him. After what his brother had done to her, he honestly didn't want to see her hurt further. And the scorn she was facing just now lay bare his own raw memories of his mother's treatment at the hands of her contemptuous English in-laws.

He felt fiercely compelled to defend Miss Kendrick, although she seemed to be holding her own well enough against her dragon of an aunt. She was trembling with courageous anger. The stubborn set of her jaw couldn't disguise the loveliness of its line, or suppress her inner fire. The kind of fire a man could sink right into . . .

Shaking off his errant thoughts, he reluctantly stepped into the fray. "Might I have a word with you, Miss Kendrick? In private?"

She broke off her heated argument with her aunt to stare at him, while Lady Dalrymple snapped, "What can you possibly have to say in this matter? You have done quite enough damage!"

"Leave him alone, Aunt Catherine!" her niece responded. "You have no right to take your anger out on Mr. Lasseter. And I would be pleased to speak to him."

Impulsively she grasped his hand to draw him out of the salon, and Kell was stunned when his body reacted at her merest touch; without warning he felt hot desire pulsing to life within him—unexpected, unwelcome, but undeniable.

He voiced a silent oath and allowed Miss Kendrick to lead him from the room and along the corridor to the adjacent dining room.

Releasing his hand then, she shut the door behind them and began to pace the Aubusson carpet, her eyes glittering with some wild, reckless emotion. Kell watched her curiously, but she seemed to have forgotten his presence.

Finally she recalled herself and sent him a disapproving glance. "Given your wound, you should sit down."

"It would hardly be the act of a gentleman to sit while you stand."

"*Now* you are claiming to be a gentleman?" she asked tartly.

He found it hard to repress a smile. "I know your dander is up from doing battle with the dragon, but there is no reason to flay me with your tongue."

She took a calming breath, obviously trying to gain control of her emotions. "Yes, you are right. Forgive me. I should not have allowed her to goad me."

It gave him some measure of satisfaction that she

had actually offered an apology, and he felt less resentment about what he was obliged to do.

"I have a question for you, vixen," he said. "Why did you lie about your abduction? Why didn't you give up my brother?"

She hesitated before exhaling in a sigh. "Because I realized that I owed you a debt. You saved me from your brother's revenge, possibly even rape. Moreover, I wasn't certain what my grandfather would do to you if he knew the role you played. At the time, I feared he might call you out. With his heart condition, he is much too frail to duel—or he might have been wounded or killed. And then there was the matter of justice. As you said, your brother had suffered a great deal already." She shrugged. "So now we are even."

His mouth curled at the corner. "We're hardly even. You seem to be forgetting that you shot me."

"But you held me prisoner." Her blue eyes held a renewed spark of defiance.

Deciding to retreat rather than fight that battle once more, Kell changed the subject. "I assume it is beyond question that your duke will still have you?"

Suddenly reluctant to meet his gaze, she looked away. "Entirely. You heard my aunt . . . Halford has washed his hands of me. And I cannot really blame him. Several hundred people saw me jilt him at the altar."

"You don't believe he could be persuaded to change his mind?"

"I am certain of it. The Duke of Halford is a stickler for propriety, and his pride is legendary. I came to know him well enough over the course of our betrothal. He would have been enraged by so public an humiliation. Besides, he would never accept a bride who had spent the night in another man's bed. Even if I could somehow manage to conceal . . . what happened last night"—her face flushed—"I couldn't lie to him on so important a matter."

"I don't suppose so," Kell said broodingly.

"So what did you wish to discuss with me?" she asked.

He drew a slow breath, steeling himself. "I am prepared to offer for your hand in marriage, Miss Kendrick."

Her sharp intake of breath proclaimed her shock. She stared at him a long moment before finally speaking. "You have no desire to marry me, I'm certain. Why ever would you make me such an offer?"

Kell raked a hand roughly through his hair, torn by the instincts that were warring inside him. He'd known from the first moment he found Raven Kendrick in his bed that her abduction could have disastrous consequences. He just hadn't wanted to face the possibilities. Nor did he want to be forced into matrimony with the heartbreaker who had made his brother's life such a misery.

But his conscience was smiting him now. And he felt honor bound to make amends for what Sean had done to her. He had to at least give Miss Kendrick the option of marrying him, even if he fervently hoped she would refuse his proposal.

"Because marriage would salvage your reputation to some extent. And I am interested in keeping my brother out of prison. I am willing to wed you if you will agree not to press charges."

She raised a hand to her temple as if dazed. Moving to the dining room table, she pulled out a chair and sank into it. "I presume you are proposing a marriage of convenience?"

"Yes. Afterward we can go our separate ways. Something could be arranged so that we needn't see much of each other."

She remained silent, looking down at her hands.

"Before you answer, Miss Kendrick," Kell commented, "you should be fully aware of my reputation. You think me an ill-mannered blackguard, and I won't dispute it. And society does not exactly hold me in high esteem. I own a gaming hell. And my Irish blood ensures that any number of doors are closed to me. Not to mention that I lack a title of any kind."

She winced as if that realization pained her. "I know," she said in a low voice. To his surprise he saw tears spring to her eyes, but she brushed them away furiously. Eventually she glanced up at him, as if a new thought had struck her. "What did my aunt mean when she said it was common knowledge that you murdered your uncle?"

All the muscles in his body went stiff. Finally Kell said, "There have long been rumors that I killed my uncle in a fit of rage."

Her intent gaze searched his face. "And did you?"

"Would you believe me if I said no?"

"Yes," she answered slowly. "I think I would. I don't put much stock in rumors. Last spring my bro— a dear friend of mine was accused of being a murderer and sentenced to hang, but he was entirely justified in his actions."

She had surprised him once again, Kell realized, with her novel attitude. He would have to learn not to underestimate the unconventional Miss Kendrick.

As for answering her question, however . . . he had no intention of divulging the truth, although he was indeed suspected of murder. The dark rumors about his past had followed him from Ireland where his uncle had died, and Kell had never made any attempt to deny them.

"I think I can safely say that my uncle's death was justified," Kell replied enigmatically.

She nodded slowly, then rose to her feet to pace the room again. At length she stopped and clasped her hands together, possibly to still her agitation. "Perhaps you are right," she said, looking at him. "Marriage is my only option. I am facing ruination. I will be branded a total pariah in society if I don't find a husband at once."

Kell didn't care for her reply at all. "Keep in mind that your family will have fierce objections to our marriage. Your great-aunt thinks me a criminal."

Her mouth twisted briefly in a grimace. "The fact that my aunt holds you in aversion is frankly an argument in your favor."

"And you would wed an unsuitable husband just to spite her?"

"No, of course not. But I won't allow her to dictate to me."

The rebellious flash of heat in her eyes struck another chord in Kell. He understood rebellion; he was a rebel himself. But that didn't mean he wanted to encourage her to accept his offer.

He gave her a measuring stare, deliberately trying to unsettle her.

In response she squared her shoulders. "No matter how notorious your reputation, Mr. Lasseter, you would still be immeasurably better than no husband at all. Unwed, I stand no chance of ever showing my face again in society. I think it vastly unfair, but it is a fact of life. And I am hardly in a position to be overly discriminating."

"Yet you just told your aunt you refused to marry."

"No. I said I refused to accept her choice."

"There is a difference?"

"A tremendous difference. It is a long story but . . . my mother was compelled by her family to marry a man she . . . disliked. And I have no intention of following in her footsteps."

Her blue eyes were filled with pain, Kell noted. "Still, there must be other better marital candidates than I."

"I can think of no one on such short notice. Even if I were to try to find someone willing to wed me, I run the risk of exposing myself further. If I were turned down . . . there would be no possible way to keep my circumstances a secret."

"You could leave the country, as I suggested earlier."

"And live as an outcast? That is even more repugnant to me than being compelled to wed." Her voice dropped to a murmur, but it was filled with trembling anger. "My mother spent most of her life preparing me to join the society she was denied, and she would have been devastated to know she'd failed in her life's goal.

And I'm certain my grandfather will rest easier if I can manage to avert disaster. My aunt as well."

Kell raised a skeptical eyebrow. "After your aunt's virulent display of sympathy, I fail to comprehend why you would want to comfort her."

"Because I don't want my family to suffer because of me. But to have any hope of shielding them, I will have to wed immediately. The servants have already witnessed my return, and they will not keep quiet for long."

Denial was Kell's first impulse, but he couldn't refute that her points were good ones.

"You appear to be regretting your offer already," she said when he was silent.

Kell shifted uneasily, not knowing which was causing him more discomfort, his injured thigh or the knot that had formed low in his belly. "I am a bachelor, Miss Kendrick. You'll understand if I'm not eager to hang in the parson's noose."

Her brow furrowed, and she hesitated a moment before asking, "Do you have someone in mind you would prefer to wed?"

"No, vixen, I don't," Kell said dryly. "I hadn't intended to wed at all. Certainly not anytime in the near future."

"I suppose you keep a mistress. Most men of means do."

His eyebrows shot up at her plain speaking, but the flush on her cheeks suggested the topic wasn't a comfortable one for her.

"Truly," she added, "I wouldn't mind if you continue to have your paramours."

"Your generosity overwhelms me," he drawled.

"Well, you might find our union financially advantageous. I have an adequate income of my own—a fund provided by my . . . father. And my grandfather promised me a significant dowry when I wed."

"I don't require your wealth," Kell declared, annoyed at her assumption that he could be bought.

She moistened her lips, drawing his attention there against his will. "Well, unless you mean to withdraw your offer, I think I must accept it."

Still fighting the inevitable, Kell narrowed his own gaze at her. "You really should consider carefully, vixen. I promise you, I would make you a terrible husband."

Pinning her with his midnight eyes, he moved toward her.

Raven took a defensive step backward, finding his intense stare unnerving. She was still amazed by his offer. And he would no doubt make her a *dreadful* husband. He was a notorious gamester, a stranger who didn't even like her. Without question, he would be disagreeable and unmanageable as a spouse. And she had deliberately shot him. . . .

It was a marriage doomed to failure. But she had little choice in the matter. Any husband would be better than no husband at all. She needed him.

"Are you certain you want to be my wife?" he murmured. When he grasped her elbow in a velvet grip, Raven felt her breath catch.

"Well?" His silken tone made her shiver, and so did his nearness.

Her gaze focused on his scarred cheek, which suddenly made him seem menacing, then shifted lower to his striking, sensual mouth, which was even more dangerous. Did he intend to kiss her? Her pulse quickened into a rapid, erratic rhythm.

But he didn't kiss her. Instead his arms folded tightly about her in a merciless embrace that wouldn't permit her to move. The surge of primal heat shocked her body into stillness; the hot darkness of his gaze filled her with the stunning memory of how he'd pleasured her all through the night. . . .

"Aren't you afraid of me, Miss Kendrick?"

Was she afraid of him? He was an intense, dangerous man, with a hot vitality that seemed to charge the very air she breathed. She should fear for her virtue at the very least. Yet inexplicably she didn't fear him. Perhaps because she had seen him so many times in her fantasies.

His eyes glittered darkly, reminding her so keenly of her pirate lover.

"No . . . I am not afraid of you," she managed to whisper unsteadily. "Especially not when I think you are deliberately trying to intimidate me."

He stared down at her a long moment, his eyes unreadable. "I can't frighten you away then?"

"No, sir, you cannot."

His mouth compressed in a sardonic line. "My name is not sir."

"Mr. Lasseter, then."

"My name is Kell. Say it."

"Kell, then. I am *not* afraid of you, Kell."

She felt her heart pounding as she waited an interminable moment for his response.

Cursing under his breath then, he abruptly released

her and turned away. For the span of another dozen heartbeats, he stood there, his jaw muscles working as if he were struggling with himself.

Finally he shot her a hooded glance over his shoulder.

"Very well, vixen," he said, his tone rife with resignation. "We will marry as soon as arrangements can be made."

Chapter
Six

He never should have touched her, Kell reflected darkly as he watched Raven Kendrick attempt to explain their sudden engagement to her disbelieving relatives. He'd hoped that physical intimidation might influence her to refuse his reluctant proposal of marriage, but regrettably, wrapping his arms around her had only reminded him of their feverish night together: the incredible feel of her aroused body, her passionate hunger for a man, his yet unfulfilled ache. . . .

Bloody hell, but his ill-considered embrace had been a mistake, affecting his body and his senses on the most primal level. His body still throbbed, while his mind spun, unable to focus on the current conversation.

Moments ago they'd returned to the salon to announce their intention to marry, and for a brittle instant, both her great-aunt and grandfather had sat stunned. Then Lord Luttrell had practically exploded in protest, leaping to his feet and waving his cane in the air to punctuate his objections while Raven tried to calm him and prevent him suffering a true apoplectic fit.

His own mind distracted, Kell settled in a chair and watched his prospective bride, wondering exactly why he had felt compelled to save her. He didn't want a wife of any kind. Certainly not a blue-blooded temptress who drove men like his impressionable brother wild. And he'd had at least one other option besides the parson's noose. Determined to keep Sean out of prison or worse, he could have spirited his brother out of the country to avoid any retribution by Miss Kendrick or her enraged family.

There was his sense of honor, of course. Any man with a shred of decency would feel obliged to make amends for the violence she had been shown. And *he* actually had been the one to compromise her. It was his bed she had spent the entire night in.

But Kell suspected there were other, more profound reasons he hadn't fought harder against having to make her his bride.

Simply put, if he didn't wed her, she would have no defenses against society's savagery. He didn't want the image of her desperate and alone haunting him, the way the stark image of his mother still haunted him.

His mother had been an Irish physician's daughter who'd fallen in love with one of her father's patients— an Englishman injured in a hunting accident while touring Ireland. Fiona had married considerably above her station, into the wealthy English gentry, and was never accepted by the haughty Lasseters, even though her husband and her two sons adored her. Within months of being widowed, Fiona was banished to Ireland by the boys' uncle William, who took over their guardianship, despite their anguished pleas and bitter protests. A year later she'd died in poverty.

Kell had blamed his uncle entirely for her death and came to hate William with an unforgiving ferocity. And that was before the bastard had violated his youngest ward's innocence with his perversions. . . .

Grimly Kell forced away the memory. He'd been unable to shield either his mother or brother all those years ago, but he didn't intend to bear that burden of guilt again by standing idle while Raven Kendrick suffered.

For whatever reason, he felt a fierce, almost savage need to protect her. He wouldn't abandon her now. Even if wedding her was wholly contrary to his own personal desires.

Kell gave a silent, humorless laugh. He'd once vowed he would never marry an aristocrat. Indeed, if he'd thought about it, he would have said he wanted to marry only for love; that he wanted a love match like his parents'.

But at least Raven Kendrick wasn't the typical wide-eyed schoolmiss without an intelligent thought in her head. As husband and wife, they would doubtless frequently clash, but he would rather risk being shot again than be tied to a milksop for life. And while the singular Miss Kendrick might be virginal, last night he'd been given a tantalizing glimpse of another woman entirely. A staggeringly passionate woman with strength and fire and spirit enough to keep him constantly intrigued . . .

Too damned intrigued.

Kell cursed under his breath. He didn't want to be

fascinated by his unwanted bride's spirit or her capti-
vating beauty. He knew too well the danger she presented. Thankfully they'd agreed only to a marriage of
convenience, a dispassionate arrangement that could
be entered into without any emotional or physical in-
volvement. After the obligatory consummation, they
needn't ever share conjugal relations. He would have
to do his utmost to see their union never became more
intimate than that.

Her grandfather, however, was acting as if he didn't
want the marriage to take place at all, Kell realized as
he refocused his attention on the conversation. Oddly
enough it was Lady Dalrymple who was championing
the union.

"You cannot be thinking clearly, Jervis," the dragon
said in her usual frigid tones. "Raven has no option but
to wed—"

"My thinking is quite clear, Catherine! You are the
one who has gone maggoty. You said he was a damned
murderer!"

"Well, I don't know that for a fact. The rumors could
be mere gossip."

"But he is still a gamester."

"True. Mr. Lasseter is the scandal of polite society.
But Raven is just as notorious at the moment. And disreputable or not, his marrying her will at least provide
her with a crumb of respectability. Furthermore"—
Lady Dalrymple shot her great niece a glance full of
dislike, if not actual malice—"I hazard to say they deserve one another."

The undercurrents of tension in the room were palpable, and Lord Luttrell's next accusation only added to the turbulence.

"Doubtless he's nothing but a damned fortune hunter."

Kell stiffened at that groundless indictment. He'd rightfully inherited the Lasseter wealth upon his uncle's death but refused to touch it, turning the income and the use of the entailed estate over to his younger brother, along with the London town house, as recompense for what Sean had suffered. Instead, Kell had made use of his considerable skills as a gamester to amass a small fortune, which had allowed him to open his private gaming club. That success, along with several subsequent judicious investments, had increased his worth tenfold and made him sufficiently rich to earn a certain deference from any but the noble class.

Before he could respond, though, Lord Luttrell continued in a voice full of contempt. "And you can't deny he's a bloody Irishman!"

Raven broke into the altercation then, her tone grim. "I think you are forgetting that Ian Kendrick was part Irish. If he was good enough to be my father, then Mr. Lasseter is good enough to be my husband."

Kell scarcely heard her argument, for he was fighting his own deep resentment and barely controlled rage. The notion that he wasn't worthy of marrying a British viscount's granddaughter made him seethe. He could never forget that his mother hadn't been good enough for the English Quality; that even Irish gentry were considered beneath them.

That sort of upper class bigotry roused his defiance enough to have the opposite effect from the one Lord

Luttrell intended; now Kell felt inclined to marry Miss Kendrick simply to spite her disdainful kin.

"But his bloodlines," Lady Dalrymple broke in, "are inconsequential at this point, Jervis. If she doesn't wed him at once, the scandal will descend upon all our heads."

"The scandal be damned." The elderly nobleman looked directly at his granddaughter, his eyes softening. "I'll not force you to wed against your wishes. I'll not repeat the mistake I made with your mother."

"It won't be against my wishes, Grandfather," Raven replied, a stubborn edge to her voice.

Kell finally was able to control his anger enough to interrupt. "I don't deny your charges regarding my profession, Lord Luttrell. But I'm not at all ashamed of my Irish heritage. As for my being a fortune hunter, you are far off the mark. I am quite capable of caring for your granddaughter and keeping her in her accustomed style. In fact I'm prepared to be exceptionally generous. I will provide her with a house and income of her own. And if you are still concerned for her welfare, your solicitors can draw up a marriage contract to tie up whatever fortune she now possesses and keep it out of my reach."

Lord Luttrell gave Kell a fierce glance, but Lady Dalrymple conferred an imperious nod of approval on the plan. "There, then. It is all settled."

A long silence followed while his lordship's scowl gradually faded to frustration and then finally resignation. At last, he sighed and surrendered to necessity, just as Kell had. "I suppose there is no other choice."

"No, Grandfather, there isn't," Raven agreed.

"Now," her aunt said briskly, obviously determined to take charge, "we must somehow come up with a credible story to explain Raven's disappearance yesterday. If she is to suddenly reappear married, then no one will truly believe she was ill as we claimed. And there will still be the disgrace of her publicly jilting the Duke of Halford." She hesitated, frowning. "But what story could be considered credible?"

"We would do best to keep as close to the truth as possible," Kell said. "Too many people saw Miss Kendrick's abduction for us to deny it, but we can suggest our own interpretation of events."

"What do you mean?" Raven asked.

He met her curious gaze with cool detachment. "We should put about a new story: we met sometime in the past and fell in love, but you rejected my suit because of your family's objections. On the eve of your wedding, I realized I couldn't live without you, so I abducted you and convinced you to wed me."

"You want to concoct a tale of a love match?" her aunt asked.

"We would pretend to be in love?" Raven echoed, startled by the unlikely prospect of Kell Lasseter loving her. Judging by his expression, he saw her as a regrettable obligation. "But when would I have had time to meet you and fall in love? Until this past spring I was still living in the Caribbean."

"Then we fell in love in the Caribbean when I visited years ago."

"It just might suffice," Lady Dalrymple said thoughtfully. "A former romance could explain why Raven would be foolish enough to jilt a duke. And it could possibly avert further disastrous consequences. Halford might be inclined to call out Raven's abductor, but if he believes her in love with someone else, he will be less likely to brawl over her. The ton, as well, could be a trifle more forgiving in judging her."

"We should probably claim to have been married last evening," Kell added, "and make it a reality as soon as possible."

"Why not elope to Scotland," Luttrell demanded, "and be married over the anvil?"

"An elopement wouldn't help Miss Kendrick's reputation," Kell answered. "For one thing, she would be unmarried and in my sole company for too long. And your servants would know differently. Moreover, with my leg wound, I would prefer not to endure countless days of jostling in a carriage." He glanced at the ormolu clock on the mantel. "There is still enough time to apply for a special license so that we can be married this evening."

"You will need a clergymen to perform the ceremony," his lordship said tersely.

"I can arrange for a clergyman. But we cannot be married here. There would be too many witnesses who could later contradict our story. The ceremony will have to take place in a private location."

"Where do you suggest?"

"I have a house in Richmond that is lightly staffed at the moment and should be adequate. The servants are discreet."

Raven shot her future husband a curious frown. Quite often gentlemen of leisure had pleasure houses close to London so their mistresses would be nearby.

Was Kell Lasseter one of those gentlemen? Was he even a gentleman?

The thought was interrupted by her grandfather's continued questioning. "What of the marriage contract? I want my granddaughter to be well provided for."

"Jervis, there is no time to draw up any contracts," his sister insisted. "That can wait until after they are safely wed."

Lasseter returned a cool look. "I don't intend to cheat your granddaughter out of a settlement, if that is what concerns you."

"Of course it can wait," Raven said. "I trust Mr. Lasseter to keep his word."

And strangely enough, she did. She had little doubt he would do as he promised. Her bigger fear in marrying him was that she could completely lose her independence, since a wife had few rights. She wouldn't be able to manage him the way she could have managed Halford. On the contrary, if any husband could prove to be domineering and difficult to control, it would be Kell Lasseter.

He was watching her with that enigmatic look again, as if trying to determine her motives. Subjected to his dark-eyed scrutiny, Raven suddenly felt her stomach twist in knots.

This man would soon be her husband. She was actually about to marry a notorious stranger, heaven help her.

If her misgivings about marriage were profuse yesterday when she was about to fulfill her long-held dreams with her ideal match, they were utterly rampant now. But she had no choice, she reminded herself, trying to curb her panic. Indeed, she was fortunate that Lasseter had agreed to rescue her.

"Well, then," her aunt said, returning to practical matters, "we have a great number of preparations to make. Raven, while Mr. Lasseter sees to the special license, you must write Halford and give him to understand the circumstances and beg his forgiveness."

"Yes," she agreed, grateful for the distraction. "I owe him an apology of some kind. And I should send a word of explanation to Brynn and Lucian . . ."

"And I will do the same with my chief acquaintances," her aunt added, "while Jervis sends a notice to the papers."

Lasseter interrupted, addressing Raven. "It would be better for you to write from Richmond. The longer you remain here, the harder it will be to support the pretense that we were wed last evening. As it is, we can say that we only stopped here to inform your family of our union."

"Yes," Raven agreed, seeing the wisdom of his suggestion. "We should be on our way."

"Is such unseemly haste really necessary?" Lady Dalrymple protested—simply, her niece suspected, because she disliked someone else being in charge. "Raven should at least be allowed to change her gown for something more suitable."

"No, Aunt Catherine, Mr. Kendrick is right. My attire isn't overly important. But I will eventually need access to my belongings. My trunks were packed for my remove to Halford House. Were they delivered there yet?"

"Not yet. With all the chaos yesterday—"

"Her trunks can be retrieved once we decide on living arrangements," Lasseter said with an edge of impatience.

"But a valise was prepared for her wedding trip," her ladyship insisted. "She should be permitted to take it with her. She cannot go about town looking like a ragamuffin." The suggestion was accompanied by a derisive look at Raven's ill-fitting skirts.

"Perhaps that would be wise," Raven agreed, remembering that the valise would contain a nightdress among other garments.

"Very well," he acceded.

Rising, Lady Dalrymple rang for Broady and instructed the grave-faced butler to have Miss Kendrick's valise loaded at once onto Mr. Lasseter's carriage.

After that, there seemed to be little more to be said except for farewell. Raven, however, couldn't help but contrast her leavetaking now with the previous day's. Yesterday she had been about to marry an illustrious duke; today she would wed a notorious gamester who was suspected of murder. . . .

Her relatives' qualms were almost as great as her own, it seemed. Her aunt remained icily polite, while her grandfather was actually distraught. Lord Luttrell took her hands in his own trembling ones and squeezed her fingers hard.

"If you ever find yourself in need, my dear . . . I hope you know you can count on me."

A sudden ache of emotion tightened her throat: surprise, gratitude, affection. She was amazed and relieved that her grandfather didn't mean to treat her in the scurrilous way he had her mother. Her voice sounded raspy when she murmured her thanks.

Her grandfather then turned to Lasseter with a fierce stare. "If you harm her in any way, I warn you, sir, you will answer to me."

"Grandfather—" Raven objected, feeling the injustice of the remark, but Lasseter offered the elderly nobleman a cool smile.

"I intend to save her, Lord Luttrell, not harm her. You will have to be satisfied with that."

Raven intended to apologize for her grandfather's animosity once they were out of earshot, but Michael O'Malley was waiting for her directly outside the salon door, pacing the hall.

The groom's expression held despair and remorse and more than a little concern.

"Oh, Miss Raven, I feared . . . Sure and I had to see for myself that you were all right," he said in his Irish lilt.

"I'm fine, O'Malley, truly."

Beside her, she felt Lasseter stiffen at the name. He eyed the groom sharply but didn't comment.

"Who was the bastard responsible?" O'Malley demanded. "That scurvy case Lasseter, was it?"

"Yes," Raven murmured, "but please keep your voice down. I don't want it advertised. In fact, I intend to try to put it behind me." She hesitated. "This is his brother, Mr. Kell Lasseter. He has agreed to wed me, O'Malley."

"*Wed?*" The elderly groom looked shocked for a moment, before his gaze narrowed in piercing scrutiny. "Saints preserve us."

The two men regarded each other with almost dislike while Raven quietly explained the need for her unexpected union.

"I ken you've no choice, Miss Raven," O'Malley finally said with reluctance, "but I mean to accompany you. I'll not let you out of my sight again."

She looked to Lasseter, whose expression was grim. "Please?" she asked. "May he come with me?"

To her surprise and gratitude, Lasseter nodded. "He can act as a witness for the ceremony. And no doubt you will want someone nearby to protect you in case my abusive tendencies get out of hand."

It was said with irony, but Raven chose not to press the issue. Instead she had a footman retrieve a cane for Kell to use and then led the way outside, where her valise was being loaded in the boot of the waiting coach. When the task was finished, O'Malley climbed up to join the coachman while Lasseter handed Raven inside and then settled beside her.

Soon they were off, but they had gone barely half a block before Lasseter spoke.

"Your groom is Irish." It was not a question.

"Yes. He was in service to the Kendrick family when my parents wed, and he decided to accompany them to the Caribbean. Actually O'Malley has been like a father to me. He practically raised me."

"He's the one who taught you to shoot."

"Yes . . . that among other things."

Lasseter's mouth curled at her admission. "I wonder that you allow him to serve you in such an intimate capacity. Your relatives obviously scorn anything Irish."

"I am not my relatives," Raven assured him in a stern voice.

She couldn't tell from Lasseter's enigmatic expression what he felt about that, but she was inclined to think her groom's being Irish was the only reason he'd granted her request to have the servant go with her. She'd seen Kell Lasseter's anger when her grandfather had derided his bloodlines. In fact, she'd caught the slightest glimmer of hurt mixed with the fury in his dark eyes, the slightest vulnerability. His Irish blood was unquestionably a sensitive matter with him.

"Is Kell an Irish name?" she asked curiously.

"It's Gaelic. Short for Kellach. It means something like 'strife.' "

She repressed a smile but couldn't resist replying, "Rather fitting, I should think."

The responsive flicker in his dark eyes might have been amusement, but the glance he gave her was unreadable. "Kell is actually my middle name, the one my mother gave me. Sean chose to use his Irish name as well."

Any humor Raven felt disappeared abruptly at the mention of his brother, while her misgivings returned full force as a wretched thought occurred to her. Sean Lasseter would shortly become her brother-in-law.

Frowning, she hesitantly broached her concern. "After tonight your brother and I will be related by marriage. But I . . . it will be difficult for me to treat him with civility. I would prefer to have nothing to do with him."

"I see no reason why you should have to deal with him," Kell responded without inflection.

"But he may not consider his vengeance complete. I might even need protection from him."

She saw Kell's jaw harden momentarily before he spoke. "I will see to it that he doesn't abuse you again."

Deciding to be content with his assurance, Raven lapsed into silence for the rest of the journey.

At length the coach turned off the main road and onto a smooth gravel drive. The well-kept grounds were landscaped with lush foliage that offered occasional glimpses of the Thames River. And when they drew to a halt, Raven found herself impressed. The house seemed more a mansion than a country cottage, large and elegant and built of mellow red brick.

"Is this your home?" she asked Kell. "Or do you use it primarily for diversions?"

"Diversions?"

"I'm aware that gentlemen often have pleasure houses for the purpose of keeping a mistress."

He glanced at her for a long moment, but his reply was less forthcoming than Raven could have wished. "This is indeed a pleasure house, but it is unoccupied at the moment."

"Because you already have Emma Walsh? Is she your mistress?"

One dark brow lifted sardonically. "I offered to wed you, Miss Kendrick. Not to divulge the details of my personal life."

Raven found herself flushing. "I simply wanted to know the circumstances of our relationship so I would not be caught off guard."

"I believe we agreed to live separate lives. Are you acting the managing wife before we are even wed?"

"No, of course not!" Raven retorted, stung by the accusation.

Thankfully O'Malley came around just then to hand her down from the carriage. But it was Kell who escorted her up the front steps. As he ushered her inside the house, his touch on the small of her back sent a sensual shock rippling down her spine. Raven was glad he was eager for them to live apart. Enduring such close proximity with Kell Lasseter day after day would be unnerving in the extreme.

The interior of the house was just as elegant as the environs, not at all the sort of residence she would think of as belonging to a gamester . . . or to a gamester's mistress.

They were met by a butler and housekeeper, who were apparently a couple. If the Goodhopes were startled by their master's announcement of his impending marriage, they were too well disciplined to show it. Kell ordered Miss Kendrick's valise unloaded and a bedchamber prepared for her, but he waited until the servants had left to execute their respective tasks before he spoke again.

"It may take me the better part of the day to arrange for a special license at Doctor's Commons and to engage a clergyman. While I'm away, you can make use of the drawing room"—he pointed toward a door off the entrance hall—"or perhaps you would prefer to rest."

Raven shook her head. She'd had little genuine sleep the previous night, but at the moment she had more pressing matters on her mind than rest. "I should write Halford as soon as possible."

He nodded. "I will have one of my grooms deliver your letter."

"If it is all the same to you, I would rather send O'Malley. I don't care to trust such an important commission to a stranger. His grace is not likely to take the news well, and it would be better if only O'Malley were there to witness his reaction."

"I suppose so." Kell made a scoffing sound deep in his throat. "Halford is as pompous and stiff-necked as they come. I can't imagine how you ever came to be betrothed to him in the first place. He hardly seems to be your type— Never mind," Kell said curtly. "I *can* imagine. Doubtless you were enamored of his title."

Raven felt herself wince. He wouldn't understand her determination to make a magnificent match, or her distress at having those plans shattered. "I don't deny," she admitted, "that his title was one of his strongest suits."

She saw Kell's mouth harden with something like contempt, but then he shrugged. "Do whatever you like. But you may consider the staff at your disposal. It isn't large, but Mrs. Goodhope can send a maid to attend you later."

"I can make do without a lady's maid."

He looked skeptical.

"Truly, I managed to dress myself for years," Raven said. "Servants were a luxury when I was growing up. Not until I came to England did I have anyone to wait on me."

Kell's dark brows drew together as if she'd surprised him once again, but he made no comment. "Very well, then. I will see you this evening."

He started to turn away, but Raven stopped him. "Mr. Lasseter . . . Kell . . . I am grateful for your . . . sacrifice. I know this is not what you planned for your future."

His mouth curled in a cynical half smile that was not unattractive. "I can only conclude my innate chivalry overcame my good sense."

"Even so, I should like to thank you."

"You can thank me once your reputation is safe." He hesitated before giving her a pointed glance. "You realize, of course, that we will have to consummate our union. Unless you want there to be a question about the legitimacy of our marriage."

Raven's breath suddenly escaped her. She hadn't thought that far ahead. "I . . . suppose you are right."

His smile was humorless. "Are you certain you don't wish to withdraw now, Miss Kendrick? The prospect of sharing my bed doesn't intimidate you?"

She gazed up at him, at his strong, chiseled features. She was indeed intimidated. The scar slashing across one high cheekbone marred his masculine beauty and suggested he was capable of violence, while those midnight eyes were heart-stoppingly intense. His mere glance made her quiver inside—as did the thought of making love to him.

"It need only be once, isn't that so?" she murmured finally.

"Yes, it need only be once." The edge of determination in his voice implied that he didn't relish the obligation any more than she did. "Until tonight then."

With a brief bow, he left her standing there staring after him.

Alone, Raven bit her lower lip, wondering if she was making a terrible mistake by allying herself so intimately with a perfect stranger. Especially one so compelling as Lasseter. He was dark, dangerous, and handsome as sin, with a damn-your-eyes attitude that was inexplicably appealing—the precise opposite of the husband she wanted. Despite her every instinct of self-preservation and common sense, she was attracted to him against her will. The heat and vitality that throbbed from him set her every nerve ending on edge. And the thought of the night to come . . .

If her sensual memories of last night were anything to judge by, Kell Lasseter would make an exceptional lover.

Shutting her eyes, Raven made a sound of distress deep in her throat. She didn't *want* an exceptional lover. She didn't need a real lover when she had her pirate. For tonight, however, there was no hope for it. She would have to become Lasseter's wife in truth.

She took a deep breath to steady herself. Surely she could manage to resist his dangerous appeal for one night.

Determinedly attempting to dismiss her chaotic thoughts, Raven made her way to the drawing room to compose what was certain to be a difficult letter to her former betrothed.

It took over an hour, as well as a half dozen drafts before Raven was satisfied with her letter to Halford, explaining how she had been stolen on her wedding day by a man who'd captured her heart long ago.

She didn't like having to lie to him but felt the tale

was necessary not merely to save her reputation, but to provide a balm to Halford's wounded dignity. The duke had an immense sense of pride, and she had savaged it, however unintentionally. Thus she was glad that her heartfelt apology had a sincere ring of truth.

And even in the midst of her misery, she couldn't deny a vague feeling of relief that she wouldn't be required to wed Halford after all. Losing him wasn't the devastating blow it might have been had she truly loved him.

Forcibly ignoring her despondent thoughts, Raven sanded and sealed her letter, then sent for O'Malley and commissioned him to deliver it for her. A mistake, she realized, for it gave him the opportunity to quiz her relentlessly about her decision to wed the man whose brother had made her life a misery.

"I've heard tell of Lasseter, Miss Raven," the groom protested almost as vocally as her grandfather had done earlier. "His reputation is shady, without a doubt."

"I know all about his reputation," Raven replied quietly. "But I have to believe it is much exaggerated."

"But his brother—"

"Kell is *nothing* like his brother, O'Malley; I am certain of that. If he were, nothing could induce me to wed him. But as you said, I have little choice. Marrying Mr. Lasseter is the only possible way to extricate myself from this disaster."

"Maybe so," O'Malley agreed with grave reluctance, "but I'd not like to see you hurt again."

"I know. But the worst is over." She gave him a smile of reassurance and repeated her arguments until he finally abandoned the fight and complied with her request to deliver her letter.

When he was gone, Raven sighed. She couldn't take O'Malley to task for exceeding the bounds of the servant-mistress relationship, for he enjoyed the status of an old friend, and she knew he worried for her. He had looked after her since she was a young girl.

She felt her stomach clench with familiar anguish as she recalled the first time the groom had consoled her. She had been ten years old at the time, nearly dancing in anticipation of attending the birthday celebration of the Honorable Miss Jane Hewitt. Eleven-year-old Jane was the daughter of the highest-ranking nobleman on the island, and all children of the Quality had been invited.

Raven, however, had made the mistake of asking her stepfather for a new dress—a request Ian Kendrick not only denied but maliciously ridiculed.

"You will not need a new dress, Raven, because you are not going. A bastard does not belong in such elite company." He eyed her coldly, making a scoffing sound. "You would never have been invited were your low origins known."

Bastard. Savage pain sliced through Raven at the vicious word, and it was all she could do to hold back her tears. It wasn't that she needed or even wanted a fancy dress; she was much more at home in her worn riding habit than flounces and ribbons. But to be forcibly excluded because of her birth, and worse, to suffer her stepfather's implied threat to tell the world about her origins . . . His cruelty made her stomach churn.

She had fled to the stables and hid in the hayloft,

where O'Malley found her sobbing her heart out. Hunkering down beside her, he eventually coaxed from her the reason for her grief.

"I am a bastard, O'Malley. I will never be anything better. I am a *nobody*."

" 'Tis not true, Miss Raven. You're a beautiful young lady, I'll be thinking. And who sired you isn't as important as who you are inside, here." He touched his chest.

"But I have no father."

"If you want a da, I'll be your da." He patted her shoulder. "There now, dry your tears and come with me to see the new filly. She's a beauty, with a coat as black as your hair. . . ."

Ian Kendrick had died two years later, but Raven had never extinguished her private fear of being publicly branded a bastard.

Nor was it only her mother who had dreamed of the day Raven could travel to England and take her place among the nobility, of when she could prove herself worthy of joining the elite ranks that would have scorned her had they known the truth.

With an illustrious title attached to her name, Raven was certain, she could bury the secret shame of her past once and for all. No one would dare utter a word against her when she was a duchess. And at last she would belong somewhere.

But now those dreams of belonging had been shattered.

Steeling herself against the bitter despair roiling inside her, Raven forced herself to ring for the housekeeper. She had felt alone for most of her life; she could endure it again if need be.

She managed to choke down a light tea, but by the time she went upstairs to the bedchamber she'd been allotted, her feeling of hopelessness had returned full force. All the tension and emotional turmoil of the past day had taken a toll, leaving her with only desolation.

The thought of dressing for her wedding was more than she could face. Perhaps she would feel better if she could just rest for a moment.

Slipping out of her borrowed gown, she undressed down to her shift, then crawled beneath the covers and closed her eyes. In only an instant she had fallen asleep, but it was a slumber troubled by restless dreams of her fantasy lover.

His anger was something new. His eyes burned like black coals as his hands twined in her hair, tilting her mouth roughly up to his. Raven drew a sharp breath at his painful assault. He had never acted this violently before.

"You cannot love him," her pirate snarled against her lips. "He will never own your heart."

"No," she promised, "never. Only you can possess my heart."

He drew back, and she gave a start as the glitter of his gaze swept over her. This was not her pirate! He had the same intense, burning eyes, and his handsome features held the same anger. But this was Kell Lasseter.

His face filled her vision, harsh with emotion, savage with demand. He was a beautiful devil, infinitely more dangerous than her pirate lover.

Alarmed, she pressed her palms against his chest, encountering corded muscle and searing heat. She felt the forceful beat of his heart along with the frantic trembling of her own as she met his scathing glance. He was wildly angry at her—for hurting his brother, for being trapped into marriage.

And yet she was angry at him as well, for ruining her plans, destroying her life. She stared back defiantly.

His mouth crushed down over hers then, claiming her lips in a brutal kiss. Her senses reeling, she tried to fight the shivers that suffused her body. She ached to repudiate him, to conquer him. It was as if they were battling for control . . . a duel of desire that neither of them could win.

She could feel his angry passion as he drew her hard against him. Heard herself whimper as he thrust his tongue ruthlessly into her mouth, his kiss hot and compelling.

She arched against the steel band of his arm, but he pulled her closer, grinding his loins into hers, rubbing the hard ridge of his manhood against her soft mound. Her nipples tightened unbearably, while a similar ache throbbed in her lower body.

Her thighs were clamped together, but he managed to slide one finger between them, finding her hot, honeyed crease. A shudder rocked her, and he made a rough sound of satisfaction, thrusting even deeper into her slick, swollen flesh folds.

Helplessly she parted her legs and opened to him fully. She couldn't deny the hunger of her body. This was what she craved, the hard fierce lovemaking of this incredible man. Their mouths locked together, and she felt herself surrender to the wild, lashing urgency. . . .

A low, insistent voice calling her name brought her out of her disturbing dreams. Raven froze to see her lover sitting beside her on the bed. No, not her lover.

Her soon-to-be husband. Kell Lasseter had one hip resting on the mattress, a hand pressed against her arm to urge her awake.

In the lamplight, his features looked starkly sensual, reminding her of his fierce passion in her dreams. When she met his dark, unsettling eyes, the power sent a shock wave rippling through her.

Her body was aching shamelessly for him. Did he know what she had been dreaming?

Just then his gaze strayed lower, and Raven felt her face flush. She had thrown off most of the covers, while the bodice of her shift had slipped down over one shoulder, exposing the swell of her breast.

Flustered, she crossed her arm over her bosom to shield herself, but Kell pretended not to have seen her immodest display.

"It's time," he said simply, his grim tone more that of a man facing execution than his nuptials.

Chapter
Seven

Her wedding was nothing like Raven had planned. Instead of an elegant church ceremony with hundreds of elite guests in attendance, her marriage took place in the drawing room of a country pleasure house, with O'Malley and the Goodhopes to serve as witnesses. She wore a simple, long-sleeved gown of lilac kerseymere, with her hair dressed in a plain knot at her nape.

Her intended husband, too, was vastly different from the nobleman she'd expected to be united with in holy matrimony. Instead of possessing an illustrious title and vast estates, her darkly handsome groom owned a gaming hell and was shrouded in scandal. And he was certainly not the safe, comfortable spouse she had wanted. There was nothing safe or comfortable about Kell Lasseter.

As she listened to the ritual words that would bind her to him for life, Raven realized her trepidation must be showing, for halfway through the exchange of vows, Kell bent to murmur bracingly in her ear, "Smile, vixen. You're about to be wed, not attend a funeral."

She stiffened her spine and managed to pledge her troth in a reasonably composed tone, but all too swiftly it was over. Ordinarily a celebration would have followed. Had she wed her duke yesterday, she would have enjoyed a sumptuous wedding breakfast. Instead, a light repast was to be served in the dining room for the bridal couple alone.

Raven, however, temporarily forgot her misgivings when she accompanied her new husband there, for she saw him limping, even with his cane.

"My leg stiffened after all the jarring travel today," he replied to her questioning glance.

Remorse returned to smite her. "Is there something I can do to help?"

"No. But I'm afraid you will have to take the lead tonight. I am not fit for the normal exertions expected of a bridegroom."

Reminded of the night to come, Raven felt her stomach muscles clench.

Throughout dinner, she merely toyed with her food, a thrumming awareness of her new husband setting all her nerves on edge. She answered his every attempt at conversation with monosyllables.

Her reserve puzzled Kell at first. Last night in his bed, she had been so flame hot, so hungry for him, that she'd practically torn his clothes off. But then last night she had been suffering under the influence of a powerful aphrodisiac. And she hadn't known who he was—a half-Irish gamester who was rumored to be a murderer.

Resentment returned to settle in his gut. The fact that Raven Kendrick had a beloved Irish groom and professed not to be repulsed by his Irish roots didn't convince Kell that she was different from the other contemptuous, purebred English members of her class. Certainly his blue-blooded bride would be comparing him to the duke she should have wed. And naturally she would find a mere commoner sorely lacking.

Kell's fingers tightened reflexively around his wineglass—but then he swore at himself. What the devil did it matter what his bride thought of him? After tonight they would not need to see much of each other.

Yet that galled him as well. Raven considered him good enough to save her from disaster but not good enough to make a life with her as her husband—even if he didn't in the least want that sort of life with her.

He wanted *her*, though. Kell bit back an oath. The pain of his wound throbbed less than the pain in his groin.

"Shall we retire?" he said finally, struggling to control his foul mood.

His wife visibly stiffened. And when Kell pushed back his chair and came around the table to help her rise, she hesitated, staring up at him with wide blue eyes.

"I thought you said you were not afraid of me," he said tightly.

She bit her lower lip. "I am not, really."

"Then stop looking like a frightened doe. I have no intention of assaulting you. Sex is more pleasurable when the woman is willing."

His sardonic comment made her chin rise, which was precisely what Kell had hoped for. He preferred her blue eyes flashing defiance, for then he wouldn't experience the illogical feeling that he was taking advantage of her.

Kell stood back as she rose and, with a gesture of his arm, invited her to precede him from the room. He escorted her upstairs to the master bedchamber and let her enter first. The room was softly lit by a single lamp, while a fire burned warmly in the hearth—perfectly appropriate for a bridal couple on their wedding night.

As he closed the door behind them, he saw Raven stop and take stock of the huge bed with its brocade curtains. The covers had been turned down invitingly. Her glance quickly shied away to focus on anything else.

"I suppose this is where you conduct your orgies?" she asked—whether out of belligerence or curiosity or merely to buy time, he wasn't certain.

"What would a well-bred young lady know about orgies?" he drawled.

"Several gentlemen of my acquaintance are members of the Hellfire League, and I've heard rumors. . . . It isn't difficult to guess what sort of wicked perversions occur at their gatherings."

The Hellfire League, Kell knew, was a notorious group of rakes and adventurers. But he had never been invited to join their distinguished ranks.

"I haven't conducted an orgy in quite some time," Kell said dryly.

"You cannot make me believe you are not a rake."

"Then I won't attempt to," he retorted. "But I will say that I prefer one bed partner at a time. And that I am not particularly fond of perversions."

When she clasped her fingers together and looked away, he decided she was simply nervous.

"If it will reassure you, vixen, I'll promise to try to control my rakehell lusts. Should I fail, you can always shoot me again."

At his deliberate taunt, her chin shot up while a frown scored her beautiful features. "I *said* I was sorry for that."

Kell sighed. "So you did. Let's just get this over with, shall we?"

He started to remove his cravat and found Raven staring at him again. "It is customary to get undressed before bed, madam wife."

"Must we . . . so soon? I scarcely know you."

"You weren't nearly this shy last night."

"But I was drugged last night. I recall little about what happened."

Kell studied her, wondering at the truth of her claim. It was possible that in her drugged state she hadn't been entirely aware of her actions or how passionate her response had been. It irked him that he was the only one who remembered their scorching, unforgettable night together. Yet he couldn't credit that she was as innocent as she was pretending.

"Allow me to refresh your memory then. You nearly ravished me. You weren't the least intimidated."

"That is because . . . I mistook you for someone else."

"Someone else?" There was a sharp edge to his voice that Kell recognized as jealousy. Raven was a virgin, he would swear to it, but that didn't preclude her from giving out other sexual favors freely. "Then you admit you've had other lovers?"

"No, not exactly. Not . . . a real lover."

His eyebrow shot up. "Perhaps you should explain."

"I don't think you would understand."

"Indulge me."

Restlessly she moved over to the hearth and began to pace, still clenching her hands. "I'm not at all as experienced as you think me. I have never told anyone this before, but I ... I created a lover in my fantasies." Her cheeks flushed with evident embarrassment, she cast him a swift glance as if to see the effect of her confession.

"Do go on. I am fascinated. Why would you have need to create a lover when there are doubtless scores of men who would jump at the chance to fulfill that role for you?" Kell asked skeptically.

"Because ... as I'm sure you know ... well-bred ladies cannot take real lovers without risking disgrace." She hesitated, looking more discomposed than he'd ever seen her. "And because, well, it is much safer that way. One cannot truly fall in love with a fantasy."

"And falling in love concerns you?"

"Well, yes." She seemed actually flustered by his questions.

"So you invented an imaginary lover?"

"Yes," she admitted with obvious reluctance. Her voice dropped to a mere murmur. "A pirate, in fact."

Kell found himself at a loss for words; once again Raven had startled him with her uniqueness. He thought back to the previous night, remembering how she had addressed him, calling him "my pirate." She had evidently mistaken him for her lover—which might explain her eagerness but not her unmistakable sexual experience.

"You must have a very vivid imagination," he said finally. "But that doesn't explain how you learned the carnal skills you practiced on me last night. You knew precisely how to arouse me."

"Well, if you must know . . ." Her flush deepened. "I have a book—a rare book—an erotic journal written by a Frenchwoman who was once captured by Turkish corsairs. It is the tale of her grand passion and is quite . . . enlightening about carnal matters. My mother left the journal in her personal effects for me to have when I was old enough."

"Your *mother*?"

"I *knew* you wouldn't understand."

Kell stared at her. Her answer was just far-fetched enough that he could almost believe she hadn't made it up out of whole cloth. "Then educate me. Why would your mother want you to be enlightened about carnal matters?"

"Because she meant the book to be a warning to me," Raven replied uneasily. "Before I was born, my mother fell in love with someone entirely inappropriate. She spent her life futilely nursing her obsession, but in her final days, she grew to lament wasting her life away on her grand passion. By leaving me the book, she intended to remind me of the devastating effect love can have. That love is like a potent drug. It can take over your sanity, destroy common sense and logic. A woman who loves has no power over her life." Involuntarily Raven clenched her fists. "I vowed long ago I would never follow in her footsteps."

She glanced at Kell to see how he was receiving her

explanation. The expression in his black eyes was shielded by his long lashes.

"And you are worried that you might fall in love with me?" he asked slowly.

"Well ... I ... " Raven found herself stammering at having her biggest fear stated so baldly. "I don't wish to fall in love with you—or any other man, for that matter—or for you to fall for me, as your brother claims to have done."

She saw a muscle tighten in Kell's jaw at the reminder of their present circumstances. "I suspect there is little danger of us falling in love. Ours is a marriage of convenience, nothing more. I have no intention of joining the legions of men who have succumbed to your charms."

"I assure you, I don't wish you to succumb," Raven said rather tartly, feeling defensive once more.

"What is this, vixen? Wounded vanity?"

At the edge of mockery in his tone, she bristled. "I wouldn't be wounded in the least if you forgot about my existence altogether."

"I shall strive to do just that—immediately after we consummate our union."

That made Raven abruptly fall silent. In the interval, her new husband began to remove his shirt. She watched as he revealed a torso sleekly ridged with muscle, his chest lightly furred with whorls of black hair.

Assaulted by a fresh attack of nerves at the imminent prospect of seeing him naked, she worried her lower lip. "You don't have to undress entirely, do you?"

"No. But it will be more conducive to passion. You may not recall, but I had little opportunity for sleep last night. Considering my fatigue and the pain of my bullet wound, I suspect it will take more than the prospect of a perfunctory coupling to arouse me."

His lack of eagerness wasn't at all flattering, but he seemed determined to go through with the bedding. He sat to remove his boots and breeches, wincing now and then as he completely undressed.

A neat bandage wrapped his lower thigh, Raven saw, but it was the rest of him that captured her unwilling attention. His lean body rippled with muscle, while firelight played across his skin. He was quite beautiful, heaven help her.

Involuntarily she followed the fine line of dark hair down his chest to his naked loins and drew a slow breath. He was every bit as virile as she had imagined him to be—and far more intimidating. Making love to a fantasy would not be the same as giving her body to this man . . . a very real, very tangible, warm flesh and blood lover.

Realizing he was watching her, she averted her gaze from his all too piercing eyes. But only momentarily. When he rose and moved toward her, she was drawn once again into the intensity of his gaze. He looked much like her pirate lover, except that the flickering shadows made his face look even darker, more dangerous. Just like in her recent disturbing dream.

It was all she could do to remain still when he stopped merely inches from her. Unconsciously Raven reached up to touch his chiseled cheekbone, brushing the jagged line of his scar.

"Does my disfigured face repulse you?" he asked quietly.

The question startled her. He was a stunningly attractive man, with the devil's own beauty, and no scar could diminish his sensual appeal. In fact it only added to his allure, heightening his aura of danger and rousing a forbidden excitement deep within her. And yet it hurt to think of the pain he must have endured.

"No, it doesn't repulse me," she replied just as softly. "Though I did wonder how you came by it."

He frowned. "It isn't a pretty tale."

Grasping her fingers, he held her hand away, dismissing her curiosity just as easily. "I was serious when I said the honors will have to fall to you, vixen."

"I . . . I'm not certain what you mean."

"I mean that I will have to be beneath you. My covering you would severely strain my injured leg. So you will have to take the initiative."

"Oh." She flushed at the disturbing image that his plain speaking brought to mind. "I don't think I would know where to begin."

"You just said that your journal has given you an adequate carnal education."

"Yes, but reading about it is different from actually—"

"Perhaps you should use that vivid imagination of yours, then." When she returned a puzzled frown, Kell amended his suggestion. "You can start by kissing me."

Shutting her eyes, she raised her face and obediently pressed her lips to his—with no reaction. She'd expected him to ravage her mouth, as in her dream, but he remained as cold and unresponsive as a statue.

She pressed harder and felt a slight stirring of warmth in his lips. A moment later, his arms came around her, but his kiss was still tentative, reluctant, as if he were forcing himself even to touch her.

More determined now, Raven slid her fingers through the heavy, dark waves of his hair and drew his face closer. The resultant spark that flared between them was unmistakable.

And she had succeeded in arousing him, she realized. When he pulled her against him, letting her feel the swollen ridge of his erection against the softness of her belly, Raven swallowed a gasp.

In response, he lifted his head to stare down at her, unsmiling. She was certain he could see the flare of mingled desire and panic in her eyes. He knew what was happening to her, how her heart beat unevenly, how her skin had become overheated.

He truly kissed her then. No longer holding back, he bent his head and covered her lips with his, like a man intent on claiming what was his. His tongue moved deep into her mouth in a kiss that was everything she'd ever fantasized and more.

Raven heard herself moan. She should try to resist his allure, she knew, but he made her feel so faint and hot, so unlike herself. Warmth was gathering in her body, seeping down to pool in her loins.

He pulled back without speaking, still staring at her. His lashes were absurdly long for a man, she thought, black as ink, framing eyes that burned.

He silently undressed her then, unfastening the buttons of her gown and slipping it off her shoulders for her to step out of. His expression tightened in sympathy when he caught sight of her bruised wrists, but he continued wordlessly, removing her slippers and peeling down her stockings, then attending to her corset and chemise, tossing the garments aside one by one until she stood naked and defenseless before him.

She quivered as his black velvet eyes slowly swept over her . . . her breasts, her waist, her hips, her legs. . . . Raven felt a scalding heat wherever his eyes touched, while a throbbing ache began to pulse between her thighs—

Drawing a deep breath, she tried to ignore the longing that was flooding her. She needn't surrender to her wanton desires. She needed only to get through this night and then she would be free of him.

But it was difficult to remain unaffected when he stood so close. She could feel the heat from his body as he removed the pins from her hair, unraveled the knot at her nape, smoothed out her raven tresses. His eyes were so beautiful, dark as midnight and just as fathomless.

Without a word then, he turned away. She followed the graceful motion of his body with unwilling fascination—his broad shoulders that tapered to narrow hips and taut buttocks, his powerful thighs and sinewed calves that evidenced he was a sportsman. And when he settled himself on the bed and leaned back against the pillows, she was far too aware of his massive erection.

"Come here, Raven." He touched the mattress beside him.

Almost helplessly, she moved to join him, climbing up to kneel beside him. When she gave him a questioning glance, though, he remained impassive.

He expected her to take the lead, she remembered;

she was responsible for arousing him, not the reverse. Yet the chance to retain control actually relieved Raven, since it would give him less power over her.

"What should I do?" she murmured.

"Whatever you wish. You'll know soon enough what I think of it."

She glanced down at him, wary of his enormous, pulsing size. Tentatively, she leaned forward and pressed her hands against his chest, feeling smooth, hot flesh over corded muscles, dusted with silken hair. His expression never changed, but when her exploring hands traveled over the hard ridges of muscle and lower to his flat, hard belly, she felt tension quiver through him.

Bolder now, she moved her hand even lower to his blatant erection, letting the surging, silky flesh brush her knuckles. His rampant member jerked involuntarily, making her breath catch. Raven bit her lip. She could imagine having that engorged length inside her, like in her fantasies.

Treacherous excitement spread through her body at the thought and made her breasts ache.

Gathering her control, she trailed her hand lower, letting her fingers curl around him. When his breath drew harshly between his teeth, she looked up, caught by the hypnotizing heat of his eyes.

His hot vitality seemed to thrum through her. The very firelight seemed to caress his male features . . . the skin pulled taut over high cheekbones, the stark line of his scar. She felt the strangest urge to touch that old wound, along with an inexplicable anger at whoever had hurt him.

Determinedly quelling her sympathetic urges, she

tried to remember what she had learned from the journal about arousing a man. Holding her breath, she bent down to taste him with her tongue. A shudder ran through him, sending a sense of power into Raven. It was a heady feeling, knowing she could evoke such a response from him.

But then he deliberately took control from her. He reached out to cup her breasts, the heat from his palms searing her skin. Her nipples changed in a rush, answering the caress of his hands.

When she would have pulled back, his fingers tightened on the stiff crests, sending shocking waves of sensation rippling through her. Her resolve weakening, she shut her eyes and let him have his way.

His touch was magical as he continued to stroke and squeeze her throbbing breasts, arousing her with controlled expertise, obviously skilled in the art of prolonging pleasure. Then drawing her forward, he bit her nipple with his teeth, hurting her and yet not hurting her.

With a moan, Raven arched against his mouth, offering herself to him. As if he knew what she needed, he sucked her nipple, his tongue lightly flicking the turgid peak. Then without breaking contact, he reached down and slipped his hand between her thighs to touch the swollen dampness there. She was slick with her own desire, Raven realized as his touch dredged a whimper from deep in her throat.

She almost came off the bed when slowly he slid two fingers inside her, penetrating her heated tightness. Her thighs closed reflexively around his hand, and she squirmed restlessly, remembering how he had done precisely this last night. But this time she was totally aware of the man who was giving her such pleasure.

In a slow, tantalizing rhythm, his deft fingers withdrew and penetrated again. Breathless, she clutched at his shoulders, incapable of defense against the explosive sensation centering in the shimmering core of her body. His thumb found the dewy bud of her sex then, stroking, teasing, while his fingers continued gently thrusting, urging her closer and closer toward the edge of an orgasmic precipice.

The sensual pressure built relentlessly until her hips writhed, until she thought she could bear no more.

"Now, vixen," he commanded, his dark eyes glittering in the firelight.

She needed no further encouragement. Almost blind with need, she straddled his hips, instinctively trying to avoid putting pressure on his wound.

His palms shaped the backs of her thighs, lifting her up, positioning her where he wanted her, the searing tip of his shaft poised at the very heart of her.

Fierce, urgent longing gathered in the pit of her belly. She held her breath as he gripped his hard shaft and very gently eased its silken head into her quivering flesh, growing rigid when he lowered her slowly onto him, guiding her.

She gasped at the alien feel of him, at his fullness stretching her, and gave a soft cry at the moment of sharp pain. Instantly he stilled, waiting for her to become accustomed to the penetration of his rigid flesh.

"Steady," he murmured, moving one hand to gently stroke the base of her spine while his lips pressed light, soothing kisses over her face. "Try to relax."

She was panting softly, but he held her still, letting her accept his invasion. And in a short while the pain began to fade.

"Better?" he asked softly, as if reading her expression.

She nodded, staring into eyes that seemed to scorch her with searing heat. Those burning eyes were so much like her pirate's, and yet her imaginary lover had never made her feel this particular way ... stunned, breathless, overwhelmed by sensation ... as if she might erupt in flames at any moment.

Reaching down between their bodies, he cupped her soft triangle of curls and resumed his delicate tormenting, caressing that wonderful point of pleasure with his circling thumb.

She couldn't fight the growing rapture; she could only cling to him, her breath coming in short, ragged gasps.

Holding her hips steady, he pressed upward with his rampant length, urging her thighs wider to take more of him. And then he kissed her, his tongue plunging deep while his tumescence seemed to swell inside her, filling her to near bursting.

This is what I have been missing, she thought, dazed. *This incredible intimacy, this joining, this merging with a passionate man made of real flesh and bone.* A magnificent lover she could feel and taste and smell. His very heat ignited fiery sparks in her blood. ...

The primal force of it excited her beyond anything she'd ever known. The fierceness rising in her made her arch and mold to him, as if she could make him part of herself.

Gritting his teeth, visibly striving for control, he

thrust upward one last time. The sensual fury that seized Raven was so intense, she shuddered and cried out, shaking in spasms of ecstasy.

Beneath her his body clenched as he was caught in the wild delirium. At the last instant, though, he lifted her up urgently so they were no longer joined. His seed spurted explosively onto her belly, while contractions continued to convulse his lower body.

Her flesh continued to pulse sweetly long after the moment of climax. Raven was dimly aware that she had fallen limply against him, her face buried in his throat. But it took longer for her to realize why he had withdrawn from her. He hadn't wanted to get her with child.

A strange twinge of sadness pierced her, before common sense caught up with her. She wouldn't want a child, not if it meant bringing one into the world with an uncaring father.

There had been no chance for her to discuss the matter of children with Kell, Raven reflected. Indeed, she'd been so overwhelmed by the disastrous change in her future that the issue hadn't even occurred to her until just now. But she doubted the man she had just married would want to be a father to her child. He didn't even want to be her husband.

Nor, after tonight, her lover.

He was lying still beneath her, his heart thudding against her breast, each beat slow and heavy. Eventually she felt him stir, felt his fingers brush a tress back from her forehead.

"Tell me, does that compare to your fantasy?"

She was startled by his question, spoken in a low

husky voice. She was more unnerved to realize her answer. The passion she'd felt a moment ago was more intense, more powerful, than anything she'd experienced during her most erotic sexual fantasies with her imaginary lover. Kell had driven her to a place of wild abandonment, pushing her headlong off the dizzying cliff of desire and need.

Deploring what he had made her feel, she eased off him and onto her side, wincing at the raw ache between her thighs. "I believe I prefer my fantasy," she prevaricated, avoiding his penetrating gaze. "Illusion is less painful."

"Did I hurt you?"

"No ... not really. At least no more than I expected."

"Your next time won't be as painful."

"There won't be a next time."

When she reached down to draw a sheet up to cover her nudity, he stayed her. "Wait a moment."

He rose from the bed and went to the washstand, returning with a basin and cloth. To Raven's keen embarrassment, he tugged the sheet from her grasp and used the cloth to clean away the evidence of his seed and her virginity, first from her body and then his own.

His tenderness was at odds with his dark expression, yet other flashes of memory assailed her—of him soothing her the previous night during her drugged fever, of him gratifying her desperate carnal need again and again. The reminder of his searing sensuality set a new throbbing ache pulsing between her thighs.

She was glad when he was done. He allowed her to pull the covers up as he disposed of the basin and turned down the lamp. The red-gold glow of firelight was the only illumination when he returned to bed.

Raven stole an unwilling glance at Kell. He wasn't her pirate lover, no matter how intimately his dark eyes reminded her of her fantasies, how devastatingly sexy his mouth was, how vulnerable he made her feel.

And the longing he stirred in her was a graver threat than even the scandal she faced. She'd hoped to salvage a shred of reputation from this disaster by wedding him, but it would all be for naught if she fell prey to the madness of desire.

He didn't look at her as he joined her. Instead he lay back, lacing his hands behind his head, staring thoughtfully up at the brocade canopy.

"You honestly intend to embrace a life of celibacy?" he asked after a moment.

"Yes. Why do you find that so surprising?"

"Because no matter how vivid your imagination or erotic your reading material, it can't compare to real passion. I'll wager you will eventually come to regret what you're missing."

"I doubt it. My fantasies will be enough."

He turned his head on the pillow to appraise her. "You realize, of course, that there is such a thing as passion without love?"

"Perhaps, but I don't intend to take the risk. I won't take a real lover."

His mouth curled at one corner. "I suppose that as your husband, I should be gratified. I wouldn't relish being cuckolded."

"You needn't worry on that score."

"But you don't expect your proscription against taking lovers to apply to me?"

"No. I have said so more than once."

Hearing the sincerity in her voice, Kell felt an unaccountable stab of resentment at her tolerant attitude, especially since he couldn't reciprocate. He couldn't feel at all tolerant about her making love to other men.

His brows narrowed in a frown. There was a reasonable explanation for his proprietary feelings toward Raven: it was no more than pure primal instinct. By taking her body, by being the first to claim her, he'd created an intimate bond between them as old as the laws of procreation—the primitive animal hunger of a healthy male for a ready female, the exultation of the conqueror. It was only natural that he would feel a certain possessiveness toward his beautiful new wife.

Scoffing at himself, Kell abruptly changed the subject. "We should establish some other rules for our relationship," he said brusquely. "I have a house in London. You may use it as it suits you, but eventually you will want to find one of your own."

Her blue eyes searched his. "You don't mind if I live with you?"

"Whether or not I mind, we will have to reside together for a time if we want to keep up the pretense of a love match. Afterward we can go our separate ways. I will take you there tomorrow."

"Thank you," she murmured.

"Why don't you get some sleep?"

She turned over, giving him her back, her hair a curtain of tousled silk that flowed to the pillows.

It was a long while before Kell heard her breathing

soften into a low and even rhythm, longer still before he could relax the tension in his own body.

Despite his exhaustion, however, sleep eluded him, for his thoughts kept returning to their consummation. What should have been a perfunctory coupling had turned far hotter than he'd anticipated—and it had dismayed the hell out of him. Raven was so exquisitely responsive, so startlingly vibrant that he'd wanted to bury himself endlessly in her.

He'd fought his desire. It had taken every ounce of control he possessed to resist her wild sweetness and withdraw from her. That brief, explosive encounter hadn't been enough to sate him, either. He could still feel the lushness of her slim body moving against him, the hot, soft tightness of her virginal passage as he sheathed himself inside her, the way she fit perfectly in his arms.

The savage rush of hunger that memory inspired made Kell curse.

Unable to help himself, he reached out and caught a stray lock of her silken hair, letting it drift through his fingers.

Raven Kendrick . . . no, she was Mrs. Kell Lasseter now, his wife. And she was an enigma. A vixen whose spirit and sensuality concealed a deep wariness. If she could be believed, she feared any man whose touch could arouse her passion.

He feared her as well. He'd been shaken by the experience of making love to her. Shaken by her mouth, her touch, her scent. By his own need.

She was a supremely dangerous temptation.

He had no difficulty understanding how she had attracted so many ardent suitors. He could fall for her without much effort—

God, what a disaster that would be!

He would have enough trouble dealing with the aftermath of their sudden marriage. He dreaded having to tell his brother that he'd wed the very woman Sean had once professed to love. And given Raven's reputation for breaking hearts, his brother's included, he would be a fool to allow her any further chance to get under his skin.

In that regard, he regretted having to offer her the use of his London house. The last thing he wanted was to be forced to share his home with Raven, where he would be enticed and tormented by her nearness.

Thankfully they needn't be together often, or in any intimate way. They could ignore each other for the most part. And he could take refuge in his gaming club much of the time.

Turning over, Kell forced himself to close his eyes. Tomorrow he would deliver Raven to his town house, and then he would be done with his duty. Afterward he should be able to dismiss her from his thoughts and focus on his brother. His chief priority would be determining what to do with Sean, Kell reflected grimly.

It only remained for him to crush his unruly feelings for Raven before they grew into something he could no longer control.

Chapter
Eight

Raven found herself alone when she woke the following morning, much to her relief. She was glad she didn't have to face her new husband. It was difficult enough to ignore the memories of his exquisite lovemaking.

The twinging ache between her thighs and the tenderness of her nipples brought to mind all too vividly images she would rather forget—of Kell's burning lips and magical hands and hard, muscular body. Experiencing his passion had far exceeded her expectations and made her long for the familiar safety of her fantasy lover.

Kell had already breakfasted and ordered the horses made ready, she learned when she came downstairs, so she hurriedly swallowed a few bites and joined him at the carriage.

The brief, dismissive glance he gave her set the tone for their relationship and Raven's mood. Their marriage was to be merely one of convenience, she had to remember. They might be husband and wife, but they would not share confidences or friendship or passion. Evidently Kell intended to begin as they would go on, with a distant civility—which suited Raven perfectly, even if the notion was unaccountably depressing.

They had little to say to each other on the drive to London. Only when they arrived at what was to be her new home did her interest perk up.

The town house stood in a quiet, elegant square—not as grand as her great-aunt's mansion, but just as luxurious and possibly more tasteful. The front entrance hall was spacious and adorned with various works of art: sculpture and beautiful tapestries and landscapes in oils.

The introductions to his staff, however, proved awkward. The varying degrees of shock and surprise on their faces told Raven very clearly how unexpected their master's marriage was.

Ignoring their responses, Kell ordered that Mrs. Lasseter be given the chambers adjacent to his and a maid be sent to help her unpack.

When the servants had been dismissed, he addressed Raven directly. "You will likely want to hire your own lady's maid. This is a bachelor's residence and not equipped for a mistress."

"My aunt can probably spare one of hers," Raven replied evenly.

"Good. And you can have O'Malley fetch your trunks."

She was grateful he had remembered. Yet she scarcely had time to glance around her before Kell took his leave.

"You are going?" she asked, caught off guard, and immediately regretted sounding so possessive.

"My staff is capable of showing you the house and helping you get settled."

"Of course," she murmured, even while wondering what they would think about a newly wedded husband abandoning his bride on his doorstep.

"I have a business to run," Kell reminded her. "And I must speak to my brother before he hears the news from some other source."

His dark tone suggested he was not looking forward to the task, and Raven felt her heart sink at the thought of Sean's reaction. "He won't be happy to learn of our marriage."

A muscle flexed in his jaw. "No, but I will see that he respects it. You needn't worry about Sean."

She nodded, making no further comment when, with a brief bow, Kell turned to the front door.

She followed his tall, lithe form with her gaze as he let himself from the house. Perhaps it was madness, but Kell inspired in her an illogical sense of safety, at least when it came to his brother. She trusted him to keep his word to shield her. Kell would make a formidable protector, she had little doubt.

Just as he had made a formidable lover last night—with scarcely any effort at all. The memory of his claiming was imprinted vividly on her mind and stamped indelibly between her thighs. . . .

Raven felt herself flushing. Even with her significant exposure to the eroticism of the journal, she couldn't have anticipated the explosion of passion he'd unleashed in her. Or the aching, overwhelming sense of fulfillment that she'd never found in any of her fantasies. The thought that she would never again know the fire of his touch filled her with a strange melancholy.

Yet she had no right to protest. Kell had already aided her more than once. First by saving her from his brother's ravishment, then by giving her the protection of his name. She couldn't ask him for more.

Squaring her shoulders, Raven turned toward the wide staircase. At the moment she had her own difficulties to face. And it looked very much as if she would have to face them alone.

"You are jesting, right?" Sean demanded, staring at his brother.

They were in the library of Sean's imposing town house—the same London mansion that had been in the Lasseter family for nearly a century.

Unaccustomed to being roused from bed before noon, Sean had thrown a dressing gown over his nightshirt and joined Kell in the bookroom, looking rumpled and bleary-eyed and worse for wear after an obviously hard night of carousing.

"It is no jest, I'm afraid," Kell replied evenly. "We were wed last evening by special license."

He watched his brother grow white around the mouth. For a moment Sean said nothing. Then he went to the side table and poured himself a tumblerful of whiskey and tossed it back in a long swallow. When at last he spoke, his voice trembled with rage.

"Forgive me if I find it hard to credit that my own brother would betray me by wedding the vicious slut who ruined my life."

Roughly Kell raked a hand through his hair. He had

known this meeting would be turbulent, known Sean would be furious and resentful, but he strove to keep his own temper under control.

"I hardly betrayed you, Sean. Rather, I saved you from prison. You should consider yourself damned fortunate that I was able to intervene. It might have escaped your notice, but by abducting Miss Kendrick, you were in grave danger of retribution from her enraged family. They threatened to prosecute you. Would you rather I allowed you to be locked away?"

Sean sent him a bitter, scathing look. "You could have found another way. I expected better from you, damn you, Kell! I trusted you not to plunge a knife in my back!"

Without warning, he hurled the tumbler into the hearth, shattering the heavy crystal with a crash. Then he threw himself into a chair, pressing a hand over his eyes as if in dire pain.

Kell clenched his jaw. He felt a measure of guilt at his brother's unhappiness, but anger as well at Sean for precipitating this disaster. "You left me little choice. If not for your means of seeking revenge, I would never have been compelled to wed her."

"She deserved what she got!"

"I'm not so certain of that. She wasn't responsible for your impressment—her groom was. And even he wasn't wholly to blame, for he was merely trying to protect her. What did you expect him to do when you assaulted her last summer?"

"She has duped you completely, hasn't she?"

"I don't think so."

"No? You believe her over me. You've sided with her

over your own flesh and blood. You've played the fool for her like countless other witless swains. You were taken in by her wiles, just as I was."

"You're mistaken," Kell said grimly.

"Am I? How else can you explain your betrayal?" His bitterness was edged with a grief that seemed genuine when tears filled his eyes. "You stole her from me, Kell. I loved her, and you stole her from me."

Kell shook his head slowly. "If you truly loved her, Sean, you would never have tormented her as you did. You would not have wanted to see her so devastated, standing alone against society, enduring the cruelty our own mother did." He felt his hands curl into fists. "I was not about to let her suffer the way our mother suffered, Sean."

Looking ashamed, Sean averted his gaze. "I did love Miss Kendrick. I do. I swear it. I would have married her myself."

"That never would have happened," Kell assured him. "She never would have accepted you as her husband after what you did to her."

His face twisting in pain, Sean ran a hand roughly down his face. Kell took pity on his brother and gentled his tone. "You should be satisfied with your revenge thus far. Think about it. You accomplished precisely what you set out to do. You've tumbled her from her elite station. She will never wed her duke, never lead society." He gave a scoffing laugh. "No doubt she'll be shunned simply because of who I am. In order to explain her sudden disappearance, we're putting about the story that we were madly in love; that I abducted her because I couldn't bear to live without her. A love match with a half-Irish gamester who possesses my notorious reputation could prove just as big a scandal as jilting a duke. The ton will never forgive her for loving so far beneath her station."

Sean's mouth twisted in contempt. He, like Kell, held a burning resentment for society's view of class differences. In truth, Kell was convinced that being unable to compete against a nobleman for Miss Kendrick's hand in marriage had outraged Sean as much or more than her refusal of his suit.

But his brother apparently was not willing to forgive *him*, at least not yet. Sean shook his head, his voice lowering to harsh fury. "May you both rot in hell."

"Sean . . ."

"Get out. Just leave me alone."

"In a moment. I have not finished what I came here to say."

"There is more?" Sean sneered.

"I want you to absent yourself from London for a while."

Sean stared. "Why the devil should I?"

"Because it will permit the scandal to die down, as well as allow time for her family's wrath to cool. They could still decide to prosecute, you realize. If you remain here, you risk prodding a raw wound."

"And just where do you expect me to go?"

"To Ireland. To the farm. You haven't visited there since last winter."

Three years ago Kell had purchased a horse farm outside Dublin, to provide Sean a place of refuge when his demons grew too fierce to bear. Now seemed an opportune time for him to return.

"I will make all the arrangements," Kell added. "You can take the opportunity to gain control of yourself. And to think about what you did."

"Just what did I do that was so terrible?"

Kell stifled a sigh. "No man of honor raises a hand to a woman, Sean. You crossed the line. What is more, you lied to me about what happened between the two of you. Raven Kendrick never gave you her body as you claimed."

Sean's green eyes filled with anguish, but he remained mute.

"I've made excuses for you in the past because I understood how you suffered. And I realize how your experience during your impressment could drive you to want revenge. But what you did to Raven Kendrick was inexcusable."

"Go to hell."

"As long as you go to Ireland."

Sean's spine went rigid. "I don't have to do what you say. You're no brother of mine. Go play the fool with your scheming bride. And don't complain to me when you are burned by her wiles."

"You will leave London, Sean, even if I have to escort you myself."

"You will have to carry me, then."

"If I must."

Setting his jaw, Kell turned away and let himself out of the house he had hated for years. His brother needed time to become accustomed to the shocking news of his marriage, but Sean's accusations had hurt more than he would have thought possible.

How had events come to such a pass? Never in his

darkest dreams would he ever have expected a woman to come between them. The last thing he'd wanted was to wound his brother by taking a bride Sean claimed to love. Yet he would still do it again, in order to protect his brother from himself.

For years now, Sean's self-destructive tendencies had alarmed Kell, although he'd always felt compelled to make allowances. Having an innocent boyhood shattered by depravity was an agony that only the strongest souls could fully overcome. And Sean had never been very strong.

His path to torment had begun the day they'd lost their father to sudden illness, when Kell was fourteen and Sean nine. Their father's unexpected death was a devastating blow, but Adam Lasseter was scarcely in the ground when their hated uncle exercised his powers of guardianship and banished their mother from their lives. Fiona had had no power or resources to fight the disdainful Lasseters—nor did Kell at the time. During his tearful farewells with his mother, he'd sworn faithfully to look after his younger brother.

A solemn responsibility at which he'd failed terribly.

Kell climbed wearily into his waiting carriage and settled back, his conscience aching, his own thoughts bitter as he remembered those grim years when he and Sean had been forced to live under his uncle's roof. They had never seen their mother again, for she'd died in Ireland barely a year later, too destitute to afford the care that might have saved her from the influenza epidemic that had raced through the Dublin slums.

Kell's hatred for William Lasseter had become irrevocable. Seething with defiance, he had let his loathing drive his every action—rebelling at every opportunity, earning himself countless beatings. Devil's spawn, his uncle called him. They had argued intensely and often, and Kell even ran away once, taking Sean with him. But their uncle dragged them back home, severely punishing them both and threatening to make Sean suffer worse if Kell's insubordination continued.

After that, he had tried to contain his smoldering hatred for his younger brother's sake, biding his time, resolving to wait until he could reach his majority and gain the power to fight his uncle.

At seventeen, Kell had gone away to university, while Sean remained at home under William's control, schooled by tutors. When Kell did come home for holidays and term recesses, Sean seemed withdrawn, despondent, but he denied anything was wrong. . . . Out of shame, Kell finally learned to his revulsion.

He'd returned home for Christmas during his second year and discovered the sordid truth: that William Lasseter had an unnatural desire for thirteen-year-old boys.

Kell had planned to attend a worship service with his brother when he found Sean huddling before a roaring fire in his room, enveloped in a dozen blankets but trembling with cold.

"I c-cannot go to church, K-Kell," he said, his teeth chattering. "N-not when I am so unclean."

"What are you talking about, pup?" Kell asked teasingly. "Do you mean to say you haven't bathed or washed behind your ears?"

The agony on Sean's face was unmistakable. "No, I have bathed. But I cannot get clean. God help me. . . . He made me do it, Kell. I couldn't stop him."

Sean had broken down in sobs then, and the tale gradually came out. For months he had been sodomized by their uncle William.

Remembering his sick horror even now, Kell rubbed his scarred cheek. He'd erupted in fury, threatening to kill William if he dared touch Sean again—

"Mr. Lasseter, sir?" a footman's solemn voice asked, interrupting Kell's dark thoughts.

His carriage had come to a halt before his gaming club, he realized.

Feeling almost ancient, his injured leg aching, he dismounted slowly and made his way up the front steps, where he was greeted at the door by his majordomo.

Timmons was too well-trained to ask about his master's unexpected disappearance, but Kell responded to his quizzical regard with a terse explanation. "I had some matters that required my attention."

"Very well, sir. Miss Walsh has managed in your absence. She has not yet risen, as she didn't retire until the wee hours of the morning. A party of gentlemen commandeered the hazard table, playing for exceptionally high stakes."

Which meant hundreds of thousands of pounds had exchanged hands, Kell knew, which meant a tidy profit for the house. At least *something* in his life was going well.

He nodded, glad that he didn't have to face Emma Walsh at just this moment. He didn't have the energy to explain about his sudden unwanted marriage.

Favoring his wounded leg, he climbed the stairs to his private study. Emma had left neat stacks of receipts and promissory notes on his desk, along with several ledgers, but he had no interest in reviewing her accounting, or really any need. She was entirely capable of running the club as well as he.

Instead, Kell entered the adjoining bedchamber and eased himself onto the bed, where two nights ago he'd spent countless passionate hours ministering to his feverish patient—

Trying to block out the scorching memory, he flung his arm over his eyes and let his thoughts return to the dark days after discovering his uncle's perversions.

They had escaped William Lasseter's guardianship and fled to Ireland, where Kell had done his best to rear his brother and try to help him overcome his tormented past. Utilizing his gaming skills, Kell had managed to claw their way out of poverty and eventually accumulate significant wealth, so that by the time he reached his majority, he no longer needed the inheritance left in trust by his father. But he'd made serious mistakes with his brother.

Guilt-wracked and filled with self-remorse for what he'd allowed to happen, he'd tolerated Sean's excesses more than was wise, providing him all the advantages money could buy, indulging him, not making him accept responsibility for his binges of drinking and gaming and whoring. He'd taken Sean to see the best doctors in Edinburgh in an effort to control his black moods, but he hadn't enforced their recommendations that Sean live a quiet life.

Perhaps if he'd been sterner . . .

It was several years before Kell realized his failure. Longer still before he finally acknowledged that his brother's simmering resentment at being abandoned to their uncle's depravity remained a festering sore between them.

Then last summer Sean's torment had been compounded when he was smitten with a heartless beauty and found himself impressed in the cruel arms of the British Royal Navy.

Raven Kendrick wasn't directly responsible for that tragedy, Kell knew now, but there was no question that her irresistible allure had led Sean into more suffering. He would always bear the brutal scars on his back as proof—even though their uncle no doubt had scarred Sean far worse than the navy ever could.

Those brutal shipboard beatings had sent Sean over the edge, Kell could see that now. Sean clearly hadn't been in his right mind when he'd abducted Raven. And no doubt he deserved retribution for his vicious treatment of her. But Kell was still desperately determined to protect his brother.

Enough to wed the woman Sean professed to love and risk his hatred.

Kell grimaced, remembering Sean's bitter accusations of betrayal and the charge that he'd fallen for the wiles of a practiced schemer.

He hadn't fallen for her, of course. Yet he would have to take care if he didn't want to be led around by his cock. He could still feel the silk of Raven's hair, the warmth of her skin, her beguiling combination of passion and innocence. He still ached with the hungry frustration of being unable to fully satisfy his own rampant sexual need. . . .

Hell and damnation, Kell swore under his breath. He would do whatever it took to remain immune to her allure. At the very least, he owed it to his brother to keep his distance. He couldn't add further insult to injury by rubbing Sean's nose in his marriage. He wouldn't fulfill those accusations of betrayal.

And that meant doing his damnedest to keep away from his new bride.

Raven's morning was as trying as Kell's, for she gathered her courage and forced herself to face her jilted betrothed, determined to apologize in person. She owed Halford that much.

Since a lady did not visit a bachelor's residence, though, and since she preferred not to risk a public rebuff, she penned a note to the duke, asking him to call on her. She waited restlessly for several hours before he deigned to appear.

Her heart was pounding uncomfortably as his grace was shown into the drawing room, but one glimpse told Raven he was not inclined to accept her apology.

Charles Shawcross, the Duke of Halford, was every inch a nobleman, tall and distinguished and rather attractive in a stern sort of way. With his brown hair graying at the temples, he looked more like her father than a prospective bridegroom, yet despite his age and studied aloofness, they had enjoyed an unexpected compatibility. She'd come to admire his keen intelligence, while he had been attracted—against his will, Raven suspected—by her liveliness and even her unconventionality.

At her murmured invitation, Halford took a seat on the damask settee, crossing one leg over the other, regarding her without speaking. He had always been a private man of few words, but his simmering silence spoke volumes. She had never seen his expression so harsh.

There was anger in his blue eyes, as well as some darker emotion. . . . Could it possibly be grief? Raven wondered in dismay. She had never expected to cause him real pain. She'd thought her defection had merely wounded his august pride.

"Well?" he said finally, his tone glacial.

"You read my letter yesterday?" Raven asked.

"I did, madam. Thus I see no purpose for this interview. You made your feelings quite clear."

She clasped her fingers in her lap, striving for patience. "I wanted the chance to explain in person, to beg your forgiveness."

"Indeed? You expect forgiveness for the dastardly trick you played?"

"Yes, Charles . . . I truly am sorry. You did not deserve such wretched treatment."

If he was surprised by her unfamiliar meekness, he gave no sign. "You are sorry for making me appear the fool? For jilting me to wed a murderous blackguard? An Irish nobody, at that?"

Raven took a deep breath, finding it difficult to defend her new husband's unsavory reputation when she knew so little about him. "He is not a murderer," she said quietly. "Nor a blackguard."

"He is a notorious gamester who made me the laughingstock of the ton by abducting my bride on the very day of my wedding."

She shook her head, knowing it was unfair to let

Halford direct his anger at Lasseter. "He was not to blame. It was my fault entirely."

Halford gave her a measuring stare, his eyes hard and mocking. "I am supposed to believe you orchestrated your own abduction?"

"No, that isn't what I meant. The abduction was real enough, but . . . I did nothing to stop it. I did not want to stop it."

Raven leaned forward, her expression imploring. She didn't want the duke for an enemy, certainly not Kell's enemy. But if she hoped to persuade Halford to leniency, she would have to convince him that she truly loved her husband.

"I didn't intend for it to happen, Charles. I didn't want to love him. But sometimes . . . we cannot predict yearnings of the heart." She took another deep breath and voiced an outright lie. "It seems as if I've known Kell forever. But I declined his proposal years ago because my family considered him so unsuitable."

"I should think so," Halford said, his voice dripping contempt.

Trying not to react to his interruption, she went on. "As the day of our wedding drew nearer, however, I began to grow cold feet. I thought I was suffering from bridal nerves, but at the final moment . . . I realized I couldn't marry you, Charles. Not when I loved another man. It would not have been fair to you."

His lips twisted scornfully. "Now you claim to be interested in fairness?"

"Yes. Do think about it. I cannot have touched your heart. You never truly loved me. You saw me merely as a prize to be won. You enjoyed the challenge of triumphing over all my other suitors. And I, in turn . . . I only wished to wed you for your title."

He winced as if from a blow, and Raven found herself aching for him.

"Charles, surely you can understand. My family had such grand plans for me. My grandfather hoped to see me well established in society, and I wanted to please him. But I found I could no longer deny my own heart. I do love Kell, Charles. I have for a long, long while."

"Where is he now?" Halford demanded, suddenly glancing around the drawing room.

Raven eyed him warily. "Why do you wish to know?"

"Because I have every intention of calling him out."

She felt the color drain from her face. "Charles, you cannot!"

"No?" he asked, his tone silken. "Are you afraid I will kill him?"

Given the lethal rumors surrounding Kell, she feared much more for Halford. If the duke issued a challenge, it might cost him his life. But no man of his grace's consequence would like having his courage or his skill impugned. She swallowed a retort.

"Charles, please . . . Your quarrel is with me, not Kell. I am the one who deserves your anger."

"And you have it, madam. It will be a cold day in hell before I can look on this occasion with any measure of equanimity."

She bit her lip. "You won't ever be able to find it in your heart to forgive me?"

Halford stood, brushing off an imaginary speck of

dust from his impeccably tailored coat. "No, my dear, I don't believe I could ever be that magnanimous. But for your sake, I won't endeavor to kill him. I will merely make it my business to ruin him." His blue eyes glittered like chips of ice. "Your libertine will rue the day he thought to steal my bride from me."

Raven was still seated in the drawing room, numb with dread, when her dearest friend was announced.

Brynn Tremayne, Countess of Wycliff, was a flame-haired beauty who, last summer, had landed the most eligible lord in England quite against her will. But despite the difficulties between them, their marriage had burgeoned into a deep and abiding love—simmering with a passion that reminded Raven uncomfortably of her mother's hopeless fervor. She was happy for her friend, of course, but she was not about to risk losing her heart the way Brynn had done.

The countess was dressed in the height of fashion; her tailored green merino walking dress and cream-colored spencer hid the slight roundness of her belly that was swelling with child, while her vivid red tresses were tamed in a sedate chignon. She said not a word, but her emerald eyes held such grave concern and love that Raven felt an ache catch in her throat.

She rose to her feet involuntarily. She had planned to put on a brave front, but when her friend held out her arms, Raven walked into her embrace and clung. After all the stress and despair of the past two days, she couldn't hold back her tears.

Brynn simply held her, stroking her hair while murmuring gentle sounds of consolation.

Finally managing to control her sobs, Raven drew back with a sniffle. "I'm sorry," she said furiously, wiping her eyes. "I hate watering pots."

"I should think you have every right to indulge in a good cry." Brynn pulled a handkerchief from her reticule and made Raven dry her face, her own gaze searching. "You really are unharmed?"

"Yes, I'm fine."

"We were frantic with worry for you. Lucian turned London upside down searching for you before your message came yesterday."

Raven didn't doubt Brynn's claim in the least. Lucian Tremayne, the Earl of Wycliff, was a spymaster for the Foreign Office and had countless agents at his disposal. "I regret putting him to such trouble."

Brynn's scoffing sound was almost amused. "Truthfully, I believe he enjoyed the challenge. He thinks town has been rather dull of late. But we were so relieved to know you were safe. And now you are wed. . . . You have to tell me all about it."

She pulled Raven down on the settee and would not rest until she had heard the entire tale.

Raven told her almost the entire truth. About her abduction by Sean Lasseter, about finding herself in his brother's bed, about her family's fury. About how she had felt herself compelled to marry her rescuer. And finally her gratitude for Kell Lasseter's reluctant sacrifice.

She refrained from mentioning her own dangerous feelings of desire. She had few secrets from Brynn, but there were simply some emotions that were too intimate to share.

When she was done, Brynn wrinkled her smooth

brow in a frown. "I know very little about your Mr. Lasseter, other than he has a wicked reputation. And Lucian is only slightly acquainted with him. But Dare knows him and frequents his gaming hell. Perhaps you should speak to Dare."

Dare was Jeremy Adair North, Marquess of Wolverton, formerly the Earl of Clune and currently the leader of the Hellfire League. Fondly called Dare by his vast number of friends, enviously known as the Prince of Pleasure by his admirers and rivals alike, he was as wicked and charming a rake as London had ever witnessed. And he possessed extensive social connections.

Raven nodded thoughtfully. If anyone knew anything about her new husband's dark past, it would be Dare.

"What manner of man is your Mr. Lasseter?" Brynn asked. "Is he anything like his brother?"

"No!" Raven replied emphatically. "Thank God, he is nothing like Sean. Kell is. . . ." She stopped, wondering how to describe the man she had wed.

He was formidable, compelling, intriguing—and vitally attractive, despite his scarred cheek and the smoldering intensity he kept tightly leashed. Or perhaps even because of it. Rather than offending her, his cutting, sardonic wit stirred her blood. Amazingly enough, she actually liked Kell when he wasn't endeavoring to defend his brother. Indeed, she was far too drawn to Kell for comfort.

"Perhaps you should judge for yourself," she said finally.

"So where is he? I should definitely like to meet him."

"I believe he has gone to his club." Raven met Brynn's

eyes. "We have agreed not to live in each other's pockets. Ours is to be purely a marriage of convenience."

"But you do mean to live here with him?"

"For a time, yes, but only to keep up appearances as newlyweds. Eventually I am to have my own house. As to where I would settle . . . I haven't thought so far ahead yet."

Brynn glanced around her with approval, eyeing the elegant furnishings done in burgundy and gold. "This is quite an attractive residence. For a wicked gamester, your Mr. Lasseter seems to have excellent taste. Better than most gentlemen I know."

The comment surprised an unwilling smile from Raven. "Since we met, Kell has been at great pains to deny being a gentleman, but I have seen glimpses. . . ."

"Hmmm," Brynn murmured noncommittally. "A true gentleman would not hare off to his club, abandoning you to your own devices at so crucial a moment."

Raven shook her head. "I don't consider it abandonment in the least. Kell has done enough. He helped me stave off the worst of disaster and saved my reputation from total destruction. I would be imposing to ask for more."

"Well . . ." Pursing her lips together for a moment, Brynn then flashed an encouraging smile. "You know we will stand beside you. We will simply have to put our heads together and determine how best to weather the tempest. You cannot remain here stewing all alone. As soon as possible you must resume your usual pursuits. Your morning rides in the park, most particularly. And we'll make calls together. And we will commandeer Lucian to squire us to evening functions. You cannot be thought of as cowering."

Raven grimaced. "I have no intention of cowering . . . although I admit I don't relish having to show my face in public. I shudder to think of all the witches who are cackling with glee over how far I've fallen, now that I am no longer to be a duchess."

Brynn's expression turned sympathetic once more. "Raven, I am truly sorry. I know how much your having a title meant to your mother."

Summoning a bravado she didn't feel, Raven shrugged. "It cannot be helped now. There is no use feeling sorry for myself. There may even be some advantages to my ruination." Her mouth twisted ruefully. "Now I needn't endure all those interminable entertainments that Halford would have expected me to attend. And a married woman has much more freedom. Being the mistress of my own household will be far preferable to living under my aunt Catherine's thumb." Raven hesitated. "What worries me more is the danger I may have subjected Kell to. Halford is furious at him as well as me."

"I can imagine," Brynn said wryly. "But surely it will blow over in time."

"I'm not so certain. Halford says he means to ruin my husband."

"Indeed? Well, that might prove more difficult than he supposes, with us as your allies. Lucian's consequence is formidable enough to contest Halford's, even if mine is not."

"Brynn . . . I cannot let you become involved in my

difficulties. You have enough to worry about at the moment."

Lucian's occupation as a spymaster had recently entangled them both in dangers that had nearly proved fatal. And with one of Britain's foremost enemies still at large, a brutal traitor named Caliban, their lives were still at risk. Lucian never allowed Brynn to go anywhere without at least two bodyguards in attendance, Raven knew.

But her friend merely arched a delicate eyebrow. "You cannot possibly think we would desert you."

"No, of course not. But I don't like to burden you with my troubles. And even your support may not make any significant difference to my situation."

Brynn shook her head. "Your ordeal must have scattered your wits more than you realized. You don't sound at all like the Raven I know. Do you truly mean to give up and allow the ton to force you to live as an outcast?"

For a moment Raven stared. Then for the first time in two days she managed a laugh. "You are right, Brynn. Forgive me." She shook her head. "I was allowing myself to wallow in defeat, wasn't I?" Her chin rose with renewed resolve. "But the war is not over, and I have not been routed yet."

Brynn gave a satisfied smile. "No, certainly not."

"I assure you," Raven added, a defiant smile claiming her own mouth, "I won't be forced to live as an outcast. I vowed long ago that the ton would accept me, and I have strived too hard to abandon the fight now."

Chapter
Nine

The scandal was the talk of the town and showed no signs of abating.

True to her word, however, Brynn did everything in her power to martial her significant resources on Raven's behalf, proving the point that in times of crisis, one learned who one's true friends were.

Raven resumed her early morning rides and accompanied Brynn everywhere during daylight hours, paying calls and indulging in shopping expeditions and attending lectures and museum exhibits, merely to be seen in public. But she refrained from attempting anything more ambitious just yet, prepared to bide her time till the moment was right.

It was wiser, for example, to avoid Hyde Park at the fashionable hour of five, when the cream of society congregated to see and be seen. And she delayed braving any glittering evening functions, where the savage horde waited to devour her like a swarm of locusts. She had violated society's unforgiving rules with a vengeance, and her battle plan had to be carefully executed if she had any hope of winning.

Still optimistic, Brynn was planning a ball to celebrate Raven's nuptials. Lady Wycliff was determined to
bully the haute ton by sheer force of will into overlooking Raven's fall from grace. Yet all but the most
courageous or reckless souls shunned her; they simply
weren't prepared to make an enemy of the illustrious
Duke of Halford for the sake of a mere Mrs. Lasseter.

Not surprisingly, Raven found loneliness her chief
enemy over the course of the next few days. Her maid,
Nan, joined the servant staff at her new home, as did
O'Malley. And she had visits by her grandfather and
her great-aunt, although Lady Dalrymple came primarily to scold.

But there was little sign of Kell. He returned home
very late each night and left for his club each morning
while Raven was riding. And although they shared a
dressing room, they had separate bedchambers.

Such arrangements were not unusual, of course.
Some husbands and wives of the beau monde barely
exchanged civilities day to day. And Raven desired
nothing more than to pick up the pieces of her life
without a notorious husband to send her tenuous future spinning into further disarray.

But there was one obvious drawback in this case.
They were supposed to be in love. And if her new husband appeared to be avoiding her, their story would be
exposed for the sham it was.

Apparently Kell had not forgotten about her entirely, however. Upon his authorization, his solicitors
met with those of her grandfather and drew up a contract that would allow Raven to retain her indepen-

dence and tie up her modest fortune for any children she might have.

Not that there would be any children . . .

Raven never discussed that particular subject with her grandfather, but from the comments he let slip, Lord Luttrell was more troubled about her potential offspring than the scandal itself.

"I want my line carried on, my dear," the earl fretted, "even if I likely won't live long enough to see it. And I dislike thinking that my great-grandchildren will have the blood of a murderer running through their veins."

Raven could do little to reassure him.

Her wicked friend Lord Wolverton was the only person who could satisfy any measure of her curiosity about her husband. Raven accompanied the marquess on a drive in his curricle one afternoon so it could be seen that he hadn't deserted her. Her riding with him in an open carriage fell within the acceptable rules of behavior, as long as they remained constantly in public view.

Dare was every inch a nobleman: tall, lithe, and fair-haired, but a rogue through and through, with a magnetic, sinful smile that could scorch the coldest of female hearts. Yet his usual laughing demeanor was noticeably absent when he explained to Raven what little he knew of Kell Lasseter.

"I encounter him upon occasion. His club is considered the prime hell in London—high stakes but with a sterling reputation for honest play. And I fence with Lasseter regularly at Angelo's salle. He's a superb swordsman; I've rarely seen anyone better. But I cannot claim to know him well."

Dare urged his spanking pair of bays past a snarl in traffic before continuing. "He's a rebel by all reports. Doesn't appear to give a damn what anyone says about him. He seems deliberately to shun polite company, although I don't doubt he would have been accepted if he had put any effort into it. His breeding is good enough on his father's side at least. But he never lets anyone forget his Irish blood."

"His mother was Irish, I understand."

"Yes. And he almost seems to take pride in rubbing our English noses in the fact. Insolent devil." Dare smiled. "I thought Lasseter rash and foolhardy when he opened his club some four years ago. Had the gall to call it the Golden Fleece. But now I realize it was a cunning strategy. That name was like a flag to a bull— a challenge for the wild bucks who fancied themselves gamesters. They fell all over themselves at the hazard table, trying to best the bank. I wouldn't be surprised if it made Lasseter a fortune. In any event, the Fleece now has the most select membership of any club in London."

Dare guided the horses onto a quieter street and set them into a trot. "As for the rumors about him murdering his uncle? I suppose they could be true. Lasseter strikes me as dangerous enough. And I've heard a wild tale or two about his profligacy. Frankly, I don't like to think of you being his wife, puss."

Raven almost smiled at the irony—a rakehell like Wolverton, the Prince of Pleasure, concerned about profligacy.

"Nick won't be happy to hear of it, either." Dare grimaced. "He'll have my head for allowing you to be abducted and forced to marry against your will."

Nicholas Sabine was the American shipping magnate and privateer Raven had never been able to acknowledge as her half brother. He'd been her legal guardian for a time, before being charged with piracy by the British navy and sentenced to hang. Upon making his escape, he had come to England in disguise, in pursuit of the wife he'd married in desperation. But with war still raging between their two countries, he couldn't remain. Nick had taken his beautiful English wife, Aurora, home to Virginia, enjoining his friends Dare and Lucian to take care of Raven.

Both men took their responsibility with deadly seriousness. Yet there was no way they could have anticipated or prevented what had happened to her.

"If I had known what that cur intended . . ." Dare's handsome features hardened, and Raven knew he was speaking of Sean Lasseter. "Impressment was far too good for him."

Raven shuddered at the reminder. She'd only just told Dare about the incident at Vauxhall Gardens last summer when Sean had accosted her. Until then, she herself had considered the younger Lasseter a mere nuisance for dogging her footsteps with his unwanted courtship. And in all fairness, he had paid a great price for his actions that night.

"He suffered a good deal during his impressment, Dare. Perhaps that is punishment enough."

"Not nearly enough." Turning his head, Dare focused

a surprisingly stern gaze on her. "You aren't possibly excusing what that bastard did?"

"No, not at all. But I see little point in crying over it or in seeking revenge. I am wed to his brother now and will have to carry on with my life."

"I mean to have a word with your husband, to make certain he understands the consequences of mistreating you."

"No, Dare, please, there is no need. I don't believe he would mistreat me. And I would prefer to deal with this myself."

He hesitated. "Very well, love. But at the first sign of trouble—"

"You will be the first I call to my rescue, I promise."

He leaned over and pressed a chaste kiss on her cheek. "See that you do," he warned. "It will be difficult enough to explain to Nick how I failed him. If I allowed any further harm to come to you, he would have not only my head but other delicate parts of my anatomy that I would prefer to keep intact."

She dreamed of Kell that night. Not intentionally, the way she did her pirate, but just as powerfully. His sensual passion invaded her body, her mind, her very senses, a dark lover who left her gasping. . . . Raven woke, struggling for breath, fighting against the feeling of being overwhelmed.

She would have liked to forget her new husband's very existence, and yet there were appearances to consider. At the very least she would have to produce Kell for the ball being planned in their honor. But she had no opportunity to ask for his escort until five days after their unexpected union, when she returned home from her morning ride.

Upon being informed that Kell was still in his rooms, she went up to her bedchamber, intending to enter his by way of their adjoining dressing room. She walked in on him just as he was emerging from his bath.

Kell froze at her unexpected entrance while Raven instantly came to halt, staring at the spellbinding sight of his naked male body. Her fantasy lover in the flesh.

His splendid anatomy was the stuff of her most erotic dreams. The powerful play of sleek muscles in his arms and shoulders. The crystals of water glistening in the dark hair of his chest, dripping in rivulets down his hard, flat abdomen to his groin . . .

Her breath caught as her attention was drawn to that masculine flesh that could give such wild pleasure. His virile maleness made her pulse race and her throat go dry. Worse, it made her recall their wedding night and the ecstasy they had shared.

For an instant she saw the same vivid memory flare in Kell's dark eyes. But then he casually picked up a towel and draped it around his narrow hips and lean flanks.

"Did you ever consider knocking?"

Her cheeks flushed scarlet. "I beg your pardon. . . ." she stammered. "I didn't realize . . . I thought . . ."

He had not yet shaved, and a bluish black shadow darkened his jaw, accenting the groove in his cheek when his mouth curled at the corner. "Did you want something of me, madam wife?"

"It can wait," Raven croaked.

Backing out, she shut the dressing room door quickly,

but the sight of Kell's magnificent nudity remained imprinted on her mind. It was only hours later that she realized she'd forgotten in the awkwardness of the moment what she had intended to ask him.

When two more days passed and she still had not managed to have a private word with her husband, Raven realized she would have to go to him.

Girding her loins for battle, as the saying went, she set out for the gaming club on St. James Street. She wore a veil and hid behind the anonymity of a closed carriage, and she took O'Malley with her for protection. But still she felt strangely tense as she mounted the front steps to the house and raised the door knocker.

Some ladies considered it a fashionable diversion to attend a gaming hell, but she had never done so, unwilling to risk her reputation when she was so close to achieving her goal of marrying into the nobility.

Now she had far less to lose. So why did she feel as if she were engaged in a forbidden sin, her heart beating as if she had run a great distance? She didn't like to think it was in anticipation of seeing her husband again. More likely, her erratic pulse was caused by her remembrance of the passionate night she'd recently spent here in Kell's bed.

A brute of a doorman opened the door. His hulking frame resembled O'Malley's, but this man might once have been a pugilist, for his nose was set crookedly and he was missing a front tooth.

She wasn't required to deal with him, however, for a stately majordomo appeared directly.

"May I help you, madam?" the august servant queried.

"I am Mrs. Lasseter. I should like to speak to my husband."

A flash of surprise and disapproval crossed his face before he schooled his features to impassivity. "I will ask if Mr. Lasseter is receiving."

Refusing to be rebuffed, Raven stepped inside. "I prefer not to be kept waiting on the doorstep."

"Very well, madam. If you will come with me."

She followed him, not upstairs as she expected, but to the nether reaches of the large gaming house. Along the way, she passed several elegant chambers, similar to those of the more famous gentlemen's clubs like White's and Boodle's she had heard described: a library boasting gleaming mahogany shelves lined with leather-bound tomes; a large dining room with several tables set with gleaming crystal and china; three smaller rooms arranged, possibly, for private games of cards; and finally what must be the public gaming room, where vast fortunes were won and lost.

Raven would have liked to explore the gaming room, but her curiosity would have to wait. She had to quell her surprise, however, when she found herself in the kitchens, of all places.

Despite the chill of the winter day, the room was warm from the great hearth fire and ovens. Kell was seated at a worktable, dressed in breeches and a flowing white cambric shirt. His sleeves were rolled up to expose muscular forearms, while his collar was opened at the neck to reveal the soft whorls of black hair that sprinkled his chest.

Raven came up short at the unmistakably pleasant shock that rippled along her spine. She kept forgetting how strikingly handsome he was, despite the harshness of his features and the scar that marred his high cheekbone.

Then he looked up and his dark eyes met hers. The ripple turned to a sizzle, with all the impact of a bolt of lightning. Raven had difficulty catching her breath, very much like when she had interrupted him at his bath.

"Mrs. Lasseter, sir," the majordomo said.

"Thank you, Timmons. That will be all."

The servant's exit left them alone, for the kitchen staff was nowhere to be seen, Raven realized.

It was then she noticed the deadly blade in Kell's hand, which he was polishing with a cloth. Any number of weapons, both rapiers and pistols, lay spread across the table—

"What are you *doing*?" she was startled into asking. Her heart leapt to her throat as she thought of the most likely possibility.

"I prefer to care for my own weapons," Kell replied, his face inscrutable.

"You aren't preparing for a duel? Halford hasn't challenged you?"

His eyebrow rose at the obvious panic in her voice. "Not as yet. Did you expect him to?"

Raven's hand went to her breast in relief. "I wasn't certain. When I spoke to him last week, he threatened to call you out at first. . . ."

"Did he now?"

"Yes." She swallowed, remembering. "Halford was so furious. He blamed you for my abduction, even though

I swore I went along willingly." She felt another stab of guilt for what she had led Kell into. "I truly am sorry."

Yet he didn't seem to want her apologies. "How touching that you are so concerned for my welfare," he murmured, his tone holding a hint of mockery.

She made a face. "To be truthful, I was more concerned for Halford. You do have the more dangerous reputation, after all."

Kell's features grew cool, and Raven immediately regretted her impetuous tongue. "I didn't mean to jest about it. I admit, Halford frightens me. He says he means to ruin you."

"He can try." The words were spoken casually, but there was an edge of steel in his voice that boded ill for his opponents.

"Why have you come?" Kell asked, abruptly changing the subject. "You shouldn't be here. It won't do your reputation any good to be seen in a gaming hell."

He didn't invite her to be seated, but Raven did so anyway, taking the end of the bench opposite him. "My reputation could hardly be more tarnished at the moment. And I cannot distance myself from your club completely, now that I am your wife. Besides, my visit is for a good cause. I had to speak to you, yet I've seen very little of you since we wed."

"I thought we agreed you wouldn't involve yourself in my life, nor I in yours."

"We also agreed we should keep up appearances for the time being. Ours was supposed to be a love match, remember?"

He bent his head to his task, removing a speck of

dirt from the deadly blade. "We both know what a spurious tale that is."

"The rest of the world doesn't realize that. And I require your presence to maintain the charade. My friends Lord and Lady Wycliff are planning a ball in our honor, to celebrate our nuptials."

Kell didn't even hesitate. "I will have to decline the honor."

"Why?"

"Because I don't care to move in your elite social circles."

"You keep away by choice, Lord Wolverton says."

Kell looked up; obviously she had surprised him. "You know Wolverton? The greatest rake in all England?"

"He is a family friend," Raven admitted without embarrassment. "Dare claims this is his favorite hell."

"I am honored," Kell said wryly, although without his usual sardonic sting.

"I asked him about you. He says you would have been welcomed by the ton had you chosen to exert yourself."

Kell lowered his long, black lashes—those thick lashes any female would envy—while his hard, beautiful mouth curled. But he didn't speak. Instead he examined the blade for imperfections.

"Dare says you are an expert swordsman," Raven said into the silence. "Is that how you came by your scar?"

He shot her a dark glance. "You have a great deal of curiosity for a mere wife of convenience."

"I suppose so," she replied, unfazed by his scowl. "Aunt Catherine considers it a prime failing of mine."

Absently he reached up and touched his scar, running his finger along the jagged ridge. "My disfigurement was courtesy of my uncle's signet ring, if you must know."

The uncle he had supposedly murdered? Raven wondered. The question must have shown in her eyes, for Kell nodded.

"I could cheerfully have killed him. He sent my mother to an early grave, after taking her sons from her. There was no love lost between us."

"And he *struck* you? In the face?" Her outrage was evident in her tone.

"Among other places. It's no secret that we fought regularly."

Raven studied him, wondering at his truthfulness. Had he told her that story merely to put off her questions? Or to gain her sympathy? Perhaps he used his scar to his own advantage, to hide the secrets he kept locked inside. Secrets that admittedly she was dying to know. She searched Kell's face. His eyes were like polished obsidian, darkly reflective and damnably unrevealing.

How many other secrets was he hiding behind those fathomless eyes?

"Is that why you despise society so?" she said finally. "Because of your mother?"

Something hot and dangerous flared in those dark depths. It was a long moment before he answered. "Primarily. As an Irishwoman she was never good enough for my father's kin—or most of the English Quality, for that matter. I want nothing to do with their ilk."

"Then we have something in common," Raven murmured with all seriousness. "I have no more admiration for many of the ton's members than you do. On the whole they are cruel, soulless, unbelievably shallow. Certainly I have no desire to suffer their contempt and condescension. If I had my way, I would tell them all to go to the devil."

His eyebrow shot up. "The toast of London professing to disdain the haute monde? Why don't I believe you?"

"It's true," Raven insisted. "One doesn't have to admire a set in order to aspire to their ranks."

"Then why were you so eager to marry one of their scions?"

She hesitated, wondering how much to reveal. "In large part because I promised my mother. In her youth, she . . . had a falling out with her father and was banished to the West Indies for life. But she always regretted losing her position in society and denying me the chance for that sort of life. It was her dream for me that I marry a title and become accepted by the ton. Indeed, it was almost an obsession with her. She made me vow on her deathbed—"

Raven felt her throat close on the familiar pain. "My promise was all that let her die in peace," she added, her voice uneven with emotion.

Kell's face took on that familiar, enigmatic look. "I understand vows like yours," he murmured. "I vowed to my own mother that I would care for Sean."

Raven suddenly flushed, realizing she'd exposed far too much of herself for comfort.

"Please"—she returned to the subject at hand—

"won't you consider making an allowance just this once? I must face the wolves sometime if I'm to have any hope for redemption. And Brynn—Lady Wycliff—thinks a ball is the best means. But I can't possibly succeed unless you stand beside me."

"Stand? That alone is a good enough reason to eschew your ball. My leg is injured—far too painful for me to stand on it, let alone dance."

"Do you even know how to dance? It is a gentleman's skill, after all."

She had meant to be provoking, and from the flash of irritation in his eyes, she judged she had succeeded.

A long moment passed while he contemplated her.

Raven held her breath, waiting for an explosion of wrath, but it never came. Instead a glint of reluctant amusement entered his eyes, the warmth softening the intensity. "You are treading a fine line with your temerity, vixen. Aren't you the least afraid your 'dangerous' husband might throttle you?"

Raven smiled. "Just this once, and I will never again ask for your presence. After the scandal dies down, we can give up any pretense of being in love."

Kell grimaced. "Very well, I'll attend your damned ball. But after that, you are on your own. Now take yourself out of here and try to salvage what little is left of your reputation. And leave me the hell in peace."

When she was gone, however, Kell sat there without returning to his task of cleaning weapons. He had no desire to attend Raven's blasted ball, but he still felt an unwilling sympathy for her. He did indeed understand the kind of promise she had made to her mother. He'd sworn a promise of his own to his mother.

Absently Kell reached up and touched his cheek, tracing the scar Raven had inquired about. He could could still feel his rage when he'd discovered his uncle's crimes against his young brother, still feel the slashing sting of being wounded that day.

"You vile bastard! I'll kill you if you dare touch him again."

He'd attacked his uncle blindly, raining physical blows and receiving punishing ones in return. He eventually won the violent fistfight, but William's signet ring had struck him viciously in the face, splitting his cheek wide open.

That night he had fled with Sean, stealthily making their way to Dublin, hoping to disappear. Those were desperate days on the streets, and they barely survived. With no time to seek medical attention, Kell's cheek had healed raggedly, leaving the skin forever marred. Yet his scar was nothing compared to the scars William had left on his brother. Sean's shame was a raw wound, festering in the dark depths of his soul.

And six months later William had tracked them down—

Forcing his thoughts away from that grim memory, Kell picked the foil he had been cleaning. Their uncle William had been an expert swordsman and should have won any contest with rapiers. Instead he'd wound up dead, slain by his own blade.

A fitting turn of events, Kell thought, setting his jaw. Even if he hadn't been the one responsible.

Chapter
Ten

The night of the ball arrived with chilling swiftness. After donning her armor, Raven dismissed her maid and stood staring at her reflection in the cheval glass. She saw a patrician young lady gowned in an elegant confection of peach and gold, her ebony hair piled high on her head and secured with a gold bandeau.

A comforting sight, she thought, encouraged. She was about to do battle and she would need every advantage she could muster. She glanced at the mantel clock. Shortly the hostilities would begin. . . .

Defiantly Raven lifted her chin and turned to pace her bedchamber while she waited for her husband's escort. Kell had returned home to dress, she knew, for she'd heard him moving around in the adjacent dressing room, speaking to his valet.

In only a few moments a knock sounded on her bedchamber door. When she opened it, a ruggedly beautiful stranger stood there. She stared at Kell, breathless.

"Well, do I meet with your approval?"

He looked dark and diabolically handsome in a blue superfine coat, pristine white cravat, silver brocade waistcoat, white satin knee smalls, and black patent pumps with silver buckles.

"Y-yes . . ." she stammered. "Yes, of course."

His own glance raked her briefly, displaying merely a flicker of acknowledgment of her own appearance, before he offered her his arm. "Shall we go then?"

. He escorted her downstairs, where they retrieved cloaks and gloves and Kell's tall beaver hat before braving the chill winter night and settling into his barouche.

They were the first to arrive at the Wycliff mansion. As she alighted on the silent street, Raven felt her disquiet rise. Had she made a grave mistake, thinking that anyone at all would attend her ball?

The house was quietly magnificent, adorned with winter roses and hothouse flowers, the crystal chandeliers sparkling with candleflame.

Their hosts awaited them in the drawing room, and both Lucian and Brynn stepped forward at their entrance. Raven felt a strange measure of satisfaction at Brynn's start of feminine awareness upon spying Kell. His smoldering masculinity would make any woman take notice, even a beautiful woman like Brynn, who was madly in love with her own stunningly attractive husband.

Brynn recovered almost immediately, however, offering Kell her hand along with a welcoming smile.

Her husband was more reserved in his welcome, but just as sincere. Tall, lithe, dark-haired, Lucian had once been one of the country's premier rakes. He shook hands with Kell, his blue eyes keen and measuring.

"Raven has told us of your generosity in coming to

her rescue, Mr. Lasseter, and I would like to express my thanks. We owe you an enormous debt of gratitude."

"You owe me nothing, my lord," Kell replied with little inflection.

"On the contrary. Raven is very special to us, like a sister"—Lucian cast her a smile that could melt stone—"and I assure you I intend to find some means of repaying you."

Seeing Kell's jaw harden, Raven thought to intervene, but she was spared when her great-aunt and grandfather were announced.

Lord Luttrell embraced her warmly, then allowed himself to be settled on a couch with a glass of sherry. Lady Dalrymple greeted Raven with chilling politeness and spoke not a word to Raven's new husband, making it perfectly clear she was here under duress.

After a few awkward moments, however, the others in the company ignored the frosty atmosphere while their hosts expertly steered the conversation to noncontroversial subjects.

Brynn had planned a quiet dinner before the ball with only the family in attendance, and the meal proceeded with unexpected cordiality. Raven was particularly surprised when Kell not only participated in the discussions, but did so with ease. He was putting himself out for her benefit, she knew, although he would not meet her gaze.

Afterward they repaired to the ballroom to await the guests' arrival. The light from myriad candles cast a shimmering glow over the vast chamber and took the chill from the winter evening, but no amount of flame could warm the growing ice in Raven's stomach.

Her tension only mounted as they formed a receiving line. Her cowardly inner voices were encouraging her to flee, while her own rebellious instincts were clamoring for her to give up her aspirations of redeeming her ruined reputation.

She glanced at Kell, who stood grimly at her side, and for some inexplicable reason, she took heart. If he could endure what must seem like torture to him, then she could as well.

The Marquess of Wolverton was the first to arrive. Shunning proper etiquette entirely, Dare kissed Brynn's cheek and then Raven's, affably greeted Lucian and Kell and Lord Luttrell, and bowed deeply over Lady Dalrymple's hand, pressing his lips to her fingers with a lingering sensuality that made the elderly lady flush.

Finally she snatched her hand away, muttering something under her breath about rogues and libertines and looking as if she would like to strike him with her fan.

Unfazed, Dare glanced around the empty ballroom, his glance touching on the orchestra that was preparing to play. "What, no one else is here? I am usually deplorably late to these tame affairs."

"You are the only guest thus far, as you can see," Raven admitted glumly.

Dare winked at her. "The more fortune for me, then. Without all your beaux for competition, I can claim half your dances."

"You may have to claim them all if no one else comes."

"Ah, no, love, they will come, if only to gawk. There's not a man jack among the upper ten thousand who isn't rabidly curious to meet the notorious pirate who stole the darling of the ton from under the nose of a duke."

His prophecy proved shrewdly perceptive. Shortly after the stroke of nine, the guests started to arrive, first in trickles, then in swarms.

Her ball would likely be a veritable crush, Raven realized with more than a little relief. But perhaps she should have expected such a response from the fickle elements of society. Few people willingly turned down a select invitation from the Earl and Countess of Wycliff, and their prominent sponsorship of her would go a long way toward easing the scandal.

And she suspected Dare was indeed right. Even the haughtiest, most discriminating members of the ton would be curious to meet the man who had stolen the Duke of Halford's bride away. Contrarily, the haute monde had a lust for scandal and a morbid fascination— even admiration—for rebels like Kell who blatantly broke their absurdly rigid rules.

As she greeted a guest in line and then passed him on to her husband with introductions, Raven surreptitiously eyed Kell, who stood beside her. He was mysteriously, broodingly handsome, and with his bold, dark eyes, he looked very much the pirate. Measured against his raw virility, most of the other gentlemen present looked weak and foppish.

Surprisingly enough, Kell appeared perfectly at ease among the elite company. His usual intensity was tempered, with no signs of the antagonism or biting sarcasm he'd sometimes accorded her.

Indeed, Raven thought, Kell seemed almost determined to put himself out to be pleasant. She watched in amazement as he charmed an elderly dowager as effectively as Dare had ever done. This was a side of Kell that she had never seen before, and it left her wondering wistfully if he would revert to form once the evening ended.

Still, no matter how fleeting his support tonight, she was grateful for it. And the size of the crowd filled her with hope that she might win back at least a toehold in polite society, if not genuine acceptance.

Many of the guests were as chillingly distant as her great-aunt had been, but Raven could detect only a handful of outright snubs as the interminable line of guests continued. The veiled insults mainly came as remarks regarding Kell's brazen ownership of a gaming club or the fact that he was part Irish.

Raven returned a cool-eyed stare or lifted an arched eyebrow in mock dismay, her answers ready:

"Yes, Lady Poindexter, my husband owns the premier club in London. I daresay Lord Poindexter has enjoyed the sport there as much as Lord Wycliff or the Marquess of Wolverton."

Or "You can't mean that you don't gamble, Mr. Smythe-Jones? I felt certain every self-respecting gentleman gambled. Didn't I just hear of a wager you made last week with Sir Randall Dewhurst about which raindrop would first reach the sill of White's bow window?"

Standing next to her, Kell watched her performance with a strange mixture of vexation and admiration. It rankled that Raven would have to defend him—and rankled still more that he cared about being defended. He was accustomed to being cut dead by these preeminent denizens of society, and he'd learned long ago to contain the simmering anger that gnarled in his gut at their infuriating presumption of superiority.

His usual anger, however, was somehow less fierce tonight, his feelings of inferiority diminished. Particularly when he observed his new wife smoothly dressing down his detractors as they moved along the line, a smile on her perfect lips. It didn't surprise him that Raven had claws, but it did that she was willing to use them on his behalf, especially when her own position was so tenuous.

She was putting up a brave front, Kell admitted. No one would guess she was under indictment for the social equivalent of murder, with her lovely neck exposed to the blade of the guillotine.

She clearly didn't like having to endure the threat of the knife, however. He had to repress a smile when he caught the unladylike oath Raven muttered in between greeting guests.

"Blast that woman for an interfering busybody," she said under her breath. "The gall of some people."

And he forcibly had to bite back laughter when Raven complained in that same peeved undervoice, "I feel like a stuffed peahen in a museum, on display for the gawking spectators."

Yet when she moved closer to him in response to a snide comment about his Irish roots, her unconscious gesture seemed more protective than defensive. He found himself watching her covertly, studying the patrician lines of her delicate profile. Raven was still an enigma to him, a fascinating one. Her eyes soft and vulnerable one moment, then flashing defiance. . . .

His gaze swept downward, over the slim, elegant

curves of her figure revealed by her empire waist gown, returning to linger on her softly swelling bosom. Remembering how those sweet, firm breasts had tasted, he felt his loins pulse.

He swore at his body's response, wishing he didn't have to stand so close to her. And yet her efforts to protect him roused an unwilling tenderness inside him—along with a need to protect her in turn. He was determined to play his role as her loving husband to the hilt.

When the reception line disbanded, he led her out on the dance floor for the first dance, a minuet.

Raven gave him a questioning look. "You don't have to do this, not if your leg is paining you."

"Ah, but I do," Kell responded with a slow, deliberate smile. "The company expects me to dance with my incredibly lovely wife."

It was the first time he had smiled at her in that rakish way, without disdain or mockery, and the effect was dazzling. Her gaze fastened on his alarmingly sensual mouth. Kell was only fawning over her for the benefit of their observers, she knew, but even so she felt a shiver of sexual awareness all the way down to her satin slippers. And his dark eyes . . .

She glanced away, refusing to be seduced by the heat she saw there. Simulated or not, it left her feeling too dangerously defenseless. Kell Lasseter was a man who made her blood run hot but her heart quiver with alarm. She would do well to keep her distance.

She breathed more easily when she was claimed by another dance partner and could leave Kell to his own devices. From that point on, she found herself in constant demand. And for the rest of the evening, there were seldom any chances for intimacy with Kell or even much conversation.

It was three in the morning before the last guest departed. Brynn declared the evening a moderate triumph, predicting that Raven would find dozens of invitations on her salver on the morrow.

Weary but relieved, Raven embraced her friends and allowed Kell to lead her out to the waiting carriage. After the heat of the ballroom the frigid air felt wonderful.

She could feel her tension starting to ease as she sank back against the squabs. Although her future was far from settled, she couldn't find the energy just now to worry about her prospects. And yet she owed Kell her gratitude.

She contemplated the dangerous man sitting silently beside her as he stared broodingly out the barouche at the dark streets.

"Thank you for attending with me," she murmured. "It went far better than I hoped."

"Yes," he agreed, a cynical edge to his voice. "I own myself surprised at how they fawned over me. Most of those self-righteous prigs consider an Irishman lower than dirt, and a gamester not much better."

A bastard would be lower than either, Raven thought involuntarily.

"My mother would never have been accepted by that horde," Kell muttered. "Damn their souls."

She heard the anger in his voice and suddenly wondered what he would say if she told him of her own origins. Would he understand the crushing loneliness of being an outcast? Of never belonging, of never being good enough? But long practice of hiding her secret kept her silent.

"I am sorry for what your mother had to endure," she said instead.

He shrugged. "I no longer let such things bother me."

But it had shaped him into the man he was, she was certain. She doubted he would be eager to debate the issue, though. After another moment, Raven turned her head away, feeling weariness overtake her.

Kell, however, only felt his own tension rising as he debated what to do for the remainder of the night. When the carriage arrived at his residence, he assisted Raven to alight and then escorted her up the front steps. A sconce had been lit to welcome them home, and the door was unlocked.

Kell opened it for her, then stepped aside to allow her to enter. But he was reluctant to follow.

"Where are the servants?" he asked, remaining in the doorway.

"I told them not to wait up for me since I would be so late returning."

Another uncommon trait, Kell thought. Few ladies of his acquaintance would be so considerate of the servants.

She started to remove her cloak but then glanced back at him. "Do you not mean to come in?"

Kell remained exactly where he stood, knowing the wisdom of taking his leave at once. He'd watched Raven during the entire evening as she'd danced and charmed her way through her critical crowd of judges. She was all laughter and wit and vivacious beauty, demonstrating how she'd drawn half the male population of London under her spell during her Season. No wonder his brother had accused her of seduction.

He himself had felt an unreasonable spark of jealousy when he saw her working her wiles on the gentlemen present, even though he'd expected such a performance.

She was a temptress, pulsing with life and sensuality. *And she was now his wife.*

He had every legal right to stay with her.

The thought sent a searing heat shooting through Kell. He could spend the night enjoying the warm, exquisite body of his wife and no one would gainsay him—except perhaps Raven herself.

"To what purpose?" he asked, probing. "You said you didn't want or need a lover."

"No, I . . . I am not inviting you to share my bed, merely your house. I don't like to think that I am driving you from your own home."

Kell held her gaze, unable to look away. "It would be best if I left now. The play at the club may not have ended yet."

"Perhaps so," she murmured, her voice low. And yet she moved closer, as if drawn to him.

Kell felt every muscle in his body tighten at her disturbing nearness, his instinct for danger warring with the powerful need to take her in his arms. He knew better than to touch her, and yet . . . the impulse was unconquerable. Gently grasping her shoulders, he drew her against him.

A lightning stroke of desire surged through him.

And from the darkening look in her eyes, he knew the fiery shock had touched her as well.

He tightened his hold—and felt himself swell with an immediate, throbbing erection.

Kell groaned silently, fighting the primal urge that was rampaging through him. He had to take care. Such hunger was dangerous, lethal. This woman could hurt him badly if he wasn't careful.

Yet he couldn't move. He gazed down into her crystalline blue eyes, seeing the color in their depths shift like richly hued gemstones. He felt as if he were drowning in her gaze, drowning in her alluring combination of fire and fragility, her vibrancy.

He wanted so badly to kiss her. To crush her mouth with his. Wanted to bury the ache of his arousal in the welcoming sheath that was made to receive him.

Kell inhaled sharply, shaken by the intensity of his desire.

Raven seemed just as spellbound. She reached up to touch his scar, and he felt something shift inside him . . . tenderness, lust, need. Desperate need.

His head lowered. . . .

"So what have we here, big brother?" a snide voice drawled behind him.

Kell gave a start, while Raven froze. Turning his head, he saw Sean mounting the front steps.

Kell cursed the untimely interruption, a curse that was swiftly followed by a surge of self-censure. He'd been caught embracing Raven when he'd resolved to keep his distance. It irked him to think he was so weak that his powers of resistance would crumble at the first test.

He would have held her away, but she stepped back on her own, into the shelter of the hall, a purely defensive gesture, eyeing Sean with wariness, even alarm.

"How inconsiderate of you, Kell," Sean sneered as he came to a halt on the upper landing. "You neglected to invite your own brother to your nuptial ball."

Biting back a retort, Kell regarded his brother over his shoulder. Sean had avoided him this past week, probably because he didn't want to be pressed into leaving London. He was the worse for drink now, and clearly infuriated.

"The ball," Kell observed with little patience, "was merely an attempt to curb the scandal you caused. A means to show our unity and support our pretense of a love match."

"You call the touching scene I just witnessed *pretense*? Admit it, brother, you're smitten with her."

"I was escorting my wife home," Kell said sharply. "A circumstance that would not have existed if not for you."

Sean jerked back as if he'd been slapped.

"But in fact," Kell added grimly, "I was just on my way to the club. Why don't you accompany me?"

Raven felt a sudden chill as Kell stepped back from her, deliberately distancing himself, a closing out of emotion. His features as hard and remote as ever, he turned to his brother.

"Come." Without waiting for a protest, he ushered Sean down the steps.

Raven watched them leave, regret coursing through her, along with a fierce surge of relief. She had despised meeting Sean again, and though it was cowardly to admit, she still dreaded dealing with him. She was glad he had gone.

And yet she was profoundly glad he had come as well. Without the interruption, she might have given in to her senses. For a riveting moment as Kell had held her in his arms, she'd almost forgotten that their marriage was a sham. She had wanted him to kiss her, to touch her. To take her, heaven help her.

Fool, she muttered fiercely to herself.

Raven shivered in the freezing night air, realizing how narrowly she had avoided peril. Muttering a curse, she shut the door firmly and turned to go upstairs to seek her bed alone.

Chapter
Eleven

As Raven's friend Brynn had predicted, the ton showed signs of relenting in their harsh judgment of the scandal. The afternoon post brought nearly a dozen invitations for Mrs. Lasseter and her new husband.

Upon seeing the size of the stack, Raven felt her mouth curve in a cynical smile, one admittedly tinged with bitterness. How fickle the ton was, following the whims of their leaders like sheep. And how blind she had been.

She had willfully fooled herself all this time, hungering for acceptance by their imperious confederates, convinced that belonging to their elite ranks meant the world to her. But their specious brand of acceptance was as much a sham as her marriage. A house of cards that had all come tumbling down with one breath.

Her course was set now, though. She was still determined to win herself back into their good graces. And she had no intention of backing down.

Raven was perusing the various invitations in the parlor when Sean Lasseter spoke from the doorway.

"How charming. The perfidious bride playing lady of the manor."

Alarmed, Raven leapt to her feet, scattering invitations everywhere.

"Beg pardon, madam," the Lasseter butler exclaimed at Sean's shoulder, "but Mr. Lasseter insisted upon seeing you."

"I came to call on my new sister," Sean drawled, sauntering into the room.

Reflexively Raven's hand went to her throat, where she could feel her pulse pounding. "What are you doing here?"

"Calling, as I said. I have a key to my brother's house, of course. And you haven't the authority to deny me admittance."

Perhaps she did have no right to order him to leave, but neither did she have any desire to be alone with the man who had used her so harshly.

"Knowles," Raven managed to say to the butler, "will you please send O'Malley to me?"

"Hiding behind your groom's skirts again?" Sean said when the servant had gone.

"What do you want, Mr. Lasseter?" Raven demanded, ashamed of the way her voice trembled. Yet the pain and humiliation he'd caused her during her abduction was still a stark memory. She had every reason to harbor a healthy fear of him.

"I told you, I came to pay a courtesy call. I thought it only polite form to welcome you into the family."

She gazed at him skeptically as Sean settled in a chair, casually crossing one leg over the other. He was impeccably dressed in a bottle green coat that brought out the deep color of his eyes. She would have considered him a strikingly handsome man but for the savage look of dislike he was directing at her.

"Somehow I doubt you consider me welcome," she returned. "Or that you are even capable of common courtesy."

"Call it curiosity, then. Tell me, what clever tricks did you employ to dupe Kell into wedding you?"

Gathering her control, Raven attempted to respond calmly. "I did not *dupe* him. He understood my plight and responded as a gentleman might, by proposing."

His mouth curled. "Kell is hardly a gentleman."

"At least he did not abduct me and drug me and ruin me in the eyes of society."

"But you know nothing of the sins he *has* committed." Sean's look turned almost sly. "He is suspected of murder; were you aware?"

She lifted her chin scornfully, unwilling to believe anything Sean said. "I refuse to listen to such ugly rumors."

"Are you certain they are rumors?"

Raven stared at him. "Are you claiming they are not? Kell said . . . He led me to believe he didn't kill your uncle."

"Would you expect him to do otherwise? He would hardly admit to murder, now would he?" Sean made a scoffing sound. "My brother is not the paragon you think him. You should take warning."

Raven shook her head, suspicious of Sean's motives. He was doubtless trying to make trouble between her and his brother. Surely there was not any real substance behind his innuendo. But whatever his aim, she only wanted to be rid of him.

She drew a deep breath. "What will it take to persuade you to leave me alone, Mr. Lasseter? Money? If so, I can give it to you. I have a modest fortune. You can have it if that will stop you from hounding me."

"You cannot bribe me," Sean returned with scorn. "No amount of money can make up for the hell you put me through."

"I am sorry for the pain you suffered. But you have had your revenge. I would call us even."

"Not even. Never even." His voice dropped to a chilling whisper. "Not until you pay in blood."

Rising, he moved toward her, his very stance menacing. If he deliberately meant to frighten her, he was succeeding. Raven took a defensive step backward, glancing behind her at the bellpull, wondering if she could reach it in time and summon a servant. If not, she could scream. . . .

When he reached out and grasped her wrist, she winced in pain. The bruises he had inflicted upon her the night of her abduction had only recently faded.

Just then O'Malley appeared. Raven gasped in relief as he grabbed Sean by the collar and yanked him away from her.

When Sean started to struggle, O'Malley drew back his meaty fist, holding it poised threateningly. " 'Tis clear you didn't learn the lesson I taught you last time."

"Unhand me, you bloody cur!" Sean demanded, his face black with rage.

When the groom contemptuously released him, Sean

staggered back, running a finger beneath his cravat as if it were too tight. "You will regret that, O'Malley."

"Not as much as you'll regret it if you dare to touch her again. Wring your neck, I will, I promise you. You'll not see your next dawn."

His scowl returning, Sean took a step forward. But then he stopped, as if considering the wisdom of fighting a man so much brawnier than he.

His fists clenched at his sides, he lowered his voice to a savage whisper. "I would watch your back, if I were you." Still bristling, Sean brushed past the groom and stalked from the room.

Raven sank into the nearest chair, trembling.

"Are you all right?" O'Malley asked in concern.

"Yes . . . I think so."

" 'Tis sorry I am that I let that bastard slip away the last time. Killed him, I should have."

She drew a slow breath. "Killing him might have been extreme. And the cost too high. You could have landed in prison or worse."

"But had I killed the blighter, he wouldn't be here to accost you now. And you would never have been forced to wed his brother."

Raven pressed her lips together, refusing to let herself sink into self-pity. "Well, it is done now. I will have to find some way to live with it."

"I don't like it, him being free to target you."

"I don't care much for the way he threatened you, either," she responded, remembering Sean's warning to O'Malley to watch his back.

"I can take care of myself, Miss Raven. 'Tis you who

should beware, I'm thinking. You should keep a knife or a pistol close at hand."

Raven grimaced. She had already shot his brother. She didn't like to think of having to defend herself by violent means, and yet it might be necessary. "Perhaps I should."

"Well, I'll be near if you should need me."

"Thank you, O'Malley."

After the groom was gone, she hugged her arms around herself, feeling unclean and afraid. It was a long moment before her shivers began to subside.

Her gaze dropped to the invitations that had fallen to the carpet. She might have made some progress in reducing the scandal, but it was clear she still hadn't removed the threat.

She still had a dangerous enemy in Sean Lasseter. And so did O'Malley.

When Raven's groom was shown in, Kell was seated at his desk in his private study, reviewing account books. He looked up in surprise as O'Malley stalked across the carpet.

"A word with you it is I'm wanting, Mr. Lasseter," the groom said grimly, coming to a halt before the desk. He stood with hat in hand, like any correct servant, but there was nothing humble about his demeanor. Rather, anger etched his craggy features, perhaps even belligerence.

Kell set down his pen. "Is this about my wife?"

"Aye, and your brother."

He felt his stomach knot.

"I'm not usually one to bear tales," O'Malley ground out, "but your brother . . . he came to your house this afternoon to threaten Miss Raven. He nearly struck her."

"Did he hurt her?" Kell demanded in a sharp voice.

"No, but he would have had I not been there to stop him. I had to show him my fives to make him leave."

Digesting the groom's information in silence, Kell felt anger spear through him. Before he could respond, however, O'Malley continued in a voice that was half-furious, half-pleading.

"That won't be the end of it, I'm thinking. Your brother said he wants revenge for the hell he suffered. But Miss Raven isn't to blame for what the navy did to him. If anyone is at fault, 'tis myself. When he attacked Miss Raven in the park, I darkened his daylights and left him there to come to his senses. But I swear, I never thought he would be taken up by the impressment gang."

"No," Kell replied in a low voice. "If anyone is to blame, it's Sean for assaulting her in the first place."

"Aye." O'Malley nodded fiercely. "He's already hurt her enough. But I've a terrible fear he won't leave it be. And I don't know if I can protect her next time."

Kell felt his jaw harden, along with his resolve. "I will deal with my brother, O'Malley," he said tightly. "I promise you, Sean won't hurt her again."

After finding Sean away from home, Kell visited several haunts his brother normally frequented, finally running him to earth at Madame Fouchet's. The most elegant sin club in London catered to aristocratic young bloods and wealthy commoners and specialized in fulfilling sexual fantasies.

The proprietor was a shrewd Frenchwoman, the same madame who had supplied the aphrodisiac used on Raven. Madame Fouchet greeted Kell personally, and with fondness.

"How good to see you, *mon cher*. You have not graced us with your presence in quite some time. We have missed you."

Kell returned a noncommittal half smile. "I am seeking my brother, madame. Is he perhaps here?"

"Indeed, he is. But he is . . . occupied at present."

"Even so, I should like to speak to him."

"Then you will find him in room number seven."

Kell started to turn away, but Madame Fouchet stopped him. "I worry about your brother, *cher*. He seems a very troubled young man. He has such delightful charm, but there are occasions when he has not been . . . nice to my girls."

"Is that so?" Kell asked with an edge of grimness. "In that case, you needn't feel obliged to endure his patronage. And you should not hesitate to call me if he oversteps the bounds."

"I will do that, monsieur. Thank you." She smiled. "Of course you must know that *you* are always welcome here. But I hear you are newly wedded. You will not want to leave your bridal bed for one of my girls, no?"

He feigned a smile and declined to answer directly. "I will keep your invitation in mind, madame."

The sporting house seemed abnormally quiet as Kell mounted the stairs. But then it was only late afternoon, far too early for the usual revelry.

He had no doubt how he would find his brother, though. And given his own past wildness, he could

hardly condemn such dissipation. Kell could well remember his younger years when he first came to London. He had thought nothing of spending the entire day
in bed with a beautiful Cyprian, indulging in decadence.

For too long, however, he'd set Sean a bad example.
He had sobered greatly since, making an effort to be
more discreet, eschewing brothels for longer-term
arrangements. His last affair with a wealthy merchant's
widow had ended badly, with tears and recriminations
on her part, and he'd refrained from employing another mistress since then.

Perhaps fortunately, Kell reflected, considering the
fact that he was now wed. Managing a wife and mistress at the same time was more trouble than he preferred to deal with at the moment. He had enough on
his hands with the problem of his brother.

Then again, he might be wise to take up Madame
Fouchet's offer to visit here. Perhaps then he would be
able to forget the searing memory of blue eyes and soft
breasts and the alluring scent that haunted his dreams.

Trying to dismiss thoughts of his beautiful, unwanted
bride, Kell rapped lightly on the door to room seven
and was sharply bid entrance.

He found Sean seated on a chaise, a scantily clad
beauty on his lap.

"If I might have a word with you in private," Kell
said, not waiting for an invitation before settling
himself in a chair opposite his brother.

With a scowl on his face, Sean patted the courtesan's derriere and sent her from the room.

"So what brings you here, brother?" he asked bel-
ligerently. "Not the entertainment, surely. You have no

need to drown your sorrows in the arms of a paid whore. You have a wife now—or is she spurning you the way she did me?"

Kell forced himself to ignore the jibe. "You crossed the line again this afternoon," he said, his tone terse. "Raven is my wife now, whether or not either of us likes it. I won't have her harmed."

Sean looked away guiltily. "I didn't harm her."

"But you threatened to."

"How do you know? Did she come running to you?"

Kell responded to the taunt by issuing a demand. "Perhaps I failed to make myself clear. You'll keep away from her in future."

"And if I don't?"

He narrowed his gaze on his brother. "I expect you to leave London tomorrow."

Lips thinning mutinously, Sean cast him a defiant glance. "Or what? What will you do if I refuse, brother?" Flinging himself from the chaise, Sean began to pace. "You are hardly in a position to dictate to me when your own reputation is so tenuous. I could ensure you have more to occupy your time than needlessly defending the heartless bitch you married."

Kell gritted his teeth at the word. "Meaning?"

Coming to a halt, Sean gazed down at him in triumph, his green eyes glittering. "Meaning that I need only find a magistrate and suggest how dear Uncle William met his demise. If I claimed I saw you kill him, you would have more trouble than you could deal with. You would likely be facing prison."

Kell's stomach clenched savagely, the depth of his brother's hostility like a knife to his gut.

For a moment he stared at the man standing before him. It was as if he no longer knew his brother. Sean had become more and more distraught over the past year, and truly violent since his impressment, but he'd never threatened outright betrayal.

Regardless . . . Even if the bond between them frayed beyond repair, Kell knew he could no longer overlook his brother's violence or tolerate his excesses.

"Claim whatever you will," Kell finally replied grimly, "but that won't change my intentions of sending you to Ireland."

His face turning red with anger, Sean brandished his fists. "This is all your fault, you know. You promised Mama you would protect me. But you didn't protect me, did you, Kell? You let Uncle William do whatever he wanted to me."

Furious himself, sick at heart, Kell drew a labored breath. He would spend the rest of his life trying to make up for his failure, but he wouldn't relent. Sean had become too dangerous. "Yes, I *am* to blame for not protecting you," he declared with quiet vehemence. "And I will never forgive myself. But there is no way for the past to be undone. If there were . . ." His own fists clenched. "I would gladly have taken your place, you know very well."

A grimace crossed his brother's face. "You would never have found yourself in my place in the first instance. You would not have let that bastard touch you. You would have fought him." His expression of anger suddenly crumpled. "I've always been so much weaker than you." Turning away, he sank onto the chaise again, burying his face in his hands.

Kell felt his own anger abate a degree at Sean's desolation. He leaned forward in his chair, searching for the right words. "Sean . . . can't you see what is happening to you? You are letting the past destroy you."

Reaching up, Sean clutched at his hair. "I know," he said hoarsely. "Sometimes I can't help myself. There is this devil screaming inside my head . . . making me want to lash out, to hurt someone, to hurt you."

Anguish speared through Kell, along with a raw desire to protect his brother. "We will get you help. There are other doctors—"

"No! I won't have more quacks poking and prodding at me, telling me my mind is diseased." After a moment, Sean looked up, tears making his green eyes shimmer. "I'm sorry, Kell," he said in a low voice. "I didn't mean what I said. I am an ungrateful wretch. God, please forgive me. . . . It is just that I . . . loved Raven. I was devastated when you chose her over me. And now she has turned you against me."

Kell ran a hand raggedly through his own hair at his brother's pleading tone. "I didn't choose her willingly, Sean. And having her come between us is the last thing I would ever want. But I can't stand by and allow you to hurt her. Can you understand that?"

"Yes." The word was a mere whisper.

"Swear to me you will leave her alone."

"I . . . I swear."

Kell could feel his brother's bleakness, his misery. Sean was in anguish, his better nature fighting the demons inside him.

Rising, Kell crossed to the chaise and pressed a hand

to Sean's shoulder. "You need to get away. If you stay here, you'll only be tormented by the past."

"Perhaps you're right," he said dully. "But where would I go?"

"I told you, to Ireland. To the farm. The breeding program was to be your responsibility, remember?"

The horse farm Kell had purchased near Dublin boasted prime breeding stock that had already resulted in several promising racers. Not that he cared much about racing or the Turf. But since Sean loved horses so deeply, Kell had hoped to provide him an interest as well as a refuge.

"Will you come with me?" Sean asked wistfully.

Kell's stomach twisted again. Sean sounded like a young boy again, like the beloved brother he'd once known. "I regret that I can't. I have obligations here. My club . . ."

"And Raven Kendrick." Sean's mouth momentarily hardened.

"Yes. Raven as well. But that doesn't mean I care for you any less. Sean, you must get away, for your own sake."

"Very well. If that will make you happy, I will go," Sean said quietly, the dismal look of defeat in his eyes.

It was nearly midnight when Kell reluctantly climbed the stairs, heading for his wife's bedchamber. Raven would be surprised that he'd returned home from his club so much earlier than usual, and even more surprised when he approached her. But he owed her yet another apology for his brother's savage conduct.

Kell moved slowly down the dimly lit hall, his thoughts still spinning around his confrontation with Sean this afternoon and the angry threats his brother had made. Their clash had dredged up dark memories of the night their uncle died.

Six months after they'd fled England, William had tracked them down. Kell knew he would never forget that night. He'd spent most of the evening gaming, milking a winning streak, trying to add to their meager savings. He returned to their stark lodgings in the wee hours of the morning to find Sean sobbing out his heart over their uncle's bloody body.

"It was an accident, Kell, I swear! I didn't mean to hurt him. I only meant to make him stop touching me."

Bit by bit Kell coaxed the story from his trembling brother. William apparently had pursued them to Ireland, concerned by the appearance that his underage nephews refused to live with him, as well as worried that they would divulge his homosexuality, a hanging offense. When William demanded the brothers return home and began shaking him, Sean revolted, unable to bear his touch. He'd stabbed William in the chest with Kell's own rapier.

Kell couldn't totally blame his fourteen-year-old brother, for he likely would have killed Sean's abuser himself, had he been present. The boy's explosive reaction was self-defense, he was almost certain.

Determined to shield his brother from further suffering, Kell disposed of the body on a deserted stretch of road outside Dublin, making William's death appear to be highway robbery. The investigation that followed pointed accusing fingers at Kell, bringing to light his violent history with his uncle, but the authorities could find no real proof. He refused to deny the rumors that he was the murderer, though. Better to take the blame himself than to have suspicion fall on his young brother.

Even so, Sean had never fully recovered. Having his uncle's death on his conscience, in addition to his sordid shame, had nearly destroyed him—a torment of the soul that no brotherly words of comfort, no passage of time, could totally assuage.

Kell squeezed his eyes shut as he paused before Raven's bedchamber door. Despite all his efforts, Sean's despondence had been inconsolable.

They'd remained in Ireland for two more years before deciding to make a fresh start where the gaming was more profitable. Returning to England, they settled in London. Kell hoarded his winnings and eventually, after a half dozen more years, amassed the funds to open a private gaming club, where the more adventurous members of society came to gamble.

The dark rumors had followed him, however. He still couldn't refute them without implicating his brother. Nor could he divulge Sean's terrible secrets. But he could at least try to make Raven understand and win her sympathy.

A light shone beneath her door, and Kell rapped softly. She was reading in bed, he saw when she bid entrance. The startled look on her face clearly proclaimed how unexpected his visit was. Hurriedly hiding her book, she snatched up the covers to her chin, concealing her nightdress from view.

Kell hesitated, wondering if he might be making a

mistake, holding this interview in her bedchamber. But this was his best chance to speak to her in private.

"Is something wrong?" she asked worriedly.

"I came to apologize for Sean's behavior this afternoon," Kell said, shutting the door quietly behind him.

She stared at him warily as he crossed the room to her. Kell found himself gratified that she didn't want him there any more than he wanted to be there.

When she remained silent, he pressed his advantage and sat beside her on the bed. Raven froze at his nearness, Kell noted with satisfaction. It would behoove him to keep her on the defensive.

"It is no excuse, I know," he began, "but I want you to understand something about Sean, how he became the way he is."

"What do you mean?"

"For some years now he has suffered periods of depression, of melancholy. When he falls into one of his black moods, he won't eat or sleep, and he drinks far too much. But until his impressment, I truly thought he had his demons under control."

Kell paused, letting his words sink in. "When he disappeared last June, I was frantic, Raven. I spent months searching for him before I uncovered the harbor manifest of a naval vessel that listed Sean's name as one of the crew. I hired a private schooner and went after him.

"When I found him he was shackled in the hold, wallowing in his own excrement. His back was a bloody strip of flesh. He had been flogged till his throat was too raw to scream."

Kell found his own throat closing at the savage

memory. "He's my brother, Raven." His fingers curled involuntarily into fists. "Perhaps you can understand my grief at finding him so broken."

"Yes—" she murmured.

"And can you imagine the pain he suffered?"

Her gaze lowered to avoid his penetrating one. "Yes . . . I can imagine."

"It sent Sean over the edge, Raven."

"And you expect me to forgive him because of that?" she asked, her voice barely audible.

"No. Not forgive. But I hope you will have an inkling of what made Sean the way he is now. How deep despair can drive a man to do unspeakable things. He is ill, Raven. How could anyone be in his right mind after that horror?"

When she didn't speak, Kell put a finger under her chin to make her look at him. "What he needs most is time to heal. I am sending him to Ireland. He won't bother you again."

"Thank you." She shuddered. "I would be happy not to be required to deal with him again."

"You won't have to."

Her blue eyes were dark and solemn as she gazed back at him. Kell suddenly found himself aware of the intimacy of the circumstances. His wife was in bed, dressed in her nightclothes, her midnight hair spilling about her shoulders, the lamplight casting a golden glow over her fine-boned face. Her high-necked nightdress was unrevealing, true, and mostly concealed from view by the covers, and yet he knew very well what lay beneath.

Kell vividly remembered her nude body from their

wedding night. He remembered her breasts, licking them, sucking them, teasing them. He remembered her slender legs and how she had mounted him. . . . Instantly he grew hard, and he swore under his breath.

Needing a distraction, he glanced down to where the book she'd been reading was peeking out from the covers. The jeweled cover sparkled in the lamplight. Reaching over her, he picked it up to examine it. He had no doubt he was seeing a magnificent and rare artifact.

"Is this the book you told me about?" he asked. "The erotic journal your mother left to you?"

Her face flushed. "Y-yes."

His gaze dropped involuntarily from her rosy cheeks to her mouth. He remembered kissing that delectable mouth, sliding his tongue deep inside to taste her, to drink of her, to steal her breath. He remembered how she had responded, her lips parting on a strangled sob as her pleasure peaked. . . .

Kell drew a sharp breath, knowing he had to leave. "Perhaps some day you might allow me to read it. It would be intriguing to discover if I could learn a thing or two about lovemaking."

"I suppose . . . if you wish," she stammered.

He could tell he had caught her off guard and realized it was a victory of sorts. He would continue to keep his beautiful wife off her guard if he could manage it. He had spent too much time of late in that position himself. Ever since laying eyes on Raven, in fact.

Steeling his loins, Kell bent down and pressed an intentionally provocative kiss to her forehead. "Sleep well, vixen."

She was still staring after him when he let himself from her bedchamber by way of the dressing room door.

Chapter

Twelve

"Thank you, O'Malley," Raven murmured when the groom had assisted her into the sidesaddle.

After arranging her skirts, she drew her cloak tight against the frigid morning air and took up the reins, eager to be off for her daily ride in the park. The moment O'Malley had mounted his own hack, Raven set out at a brisk trot, with the groom following close behind.

She didn't expect to meet Brynn since her friend had another engagement this morning. But she hoped to find Dare, for she had an alarming report to discuss with him: an ugly rumor that concerned her husband.

She hadn't spoken much to Kell during the past week, not since the night he had come to her bedchamber to discuss his brother. Except for passing him on the stairs, she hadn't even seen him. The duty of providing her escort to various social functions had fallen to her friends.

Unaccountably Raven found Kell's deliberate absence bothersome. Restlessness was nothing new to her, but she'd felt an unusual despondency of late. She tried to explain her feelings away, telling herself that her low spirits had nothing to do with her husband's pointed neglect. After all, Kell was only adhering to the bargain they had struck.

There were countless other possible reasons for her melancholy, the most logical being that with the scandal, she now found herself on the fringes of the high society that she'd been such an integral part of until now.

Or perhaps her blueness could be attributed to the winter weather, which was remarkably cold, even for late November.

Or it was her apprehension over Sean Lasseter. Raven frequently found herself glancing nervously over her shoulder, seeing threats in the shadows, fearful that he would assault her again, even though Kell had assured her otherwise.

Or it could simply be due to loneliness. Admittedly she felt more alone than at any time since her arrival in England. Her grandfather had departed London for his own estate in East Sussex, while Raven remained in town for appearance's sake. She planned to join her grandfather for Christmas, but that was still several weeks away.

At least she had O'Malley. It was comforting to have him nearby, just as it was a solace to have Brynn and Lucian and Dare—her stalwart champions and dearest friends—stand by her. But still Raven couldn't deny her stark feeling of isolation. The nights were the worst, when she lay staring restlessly at the canopy above her bed. Not even her pirate lover could console her, for oddly, she had trouble summoning him. When she closed her eyes to imagine him, all she saw was Kell.

With her uncertain future stretching out before her, empty, pointless, without any goal to strive toward, she felt keenly alone and at a loss, regardless of how fiercely she scolded herself for falling victim to self-pity.

She should be counting her blessings, Raven knew. While her dreams of making a titled match were crushed, while the scandal had resulted in a great many closed doors, she had survived. And compared to many of her peers, she was actually well off. She had contracted a marriage in name only, with no dire risk of overwhelming love or obsessive passion to threaten her. And as the wife of a wealthy, indifferent husband, she had complete freedom to do as she pleased.

But still she found herself missing Kell. He had startled her the night he came to her room, especially when he bent to give her an unexpected kiss.

"Sleep well, vixen," he'd said.

But she hadn't slept. She had tossed and turned for hours, remembering the way his eyes had darkened when they scrutinized her concealing nightdress; remembering his sudden interest when he had spied the journal and her acute embarrassment at being caught reading it.

She had put away the journal after his visit, for the erotic passages only aroused her and reminded her of the physical relations that were missing in her marriage. But once or twice when she had heard Kell come in late at night, she lay there in bed, aware that she had a husband in the very next room, her body throbbing shamelessly for him. . . . She pictured his magnificent nudity when she'd surprised him at his bath. . . .

Wondered how she would react if he returned to her bedchamber to claim his marital rights.

But he never came to her room again.

No doubt Kell was occupied with his club, but Raven couldn't even be certain of that. She had shared some of her most private secrets with him—about the journal, about her fantasy lover—and still she knew so little about him.

Moreover, yesterday she was forcibly reminded of her obligations to Kell when she learned of a worrisome development.

According to Brynn, someone had begun spreading unsavory rumors about the honesty of Kell's gaming club. Raven could only suspect the gossip was the work of the Duke of Halford, since he had threatened to ruin the blackguard who'd stolen his bride.

When she reached Hyde Park, however, there was no sign of Dare, so she enjoyed an easy gallop along Rotten Row. It was perhaps a half hour later when she spied the marquess riding toward her. She barely waited for his charming greeting before she brought up the matter of her former betrothed's possible vindictiveness.

To Raven's dismay, Dare only confirmed her fears.

"Yes, I'm afraid Halford has been disparaging your husband's club. He has persuaded a number of his acquaintances to shun it, claiming the Golden Fleece is living up to its name—fleecing its customers."

"Does he have the slightest bit of proof?"

Dare gave her an arch look. "Proof isn't necessary to paint a man as dishonorable. The mere accusation from someone of influence can be just as lethal. I wouldn't be

surprised if Halford has never stepped foot inside the
Fleece."

Raven frowned in dismay. "Surely something can be
done to stop him."

"Well, I can help Lasseter make up for lost business
by patronizing his hell more often. And I could ensure
that my fellow Hellfire League members do the same."

"Would you, Dare, *please?*"

"Of course. But no amount of patronage can repair a
club's tarnished reputation. It's much like a lady's good
name. Once lost, it is almost impossible to regain."
Dare pursed his sensual lips thoughtfully. "It would no
doubt help if Lasseter made an effort to become better
known to his more celebrated clientele—give them
the opportunity to size up his honor and character. As
it stands now, he's merely a notorious enigma."

"But how is that to be accomplished?"

"He could start by getting about in society more. I
would be perfectly happy to sponsor him, as I'm sure
would Lucian, but your husband must be willing to
take part."

"I don't think he would," Raven said ruefully. "He
despises society."

"Even to save his club?"

"I don't know. I will have to ask him."

She visited the club that afternoon but was informed by the hulking doorman that Mr. Lasseter was
away. Emma Walsh, however, came down the stairs at
just that moment and greeted Raven with a gracious-
ness that seemed unfeigned.

Raven felt herself flush with embarrassment. She

had not seen the beautiful hostess since her abduction and wasn't quite certain how to act.

But Emma seemed determined to put her at ease. "Kell is at a fencing match, but he should return within the hour. Would you care to wait for him?"

Absurdly, it irked Raven that she knew less about her husband's whereabouts than this woman did. Surprised by the invitation, though, she accepted readily. When Emma had directed the doorman to have a tea tray sent into the bookroom, Raven surrendered her cloak and followed the hostess, gazing about her covertly.

Everywhere she looked, she saw evidence of tasteful richness: the sheen of waxed wood, the sparkle of crystal chandeliers, the sumptuousness of velvet and brocade furnishings.

Emma evidently noticed her interested glances. "Have you ever seen the inner workings of a gaming club?"

"No, but I admit to a vast curiosity."

"After tea I would be happy to show you about if you wish."

"I would like that very much."

"This is the most comfortable room in the place," Emma said, leading Raven into the library. "It is designed to give the club an air of refinement and remind our patrons of their libraries at home. Here they may enjoy a cheroot or a short respite from the gaming tables."

When they were seated around the tea table, Emma gave her an assessing glance. "Perhaps you might be interested to know that Sean has left for an extended stay in Ireland."

Raven drew a hopeful breath. "Truly? He is gone?"

"Yes. Kell persuaded him to go."

"I wonder how he accomplished that?"

"I am not quite certain, but Kell is the only one who can influence Sean when he turns wild. They are very close, even for brothers. I expect you must be relieved."

Pressing a hand to her temple, Raven managed a smile. "You cannot imagine how much."

Emma's own smile was sympathetic. "I am truly sorry for your ordeal. I tried to stop Sean that day, but all I could do was send for Kell."

Remembering, Raven shuddered.

"If I may be of any assistance to you," Emma offered, "you need only ask."

"Thank you," she replied. "Actually . . ." She leaned forward. "There is a way you could help me. I find myself in . . . an awkward situation, wed to a stranger. I don't doubt you know far more about my husband than I do. It would be helpful if you could tell me more about him. I have only heard bits and pieces regarding his past, and some of those were ugly rumors."

Emma hesitated a moment before answering. "I suppose you mean the rumors about him murdering his uncle."

"Yes. Sean intimated to me that they were true."

Anger filled Emma's eyes, while her mouth pressed together in a tight line. "I don't know how their uncle came to die, but I would stake my life on it—Kell Lasseter is not a murderer. And Sean is an ungrateful wretch to imply otherwise after all Kell has done for him!"

Her vehement defense of Kell pleased Raven and only strengthened her own belief in his innocence. "I didn't think Kell guilty," she observed. "But he wouldn't confirm or deny the rumors. All he would say was that his uncle sent his mother to an early grave after taking her sons from her. And that his scar was the result of a blow from his uncle's signet ring."

Emma nodded. "I don't think I would be betraying Kell's confidence to share what is common knowledge. You know his mother was Irish?"

"Yes."

"Well, she was not of the gentry, merely the daughter of an Irish physician, and the Lasseters despised her for it. When she was widowed, William Lasseter became her sons' guardian and threatened to withhold every cent of their inheritance unless Fiona gave up all claim to them."

"And did she?"

"Yes. From what Sean told me, she couldn't bear to deprive her sons of their birthright. And she didn't have the means to fight so powerful a family. She returned to Ireland and died there of an ague, alone and penniless. William refused even to let her sons go to visit her grave."

"Then it is understandable why Kell would loathe his uncle."

"Yes, but that isn't the only reason. According to Sean, William was a tyrant. And someone with Kell's rebellious nature wouldn't take kindly to such dictatorial control. Some years later, he became involved in a violent dispute with his uncle, which is when Kell received his scar. He escaped with Sean to Ireland and hid out on the streets of Dublin, barely managing to survive. Sean told me that more than once they had to resort to eating rats—although he might have made that story up simply to unsettle me."

Raven felt herself shudder. "So what happened next?"

"That isn't so clear. Eventually William pursued them to Dublin, where he took up lodgings and spent weeks searching for his nephews. But one day he simply disappeared. His body was discovered on a road outside Dublin. Apparently he'd been set upon by highwaymen and killed for his purse."

"Then why was Kell suspected of his murder?"

"Because William had been run through with a sword blade—an unusual choice of weapons for road agents, who normally use pistols. And Kell was a skilled swordsman. Sean says Kell learned the sport so he could hold his own with his uncle, who was a champion fencer. The theory was that Kell killed William in a duel and then disposed of the body."

"That seems flimsy evidence on which to base charges so serious as murder."

"Well, the charges actually came a bit later, from William's family. They were outraged by his death and felt certain Kell was to blame, but they could never prove it. And it didn't help that Kell never expressed any grief over his uncle's demise, or that he refused to return to England. He wanted nothing to do with the Lasseters or their wealth, even though he had to turn to gaming to scrape out a living. He was determined to raise Sean on his own, away from their influence. Kell even refused to accept the inheritance that was rightfully his. Everything you see here, he earned through his own efforts."

Raven glanced around the lavish room, feeling a touch of guilt. Despite the trials of her childhood, she'd had an easy life compared to Kell's. She had to admire a man who would make such a sacrifice for his brother. And even though his past was shadowed in secrets, she thought she knew Kell well enough by now to be certain he couldn't be guilty of cold-blooded murder.

Emma started to speak again but was interrupted when a boy of perhaps ten entered the library, unsteadily carrying a tea tray. He was followed by the majordomo whom Raven had met before.

Under Timmons's watchful regard, the boy carefully set the tray on the tea table, then looked up at the servant, seeking approval with a hint of fear in his eyes.

Raven could scarcely contain her dismay at the boy's appearance. Even though he was clean and well-groomed, he was thin to the point of emaciation. Worse, his face and hands sported numerous bruises and open sores that looked suspiciously like burns.

"Thank you, Nate," Emma said gently. "That was well done of you."

"Oi, mum." His coarse accent suggested his lower class origins.

When both the butler and boy had gone, Emma took up the teapot to pour, but she evidently saw Raven's troubled frown and hastened to explain. "Nate was a climbing boy until last week. Kell discovered him in an alleyway being beaten by his master and forcibly purchased him."

Raven winced at the image. Climbing boys were little more than slaves and so often ill-treated—by being prodded up chimneys with knives and flaming torches—that they sometimes died.

"I know." Emma agreed with her unspoken thought. "A life of hell. But at least he has a future now. When his wounds heal, he will go to the foundling home that Kell supports."

"Foundling home?"

"For orphaned boys." Emma smiled. "Nate makes the thirteenth street urchin that Kell has rescued. A baker's dozen. Kell feeds and clothes them, provides for their education, and sees they learn an occupation."

"How admirable," Raven murmured, thinking how few true good deeds she had rendered in her own life.

"Yes," Emma replied. "I owe Kell a great deal myself. He saved me from a . . . a difficult situation with my former protector."

And me as well, Raven thought. Kell had saved her from a life as an outcast. "He seems to make a habit of rescuing people."

"Indeed," Emma said softly. "He claims not to care, but he continues to protect the innocent and the abused."

Hearing the note of tenderness in Emma's voice, Raven couldn't help but wonder if more than admiration was its cause. Not for the first time, it occurred to her that Emma could be Kell's mistress. It was even possible she might be in love with him.

The thought sent an uncomfortable pang to the

depths of Raven's stomach. This woman knew her husband far more intimately than she herself ever was likely to. And she could well understand if he was attracted to the golden-haired woman in return. The hostess was older than Kell, perhaps nearing forty, but still incredibly beautiful.

Yet in spite of her instinctive jealousy, Raven found herself liking Emma and feeling ashamed of her ungrateful thoughts. Thus far Emma had proven a firm ally. Admittedly her cordiality surprised Raven. She would have thought a mistress wouldn't relish having an unexpected wife for a rival. But then, perhaps Emma didn't consider her a rival for Kell's affections, since he wasn't sharing her bed.

Raven was glad, however, when the talk turned to less serious matters, namely how a gaming hell was run. She was extremely curious about the notorious male world that had always been denied to her, and asked numerous questions, which Emma patiently answered.

Her fascination was piqued further after tea during her guided tour of the club, when she was shown the large, richly paneled gaming room where the hazard table stood. O'Malley had taught her how to shoot dice, but she knew the game of hazard involved far more than tossing bits of ivory. It was a complex betting game where players wagered on the combinations thrown.

The oval-shaped mahogany table was indented on either side—to provide a place for the croupier to stand, Raven presumed. The surface was covered with a fine green cloth marked with single and double yellow lines.

Completing the table were chairs for the gamesters, boxes, bowls, and small hand rakes.

"What are these used for?" Raven asked, indicating the accessories.

"Those are dice boxes," Emma explained. "The bowls are for holding counters—worth differing amounts of money—and the rakes are for drawing them in."

"And one player casts the dice?"

"Yes. His initial throws establish what are called the main and the chance. How subsequent throws match those determines who wins and loses. The most successful players are able to calculate the odds of various casts. Shall I show you?"

Raven started to reply that she would enjoy a demonstration, but just then a masculine voice sounded from behind her.

"Would you care to explain what you're doing in my gaming room?" her husband asked in a disapproving tone.

Her pulse quickening, Raven glanced over her shoulder to find Kell moving toward her. Awareness shivered down her spine as she met his unsettling gaze. The physical effect he had on her never failed to startle her. The mere sound of his voice stirred her senses, while her blood seemed to thicken at his nearness.

Disciplining her thoughts, however, she fished in her reticule and withdrew the dice she had brought with her, but kept them hidden in her closed fingers.

"I was just showing Raven around," Emma answered for her.

"Thank you, but I will take over from here."

For a moment Emma looked as if she might argue, but then she offered Raven a smile and took her leave.

"What are you doing here?" Kell repeated when the hostess had gone.

"I was curious," Raven replied. "I have never seen a game of hazard played."

"This is no place for a lady."

Raven arched an eyebrow. "You sound remarkably like my aunt. Do you really mean to suggest my presence here offends your sense of propriety?"

Did it? Kell asked himself. It would be hypocritical to claim he didn't want his wife at his gaming hell because it was improper. Some men, even rakes and libertines, became excessively conservative about their wives upon marriage, but it was absurd to be entertaining proprietary notions or feelings of possessiveness toward Raven. She wasn't his wife in the true sense of the word—or even his woman.

Yet he didn't want her here. His club was his one haven from her. Ever since Raven had begun sharing his house, he'd found it impossible to shed his awareness of her. He didn't want her invading his sole refuge. Not that he intended to let her know how profoundly she affected him.

"Besides," she was pointing out, "I understand from Emma that several ladies frequent your club."

"Perhaps, but they don't have a scandal hanging over their heads. Or they don't give a fig about their reputations. And you haven't answered my question. Why are you here?"

"Actually, I wished to speak to you. I wanted to

thank you, for one thing. I am profoundly grateful that you sent Sean away."

Kell nodded. "Very well, I'll consider myself thanked. Now you can go."

Raven made a face. "You can't evict me without undermining our pretense of being happily married."

Kell's gaze narrowed. "I believe we had an agreement. If I escorted you to the Wycliffs' ball, you pledged never to ask me for another favor, remember?"

"This has nothing to do with favors. This concerns the fate of your club." She hesitated. "Have you heard what Halford has been saying about you?"

His lips thinned in a hard line. "I've heard," he replied grimly.

"Well, we must *do* something. We have to try to stem those terrible rumors."

"I doubt anything I could do would have an effect."

"Lord Wolverton has offered to sponsor you in society. Dare believes that if you would only ingratiate yourself with the ton's leaders, you might be able to weather Halford's accusations."

Kell shook his head. It rubbed painfully against the grain to accept help from anyone; most certainly he didn't want to be beholden to Raven for her friends' intervention. "I'm not about to accept charity from the Marquess of Wolverton."

"It wouldn't be charity in the least. He would be doing it for my sake. Besides, you are always aiding others. Emma told me about all the street urchins you've rescued. It is only fair that you be the recipient for a change."

Kell grimaced. He didn't like having his secrets probed

any more than he liked having to deal with his beautiful wife's nearness. "You are much too interested in my affairs," he observed.

She didn't respond to that charge but took another tack. "Kell . . . I can understand why you scorn society, but this is another matter altogether. Your club is in danger."

"It isn't your concern."

"But it is." Raven gave him an imploring look. "I am the reason your reputation is being maligned. I cannot simply meekly return home and forget the trouble you are in. I won't stand idly by while you are ruined."

"I'm not giving you a choice. I don't need or want your help."

Frustration shone in her blue eyes. "I don't understand why you must be so stubborn!"

Kell steeled himself against his own frustration, wishing Raven would just go away and leave him in peace. Her very nearness was a temptation. Yet if he wanted her gone, he would have to drive her away. But how, other than physical threats . . . ?

Assessing her, he responded to the devil prompting him. "There is only one thing I might want from you, vixen."

She looked taken aback. "Oh? And what is that?"

"Perhaps you can guess." He reached out to brush her breast through her gown, making her start in alarm. "Carnal relations. You can fulfill my carnal needs."

Her sharp intake of breath was supremely satisfying.

"I see I have shocked you," Kell murmured. "How entertaining to render you speechless."

Raven ignored his baiting, however, and searched his face, her gaze both serious and wary. "Do you truly want relations between us?"

Kell felt his loins pulse at the prospect. Too clearly he remembered the tight, glorious fit of his hard flesh in the hot, wet softness of hers. "No," he denied swiftly. "I'm perfectly satisfied with our mock marriage, with neither of us demanding or expecting anything from the other."

"But will you at least consider taking Dare up on his offer? I know it wounds your pride to consider accepting help—"

"My pride is none of your concern."

Her lips pressed together for a moment, but then she narrowed her eyes, the picture of determination. "Very well, then. I have a proposition for you."

Kell gave her a measuring look. "Why would I be interested in any proposition of yours?"

"Because you are a gamester, and you can't resist a wager. I will gamble with you for your agreement, Kell. A few throws of the dice. If I can roll seven or eleven three times in a row, you will allow Wolverton to help you."

"And if not?"

"Then I will never bother you about the subject again. I will stand back and let your good name be ruined and your club destroyed with my blessing."

Kell eyed her in speculation, wondering what she was up to.

"Are you afraid I might win?" Raven taunted, a bright challenge in her eyes.

He wanted to tell her to go to the devil, but curiosity

got the better of him. He pushed the dice box toward her, then leaned indolently against the table, crossing his arms over his chest. "Go ahead then, roll."

Shaking her head, she opened her fist, showing a pair of dice. With a smug look, she juggled them a time or two and tossed the bits of ivory on the table, rolling a combination of eleven.

When Kell raised an eyebrow, Raven smiled serenely.

The second throw was just as successful. A seven. She gathered the dice and started to throw again.

His hand reached out to close over hers, staying her. Prying open her fingers, Kell captured the dice, hefting them in his hand.

Understanding dawned, as did anger. "These are weighted," he said harshly.

"I never claimed they weren't," Raven responded, her own tone dulcet. "You merely assumed I would use your dice."

Kell took a step toward her, reaching up to wrap his fingers around her throat in a gentle vise. "I don't tolerate cheating in my establishment."

A fleeting smile wreathed her mouth. "I never doubted it for a moment. But we must make everyone else see that."

Praying for patience, Kell shut his eyes. "I've been gulled like the veriest greenhorn, haven't I?"

"I'm afraid so." Pulling his fingers from her throat, Raven eased from his grasp. "But I cheated for a good cause."

Seeing the mirth trembling on her lips, Kell choked back his own bark of laughter and cursed instead.

"Where in hell did you get a pair of loaded dice? No, don't tell me. O'Malley."

"Yes. He taught me to play cards and shoot dice."

"And pistols as well," Kell said darkly, remembering.

"Well, yes. He contributed a great deal to my education."

"Your education was damned peculiar for a young lady."

"I won't argue with you on that point. My mother would have been appalled had she known."

She took the dice from him and threw again. Another seven. "I believe I just won," she said, her tone unwisely triumphant.

But Kell wasn't willing to let her escape so easily. Grasping her arm, he turned Raven to face him and, with his body, crowded her against the hazard table, bracing his arms on either side of her to prevent her escape.

"Do you know what I do to cheats?" he asked, his voice a silken menace.

"No, what?" she said breathlessly.

His gaze dropped to her mouth. He wanted to shake her. He wanted to kiss her and wipe that knowing gleam from her incredible blue eyes. "I throw them out on their ears."

"Would you really be so cruel to me?"

At the laughter in her question, a dozen thoughts rushed through his mind; foremost was how badly he wanted her. It would be so simple to lift her onto the table and drive himself home between her parted thighs. . . .

Without volition, he reached up to trail his knuckles

along the delicate curve of Raven's jaw. Instantly he heard her breath catch, saw her lips part in surprise at the heated tension that suddenly sizzled between them.

Riveted, Raven stared back at him. Kell's unexpected caress had made her stomach muscles contract, made her nipples stiffen. The feel of his hard, powerful body pressing against her own aroused a yearning ache between her thighs. . . .

He bent closer, his eyes dark as polished onyx, his lips hovering above hers. She trembled at the warm breath dazing her senses, fearing how she would respond if Kell decided to kiss her, wondering if she could possibly deny him.

But she wasn't required to make a decision, for suddenly he gritted his teeth and stepped back, putting a safe distance between them, his features totally shuttered.

"Go. Now," Kell demanded. "Get out before I think of something even more cruel to do to you."

Raven wisely decided to take his advice. Shakily she picked up her dice and fled the room.

Emma was in the entry hall, apparently waiting to say farewell. Raven exerted herself to respond calmly as she accepted her cloak from the doorman.

She had turned to go when she felt Kell's presence. When she glanced back, she saw he had moved to stand beside Emma, one hand resting lightly on the blond-haired woman's shoulder.

Raven felt her stomach twist with a different kind of awareness; that intimate gesture was one of a man toward his lover.

She drew a painful breath. It stung to think that the

beautiful hostess was the one claiming Kell's attentions at night while she lay alone in her bed.

Pasting a frigid smile on her mouth, though, she made a dignified exit, her head held high.

She stirred restlessly in the twilight between waking and sleeping, seeking release from the growing wildness inside her. Her pirate's worshiping mouth was on her naked breast, roughly tender, his lips suckling her taut, straining nipple. She quivered with her quickened breathing as his rasping tongue laved in a fiery circling.

Below she felt the brush of his fingers stroking possessively against her moist cleft, rimming the slick, honeyed entrance to her body. She arched, wanting him, aching for him.

In response, his caressing lips left off tormenting her bare breasts and moved lower, his open mouth seeking her sex, his breath hot on her exposed, sensitive flesh. She released a choked moan of pleasure as he probed the swollen, aching folds with his tongue.

When she began to writhe, he pressed his face harder between her legs, both hands gripping the curves of her buttocks to hold her to him while his tongue licked and stabbed her with fire, making her burn with desire.

Her body clenched unbearably, her fingers clutching in his hair.

Yet he refused to satisfy her. Pressing one last tantalizing kiss to the core of her, he rose above her. His face was shadowed, but she could feel his intensity, his burning sensuality as he stroked the velvet hardness of his arousal against her.

Then he lowered himself upon her, the sleek heavy weight of his body pressing her shivering thighs wide.

"You are my passion and my pain," he whispered, his voice rough.

The restlessness inside her stirred harder, hotter.

When his rigid flesh sank into her, she gasped and held him closer, drawing him even more deeply, sheathing him tightly. And when he began to move, she wound her legs around him and lifted herself to match his fierce thrusting.

It was a short, almost violent mating, her soft whimpers turning to cries as her senses erupted in climax. She shuddered as the spasms convulsed through her.

Yet when the throbbing of her body finally ebbed, when the heated pulses faded away, she still felt unsated.

Raven stirred to wakefulness, feeling the sharp lash of disappointment. She had let her mind slip into her dream world of illusion where she usually found fulfillment, but this time the usual pleasure had been missing. Even now the hungry yearning was still there, clamoring inside her. The wildness still pulled at her, along with a strange emptiness. . . .

Rolling over, Raven drew the sheet to her naked breasts. What had gone wrong? Her fantasy lover had never before failed her like this.

She had created him to fulfill her ideals. He was all she could ask for in a lover—tender, commanding, passionate, sharp-witted. A nameless, faceless soul mate who stirred her blood and calmed her restless spirit. He rarely spoke except to challenge her, seeing her as his equal, not a conquest to be dominated or subjugated.

With him she found the tenderness she craved, the love she dared not seek from any real man. Her pirate was her protection from heartache. She could surrender to him without fear of losing herself.

But he had never seemed so insubstantial as now.

Raven shut her eyes, envisioning her pirate lover. The hard, virile face. The thick, dark lashes. The eyes that were hot, intense, passionate . . .

Oh, God . . . *Kell*.

She groaned softly, trying to shut out his powerful image. He bore too damningly close a resemblance to her imaginary lover.

A twinge of panic coursed through Raven as she tried to rationalize this disquieting turn of events. There was a logical reason she'd found her fantasy so disappointing. She now had a standard to compare to.

For the first time in her life, she knew what real passion was. She knew the touch of a flesh and blood man, his taste, his scent, his fiery heat. . . . She knew Kell.

She groaned again, remembering how he had aroused her passion on her wedding night.

Murmuring a low oath, Raven buried her face in the pillow, determined to crush her vivid memories of that night. Of him.

She couldn't deny the distressing realization, though. Her fantasy lover was no longer as satisfying as her very real husband.

The elusive husband who wanted nothing to do with her.

Chapter
Thirteen

Raven couldn't regret her underhanded means of forcing Kell to cooperate in his own salvation, yet she worried he wouldn't take their wager seriously. Determined to press her case, she canceled her ride the next morning and instead surprised her husband by joining him in the breakfast room.

Kell briefly looked up from reading *The Morning Chronicle*, appearing disgruntled that she would invade his domain. After a terse greeting, he returned to perusing the news.

Raven didn't let his displeasure distress her. She filled her plate from the sideboard and took the seat at his right hand, addressing him as she spread strawberry jam on a muffin.

"I spoke to Dare and Lucian yesterday about our scheme to redeem your reputation. They intend to do their utmost to help, now that you have agreed to participate."

The sound Kell made was something between a grunt and a sigh. "I know. They attended my club last evening."

"Did they?" Raven smiled in relief. "I was certain I could count on them."

She took a bite of coddled egg and studied Kell. He was dressed informally again with no cravat, but his rust-colored coat molded his muscular shoulders to perfection, while the pristine white of his shirt heightened his dark good looks. She was growing accustomed to his scar, but his unabashedly sensual appeal still had the power to unsettle her.

Chastising herself, Raven mentally searched for a subject to distract her thoughts from her husband's dangerous masculinity.

"I have been wondering, Kell, about the climbing boy I met at your club yesterday. How is Nate doing?"

He didn't look up from his paper. "Well enough."

"I've been thinking . . ."

"That strikes me as hazardous," Kell murmured, his tone dry.

Raven bit back a smile. "It seems to me that a gaming hell is no place for a boy to be raised."

Kell did lift his gaze at that, regarding her intently over the paper. "You consider yourself an expert on how boys should be raised?"

"No—and I intended no criticism. I just thought that perhaps Nate would be better off living here. In your house, I mean, rather than at your club."

His eyes held hers in a level stare. "You would actually consider taking in a wretch from the streets? You don't fear he would purloin the silver or murder you in your bed?"

"Not in the least," she responded, surprised he would ask such a question.

"Most ladies would."

"Well, I don't. And I should like to help."

When Kell finally answered, his tone had lost its gruff edge. "It is generous of you to offer, but Nate has come to know the staff at the club, and I'm certain he would feel less apprehensive there than he would here. In any case, he will remain at the club only a few more days. I'm taking him to a foundling home once his bruises heal."

Raven frowned. "I have heard some unpleasant tales about foundling homes. About the cruel lives their inmates lead."

"Not all such places are cruel. And it will be best for Nate to be around boys his own age and to learn a trade. The lad is sharp-witted for all that he seems so cowed."

"But it must be frightening for him to go to live in new surroundings."

"This home is not so frightening," Kell replied. "The headmistress is a jovial sort and gives out gingerbread to the newcomers to make them feel welcome."

"I should like to see that," Raven said thoughtfully. "Would you consider allowing me to accompany you when you deliver Nate there?"

Kell's eyes narrowed with something like suspicion. "Why would you wish to?"

"Because I have little to occupy my time. And I would like to do something worthwhile, rather than moping around here, feeling lonely and sorry for myself. Please? I promise I won't make a nuisance of myself or cause you any trouble."

Reluctant amusement lit his eyes. "Your middle name is trouble, vixen. But if you seriously want to go . . ."

Raven gave him a brilliant smile. "I do."

"Very well. Now will you permit me to finish my breakfast in peace?"

"Certainly," she agreed, "if you will hand me a page or two of the paper. Are you always such a bear in the morning?" she couldn't resist asking when he had complied.

Kell's stare turned to one of exasperation. "Might I remind you that you were supposed to be a wife of convenience, not a termagant?"

Forcibly Raven swallowed her amusement and applied herself to the society page, content to retreat after her small victory.

Four days later she found herself accompanying Kell and Nate on the drive from London to Hampstead, where the Charity Home for Indigent Boys was located.

Nate at first seemed overwhelmed by the luxurious interior of the coach and by the unfamiliar sights of the passing countryside. He sat rigidly, not daring to speak as he stared out the window, yet he was obviously listening avidly to every word Kell said.

It amazed Raven to watch Kell reassure the boy.

"If you don't like the place, you don't have to stay. But there will be other lads your own age. And you will learn a trade that will allow you to be your own master some day."

"Not a sweep?" Nate asked in a small voice.

"No, never again. But you will have to learn to read and cipher."

His nose screwed up in distaste. "Why must oi learn to cipher, sir?"

"Because if you can calculate numbers, you won't have to toil at physical labor. You could be a tailor's apprentice or shopkeeper's assistant or perhaps even a clerk. And you will be less likely to be fleeced by merchants who are eager to cheat you out of your hardwon earnings. Trust me, when you are at the beginning of your career, you can't afford to forfeit even a penny."

With a sleight of hand, Kell pulled a penny from behind the boy's ear and presented it as a gift.

Nate stared wide-eyed in wonder and delight.

"Here, lad," Kell added, fishing in his pocket for a small purse. "You will need a little spending money to see you through your first weeks."

The boy was speechless, while Raven felt tears sting her eyes. Doubtless such kindness was rare in Nate's young life.

When they arrived at the charming village of Hampstead and dismounted from the coach, the boy clung to Kell's hand. The large, mellow brick manor covered with ivy looked much like a country gentleman's residence, but behind the house stood outbuildings and fields more appropriate to a farm, with chickens and pigs and grazing livestock in view.

Much to Raven's relief, the headmaster who greeted them seemed kind and intelligent. And his wife was indeed a jolly soul who won Nate over with gingerbread and soon had him answering gentle questions about his origins.

Nate knew nothing of his father, but apparently his mother had been a Covent Garden doxy who'd sold

him into the hellish life of a sweep when he was five.
And he was clearly terrified of the man who had been
his master.

Mrs. Fenton assured him solemnly that no one here
would beat him or force him to climb anything except
perhaps a ladder to the haylofts in the barns. Eventually she introduced Nate to a half dozen other boys
who took him off to tour the outbuildings, while Mr.
Fenton explained the workings of the place to Raven.

The home housed perhaps forty orphans, many of
whom were former beggars, cutpurses, or climbing boys.
They slept in dormitory rooms according to age and
were required to do daily chores around the farm, but
they spent several hours each day in the schoolroom
and the remainder apprenticing with masters of various
trades.

When Mr. Fenton asked what trade Nate might be
best fitted for, Kell answered thoughtfully. "He can't
read a word, but he shows an aptitude for mathemat-
ics. He can accurately tally the counters at my gaming
tables." Kell gave a wry smile. "He also has a vocabu-
lary that would make a sailor blush. And I should warn
you, he isn't partial to bathing. With some decent food,
his scrawny form should fill out in time, but I doubt he
will ever be cut out for heavy physical labor."

"We'll do our best to make him prosper, sir, God love
you," Mrs. Fenton said.

"I'm certain you will," Kell replied. "You've managed
to work miracles with the other poor wretches I've
brought here."

The healing miracles had already begun for Nate,
Raven realized. When he came running back, his eyes

shone with the delights he had seen at this, the first real home he had ever had known. His happiness was so palpable, he might have been in heaven—a happiness that only dimmed a bit when Kell and Raven took their leave.

Kell remained silent until they were seated in the coach on their way back to London. "Well, are you satisfied he isn't being condemned to a life of cruelty?"

"Yes," she said softly. "I cannot imagine a better place for him."

It was true, Raven reflected, thinking of the terrible life the boy had led. Recalling that he was a bastard, she felt rather humbled and ashamed of herself for bemoaning her own origins all these years. She had been so much better off than poor Nate. At least she'd had a loving mother, but Nate had had no one until Kell literally hauled him off the streets.

Kell cared a great deal for the boy, that much was obvious. "It was exceedingly good of you to save him," Raven added.

Kell's mouth twisted as he shook his head. "I am no saint, if that is what you are thinking."

"No, I would hardly call you a saint. But certainly a guardian angel. Tell me . . ." She regarded Kell seriously. "Why would you go to so much effort for a boy you don't even know?"

He was silent for a long moment. "I suppose because his plight strikes too close to home. I know what it's like to be helpless. To be on the streets. To be alone and have nothing and no one to turn to."

She heard the pain in his voice, the loneliness he let

her glimpse, the man behind the mask. Regretting having probed such a raw wound, Raven mentally berated herself. "Surely you were never so wretched as Nate."

"No, but for a time I was just as powerless. I came to despise that feeling. And Nate reminds me of my brother. Sean was his age when we were delivered to the tender mercies of my uncle. I admit it became a compulsion of mine, to rescue any helpless creature that crosses my path."

"Including me? Is that why you came to my rescue and wed me?"

Kell frowned at her, deliberately trying to discompose her, she suspected. "You are an extremely nosy wife."

"I suppose I am."

"I thought you promised not to make a nuisance of yourself."

"But sometimes I cannot help myself. You may beat me and restrict me to bread and water if that will make you feel better."

"Don't tempt me," he warned, although his wry smile took the sting out of his words. He leaned back against the leather squabs then, shutting his eyes and effectively dismissing her.

Raven watched him for a moment, marveling at the compassion she'd seen in him. Kell was a hard man, with a brusque temper and unforgiving manner, especially toward her. But she was beginning to suspect that inside, he was closer to melted wax than granite. Clearly he couldn't bear to see anyone helpless and downtrodden.

It had been Nate's good fortune to be rescued by Kell. Was she as fortunate?

Uneasily, Raven banished the thought, unwilling to admit that wedding Kell had been anything but misfortune for her.

Tearing her gaze from him, she stared out the window. She would do better to heed the warning voices in her head. If she didn't take care, she could grow to like Kell far too much, but it was folly to entertain feelings of warmth and admiration toward her unwanted husband.

Kell's genuine kindness, however, made Raven even more determined to see that he didn't suffer for her sake. Yet judging by the daily accounts she received from her friends, the progress was not encouraging.

She had hoped that with the Marquess of Wolverton and the Earl of Wycliff promoting her husband's acceptance into the elite ranks of the ton, Kell at least stood a chance of living down his notoriety. Reportedly, he attended several events with Dare and rubbed shoulders with the prime social leaders, including the Prince Regent himself. Dare also related that the Hellfire League members were patronizing the club regularly.

And yet, as Raven had feared, her friends' earnest efforts to rally around him were in vain. According to Emma, attendance at the club had fallen to record lows. And the spurious rumors about his gaming hell only worsened.

By the following week, Raven concluded there was only one course open to her—to confront the source of the slander directly.

It took some maneuvering, but she managed to discover through the servants' grapevine that the Duke of Halford was expected to attend Drury Lane Theater that evening. When she expressed an interest in seeing the play there, both Brynn and Lucian dropped their plans in order to accompany her.

She dressed carefully in an empire waist gown of royal blue velvet that was Halford's favorite shade, knowing it brought out the vivid color of her eyes, while the low, square neckline showed her bosom to advantage.

Halford was already at the theater when they arrived, seated in a box opposite the Wycliffs'. But he refused even to look at Raven—a deliberate cut, she knew. Half the opera glasses in the theater were trained on her, but she paid no attention to the spectators or to the play. She could not even have said what she saw, her attention was focused so intently on her task.

At the first intermission, when she saw Halford leave his box, she persuaded Brynn to stroll the halls with her. As she hoped, they encountered the duke shortly, but he was surrounded by friends.

Keeping a discreet distance, Raven waited until he left his party. Then taking a deep breath, she stepped forward into his path.

Halting abruptly, Halford raised his quizzing glass, looking at her as if she were a particularly odious species of bug.

She endured his scathing perusal without visibly flinching. "Good evening, Charles."

"Madam." He made no effort to bow. "I confess you astonish me, brazenly accosting me in public like this."

"I presumed this would be my only chance to speak to you," Raven replied. "No doubt you would have refused to see me had I applied to you in private."

Raising a mocking eyebrow, Halford looked around them. "I wonder that your husband didn't accompany you here."

His very tone was a taunt, but Raven tried to remain calm, not wishing to antagonize him. "My husband is occupied at the moment. He has a club to run, as perhaps you know."

"Ah, yes." The duke's lips curled with contempt. "I recall now that he is a gamester. I should have perceived your presence, since the stench followed you here."

Raven bit her tongue. "Charles, I only hoped to have a word with you."

"You may spare your breath, madam. Nothing you have to say could possibly interest me."

He turned abruptly and left her standing there.

Her determination only rose, however.

Near the end of the play, Raven pleaded a headache and told her friends she intended to take a hackney home. Lucian escorted her below and found her one, but several blocks away, she instructed the jarvey to double back.

He dropped her at the end of the long queue of carriages waiting for the theater patrons. Fortunately most of the coachmen and footmen were hovering together, laughing and dicing and simply trying to stay warm in the frigid night air.

Raven kept to the shadows until she spied Halford's town coach with the ducal crest emblazoned on the door, then slipped inside, hoping she hadn't been seen. She was risking fresh scandal with her brazen plan, no doubt; ladies did not closet themselves in closed carriages in order to confront irate noblemen. But she felt she had no choice.

She curled herself in the far corner, in the rear-facing seat, and pulled a carriage rug over her head, praying she wouldn't be detected until they were under way. Then she lay shivering in the darkness.

It was quite some time before the line of carriages began to roll forward, and longer still before she heard Halford enter his own vehicle. She waited until they were well in motion before pushing off the rug and sitting up. She could barely make out his form across from her.

"Charles?" she murmured quietly.

With a violent start, he snatched up his cane to defend himself.

"Charles, it is I, Raven," she said hurriedly.

He reached up to rap on the roof, but she leaned forward to grasp his arm, staying him. "Please, I beg you, just hear me out a moment."

"Are your powers of comprehension defective? I told you, I have no interest in anything you have to say. Now, pray be gone. I want you out of this carriage—"

"Charles, I lied to you," she said quickly before he could throw her out. "My marriage to Lasseter was not a love match in the least. Merely an act of desperation."

Her confession made Halford hesitate. "What are you talking about?"

Raven took a deep breath. She could see no other way to gain his sympathy than to tell him the complete truth and throw herself on his mercy. "It was not Kell Lasseter who abducted me. It was his brother, Sean."

"His brother?"

"Yes. Sean was intent on revenge because I once spurned his suit. But Kell had nothing whatever to do with my abduction and only became involved afterward."

Halford settled back in his seat, his attention captured for the moment. "I suppose you should explain after all."

"It is a long story. . . ."

"I'm listening," he said gruffly.

She told him then about Sean once being her suitor and his accosting her in the Gardens. About his subsequent impressment and his desire for revenge. About his hired thugs violently seizing her when she was on her way to the church to be married.

"Sean rendered me unconscious and drugged me and kept me tied to a bed. I have no doubt he meant to torture me and worse, but Kell Lasseter intervened. He saved me from ravishment, I'm certain. But until that day Kell was a perfect stranger to me."

"A stranger?"

"Yes. I never saw him before the day of my abduction. He was only protecting me from scandal by wedding me."

"So you didn't love him?" Halford asked slowly, his first sign of uncertainty.

"No, not at all."

"Then why the devil did you lie about making a love match?"

"Because I feared you would call him out otherwise."

The duke shook his head. "I am still not certain I comprehend. You made me look the fool rather than admit the truth?"

"Would the truth have served any better purpose? Your being jilted for love was humiliating, certainly, but having your betrothed abducted would have been nearly as shameful—and much more dangerous. If you had felt compelled to duel to defend my honor, you might have killed or been killed yourself. I didn't want that to happen."

Halford remained silent, giving no indication if he believed her.

"By claiming a love match," Raven continued, "I stood a chance of salvaging some shred of my reputation. I promise you, Charles, I had no desire to wed anyone but you, but Kell Lasseter was my only option if I hoped to diminish the scandal. As a married woman, I could possibly survive, but without a husband . . . I was almost certain you would have refused to wed me after my abduction. Yet there was another possibility: You might have felt obliged to honor our betrothal. I could not have let you make that sacrifice. Your duchess should be above reproach, and I was damaged goods."

He turned his head away, not answering.

"Truly," Raven pleaded, "I thought it was for the best. It was too late for me. My future was already ruined, and I didn't want to ruin yours as well."

"My future was indeed ruined that day, my dear," he said quietly. "I lost you."

Raven felt an ache squeeze her throat. "Charles, your heart was never engaged. You never loved me."

"Ah, but you are wrong. I cared for you a great deal." He turned back to her. "I wish you could have trusted me."

She heard the sorrow in his voice, recognized the genuine pain. Her eyes burned with sudden tears. "I'm sorry I hurt you, Charles. I would not have done it for the world."

Removing his glove, he reached forward and touched her wet cheek. "I think you honestly mean it."

"Of course I do," she said, her voice unsteady.

Halford sank back in his seat, observing her in the dim light. "So now you are wed to a notorious gamester."

"I am making do." She wiped absently at her tears. "But I owe Lasseter a huge debt of gratitude. He doesn't deserve your anger, Charles. He only rescued me from becoming a pariah in society. If you must be angry, then please, be angry with me."

The duke sighed. "I can't be angry with you, my dear. You were not to blame for what befell you. But I wish you had come to me for help."

"I'm sorry, Charles, but I didn't think I had any choice. Can you not understand that?"

"I suppose I can. Very well, then . . . I should take you home."

"Charles . . ." She hesitated, wondering if she could risk asking him for a favor. "I would rather you accompany me elsewhere."

"Where?"

"To the Golden Fleece." Raven hastened to explain. "As I said, I owe Lasseter a great deal, but he is suffering because of me. Your accusations have nearly ruined him, Charles. If you would only make a brief appearance at his club, perhaps spend a little time at his gaming tables, it would go a long way to refute the rumors you've been circulating about his dishonesty. Please, for my sake, won't you at least consider helping him?"

"You forget, I don't gamble."

"But you could make an exception just this once. I will gladly stake you the funds. A few thousand pounds should be more than adequate. If you could just manage to lose it with good grace—"

"Don't be absurd." His tone was stiff but held a wry note. "I can afford to lose a few thousand."

"Then you will come with me?"

Halford sighed again, this time with exasperation. "I cannot imagine how I manage to let you talk me into the very things I despise."

Smiling with fervent relief, Raven grasped his ungloved hand and pressed it to her lips in gratitude. "Because you are a wonderful, magnanimous man who believes in doing what is right."

For the hour of midnight, St. James Street was surprisingly well-populated by revelers and gamesters and swells making their way about town. But there was little traffic passing through the doors of the Golden Fleece.

When Raven and her guest were admitted by the majordomo and escorted to the gaming room, she hesitated, surveying the small crowd with dismay; the number of gamblers was far smaller than on previous nights, she suspected from what Emma had told her. She could only pray that would soon change.

Her heart in her throat, Raven took the duke's arm and stepped forward, then paused for effect. A hush slowly fell over the room, just as she had hoped; they were the focus of all eyes.

When she spied Kell, her heart took up a rapid rhythm. His expression remained impassive as he unhurriedly moved her way, but she didn't presume he was pleased to see her, or the Duke of Halford, either.

He came to a halt before them, neither bowing nor greeting them.

Tension hung heavy in the air as the two men regarded each other—combatants sizing up their foe.

Raven took a deep breath and hastened to make the introductions. "Your grace, may I present my husband, Mr. Kell Lasseter. Kell, this is Charles Shawcross, Duke of Halford."

"Your grace," Kell said tersely. "To what do we owe the honor of this visit?" His slight emphasis on the word "honor" suggested it was no such thing.

Halford returned a stiff smile. "It seems that I owe you an apology, Mr. Lasseter. Regrettably I have made some unfounded accusations against your establishment, impugning your honesty and your reputation. To my shame, my motives were hardly pure. I confess I was insanely jealous after you won my bride from under my very nose. But I sincerely hope you can find it in your heart to forgive me."

When Kell's dark eyes narrowed, Halford turned to glance at Raven. "There, is that adequate, my dear?"

His generous apology was more than she had even hoped for. She might have kissed his hand again, but knew he wouldn't appreciate such a public display. Nor did she wish to give rise to further gossip.

Instead her lips curved in a brilliant smile. "Thank you, Charles," she said softly. "I think you must be the kindest man I have ever known."

Halford's cheeks took on a slight flush as he returned his attention to Kell. "And you are a fortunate man, Lasseter. I trust you will take good care of her."

Raven felt Kell's sharp gaze sweep her before he replied, "I intend to, your grace."

Glancing around, the duke eyed the hazard table with curiosity. "I am not much of a gambler, but I am willing to attempt it, if I could prevail upon you for some instruction."

With a single glance, Kell summoned his hostess, who had been watching the exchange along with everyone else in the room. "This is Miss Emma Walsh, your grace. She will assist you in every way possible. And whatever gaming you do will be on the house. If you will excuse me, I should like to have a word with my wife."

If Halford was put out by being relegated to an underling, he didn't show it. His bow was all politeness as he acknowledged the beautiful hostess. "I am honored, Miss Walsh."

Emma returned a pleasant smile. "I would be delighted to show you how hazard is played, your grace, if you will come this way. . . ."

Raven was left alone with Kell and his simmering anger. She nearly flinched as she met his dangerous gaze.

"And just what did you promise your duke in exchange for his apology, dear wife?" he asked in a silken tone.

She stiffened at his insinuation. "I promised him nothing. I simply told him the truth about our marriage, that it wasn't a love match, and that you were a perfect stranger who saved me not only from your brother, but from the wretched fate of becoming an outcast. It so happens that Halford has a generous nature—more generous than I even hoped. I merely asked him to make a public appearance here, to help refute the rumors that he himself started, but he added the rest." Her own gaze narrowed. "And you might show him the smallest measure of gratitude. Your club should be safe now."

She turned on her heel then and walked away, leaving Kell to fume alone.

He didn't *want* to show any gratitude toward the duke. It infuriated him to be obliged to anyone, particularly to a man of Halford's elevated rank. It infuriated him more that a nobleman could wield such power over his life, rousing his dormant sense of inferiority and impotence.

As for his meddling wife . . . she'd brazenly disregarded his wishes. Kell's gaze settled upon Raven as she stood with her duke at the hazard table.

Her duke.

His rival.

Kell clenched his fists, jealousy an unexpectedly fierce emotion inside him. As much as he despised admitting it, the sight of them so close together fired every possessive male instinct in his blood—and stirred unwanted images in his mind as well of Raven surrendering to her lover.

It made his blood boil to think of his aristocratic rival touching his wife, enjoying her lovely body, caressing her full, ripe breasts, her long, slender legs. Hell and damnation, *he* wanted to be the one suckling her rose-hued nipples, stroking her creamy ivory skin, so velvet smooth beneath his hands. . . .

The very thought made his loins ache.

Cursing again, Kell turned away. He had to get hold of himself before he became no better than his brother, filled with lust and insane jealousy, ready to do battle for the tempting Raven Kendrick.

As she absently watched the gaming, Raven was highly aware of her husband's brooding gaze surveying the crowd. Kell stood to one side, seeming alone even in a room full of people. A breed apart. A rebel.

His smoldering intensity only added to his appearance of isolation, as did the scar that marred the chiseled perfection of his face.

It was no wonder he was considered an outcast, she thought, remembering his almost grudging acceptance of the duke's apology. Polite society didn't take kindly to a man who showed so little deference to their rules, and Kell seemed to relish his defiant, black-sheep image.

Raven found it impossible to keep her glance from him. He was remote, enigmatic, notorious. And she was more drawn to him than any man she had ever known.

Was it because at heart, she was something of a black sheep herself? Because she understood what it meant to be alone? Or was it because Kell didn't want her? Because he was eminently capable of resisting her charms? Or perhaps it was the lure of forbidden danger that she found so potent.

From their first moment together, she'd felt that perilous pull to danger, the breathless thrill of walking a cliff edge. A primal threat that only stirred the restlessness inside her . . .

Raven shivered. How could she be so enticed by a man who made her feel this vulnerable? So fiercely attracted to one who didn't need or want her?

Casting another glance at Kell, she suddenly stiffened. Emma Walsh had joined him as he stood on the sidelines. Seeing them with their heads close together aroused a hot sting of jealousy within Raven.

She scarcely noticed when Dare came up to her.

He followed her narrowed gaze for a moment, then said in an amused drawl, "If I were Miss Walsh, I would take great care. You look as if you want to scratch her eyes out."

Pressing her lips together, Raven dragged her thoughts away from her irksome husband and his beautiful mistress and focused her attention on the marquess. "Have you just now arrived?"

"Yes. I had a prior engagement. A pity," Dare remarked. "I hear I missed all the excitement. Word has already flown around town about Halford's public apology. I suppose you orchestrated it?"

"I only asked him to make an appearance here. Halford did the rest."

"I should have thought your husband would be more pleased."

"Not Kell," Raven muttered. "He considers the duke's gesture charity."

"Well, a man has his pride. But even so, Lasseter should be grateful to you."

"He wants nothing to do with me."

At her morose tone, Dare gave her an assessing look. "And it disturbs you that your husband's amorous interests lie elsewhere?"

Raven averted her gaze from Dare's knowing one. "I shouldn't allow myself to be disturbed, I know. Ours was merely a marriage of convenience. He has every right to keep a mistress, or an entire harem, if he wishes."

"You could change the situation, puss. I have no doubt you could have Lasseter fawning at your feet if you chose to."

The image was an appealing one, Raven admitted to herself. She cast Kell another glance. He was watching her intently now, with those dark eyes that could hold her spellbound. Yet there was a decided coolness to his features, even disapproval, Raven noted. Perhaps he didn't like her associating with the Marquess of Wolverton any more than she liked her husband dallying openly with his mistress.

Forcing her gaze away, she gave Dare a deliberate smile. "I suppose I should apply to you for advice. No doubt the Prince of Pleasure could instruct me on how to keep a philandering husband from straying."

He laughed. "You don't need instruction on how to

secure a man's attention. You had half the males in London swooning over you last Season."

"I'm not sure how I managed that."

"I can tell you how. Because you were so refreshing. With your frankness and your high spirits, you were unlike every other debutante in existence. A tart lemon ice to their blancmange."

Raven made a face. "How gratifying to be compared to a vanilla pudding, Dare. And to think I tried so hard to conform."

"You succeeded admirably, but you still stood out in the crowd." Dare hesitated. "If you're serious about keeping your husband from straying, a little effort at seduction would not go amiss." He glanced toward the hazard table. "Perhaps I should see how Halford is getting along."

He left her then to stew over his advice.

Raven frowned thoughtfully as she eyed her husband. Did she wish to keep Kell from straying? Did she want to risk a mortifying rebuff?

It would be undeniably brazen to try to seduce him. While her upbringing had been unconventional, she possessed enough ladylike sensibilities to hesitate at such flagrant boldness. And yet she was immeasurably weary of conforming to society's rigid rules.

Furthermore, she was not the unsoiled virgin with a spotless reputation to protect that she'd been a few short weeks ago. In that sense, the scandal had been liberating. She had much more freedom now from the stifling strictures of the ton, the trivialities of London drawing rooms, the vapidness, the pretense. If she wanted to seduce her notorious husband, she could do so without feeling shame or guilt.

And she had to confess she was tempted. So tempted.

She was also dismayingly, idiotically jealous, Raven realized when she saw Kell laugh at something Emma said.

The intimacy of the gesture sent rebellion flaring inside Raven. Involuntarily her hands curled into fists, and she moved forward, unable to stop herself. She found herself standing before Kell, demanding an interview of a man for the second time that evening. But this time there was fire in her heart.

"Might I have a word with you, *dear husband?*" she said through gritted teeth.

Kell raised an eyebrow, while Emma's smile of greeting faded.

The hostess looked from Raven to Kell, who gave a brief nod.

The moment Emma was out of earshot, Raven launched her impulsive tirade. "Publicly flaunting your mistress is hardly the way to avoid scandal."

He regarded her levelly, not remarking on the unfairness of her attack. "I had no idea you cared about my mistresses."

"I don't, except when you make such an obvious display of your affections."

"If you are so concerned about appearances, perhaps we should continue this argument in a less public forum."

"Very well," Raven replied tightly, realizing they were once again the focus of all eyes. "Where do you suggest?"

He gave her a curt, mocking bow. "I will meet you shortly upstairs in my apartments. I believe you know the way."

Chapter
Fourteen

She waited for him in his private study rather than the intimacy of his bedchamber. The fire had died down to embers, so she added more coal and stood at the hearth, warming her hands and wondering what madness had overcome her.

Did she really want to make an issue of Kell's mistresses? Did she want to acknowledge her jealousy, even to herself?

At least she didn't have long to wait. Only moments later Raven heard the study door shut softly. She whirled to find Kell leaning indolently against the doorjamb, watching her with narrowed eyes.

"I suppose you mean to explain your tantrum just now, *dear wife*," he said finally, his tone cool.

Raven swallowed, regretting her earlier outburst. She hadn't meant to make her possessiveness so obvious. "It was hardly a tantrum. It was more along the lines of a complaint."

"And just what do you have to complain about?"

"Your indiscretion," she prevaricated. "It is mortifying to have to watch your dalliance before a roomful of people."

"If you had taken my advice and kept away, you wouldn't have to watch my dalliance, as you put it."

Pushing off from the door, Kell crossed the room toward her. Raven held her ground, but he only went to the hearth and bent to stir the fire.

"You were purposely flaunting your mistress directly under my nose," she said tightly, "and I won't stand for it."

That drew a quick, challenging stare from him.

Raven flushed at his measuring appraisal, and she hurried on. "You agreed we would try to preserve the appearance of being in love. And publicly lusting after Miss Walsh is hardly the way to do it."

"I trust," Kell responded in a drawling voice, "you don't expect me to live like a monk. I believe I mentioned that I'm not overly fond of celibacy."

"No, but you might try to contain your passion for that woman and keep out of her bed."

His eyebrow shot up. "Are you perhaps demanding fidelity from me, vixen? That was not part of our bargain, nor is it exactly fair. You have not been any kind of wife to me thus far."

"And you have been no kind of husband!"

His gaze raked her. "If you don't want me to seek my pleasure with Miss Walsh, perhaps you would care to take her place."

Raven felt her heart skip a beat. "What exactly are you suggesting?"

"That you see to my pleasure yourself. You are perfectly capable of assuming the duties of a mistress, or at least fulfilling the carnal obligations required of a wife."

Their gazes locked and held.

"So, love," Kell murmured tauntingly, "are you willing to be a proper wife to me?"

Was she willing? Raven asked herself. She wanted Kell; there was no denying it. And she wanted to keep him from his beautiful hostess's bed.

She stared back into his impenetrable eyes, the tension stretching like a taut cord between them.

"Very well," she murmured.

"What did you say? I couldn't hear you."

"I said I was willing!"

He let his gaze slide down her. "You agree to satisfy my sexual needs?"

"Yes! Although I can't imagine it will be easy to satisfy a libertine of your vast appetites."

Her muttered comment was meant as an insult, but Kell returned a tolerant smile. "I expect you will be a quick study. After all, you have an unusual depth of knowledge gleaned from your erotic journal. And experience with your fantasy lover as well."

Annoyed by his reminder, Raven frowned. Perhaps it had been unwise to tell Kell about her fantasies; certainly it was if he meant to throw her confessions back in her face.

"Well, what are you waiting for?" he asked as she stood trying to think of a suitable retort. "You just agreed to satisfy me."

"You want me to— *Now?*"

"Why not now? What better opportunity to show me that you are serious? You can start by undressing me."

"You cannot undress yourself?"

His smile was one of amused patience. "Where would

be the satisfaction in that? I will find it much more pleasurable if you assume the honors."

Biting back an oath, she reluctantly went to him and helped him out of his coat. Then she removed his waistcoat and untied his cravat. The open throat of his shirt revealed a glimpse of bronze-hued skin lightly sprinkled with hair.

"Please me, Raven," he commanded softly when she hesitated. "Take off my shirt."

Obediently she slid her hands beneath the fine cambric to touch his flesh, finding it warm and silky. With his help, she raised the shirt over his head but found herself distracted by the elegant patterns of dark hair on his chest.

"Raven?"

Dragging her gaze away, she glanced up at Kell. A cool smile played around his impossibly sensual mouth; he knew quite well how appealing she found his stark masculinity.

"Now my breeches."

Her cheeks flushing at his knowing look, she took a deep breath and unbuttoned first the straining placket on his breeches, then his drawers. His rampant member sprang free, brushing her fingers. He was fully aroused, his erection as hard as marble.

Raven drew back as if she'd been burned. Merely touching him felt like playing with fire. Yet she wasn't nearly as bold as he thought her. It was one thing to make love to a fantasy image, quite another to take the initiative with this beautiful, vital man.

She glanced up at him, hoping that her racing heart

wasn't obvious. "You are laboring under a misapprehension if you think I know how to pleasure you. I don't have your prowess or experience."

To her surprise, Kell didn't pressure her. Instead he moved over to his desk and pulled out the chair, then settled in it.

"Come here, then." He held out his right arm, indicating that she should sit on his lap. His blatantly rigid manhood jutted out from the opening in his breeches, beckoning as well.

His brazen arousal held her fascinated gaze as she crossed to him. But then she remembered his bullet wound and hesitated, eyeing his left leg. "Has your thigh healed?"

"Enough to allow me to perform, at least if I am careful."

She sat gingerly on his right side, feeling the hard, lean muscles of his thigh flex beneath the tight-fitting satin breeches.

His arms encircled her loosely as he settled her more securely on his lap. His eyes had taken on a slumberous look, his black-velvet lashes hooding the dark intensity.

"With my body I thee worship," he murmured, repeating a line from their marriage vows. "Do you intend to properly worship me, wife?"

Not answering, Raven held herself stiffly, despite the heat rising up in her at his suggestive words. She continued to remain immobile when he reached around her, his fingers expertly unfastening the hooks of her gown.

"Relax," he said, evidently feeling her tension. "I won't make you do anything you don't want to do."

Yet she couldn't relax. His alien hardness was a hot brand against her thigh, and she could only think of what was to come, how it would feel to have that swollen length thrusting inside her, filling her. . . .

He leaned forward and, with his tongue, touched the rapidly beating pulse in her throat. "Draw down your bodice for me."

The heat of even that brief caress flared through her, setting fire to every nerve. After a short hesitation, she lowered the neckline of her blue velvet gown, leaving her bosom still covered by her chemise. When she looked down, she could see the rosy outline of her peaked nipples.

Bending, he kissed one through the thin fabric, his tongue finding the tip, drawing it against his teeth.

Raven shivered.

"Your shift, too. I want to see all of you."

When she had difficulty freeing her arms, he aided her, unfastening the buttons at her back, then drawing off the sleeves and pulling down her garments till she was bare from the waist up. Everywhere his fingers touched, her skin seemed to burn.

His gaze was almost leisurely, appreciative and very male as he surveyed her naked flesh. "I keep forgetting how beautiful you are," he said, his voice low and husky. "Your breasts are more lush than I anticipated, given your slenderness."

Raven shifted restlessly in his lap, her breasts tingling for want of his caresses.

His gaze focused on her taut nipples, his eyes glittering with a heat that had nothing to do with his earlier anger. "Your nipples are hard and I haven't even suckled them yet. . . . Do you want me to suckle them?" He touched the sensitive tip teasingly with his mouth.

Raven closed her eyes, unable to deny her need. "Yes . . ." she breathed.

"Then offer your nipples up for me," he ordered, his voice as smooth as velvet.

Her eyes flew open. Kell was watching her, challenge in his dark eyes. He was perfectly serious, Raven realized. He was demanding she act the wanton. But if he meant to intimidate her, he would not succeed.

"You aren't very accommodating for a mistress," he said, his voice a silken taunt. "Didn't that journal of yours teach you anything?"

"Yes, but obviously not the sort of thing you are proposing."

"Then I shall have to give you lessons in how a woman satisfies a man."

"I suppose Miss Walsh knows how to satisfy you."

He surveyed her with a level gaze. "She knows very well what it takes." His eyes were suddenly intense, his tone harder. "What of your fantasy lover? Does he know how to satisfy you?"

"Yes," Raven retorted, glad to have something to throw in Kell's face.

"Then think of me in his place. I intend to be your lover tonight. Now do as I say and give me your nipples."

Another sensual shiver rippled through Raven. Kell was bold, brazen, commanding, just like her pirate lover—and it excited her more than she could have imagined. Swallowing her misgivings, she did as he bid, cupping her breasts till they were raised high and mounded in her hands.

Kell nodded with a charming, predatory smile. "Now say 'please suck on my breasts, lover.' "

"Kell . . ."

"Say it."

"Please . . . suck on my breasts . . . lover."

"As you wish, my sweet."

He bent his head, seeking and finding. His warm, sculpted mouth sent a shocking trail of fire curling deep inside her.

Without volition Raven's fingers clutched in his silky black hair as he suckled her. He was rousing her to a warmth she had not thought possible. His mouth was a searing flame upon her bare, aching breasts, and she could only fight the pleasure.

Moments later she felt his hand move between her legs, and she shuddered. Without her knowledge he had raised the hem of her gown to stroke his palm up her bare thigh. When he cupped her woman's mound, the gesture was so sexually possessive that Raven gasped.

"Touch yourself. See how wet you are."

She didn't need to touch herself. She knew her secret places were damp and swollen, throbbing with need for him.

But Kell refused to take no for an answer. Clasping her hand, he guided her fingers to the juncture of her thighs, deliberately making her explore her own tender flesh.

He was right; she was sultry, yielding, weeping

passionately for him. Raven felt a tremor of excitement ripple through her.

Then brushing the point of hot pleasure with his thumb, he slid a long finger deep inside her. She whimpered, her body pulsing to his touch as if she had been made for him alone.

For a long moment he stroked her, sending all her senses reeling.

"I think you are ready for me," he said with satisfaction.

Wrapping his arms around her, he lifted her up and set her on the desk facing him, then pressed her back to lie on the hard, unyielding surface. Raven was scarcely aware of the discomfort, though, for Kell was pushing up her skirts, baring all her secrets to him.

In the firelight his eyes gleamed like onyx as his hands parted her legs and slowly smoothed up the insides of her naked thighs. The way he looked at her was rawly sexual and made her heart race.

Holding her thighs spread wide, he bent down to her. Lightning speared through her body as she realized his brazen intent.

Raven gasped in protest and pushed against his shoulders, trying to stay him.

Kell raised his head, his eyes gleaming. "Does your fantasy lover kiss you here?"

The question was too intimate for comfort.

"Does he?" Kell demanded roughly when she was silent.

"Yes!"

He bent his head, his warm breath hovering over

her aching flesh. "Then don't withhold from me what you so eagerly give him."

At the first touch of his mouth, she whimpered. She wanted Kell to kiss her there. Her body was begging for it, craving it; she didn't care if it was foolish or wise. She could almost feel her feminine folds moving like real lips in anticipation, pleading for his caress.

"I want to taste your nectar," he murmured softly before his tongue found her, gently stroking.

The pleasure almost shattered her. With a breathless moan, Raven put both hands in his hair, not to push him away but to hold his face between her burning thighs. Kell obliged her by sucking in a kiss. His passion was a brand, searing her flesh. A heartbeat later, his tongue slid deep inside her. Her breath caught on a sob, and she desperately tried to shift her hips, seeking to escape his ravishing mouth.

He wouldn't let her move. Holding her still, he hooked his arms under her thighs and draped her legs over his shoulders. His tongue was still attending her, softly licking, savoring, thrusting, giving her the most frightening pleasure she had ever known. Under his ruthless assault Raven nearly went wild. Urgently she arched against his hot mouth, her hips moving in a rhythm that was ancient, mindless, elemental, the growing sounds of frenzy in her throat filling the hush of the room.

In a few moments more, she climaxed, dissolving into throbbing, impassioned release, crying out at the showers of sparks that fountained upward, drowning in black fire and glittering darkness.

Even as she was recovering, Kell moved upward,

kissing her breast, her damp throat, the corner of her mouth. Raven lay panting for breath, replete, yet vaguely dissatisfied.

He had left her shaken with the realization of her own passion and filled with a desperate yearning. She wanted them joined, wanted to have him deep within her.

"Come inside me," she whispered.

His eyes narrowed with heat and dangerous lust at her invitation, but he didn't obey. Instead he stepped back to shed the rest of his clothing.

Shakily Raven pushed herself up to watch. He still wore a bandage around his thigh, she saw when he stood naked before her. But the beauty of his finely honed athletic body made her throat go dry. She felt her loins clench painfully. He was boldly a man and he wanted her. Just as she wanted him. All she could think about was how Kell's splendid arousal would fill her. . . .

He must have had the same thought for the glitter of his gaze swept over her as he moved toward her.

Her breath faltering, Raven reached up to touch his chest. His skin was hot and smooth as velvet, his muscles rippling beneath her fingertips. Her hands were actually shaking, she realized.

Yet Kell seemed undismayed by her distraught state. With a cool smile, he stepped between her parted legs and gathered her against his chest until her nipples nestled against his hard muscles, until the big rod of his straining arousal teased her throbbing feminine warmth.

Raven felt the shock of his naked flesh against her and quivered.

"Want me?" he asked, his masterful arms holding her lightly.

"Yes," she answered, desire flooding in a mad rush, sweeping resistance before it.

She yielded willingly when he lay her back again upon the desk, trembling to feel the hard length of his body pinning her against the surface, anticipation taut and screaming through her senses. She hadn't realized how desperate she was for this. It was as if her body had been starved for a man's hardness, for Kell's hardness. She wanted, needed, craved an end to the restless, hot longing he had created in her.

She could feel the heat of his rigid flesh probing her soft folds. . . .

The same heat was in his eyes as he entered her slowly, gliding into her yielding, wet flesh. Raven drew a sharp breath as the fiery brand intruded into her delicate softness.

His kiss scorched the arch of her throat as he pushed into her. "Can you take all of me?" he murmured, his voice a rough rasp.

"Yes . . ." she panted. And she gasped aloud at the feel of him, huge and hot and urgent, forcing her wide open.

He held himself still then, waiting for her to grow accustomed to the feel of his engorged shaft inside her. It was a long moment before Raven relaxed beneath him.

"That's it," he praised in a hoarse whisper. "I want you flowing all around me like hot wild honey. . . ."

He kissed her then. He cupped her breasts, eroti-
cally kneading them, while his tongue plunged rhyth-
mically into her receptive mouth in a bold, sexual way.
His taste, his scent, his touch filled her senses as he began moving inside her.

Raven whimpered into his mouth, her inner muscles
tightening at the wet, white heat scalding her. She felt
frenzied, unable to get enough of him.

Kell felt the same pulsing urgency in his body. Knowing his control was nearly at the breaking point, he gathered up the trembling, sexually aroused woman in his
arms and lifted her. Still iron-hard within her, he swiftly
crossed to the connecting door to his bedchamber.

He had planned to carry her to his bed but suddenly
knew he couldn't make it. So he pressed her up against
the door and thrust deeply.

The painfully intense pleasure made them both shudder wildly.

He took her against the door, hard. His hand raked
through her hair, sending the anchoring pins flying,
while his mouth found hers, not letting her move or
twist away. He felt her response, felt the convulsive
movements of her hips arching into him as the heat of
animal hunger flared between them.

Raven felt the same intense heat as his hard, straining body moved against her, branding her with his desire. He ravished her with fierce demand, yet she wasn't
afraid; she welcomed his fierceness.

Shuddering under the force of his thrusts, she
rocked forward against him with desperate yearning. A
roaring sounded in her ears as the exquisite pressure

built. Raven tossed her head wildly, pumping her hips against him with frantic need.

Suddenly his muscles clenched. His head thrown back, his neck corded, he drove into her one final time. A moan burst out of him as his orgasm exploded in a powerful stream, pushing Raven over the edge. With a scream, she sank her teeth into the raw silk of his bare shoulder and gave herself up to the savage, unrestrained pleasure ripping through her.

They clung to each other in the aftermath, gasping for breath. An eternity later, Kell returned to earth to find Raven hiding her face against the base of his throat, her heart beating in a frenzied echo of his own.

Concern swept through him. His use of her had been devastatingly thorough; he had taken her with a pirate's passion, with little regard for her inexperience.

Leaning back, he studied her flushed face, her swollen, bruised lips. "Did I hurt you?" he rasped.

"No," she said quickly. And yet there was a vulnerable look about the mouth he had just ravished.

Searing heat and fierce tenderness filled him. He wanted to make it right. Next time he would show her more gentleness.

And there would definitely be a next time. He was tired of fighting his desire for her. Raven was his wife, and he wanted her; he should be able to have her.

Surely he could command enough strength of will to enjoy her body without falling for her. To slake his urgent need and still resist her incredible allure.

It would be difficult, but he was through denying himself.

His arms tightened about her for a moment, crushing her naked breasts to his chest. Keeping her legs wrapped around his hips, he managed to open the door and carry her to the bed, where he laid her down and stood staring down at her.

The room was dark but for the low-burning fire in the hearth, but Raven had no trouble seeing the glimmer of heat in his gaze or her own dishevelment. Her skirts and bodice were both tangled around her middle.

Blushing at her near nakedness, she stirred restlessly. "My gown is ruined. . . ." she murmured, plucking at her bodice.

"I'll buy you a new one," he replied as he began to strip her of her garments.

"Kell . . . what are you doing?"

"Undressing you. You'll stay here tonight. You haven't fully satisfied me yet."

"Kell . . ." Raven bit her lower lip. She had agreed to attend to his sexual needs, not spend the night in his bed. "I don't want to stay here with you."

"Why not?"

"Because . . . it could lead to unwanted complications."

That made him pause. "Physical intimacy can breed too much emotional intimacy, is that what you mean?"

She shivered. "Yes."

Without replying, he removed her clothing completely, then eased the covers from beneath her hips and drew them up over her naked body. After going to the hearth and stoking the fire, Kell returned to the bed and slid in next to her. For a moment he lay beside her, staring at the ceiling, his arms laced behind his head. Finally he spoke.

"Do I understand your reservations correctly? You're afraid to have a real lover because you're determined never to fall in love?"

"Yes." In a defensive gesture, Raven clutched the cover to her breasts.

Kell turned onto his side, supporting his head on one hand. "And yet sex and love are two entirely different matters. Passion doesn't necessarily lead to love. If it did, most of the men of the beau monde would be in love with their mistresses."

When she didn't reply, he reached out to brush a tendril of hair from her cheek. "I see no reason we cannot be lovers, Raven. A relationship based purely on sensual pleasure. Like you, I'm not interested in anything deeper."

Raven held herself rigid, wanting to look away from his eyes that seemed too burningly intense.

She couldn't deny that she was afraid. Passion was dangerous; it could lead to terrible vulnerability. Yet perhaps Kell was right: the true danger didn't lie in physical intimacy but in that of the emotional kind. A man could take pleasure from her body, but if he ensnared her heart, he took control.

Raven shuddered. She would never suffer a tragic love as her mother had. No man would ever render her senseless, without a will of her own.

Still, passion of the flesh didn't always result in passion of the heart. . . .

As if sensing her inner turmoil, Kell slipped his hand beneath the covers, resting his palm lightly on her breast. "Since we are tied together as man and wife, we might as well indulge ourselves."

His warm, erotic touch distracted her, preventing her from forming a coherent reply.

"You enjoy my lovemaking, vixen," he added in a low tone. "Your response a moment ago very clearly proved that." He smiled knowingly. "Not many women are as responsive as you are. Your body craves my touch." As if to prove his point, he brushed her peaked nipple with his thumb, making her arch involuntarily.

She did crave his touch, Raven thought in desperation, perhaps too much. And his brazen lovemaking . . . Trapped in his dark gaze, she stared back at him. It had thrilled her to have Kell take her like he had, as her pirate lover would have.

She swallowed against the dryness in her throat, struggling to break the hold Kell's eyes had upon her. Was it possible, what he was suggesting? Could they engage in purely carnal relations without physical intimacy blossoming into anything deeper? Could she indulge in a passionate affair with her convenient husband without losing her heart?

Perhaps so . . .

But there were other considerations as well.

"What of the possible consequences?" she asked. "What about children?"

His features darkened in a frown. "What about them?"

"I don't want to bring a child into this world without a father to love him, to care for him. . . ."

"There are means of preventing pregnancy. We failed to take precautions tonight, but that can be remedied."

Raven frowned as well, remembering how Kell had

withdrawn from her body on their wedding night. "You are not interested in having children?"

"I'm not anxious to, no."

She couldn't read his impassive expression. "Not even to gain an heir? You wouldn't want one someday?"

"Sean is my legal heir. That is enough for me."

Raven stiffened at the mention of his brother and hastened to change the subject. "I know from the journal how to prevent pregnancy, but I have no idea how to obtain the necessary means."

"Leave it to me," Kell said brusquely before his tone softened. "Meanwhile . . ."

With slow deliberation, he pulled the covers from her grasp and reached down to stroke her inner thigh. His burning touch made her body clench with longing.

"There is still the matter of satisfying my sexual needs. . . ." he murmured, his voice warm and rough like velvet. "And your own."

Raven drew a steadying breath, vainly fighting the rush of desire that flooded over her. She wanted Kell to satisfy her. Desperately wanted him . . .

As his mouth slowly descended toward hers, she shut her eyes, ignoring the warning voices in her head. Surely she could manage a sexual relationship without tumbling into the quagmire of love.

Her chief goal would be to keep her heart safe, she vowed silently, trying to convince herself. She would never surrender her heart to this man. . . .

Then the thought fled her mind as his scorching mouth met hers, and with a sensual shudder, she gave herself up to his caresses.

Chapter
Fifteen

Raven woke disoriented. The crackling fire looked familiar, however, as did the masculine bedchamber. She was alone, she realized, lying naked in Kell's bed at the gaming house. The same bed where she'd spent her abduction.

Heat flooded her entire body as she recalled the mindless passion between them last night. She'd behaved just as wantonly as her first time in Kell's arms, only last night she hadn't had the excuse of being drugged.

Flushing, Raven sat up and saw her ruined gown draped over a chair along with her other garments. When she climbed from the bed in order to dress, she found herself wincing at the unaccustomed aches and twinges from too much sensual indulgence.

Then she caught sight of herself in the cheval glass. She looked like a woman who had been deliciously ravished all night long and who was more than eager to repeat the experience. Her hair was a wild tangle around her face, her lips bruised and swollen, her nipples rasped red from the attentions of his hot mouth. . . .

Raven closed her eyes, remembering Kell's exquisite

lovemaking and the explosive desire he had aroused in her. The memory was a wild hunger in her—

A soft rap on the door made her snatch up her gown to cover her nakedness.

It was Emma, carrying a tray. "I've brought you breakfast," she said with a cheerful smile, "or luncheon, really."

Raven glanced at the brocade draperies, which were still shut against the morning light. "What time is it?"

"Nearly noon."

"So late?" She blushed, feeling unexpectedly flustered to have been caught in Kell's bed like this, by his mistress.

"Kell thought you needed to sleep. Your groom— O'Malley, is that his name?—was here at the crack of dawn, looking for you. He wanted to make certain you were all right. But Kell assured him you hadn't been abducted again."

Absurdly Raven found herself stammering. "I suppose . . . you are wondering what I'm doing here. . . ."

"Not in the least," Emma replied, setting down her tray on the small table near the hearth. "You are Kell's wife, after all."

"But still this is awkward with you being his . . ."

Emma's eyebrows shot up. She studied Raven a moment before understanding dawned. "Did you think I was his paramour? Oh, Raven, Kell and I are not lovers, nor have we ever been. I have no claim to him."

Raven stared, frowning. Had he deliberately misled her about the nature of his relationship with his beautiful hostess? She thought back to what he'd said about

Emma knowing how to satisfy a man. He'd never actually declared in so many words that they were lovers, but he'd certainly implied as much, never taking the trouble to deny the accusation. . . .

Relief and vexation roiling though her, Raven muttered an unladylike oath. She would have a few choice words to say to Kell about his deception when she next saw him. If not for her jealousy, she would never have agreed to share his bed last night—

Emma interrupted her vengeful thoughts with a faint, self-deprecating smile. "I admit I would have welcomed such an arrangement with Kell," she confessed with surprising candor. "In fact, when he rescued me from my former situation, I offered to become his mistress, but he declined, claiming I was acting out of gratitude. He wouldn't take advantage of my vulnerability. But if he had shown the slightest encouragement . . ." Her gaze focused on Raven. "I think you are very fortunate to have captured his interest," she said softly, then shook herself out of her reverie. "Come, put something on and enjoy your breakfast before it grows cold."

Raven felt herself flushing again, both at her state of undress and this strange turn of events, discussing Kell's romantic inclinations with another woman. Rather than argue, however, she found a brocade robe of Kell's in the wardrobe and settled before the hearth to eat. When she invited the hostess to join her, Emma hesitated only a moment before sitting in the adjacent chair.

"If I may," the hostess murmured, "I have a question to ask you. It concerns his grace, the Duke of Halford."

"Halford?" Raven repeated curiously as she sipped her hot coffee.

"Yes. Last night he . . . expressed an interest in seeing me again. Would you mind terribly if I were to agree? He seems in need of comfort after . . . well, after losing you to Kell."

Swallowing her surprise, Raven shook her head. "No, I would not mind in the least. I have no claim to Halford."

"I wouldn't accept a permanent arrangement," Emma remarked, "even if he offered. Kell pays me extremely well, enough to allow me a large measure of independence, so I can choose the gentlemen I see. But being alone as I am . . . well, it sometimes gets lonely."

Raven felt a pang of sympathy. She understood loneliness; she'd known a great deal of it since her mother died, a feeling that had only been exacerbated since her marriage.

"I know Kell suffers from loneliness as well," Emma said softly, "even though he would be the last to admit it. That's why I am so glad he has you. I hope you will be spending more time here, Raven."

She shook her head. "It's unlikely, for I'll be leaving town soon. I plan to celebrate Christmas in the country with my grandfather."

"Oh, is Kell accompanying you?"

Raven hesitated. Her grandfather had expressly written in his last letter that her new husband would be welcome, but she hadn't mentioned the invitation to Kell. "We haven't discussed it yet, but I doubt he would want to go."

"I do hope you can persuade him. It would do him a world of good to be with you."

Raven wasn't certain she wanted to persuade him, for sharing a holiday with Kell could only lead to more intimacy and complicate their relationship further.

And yet . . . Emma was no doubt right about his loneliness. She had sensed that in him almost from the first. Beneath his air of disdainful detachment, he was hiding more pain and loneliness than he would ever reveal. She just didn't know if she wanted to do anything about it.

She had started to cut a bite of ham when the door opened and Kell walked in. As Raven glanced over her shoulder, he met her gaze, and heat crackled between them like a bolt of lightning. Raven found herself suddenly breathless.

An instant later, he dropped his gaze to survey her attire. The rakish gleam in his dark eyes told her clearly that he recognized the dressing gown she wore, and that he knew she was naked underneath.

Raven flushed and swiftly tucked her bare feet beneath the hem.

His attention turned to Emma. "I have a fencing match in a short while, and I need to dress."

"Then you will wish me to leave," the hostess said with a smile as she rose.

When the door shut behind her, Raven found herself unexpectedly tongue-tied. After their passionate encounter last night, she wasn't certain what to say to him.

Kell, however, seemed perfectly at ease as he went to the bureau and fetched a length of starched linen for a cravat. "What of your plans for the rest of the day?" he asked Raven casually. "I can drop you at home on the way to my match . . . unless you prefer to remain here?"

The thought of staying here in his bedchamber made butterflies dance in her stomach. "No," she said at once. She needed a bath but that could wait. "I intend to go home—but I should get dressed . . ."

She started to rise but Kell stayed her with a wave of his hand. "You have time to finish your breakfast."

Raven sank back down in her chair, relieved that she wouldn't have to dress in front of him. She applied herself to her food, but when Kell stood before the glass to tie his cravat, she found herself covertly watching him, fascinated by this routine male task. Then she realized what she was doing and averted her gaze. It was such an intimate act, a wife watching her husband dress. . . .

"You seem to be extremely fond of fencing," she remarked, anxious to break the private mood.

"I am. Beyond that, physical exertion tends to burn off sexual frustration." He gave her a wry glance over his shoulder. "I've been fencing a good deal of late."

Raven could feel her cheeks flush with heat.

"I wonder, did O'Malley teach you to fence?" Kell asked when she was silent.

"No, only to shoot."

"And to cheat at dice."

The mention of cheating brought to mind her own grievance with him. "I am not the only one to resort to duplicity when it suits me. You were plainly dishonest last night when you led me to believe Emma was your mistress."

Kell raised an eyebrow. "Am I to blame if you leapt to such an erroneous conclusion?"

"Certainly you are to blame," Raven retorted. "If not for your deception, I would never have agreed to . . . to what you proposed."

His grin was slow and unequivocally rakish. "To satisfy my sexual needs, you mean?"

"Yes . . . *that*. I consented only to keep you from lusting after other women when you are supposed to be showering me with the attention due a new bride."

"I hope you don't intend to back out of our agreement now."

"I would have every right! My decision was made under false pretenses."

Having finished tying his neckcloth, he drew on a simple leather waistcoat. "I don't see that the circumstances have changed since last evening. Regardless of Miss Walsh's status, if you want me to show you fidelity, the surest way is to honor your conjugal obligations." He gave her a penetrating glance as he fastened the buttons. "That's more than you've promised me, vixen. I don't see you offering to give up your fantasy lover for my sake."

Raven's brows drew together. "The situations are not at all similar. Having an imaginary lover cannot be compared to taking a real live mistress—which legally could be considered adultery."

"Some men might consider it more insulting," Kell said softly, "being cuckolded by a fantasy."

"You know very well why I resort to fantasy."

"I think I do. You're acting the coward."

Raven gave him a genuine scowl this time. Biting back a tart retort, however, she managed to say with remarkable calm, "I don't intend to let you provoke me. And in any event, I won't be able to see to your . . . carnal needs for much longer. I will be leaving at the end of next week to join my grandfather for the holidays."

"I know. Luttrell said as much in his letter."

"What letter?"

"He sent me an invitation of my own, asking me to spend Christmas at his estate."

Raven stared at Kell in surprise. "He did? Whatever for?"

"How the devil do I know? Perhaps because I'm your husband."

"I suppose he wants to make amends for the shameful way he treated you."

Kell made no reply as he shrugged into his tailored burgundy jacket.

"Well, do you mean to go?" Raven asked impatiently.

His expression remained infuriatingly enigmatic. "I haven't decided yet."

She wanted to hit him.

"I expect it would be good for appearances," he added casually before she could erupt. "We could keep up the pretense of marital bliss and lay to rest once and for all the question of our union . . . about it being a love match."

"Yes," Raven replied with a troubled frown. "I imagine we could at that."

"I'm presuming, of course, that we can refrain from indulging in anything more intimate than sex." He shot her another arch look. "I believe I could manage it; could you?"

"I suppose so," Raven said reluctantly, although with far less conviction than she felt.

Kell flashed her a crooked smile. "You needn't be so afraid. Our agreement is for conjugal relations, nothing more. Merely a convenient physical arrangement."

When she didn't reply, he crossed to her. "I will see you tonight then."

"Tonight?" Raven echoed, looking up at him in surprise.

"I intend to leave the club early and be home by midnight." Bending, he gave her lips a brief, hard kiss. "I want you to be waiting for me. In bed. Naked."

Speechless, she stared after Kell as he turned away and let himself from the room.

For the entire remainder of the day and evening, Raven wavered in indecision.

One moment she had every intention of refusing Kell her bed. It vexed her thoroughly, his assumption that he only had to command her and she would obey. And he had deliberately misled her about Emma's status as his mistress.

Yet when Raven recalled the incredible passion they had shared last night, her resolve faltered. Why shouldn't they enjoy each other physically? What would be the harm? If they kept their intimacy to a minimum, there would be little risk of falling in love with him. Was she really such a coward that she had to deny herself what little pleasure her marriage could offer?

Admittedly, she wanted Kell. In his presence she felt more alive than she had imagined possible. Like her fantasy pirate's, Kell's erotic touch excited her and challenged her restless soul.

As the evening drew on, Raven couldn't quell her sense of anticipation at the night to come. By the time midnight struck, her nerves were screaming with sensual tension. A short while later she heard Kell in their dressing room.

When eventually he entered her bedchamber and shut the door behind him, her heart leapt. She had turned down the bedside lamp, but in the dim glow she could see he wore a dressing gown of black and gold brocade. Even across the room, his intense magnetism affected her.

He went to the hearth first and stirred the fire before coming to stand beside her bed. The heat of his gaze was just as arousing as it had been this morning; his first comment just as provoking and provocative. "Are you naked as I asked?"

Raven drew a sharp breath. "As it happens, I am," she observed coolly. "But if you expect me to be your obedient servant, you can think again."

His mouth curved in a sensual smile. "I cannot imagine you being obedient unless you choose to be. But I'm pleased that on this occasion, you decided to honor my request." His gaze skimmed the outline of her body under the covers. "I have thought of you all day, vixen. . . ." Untying the sash of his dressing gown, he let it fall open to reveal his own nude body. "As you can see." His arousal stood pulsing and erect.

Raven's blood began to race.

"Have you been lying here, thinking of me coming into you?" he asked in a rough-velvet murmur.

She couldn't deny she had been doing exactly that, but she didn't wish to give Kell the satisfaction of knowing it. Before she could think of a retort, however, he held out a black satin bag.

Raven suspected the contents even before Kell sat beside her on the bed and showed her. There were several sponges with thin strings attached, along with a small bottle of amber liquid.

"The precaution you requested," he said as he wet one of the sponges.

"What is that?"

"Brandy." He gently tugged down the covers to bare her body. "Open your legs."

She shivered in the cool air, yet she didn't protest when his fingers probed between her thighs. Instead she shut her eyes and let him press the brandy-soaked sponge deep inside her. The sensation was thrilling, and even more arousing when his thumb deliberately stroked the bud of her sex. Raven bit back a moan.

"I would say you are ready for me," Kell said in approval. "Hot and wet and eager . . ."

When his fingers buried inside her, her hips arched up off the bed, but he left off teasing her.

"Not so quickly," he murmured with an edge of amusement. "Last night I did most of the work. Now it is your turn."

When she opened her eyes to stare up at him in

frustration, he shook his head. "You are supposed to be pleasuring me, wife, remember?"

Shrugging out of his dressing gown, he pushed the covers aside and lay back upon the bed.

Disbelieving his audacity, Raven raised herself up on one elbow but found her gaze riveted by the sight of him. His male nudity enticed her senses; he was beautiful, so beautiful she forgot to breathe.

"Well?" he taunted softly. "Do you intend to take all night?"

She cursed beneath her breath, trying to deny the pulsing need running rampant inside her. Yet his vital intensity was like a magnet, drawing her to him.

She let her gaze roam over him; over his erection that lay arched against his belly, over the powerful thighs and calves that were lightly dusted with hair. . . .

When he saw where her fascinated gaze was fixed, he arched his back slowly, like a big sleek cat stretching, flaunting his manhood even more. "Are you afraid to touch me?"

"No, I am not afraid," she lied. "Only vexed by your insufferable arrogance."

Kell gazed at her steadily, the promise of sexual pleasure gleaming in his dark eyes. "Then touch me," he demanded, his voice seductive.

Steeling herself, she reached down to brush his loins with her hand. His phallus surged eagerly against her fingertips, almost burning her.

"If you need instruction . . ." he said when she hesitated.

"I don't."

Defiantly, she rose to kneel over Kell and placed both palms on his hard-muscled chest, determined to make him swallow his taunts.

His skin was heated velvet when she caressed him, his muscles smooth and firm beneath her fingers. She ran her hands down his body, exploring his tapering chest, his lean waist, his flat belly . . . his towering erection.

He tensed when she stroked him there, but she didn't stop. Deliberately she fondled him, applying the erotic methods she'd learned from the journal, the same exquisitely sensual methods Kell had used on her last night.

She suspected, however, that her assault was proving just as arousing to her as to him. She loved the feel of him under her hands, the way he pulsed and hardened to her touch, the way he seemed to relish the pleasure she was giving him. But she knew from the journal how she could increase the pleasure.

She left off stimulating him and reached for the brandy bottle he had left on the bedside table. One dark eyebrow shot up in question when she wet her fingers with the liquor, but when she touched him, Kell shuddered and gave a low groan of sensual pain. His response delighted Raven and sent her pulse thrumming in her veins.

"Does it please you when I do this?" she asked, her own tone provocative.

"You know it does."

Bracing her hands on either side of his hips then, she bent to him, first trailing her lips along the huge, swollen length of him, then touching his flesh with her tongue, tasting the brandy, along with his own musky masculine flavor. When he drew a sharp breath, she closed her lips around the hot blunt tip.

In only moments his hips were flexing restlessly beneath the soft suckling of her mouth.

"Witch," he muttered in a voice rough with need. "You had best stop before I spend myself."

"Not yet . . ."

For several long heartbeats more, she pleasured and aroused him, until he was nearly writhing. Her sense of power swelled to bursting as he fought for control.

"Do you intend to make me beg you?" he rasped.

Raising her head from his straining shaft, Raven sent him a challenging look. "Would you really beg?"

"Yes . . . sweet mercy, yes. Please, my lovely Raven . . ."

"Well . . ." To give like this was ecstasy, but she wanted to take as well. She gave Kell a taunting smile. "Since you insist . . ."

Straddling his waist with her thighs, she leaned forward, deliberately letting her breasts lightly caress his chest. "I don't believe you are hot enough yet."

Her teasing made him clench his teeth. "Damn you, vixen. . . . Any hotter and I will burst into flame."

Indeed his eyes smoldered as she eased downward over his rigid sex, slowly impaling herself.

Kell shuddered as if it were almost more than he could bear, and her sense of power intensified. She loved having him fill her this way—and yet it wasn't enough. She wanted him to participate in his own ravishment.

Bending, she grasped his wrists and drew his hands

to her breasts, her hard nipples stabbing his palms. Immediately he understood her need and complied, rubbing the aching peaks. Raven gave a sigh of rapture at the exquisite sensations and arched her back.

She nearly moaned when his magical hands left her, but he only pulled her thighs wider, lifting his hips to thrust more deeply inside her.

Raven quivered at the scalding hot feel of him urgently filling her, at the clawing need that began to build within her. It was terrifying and thrilling at the same time, how her tenuous control vanished while his only seemed to grow.

He took command then, tangling his hand in her hair, forcing her head down until her mouth met his in a feverish kiss. Raven clutched his shoulders while her hips helplessly rocked against his, trying desperately to assuage the hungry primitive ache.

His kiss burned her to near oblivion, while the vibrant fiery pleasure mounted to a sudden, startling explosion that made them both shatter. Her cry of ecstasy mingled with Kell's groans as the powerful climax swept them both away.

Gasping for breath, Raven collapsed bonelessly on top of him, her hair falling around his face, a curtain of silk. Weakly his arms came up to encircle her, and he lay unmoving.

When finally she regained her senses it was to find Kell stroking her naked back, nuzzling her temple with his lips.

"Did you find that adequate?" she murmured when she could summon the energy to speak.

She felt him smile against her hair. "Unequivocally."

Easing her off him, Kell drew the sheets up to cover their nakedness, then lay back and gathered Raven closer. Languidly she curled against him and shut her eyes.

It was a long moment before he broke the silence. "What do you call him, your fantasy lover?"

Raven stiffened at the question. "I don't have a name for him."

"What does he look like then?"

She hesitated. "Like a pirate. He has black hair and dark eyes."

"As I do?" He rolled on his side, his gaze finding hers. "Should I be flattered?"

"I don't think so. I imagined him long before I met you."

Kell reached up to brush a tendril of hair from her forehead, but he seemed thoughtful when he spoke. "If I had a fantasy lover, I think she would be very much like you. . . . Flashing blue eyes, a heart-shaped face, a beautiful, slender body with lush breasts . . ."

Raven stirred self-consciously as his voice washed over her, but Kell wasn't done.

"She would know not only how to pleasure me, she would know how to make my body sing, to wring me dry and make me ache with need. . . ." A smile flickered across his mouth. "Does your lover do all that?"

Moving away from him, she drew the covers to her breasts.

"Does he?" Kell repeated, his tone curious.

"Yes," Raven replied defensively. "He does all that and more. He not only gives me pleasure, he makes me feel cherished, desired. As if I am the only woman in the world."

Kell raised an eyebrow but his measuring gaze was entirely serious. "Is that every woman's secret fantasy? To be cherished?"

"I wouldn't know about other women's fantasies," Raven replied, deploring the turn their conversation had taken. "But I am perfectly content with mine."

"Still, I should think the real thing would be more satisfying. An image can't fill you like a flesh and blood man can. He can't stroke your nipples like this. . . ."

When Kell caressed her breast, Raven jerked back, away from his sensual touch. "Perhaps not, but neither does he incite a desire in me to commit mayhem, as you do."

Kell's lips pursed in a frown. "I confess, I don't like the thought of you seeking pleasure from your fantasy lover."

She gave him a sharp look of disbelief. "You cannot possibly be jealous of a fantasy."

"No? How do you think a man feels when his lover . . . his wife . . . constantly dreams about another man? It arouses a primitive male instinct to do battle."

Raven gave a sigh of exasperation. "It is not a contest, Kell."

"What if I were to make it one?"

"What do you mean?"

He shrugged. "Nothing. Never mind. Why don't you go to sleep?"

He shut his eyes as if prepared to do just that, but Raven made a sound of protest in her throat. "Kell . . .

I think you should sleep in your own bedchamber tonight."

His eyes opened. "Sleeping together is too intimate, is that your assumption?"

"Yes. We agreed merely to carnal relations, nothing more."

"Very well," he said easily, surprising her. "If you insist . . ."

Rising from the bed, he scooped up his dressing gown and shrugged into it. Then he bent and pulled the covers up over her shoulders, tucking her in. "Sweet dreams, vixen."

He didn't seem at all angry that she had ordered him from her bed. Instead he pressed a chaste kiss to her temple and left the room.

Raven frowned, somewhat bewildered and more than a little suspicious that he had been so accommodating.

Had she questioned him, however, Kell would not have told her his intent. It would be foolish to rekindle Raven's resistance by revealing his plans.

He was set on taking over her fantasies.

Her decided preference for her dream lover had roused his new resolve. Irrationally or not, it incensed Kell that Raven had another lover, however illusory. Whether driven by male pride or simple jealousy, he wanted to be the only man in her life. He *intended* to be the only man in her life.

It would be a challenge, but he meant to win her away from her imaginary lover.

Chapter
Sixteen

He came to her the next night and every night that week. They made love with passionate abandon, but Raven always insisted that Kell return to his own bedchamber. She was willing to give him her body, but nothing more intimate.

It disturbed her, however, that the line between Kell and her fantasy lover was becoming more and more blurred—and never more so than when Kell escorted her to a brothel.

Merely his offer surprised her.

"I think it's time we furthered your education and introduced you to some genuine fantasies," he said as they lay in bed after a particularly intense bout of lovemaking.

"What do you mean?" Raven murmured, enjoying the warmth of Kell's hard body as she lay curled against him.

"Madame Fouchet's salon is the most elegant sin club in London. It specializes in some unique pleasures of the flesh and excels at fulfilling fantasies. I mean to take you there. It will be an experience I doubt your imaginary lover could give you."

Raising her head from his shoulder, Raven eyed Kell

skeptically. "All this time I have been attempting to salvage my reputation, and you expect me to comport with you at a brothel?"

"Your reputation seems to be repairing itself well enough. And as a matron, you are no longer bound by the same restrictions you once were."

"Even so . . ."

"Where is your spirit of adventure, love? Haven't you conformed to propriety long enough?"

Raven had to admit that the forbidden allure of a brothel held an unmistakable appeal. Two nights later she found herself accompanying Kell up the steps of Madame Fouchet's house of pleasure.

They were admitted to an antechamber by a major-domo and greeted by Madame Fouchet, who expressed delight at their patronage.

"All is arranged as you asked, Monsieur Lasseter," the Frenchwoman said. "My house is yours. You have only to ring for whatever you require."

"Thank you, madame."

"I shall leave you to your pleasures, then."

With a bow, she disappeared through a rear door, leaving Raven alone with Kell.

He led her through another door to a long hallway, explaining as he went. "The rooms on this floor are used for group affairs, but there are a number of bed-chambers above that provide more seclusion."

Raven noticed the quiet and suspected that it was unusual. "There seems to be no one else here."

"Because I hired the place for the night."

"The entire house?"

"Yes, to allow us privacy."

It amazed her that Kell would have gone to such trouble and paid what undoubtedly was an exorbitant expense, and yet she was grateful he intended to keep their tryst private. She might be unconventional at heart, but the prospect of a group fantasy enticed her not at all.

"Ordinarily," he continued, "clients select their partners for the evening and dress in appropriate costume. The Turkish harem is one of the prime entertainments."

He paused at an alcove that had a small viewing window. Raven could smell the scent of incense as she stepped up to the glass. The exotic scene was of an Eastern palace, with swaths of filmy draperies and wisping smoke and silken cushions.

He led her to another alcove, but the viewing window was curtained, Raven saw as they entered the fantasy room through a door. This scene was lit by flaming torches and resembled the deck of a ship with railings and sails and a tall wooden mast.

"The pirate ship is also a favorite here. The clients dress up as pirates and take captive a ship of female passengers."

Raven raised an eyebrow. "And what do they do with their captives?"

"What do you suppose?" Kell asked, flashing a provocative half smile. "Ravishment is quite a popular fantasy. Here a man can have his wicked way without consequence. And adventurous ladies can pay for the pleasure of being one of the captives."

"I collect that I am to play the role of captive?"

"And I will be your pirate lover. You said your fantasy lover is a pirate, did you not?"

She nodded hesitantly, not certain she liked where this game could lead.

"Tell me, has your lover ever ravished you or threatened your virtue?"

Raven felt herself flush. "My fantasies are my own," she replied, unwilling to answer.

"Not tonight, vixen. Tonight I will be your fantasy."

He ushered her across the deck to a small door. Beyond was the captain's cabin, Raven presumed. It was lit by flickering sconces and luxuriously appointed, unlike any real pirate ship she could imagine. Black satin sheets and red silk pillows embellished the large bunk, while gilt mirrors adorned the opposite wall.

On a peg hung a filmy garment, which Kell handed her. "Your costume, my sweet."

Raven eyed the gossamer nightdress. "That fabric will be as revealing as wearing nothing at all."

Kell's wicked grin flashed again. "I believe that is precisely the point."

On the captain's desk lay a jeweled chest from which he withdrew a demimask. "For anonymity," Kell explained, handing it to her. He also withdrew several gauzy scarves.

"What are those for?" she asked, although suspecting.

"For tying your wrists. Have you never indulged in bondage with your fantasy lover?"

Raven shook her head, and yet Kell's suggestion didn't shock her; there were several incidents of such erotic delights described in the journal.

"Then you can let your imagination run riot," he said. Her uncertainty must have shown on her face, for he added in an amused voice, "Do you think I would hurt you?"

"No . . . not really."

"Here, you will need these as well."

He gave her the bag of sponges and left her to undress while he donned his own costume.

When she was attired in the diaphanous nightdress, Raven sat in the captain's chair to wait. She was glad for the coal brazier that warmed the cabin, yet she found herself shivering, not because of the cold or her near nakedness. Despite her misgivings, the thought of the night to come was dangerously exciting.

Moments later her heart turned over when she looked up to see her pirate filling the doorway. He wore a billowing white shirt and tight black breeches and thigh-high boots, while a dagger was tucked into his sashed waist. The demimask concealed the upper part of his face, but she could make out Kell's gleaming gaze as it roamed over her revealing nightdress.

"Stand up," he commanded in a low voice. "Let me see what treasure my men have brought me."

She rose slowly, her heart thudding in her chest as he boldly surveyed her, measuring her rose-hued nipples and the dusky curls crowning her thighs.

"Exquisite," he said with a satisfied smile. Taking her elbow, he drew her toward the door. "You will come with me, captive."

When she held back, he withdrew his dagger from his sash and held it menacingly to her throat. "Remember you are my prisoner, mademoiselle. I can have you thrown overboard in an instant."

Uneasily Raven complied, telling herself she should enter into the spirit of the fantasy.

The pirate led her from the cabin and across the deck to the mast, where he turned her to face him. Sheathing his dagger, he forced her arms behind her and secured her to the timber with the scarves. Then he leaned forward to kiss her, pulling her lower lip between his teeth and nipping softly.

When she made a sound of protest, his hand went to her throat and held her still as he pressed his full length against her. He kissed her more thoroughly then, his tongue plunging deep while he moved his hips in a slow, rotating motion that made her pulse race.

Raven's breath was coming in soft pants when he finally drew back. Reaching to his waist, he brandished the dagger again, startling her. With the point, he drew a slow line down the valley between her breasts. Then turning the blade, he deliberately sliced her nightdress from throat to hem, exposing her pale body to his view.

Raven couldn't stifle a gasp.

"There is no use crying for help," he chastised. "My crew does my bidding."

The cool air caressed her naked skin, puckering her nipples. Raven wet her lips, staring at him. She was completely at his mercy. The knowledge made her tremble, even as it thrilled her.

He saw her convulsive shiver and smiled. Returning the dagger to his sash, he lifted the curtain of her hair, drawing the long tresses over her pouting breasts. He was playing with her, prolonging the moment, Raven knew.

"Such smooth, white skin," he said in approval. He

stroked his hand over the swelling mounds of her breasts, cupping the ripe fullness in his palms. "Such lush flesh."

His fingers traced a circle around her jutting nipples, making her arch against the delicious sensation. "These ripe buds are just waiting for me to taste them."

She bit her lower lip hard, trying not to respond as he pulled at the swollen crests. Yet shameful pleasure flared wherever he touched her.

"I think I will suck on your nipples until you come." He bent his head, his breath hot and moist against her skin, sending liquid warmth coursing downward between her legs. Yet he didn't kiss her. Instead his tongue barely flickered over the taut peaks.

Raven twisted against her bonds, fighting the keen sensations he was deliberately arousing in her.

A moment later he stood, a frown of disapproval drawing down the corners of his sensual mouth. "What, no response, my beauty? No matter. You will soon be begging me, offering me anything I choose to take."

She raised her chin in defiance. "I will never beg."

His smile was utterly devilish. "You will do as I say. If you are disobedient, I will give you to my men."

"You wouldn't," she replied, although her tone held uncertainty.

"No," he said, his voice husky. "I wouldn't. I intend to keep you all to myself. I won't share my treasure with any man. You are *mine*."

Possessively, his palm covered her breast, then glided down the silken skin of her belly to her loins.

"Tell me, are you a virgin, mademoiselle?"

She hesitated before answering honestly. "No."

"Excellent. The better for me to enjoy you. I am a man of strong appetites, and I am not easily appeased."

He slid a probing finger between her thighs, along her wet, slippery cleft. Already it was pulsing eagerly.

"You're very hot, mademoiselle, are you not?"

Raven arched her hips convulsively, feeling her bonds tighten in warning at her wrists.

"How easily aroused you are."

One of his hands remained between her legs, while the other moved up to fondle her swelling, aching breasts. When he pinched her nipple, a needy whimper escaped her lips.

"Be silent, captive," he ordered. "You mustn't scream, or my men might come to watch. You don't want them to see you naked and helpless like this, do you?"

Raven swallowed her moan, yet the thought of his lusty, rugged crew seeing her ravishment roused a shameless throbbing heat between her legs.

"Good, you know who is your master." His indulgent, arrogant smile made her blood boil and race at the same time.

"You must remain completely still, or I won't satisfy you."

He was teasing her, making her wait, and the delay excited her beyond bearing. She strained against his hand, shamelessly seeking his penetration.

"I said be still! You will obey me if you want me to take you." His fingers thrust inside her a mere inch and then stopped. "Do you want me to take you, captive?"

She drew a long shuddering breath. "Yes," she said through gritted teeth.

"Then you will beg me."

"I won't."

"We shall see how long you resist when I put my mouth on you."

Going down on one knee, he parted her thighs and pressed his lips to her sleek folds, seeking the point of feminine pleasure. Raven sucked in a sharp breath, her legs instinctively parting even more.

His long tongue lapped at her slowly, thoroughly, rasping against her sensitized flesh until she burned with frenzy.

"Are you ready to beg me yet?" he asked at length, his voice husky.

Wildly excited, she squirmed against his assault. His hands moved to clasp her buttocks and hold her still, his tongue and lips and teeth ruthlessly pleasuring her.

"Are you?" he demanded.

"Yes . . . please, yes! I beg you. . . ."

She writhed in helpless rapture as, with a final hard kiss, he dredged a shattering climax from her. Wanton cries of delight rippled from her throat until the fiery waves of sensation ebbed and she sagged limply against the mast.

"Perhaps next time you will be more obedient," he remarked, his husky murmur holding a note of triumph.

Rising, he took a step backward. Through her haze of pleasure Raven watched as he unbuttoned the straining placket of his breeches and released his phallus, already massive and darkly engorged.

"My cock is hungry for you. Are you hungry for it? Do you want to feel it sliding up inside your pretty, quivering flesh?"

A fevered longing filled her, and she licked her dry

lips, anticipating that hot, hard shaft coming into her, assuaging the terrible, sweet ache that all but consumed her.

"Yes." Her own voice sounded sultry when she added a plea. "But you should untie me, sir. I can give you more pleasure that way."

"Very well, captive."

He complied, reaching behind her to slice the bonds from her wrists.

"Thank you, kind sir," she murmured. "You won't regret it." Looking down, she eyed the dagger. "Do you really need this wicked blade? I vow I will be obedient."

With a provocative glance, she took the dagger from his hand. The anticipation in his smile, however, vanished when she held the blade to his throat.

Behind the pirate's mask, his eyes flashed dangerously.

"Back away," she ordered. "Farther!" she insisted, waiting until he had retreated three more steps. "Now it is your turn, monsieur."

"My turn?" She could imagine him raising an eyebrow behind the mask.

"To obey. Kneel before me."

His mouth twisting with mockery, he did as she bid, dropping to both knees.

"Now your manhood. Release it completely. I want to see it."

Opening his breeches farther, he drew up his shirt to expose his flat, hard belly and powerful loins. His erect member jutted proudly toward her, Raven saw with fascination.

"Now pleasure yourself."

"Mademoiselle?"

"You heard me! I want to see you stroke yourself, to torment yourself as you did me."

Obediently he reached down, but when his palm brushed the smooth tip of his phallus, the shaft jerked hungrily. Raven saw him clench his teeth.

"I am waiting, pirate."

Sitting back on his heels then, he cupped the velvety pouch of his heavy testicles with one hand, gripping the thick stem with the other.

"Like this, mademoiselle?" he said, slowly stroking from base to head.

Raven barely stifled a moan, overwhelmed with longing to feel that hard flesh driving deep, deep inside her.

The pirate clearly had the same goal in mind, for his black eyes were fastened on the juicy folds of flesh between her thighs.

"This will satisfy neither of us," he scoffed, yet raw desire darkened his voice.

"Do you think I care about satisfying the lustful desires of a pirate?"

"Yes."

Gazes locked, they stared at each other.

"No," she insisted. "I would rather have you at my mercy."

He gave a slow, lascivious smile. "There is just one problem, mademoiselle." He sprang lithely to his feet and stalked toward her, his magnificent shaft swaying. "You should know better than to torment a pirate."

Raven gasped as he swept her up in his arms, letting the dagger clatter to the deck.

"My revenge will be swift," he threatened, his warm mouth against her lips. "I intend to ravish you until you scream with pleasure."

He carried her into the cabin then, dropping her on the satin-covered bunk and following her down, pinioning her hands on either side of her bare shoulders.

When she struggled to free herself, he gave a menacing laugh. "Fight me, vixen," he urged, tenderly biting each of her hardened nipples in turn. "But before we're through, you will surrender to me. You'll give me everything I want, everything you have to give."

He thrust himself relentlessly within her, making her cry out in pleasure. Raven arched against him, her inner muscles clutching his gloriously hard flesh, even as she fought the onslaught of rapture.

But his hot, slick strokes drove her onward, toward the excruciating bliss. He released her hands to capture her face and kiss her fiercely, his tongue plunging deep. Yielding, straining in mindless abandon, she dug her nails into the muscles of his shoulders.

Suddenly his body wrenched in a massive shudder. At his ragged groan, fire exploded through her veins. She screamed, and his mouth captured her sobs of ecstasy, just as her pirate lover might have. They clung together through the passionate storm, lost to reality, oblivious to anything but their fantasy.

Finally he collapsed against her, spent, shuddering, leaving her dazed and exhausted.

Later, much later, Raven lay in Kell's arms as he slept, stunned by the savage pleasure he had given her, frightened by the feelings this complex, enigmatic man had incited in her.

He had become too dangerous, she reflected. Their carnal pleasure had grown too threateningly intimate, his image too irresistibly entwined with her imaginary lover.

I want everything you have to give, he had said. Dismayingly, she could envision herself giving him everything.

But she wouldn't let that happen, she vowed. She would have to stop making love to Kell before he took over her fantasies entirely.

Three nights later Kell found himself pondering how to proceed with his wife as he watched a dozen nubile female bodies cavort upon a stage.

As Dare's guest, he was attending a soiree held expressly for the Hellfire League at a different sin club. The entertainment, which had begun merely as an erotic ballet, was in danger of sinking into something of an orgy, for a few noble bucks in the audience had become overly aroused and had claimed several of the performers as their sexual partners.

The debauchery didn't surprise Kell. He had attended similar gatherings in the past at various flesh houses, although never in such elite company. Dare had seen to it that his fellow Leaguers had welcomed Kell into their ranks and supported his gaming club— much to his gratitude.

Twisting his mouth wryly, Kell took another potent swallow of brandy. Two months ago he would have scoffed had someone told him he would be grateful to be taken under wing by the Marquess of Wolverton and his ilk. But he owed a great deal to Dare—and to Halford as well, he grudgingly admitted.

His club was safe now. Halford had been magnanimous indeed, bringing the Prince Regent himself to patronize the Golden Fleece last evening. Prinny had won a small sum and pronounced the play "capital." And with the royal seal of approval, Kell's club was assured of recovery from the destruction the duke's slander had wrought.

The future of his marriage, however, was still wholly unsettled.

Absently Kell's gaze wandered over the stage, but the carnal antics had no power to arouse him, nor did the thought of coupling with any of the beauties there. Upon his arrival, several of the doves had fawned over him and invited him to partake of their frolics later, but he had politely extricated himself.

There was only one woman he desired, one pair of legs he wanted coiled around his waist, one delectable beauty writhing in passion beneath him.

Averting his gaze, he stared down into his brandy, seeing a vision of soft, creamy skin and lush breasts and laughing sapphire eyes. He could still feel every soft curve against him, stirring his body. . . .

His unsated body.

Raven hadn't allowed him to touch her since their heated night of shared fantasy. She was regretting what had happened between them, he knew.

As he was.

Hell, it had probably even been a mistake to goad her into conjugal relations in the first place. Initially he'd had the vague, misguided notion that if he made love to her, he could satisfy his hunger and drive her from his mind. And then his male pride had gotten the better of him, spurring him to see her imaginary lover as his rival.

He had fooled himself, though. The deep ache of desire hadn't eased even after their nights of passion. Raven's allure was as potent at ever. And her fantasy lover still claimed her allegiance.

Cursing, Kell tossed back the rest of his brandy.

Just then he saw Dare making his way toward him and felt another involuntary twinge of jealousy. He was jealous of the marquess and his easy relationship with Raven, for Dare shared her confidence and trust. Even Halford had a stronger claim to her affection than he himself did.

He would have preferred Raven to associate less with both men, but he could hardly order her to cut the connections. He didn't have that right. Whatever his feelings of male possessiveness, he would have to control them. Their marriage was merely one of convenience. It would be lunacy to develop any deeper emotions toward Raven, for she wouldn't allow herself to reciprocate.

He schooled his features into impassivity as Dare sat beside him.

"I must apologize for the spectacle," Dare said with an elegant grimace. "Such juvenile deportment can be so tiresome. I suspect it interests you no more than it does me."

"I prefer a more private performance, I admit."

"Shall we depart, then? The sport is far better at your club."

Agreeing, Kell accompanied the marquess downstairs, but they spoke of inconsequential matters until they were seated in Dare's carriage.

"I haven't thanked you adequately for your intervention on my behalf," Kell said then.

Dare waved a hand. "Think nothing of it. I would have acted for Raven's sake, even if I had not come to like you. I very much want her to be happy." He gave Kell a studied glance in the dimness of the carriage. "You needn't be concerned about my relationship with your wife," he added pointedly. "I think of Raven as a beloved younger sister."

"You relieve my mind," Kell remarked, his tone lightly mocking although inwardly he was quite serious.

Dare hesitated. "To be frank, I am glad for the opportunity to speak to you alone."

Kell felt himself stiffen, uncertain where this conversation would lead.

"I confess," Dare said, "I wasn't entirely displeased when Raven was compelled to wed you. She and Halford were completely ill-suited. In the long run, I believe you will be a far better choice for her."

Kell eyed the marquess skeptically. "You think me a better choice than a lofty duke?"

"Without question. You are much more likely to appreciate Raven's unique qualities. She has more spirit than any dozen other women combined, even if she's endeavored to repress it since coming to England."

She did indeed have more spirit, Kell agreed silently. A bright spirit that was irresistible.

"She has worked quite hard at attempting to fit in, trying to mold herself into what her mother wished her to be."

"And what was that?"

"A milk-and-water miss who's ruled entirely by propriety," Dare said with an edge of derision.

"You seem to know Raven well."

"I am privy to some of her secrets."

"Her secrets?"

"She would probably have my head for telling you this, but I think you should know about her past. Her half brother Nicholas informed me so I would be better prepared to look after her."

Dare proceeded to tell about Raven's mother and her passionate love for a married man, about Elizabeth conceiving a child out of wedlock and being forced to wed a younger son she disliked.

"So Kendrick was not Raven's real father?" Kell asked thoughtfully.

"No. Raven rarely speaks of him, but I gather there was no love lost between them. She cherished her mother, though. Before she died, her mother made her promise to wed a noble title. I expect Elizabeth feared the scandal might catch up to her daughter one day and wanted Raven to have the protection of rank and position, even though Nick made certain she inherited a substantial income from her real father. Wealth can make up for a multitude of sins but not questionable bloodlines."

"How well I know," Kell said darkly.

He fell silent, remembering Raven's remark about not wanting children—her concern about conceiving a child without a father who would love and care for him. Was her reluctance because of her own experience?

Kell frowned. He wasn't all that certain he wanted children himself. There was enough bad blood in the Lasseter line to fear passing it on to his offspring. His uncle for one, and his brother Sean . . .

He recollected himself as Dare spoke again.

"Despite your lack of a title, you could be precisely what Raven needs."

"You're not concerned I might do her harm?"

"Not in the least. I've seen how you look at her."

"Like every other besotted sap who sets eyes on her, you mean." Kell's mouth twisted. He couldn't deny that his worst fear had come to pass: He'd been bewitched by the bride he'd planned to ignore. "I suppose you have a reason for confiding Raven's secrets," he said finally.

"I do," Dare admitted. "I consider you a highly intelligent man. If you understand what drives her, you will know better how to deal with her. Raven is passionate in everything she does. If she came to care for you when you couldn't reciprocate . . . I would not like to see her heart broken."

"Raven is the one known for breaking hearts," Kell retorted dryly. "I expect I'm in far greater danger than she is."

"Even so . . . if you don't think you can care for her, then it would be best if you simply kept away from her."

It was Kell's turn to hesitate. "I've been invited by her grandfather to spend the holidays with Raven at his estate."

Dare raised an eyebrow. "Luttrell must have elected to accept your marriage, then. Do you intend to go?"

"I have yet to decide." Surprisingly, Sean had written of his desire to remain in Ireland over Christmas, and Kell was uncertain about whether to join him or to allow his brother the distance he seemed to crave.

"You are more than welcome to come with me to the Wolverton family seat for the holidays," Dare said. "Frankly, I would enjoy the company, for this visit will be purely obligatory. I've been there only once since I inherited from my grandfather, because it holds so many unpleasant memories of the old bastard. You would be doing me a favor."

"Thank you. I'll keep your offer in mind."

Gazing out at the dark streets, Kell sank into contemplation. He had unpleasant memories as well, both of his bastard of an uncle and of Christmas. It was during the Christmas holidays that he'd come home to discover the terrible truth about his poor brother. And then they'd fled to Ireland and to the misery of living on the streets—certainly the worst time of his life.

He didn't want to endure Christmas alone. Whether or not he should risk spending it with Raven, however, was an entirely different matter. Raven left him so dangerously vulnerable.

She'd shown little enthusiasm about his accompanying her to her grandfather's. And then there were his brother's feelings to consider. Sean would be furious if he returned to find his prediction had come to pass—that Kell had fallen for the very woman Sean blamed for causing his misery.

Mentally Kell shook his head. He couldn't continue

letting his brother rule every aspect of his life, especially one so personal as his marriage. And despite the danger, he wanted to go.

The temptation of being close to Raven for even a short while was relentless, overpowering. He was like a possessed sailor being lured by a siren's call toward the lethal rocks. He couldn't turn away.

Kell pressed his lips together in a grim line. It was no doubt madness, but he intended to accompany his wife to the country for the Christmas holidays. And God help him if he couldn't prevent his desire for her from swelling out of control.

Chapter
Seventeen

If Raven hoped to avoid intimacy with Kell during the Christmas holidays, she realized her mistake the moment she set foot in his traveling coach.

Her grandfather's estate in East Sussex was only some forty miles south of London, but spending a good part of the day alone with Kell gave her more opportunity for private conversation than in all the weeks of their marriage. Regrettably O'Malley wasn't on hand to keep the discussions impersonal, for he rode in a second carriage with the other servants—her maid and Kell's valet.

The frigid weather didn't help her keep her distance, either, for the coach windows had to remain shut against the light snow that was falling. Unaccustomed to such chill temperatures, Raven couldn't refrain from shivering, despite the hot bricks at her feet and several woolen carriage robes.

"I never realized winter could be so cold," she complained, watching her breath frost on the interior of the panes.

"The West Indies isn't exactly renowned for its snow," Kell replied, amused.

"No. Until I came to England, I never even saw snow."

"It will likely get far worse than this. Come here," he ordered, holding out his arm.

She protested when Kell drew her into the shelter of his body to share his warmth, but then he asked her about winters in the British West Indies, and somehow Raven found herself telling him about growing up on the Caribbean isle of Montserrat and revealing confidences she never intended to—about playing pirate on white crystalline beaches and swimming in aquamarine seas and galloping over green, green hills.

"I've heard that Montserrat resembles Ireland somewhat," Kell remarked thoughtfully.

"I wouldn't know since I've never been to Ireland, but the largest number of settlers on the island are indeed Irish. Did you spend much time in Ireland when you were young?"

She immediately regretted her question, though, for it was unsettling to hear Kell tell of visits to Ireland when his parents were still alive, especially when she caught his dark eyes smiling with fond memories.

"From the time I was a babe, my mother regaled me with tales of the wee folk, so whenever we visited, I spent most of my waking hours hunting them." His self-deprecating grin held an irresistible appeal. "I vow I believed in leprechauns until I was nearly a grown man."

Raven shifted restlessly and eased herself from Kell's embrace, claiming that she was warm enough. Even if it was a lie, she knew she would be wiser to maintain a formal reserve between them.

The situation grew even worse when they arrived at the Luttrell estate. There were some initial awkward moments when his lordship greeted Kell, and Raven worried that she would have to come to her husband's defense. Then they were shown upstairs and she discovered her grandfather had allotted them only a single bedchamber, even though there were dozens of empty guest rooms throughout the huge manor.

When she eyed the bed unhappily, Kell merely shrugged. "We can manage for appearance's sake."

Dressing for dinner proved a further exercise in intimacy, for they had to share the small dressing room under the curious eyes of their servants. Raven was almost grateful when they could repair downstairs for dinner.

The entire manor house was bedecked for Christmas, with holly and ivy and evergreen boughs adorning the picture frames and stairway banisters. Raven saw Kell eyeing the greenery and wondered what he was thinking.

"I haven't seen such decorations since my youth," he answered her unspoken question. "My mother was fond of observing Christmas like this."

The pleasure in his voice held a note of sadness that Raven could understand well enough. She herself had few fond memories of Christmas, but she missed her mother dreadfully.

They found the drawing room particularly festive. A huge Yule log burned in the hearth, while the mantel was brightened by red ribbons and holly sprigs.

Her grandfather awaited her in his favorite chair. At her appearance on Kell's arm, Luttrell groped for his cane and started to rise, but Raven stayed him with a quick word.

"The decorations are lovely, Grandfather," she said, bending to give him a kiss on his withered cheek.

"I wanted to make you feel welcome, my girl, so you would visit me more often. I am a lonely old man."

He turned his attention to her husband. "So tell me, Mr. Lasseter," the viscount said, plainly making an attempt to include Kell in the conversation, "how have you been getting on with my minx of a granddaughter? I trust she is not proving too troublesome?"

Kell shot Raven a provocative glance, his eyes suddenly gleaming with amusement. "Oh, she is proving exceedingly troublesome, sir, but I am managing somehow."

Her grandfather gave a crack of laughter and then asked after his sister Catherine, who had remained in London for the holiday. "I confess I didn't invite her to join us," Luttrell added in a conspiratorial undertone. "I did not want her spoiling the occasion. Catherine's shrewish tongue could vex the devil himself, isn't that right, Granddaughter?"

Raven returned a politely ambivalent smile, although inwardly she was glad she didn't have to deal with her aunt Catherine as well as her grandfather and her husband.

Dinner turned out to be far more congenial than she had expected, Raven noted with rueful surprise. Even though the two gentlemen found little in common, they both obviously endeavored to be on their best behavior.

When the sweets were finished, she looked expectantly at her grandfather, wondering if they would observe the more formal custom of the ladies repairing to the drawing room while the gentlemen remained behind to enjoy an after-dinner wine and possibly a smoke.

"Go ahead, my girl," her grandfather urged. "We will join you shortly. I have an excellent port I wish Mr. Lasseter to try."

Containing her reservations, she left them together and occupied herself by absently picking out tunes on the drawing room pianoforte from the sheet music provided, but she found herself glancing at the ormolu clock on the mantel with increasing frequency.

In the dining room, however, the viscount's after-dinner conversation had taken Kell somewhat by surprise.

Luttrell began by offering a sincere apology for the chilly reception Kell had received into the family. "It alarmed me to think of my granddaughter wed to a man of your reputation, Mr. Lasseter. But I came to realize what I owed you for saving her. And Raven seems content enough. I trust she is not pulling any wool over my eyes?"

Kell had no desire to answer probing questions about the state of his marriage, and he fended the inquiry off politely. "You will have to ask Raven, my lord."

Luttrell waved an impatient hand. "I doubt she would tell me if she were unhappy, since she wouldn't wish to disappoint me." He leaned forward, pinning Kell with an intent gaze. "I hope you will allow me to be frank, sir.

I'm an old man and not much longer for this world, I fear. I want my granddaughter to be well cared for when I am gone—and not only in the monetary sense. Raven will be all alone, except for my sister Catherine, who has all the motherly instincts of a gorgon."

"I understand Raven has a half brother," Kell said carefully.

Luttrell frowned. "You know about that, do you? Well, it's true, she does have a half brother, but she can't acknowledge the connection without dredging up the past. Furthermore, Sabine is in America, and this infernal conflict with America makes the seas too dangerous to sail. You will be the only protection she has from a cruel world."

"I assure you," Kell vowed quite honestly, "I will care for Raven to the best of my ability." He paused before adding, "I would be better prepared, though, if I understood more of her history."

"You wish to know about Raven's mother?"

"I gather you were estranged from her."

"Yes." The viscount's rheumy eyes welled up with tears. "I treated my daughter so wretchedly. I wish to God I had acted differently. . . ." Tears slipped down his wrinkled cheeks as he spoke of his lifelong regrets. "I repudiated my only child because of my stubborn pride, and I never saw her again. What a damned fool I was." Wearily he shut his eyes. "When you come to be my age, you realize the importance of family. I have only myself to blame for my loneliness."

They stayed for more than half an hour, with Luttrell lamenting his past mistakes and disclosing what little he knew of his granddaughter's upbringing. When he finally composed himself, they joined Raven in the drawing room.

Her gaze immediately sought out Kell's, but he kept his expression purposely enigmatic. Her countenance, however, clearly showed her relief that the two men hadn't done mortal battle.

Lord Luttrell made straight for his chair and gave a sigh as he sank into it. "Play a carol for us, my dear, while I warm my old bones by the fire. I vow these damned winters are getting more brutal each year. Do you sing, Mr. Lasseter?"

"I haven't in years," Kell replied, going to stand near Raven at the pianoforte. "Not since my mother was alive."

"Well, I am a bit rusty myself, but Raven has a voice like an angel and should keep us in tune. If you are willing to risk making a cake of yourself, so am I."

Thus it was that Kell, to his amazement, found himself turning the pages for Raven and singing Christmas carols he hadn't sung since his youth.

The evening was a strange one for Kell, disturbing in many ways, for it reminded him of everything he'd once had and lost. He hadn't known such familial warmth since his father died.

He found himself relishing the easy laughter between grandfather and granddaughter. Luttrell obviously cared for Raven a great deal and profoundly regretted having lost the opportunity to witness her childhood and to see her grow to womanhood.

The viscount's earlier sad utterances about loneliness echoed in Kell's mind as he stood at the pianoforte beside Raven, feeling a strange melancholy. The warmth and intimacy of the evening only emphasized his own isolation, while the discussion of family had roused unwanted reflections about his own painful past and made him acutely aware of all that was missing in his life.

For so many years he'd had Sean and no one else. . . . But now he had a wife. Raven. Unaccountably she filled him with unnamed longings, stirred desires in him that he hadn't allowed himself to feel for an eternity, desires that went beyond the physical. When he was with her, his shattering sense of loneliness faded, and he could almost envision a future that held something other than barren emptiness.

Kell gazed down at her as she completed the final verse of a carol, and the yearning intensified. He'd been so mistaken about her. He'd once considered her a conniving, title-hunting schemer and tarred her with the same brush as he did the elite society he despised. Instead Raven had proven him completely wrong, continually surprising and delighting him. Deliberately or not, she'd challenged and provoked and aroused him—both his body and his heart.

A flicker of tenderness rippled through him, and he found himself wishing their circumstances could be different, that they could have something more than a cold marriage of convenience.

Mentally Kell scoffed at the absurd notion. Raven didn't want a real marriage. Certainly she didn't want love. She didn't even want passion from him. She would rather escape into her fantasies with her imaginary lover.

A renewed arrow of jealousy suddenly stung him,

and Kell felt his mouth tighten in a sardonic line. Sweet hell, he was mad to be jealous of a damned fantasy. And yet he still wanted fiercely to tear Raven away from her fictitious lover, to drive him from her mind and take his place. . . .

She glanced up at him just then, her eyes an incredible blue beneath a poignant sweep of ebony lashes. He had little defense against those eyes—or against Raven herself. It scared him that his resistance toward her was crumbling. . . .

They both fell silent, staring at each other. A log crackling in the grate broke the spell, but it took Kell a moment to realize that the drawing room had grown quiet.

Glancing over at the viscount, he saw that Lord Luttrell had dozed off in his chair. Evidently they'd been the only ones singing for some time.

The slight flush that colored Raven's cheeks suggested she realized their circumstances as well.

"I wonder if we should call someone to put him to bed?" she whispered.

Kell shook his head. "Let him sleep. He'll likely waken on his own, and if not, his servants undoubtedly know his habits and will care for him."

Raven hesitated, glancing at the mantel clock, which showed the hour of ten. "It's late. Perhaps I should retire."

It was not an invitation to join her, Kell knew. She intended to keep as much physical distance between them as possible—her way of maintaining her emotional defenses, he realized.

Wisely Kell clamped down on his instinctive urge to

protest. He would be far better off not touching her.
He would have a hard enough time maintaining his
own defenses without the temptation of Raven's lovemaking to further arouse his heart's longings.

He returned a wry smile. "This is early compared to
the hours I usually keep. On a busy night at the club,
it's rare that I get to bed before three or four in the
morning. I think I will stay up for a while, perhaps find
a book to occupy me."

"Grandfather's library is well stocked," Raven
observed.

"Good. I'll see what reading material is available."

In unspoken accord, they quietly left the room.
When Kell escorted her to the foot of the stairs, Raven
paused with a nervous glance, as if wondering what he
intended.

"Sleep well," was all he said, putting a firm rein on
his desires.

He wanted more than anything to accompany her
upstairs to bed and resume where they'd left off last
week. But he would first have to resolve two burning
questions:

How could he break through Raven's determined
guard when she was so set on resistance?

And did he even wish to risk gambling his heart
against such formidable odds?

To Raven's dismay, keeping her distance from Kell
proved impossible during the course of their visit—
particularly since they were required to spend their
nights together in enforced intimacy.

Even though she retired long before Kell did and intended to remain well on her side of the bed, once the fire died down, the wintery chill of the room drove her to unconsciously seek the warmth of her husband's body. She woke each morning to find herself pressed against him, reveling in his heat.

The first time startled her. Raven lay gazing at Kell while he slept, her breath faltering as she studied his beautiful features. He looked slightly dangerous and disreputable, with his wicked scar and the early morning stubble shadowing his jaw. And yet his usual intensity was missing. His peaceful repose made him seem younger, more vulnerable—and roused an unwanted tangle of desire and tenderness inside her.

Savagely repressing the emotions, Raven eased away and rose to dress, shivering in the frigid air.

During the day, time hung heavily on her hands. It began to snow in earnest, with the storms sometimes developing into blizzards, so her fascination with the novelty of snow quickly wore off. Ordinarily she would have spent her mornings riding, even though her grandfather kept a meager stable, but hazarding the treacherous conditions would have been lunacy.

Raven found herself at loose ends until the viscount rose late in the mornings, when she could keep him company, reading aloud to him or playing cards. But still, her husband usually joined them, and being in the same room with Kell under such intimate circumstances for so many hours each day severely tested her nerves.

She was most discomfited by her infrequent glimpses into his past, when he shared fond memories. One was dredged up during a particularly chilly afternoon, when they had gathered before the drawing room fire to enjoy mulled cider spiced with cinnamon.

"Drink up, my boy," Luttrell commanded. "I'll wager you've never tasted better."

Kell smiled as he stared down into his steaming mug. "No disrespect, my lord, but actually I have. My mother had a decided partiality for mulled cider and had her own family recipe. At Christmastime, she would bundle us up and send us out hunting for a Yule log with my father, and when we returned, she would ply us with hot cider. It tasted like nectar to me. After she died, though . . ." Kell shrugged, making Raven suspect he had never entertained the custom again. But then he recalled himself and raised his mug to the viscount in a salute. "But this comes a close second to my memories."

Christmas came four days after their arrival and further strained Raven's nerves. It started out safely enough when they exchanged gifts.

She had gotten Kell a matched set of foils of the finest steel, and he seemed pleased when he examined them.

"Remarkable quality. How did you find these? I wasn't aware you knew anything about fencing."

"I don't. Dare selected them for me."

Kell's mouth tightened momentarily, but then he handed her his gift.

Raven opened the large package to discover a luxurious blue kerseymere cloak trimmed with marten fur, with a matching fur hat and muff.

"Emma chose them," Kell remarked evenly.

Raven was gratified that his gift was relatively impersonal, yet she felt a familiar sting of jealousy when he mentioned the beautiful hostess.

To her further chagrin, Christmas dinner held a disturbing amount of closeness and warmth. They enjoyed a repast of roasted goose and plum pudding, followed by more carols. Then her grandfather surprised them by telling ghost stories, which led to a great deal of merriment. Dismayed, Raven knew she would be glad to return to London.

The next day, however, was Boxing Day, when Lord Luttrell distributed Christmas boxes of money to the poor and to his own servants, as well as opened his grand house for a tenant ball. Raven was required to dance several dances with her husband, which only reminded her of the sacrifice Kell had made in marrying her.

Shortly after the ball, winter tightened its grip on the countryside, not only making the snow too deep for riding but delaying their departure indefinitely; the roads to London had become impassable.

Impatient and restless, Raven began to think it was a mistake to have come with Kell, for there was no avoiding him. With him sharing her bed, she couldn't even escape into dreams of her fantasy lover in an effort to dismiss him from her mind.

And then there was Kell himself. He seemed a kinder, more considerate man than the one she had wed—or at least he was making an effort to blunt the sharp edge of his sardonic wit.

He apparently noted her restlessness, though, for when Raven complained about having nothing to occupy her time, he offered to stave off her boredom by teaching her how to fence. She accepted with alacrity, desperately needing the distraction.

Thus, for several hours each morning, Kell instructed her on the use of foils, the tips of which were protected by buttons. He demanded that she work hard, but Raven found herself craving his praise. Even the slightest compliment warmed her more than was warranted.

She proved a fast learner and appeared to surprise him with her agility and quickness, but to her admittedly untrained eye, Kell's skill seemed truly remarkable. When in an offhanded tone she asked how he had become so good, he surprised her by giving her a candid reply.

"It was a retaliation of sorts against my uncle. He was a champion fencer, and I was eager to deflate his pride. So I set out to compete on his level and even excel. I relished the day I was good enough to challenge him and win." His mouth curled, evidently at some dark memory. "Uncle William considered me part devil, and I made it a point to live up to my reputation."

Raven would have liked to hear more but refrained from asking, already regretting having given Kell an opening to share further confidences.

The following week, she thought she would finally have a brief respite from Kell when the sun made an afternoon appearance. Declaring she had to get outdoors or go mad, she bundled up in her new cloak and braved the frigid temperatures to tromp about in the heavy snow.

To her dismay, however, Kell accompanied her.

The countryside sparkled a crystalline white and offered a breathtaking view, but all Raven could think
about was the man beside her, especially when he took
her elbow to help her maintain her balance on the slippery paths recently cleared by the Luttrell gardeners.
She had just begun to grow accustomed to the texture
and depths of the icy drifts when she was startled to
feel a thud on her shoulder and a burst of snow spray-
ing her face.

Kell had thrown a snowball at her, she realized in
astonishment.

"I expect you've never engaged in a snow fight," he
said with a challenging grin.

"Now where would I have learned that?" Raven demanded, placing her hands on her hips in annoyance.

"There is an art to fashioning a good snowball.
Would you like me to teach you?"

"I suppose so," she replied, intrigued despite herself.

Quite against her will, she allowed him to introduce
her to the deliciously childish pastime of a snow fighting.
For a time the air was filled with flying snow and
laughter and shrieks of protest. Raven couldn't remember when she had enjoyed herself more—or when Kell
had seemed happier. It warmed her to see him so light-
hearted. His smile had always been so elusive that she
delighted in his devilish grin as he stalked her.

But then she hurled a well-aimed missile that sent
his hat sailing, and he retaliated by tackling her face-
first in a snowbank.

"Pax!" she cried, weak with mirth as she struggled to
turn over.

When she found herself pinned beneath his weight,

Raven suddenly stilled, gazing up at Kell. The sun picked up the glinting blue highlights in the ebony waves of his hair, while the cold had flushed his cheeks and his sensual mouth. . . .

Kell froze as well, staring back at her. He was drowning, drowning in the shimmering ocean of her eyes. When he felt Raven shift uneasily beneath him, the sharp yearning welled up in him like an ache. He wanted so badly to stake his claim on her. What he wouldn't give to be in a real bed with her just now, bringing her to pleasure and taking pleasure in return.

Seeing her laughter fade, though, Kell knew he had let his feverish lust become too apparent. Abruptly he rolled off her and helped her up, and they resumed their fight, yet the moment was no longer as blithe and natural between them.

Kell muttered an oath under his breath, not knowing how much more he could take of this tormenting dance. These past days had been a sadistic form of torture for him, as well as a severe exercise in control. He'd done his best to retire late and rise early to minimize the amount of time he had to endure lying next to Raven, burning with desire yet permitted to do nothing more than share his body heat.

It was no doubt fortunate she had erected a wall between them, he thought, watching her brush snow from her new cloak. He could fall for her so easily. He had never met a woman who tied him in such knots. Her merest smile left him breathless, while her touch sent fire streaking through him.

Yet he couldn't make the dire mistake of falling in love with her. That was the surest path to heartache, for Raven would likely spurn him . . . and he would earn his brother's resentment at the same stroke.

The more determined Kell was to deny his passion, however, the more fiercely his need grew to possess her. Three mornings later, he gave up trying to fight his longing when he woke to find Raven curled against him and his erection throbbing. He lay quietly watching her, feeling a powerful tenderness for this woman who was his wife.

His heart performed a somersault when she slowly stirred awake. She looked incredibly alluring—soft and sleepy, her defenses down, her hair falling loosely over her shoulders in a wild mane.

He resolved then to overcome her resistance, whatever it took . . . and he knew it would take a great deal when she reacted. Seeing him watching her, Raven abruptly started to draw back.

Kell wrapped his fingers in her hair. "Don't go," he murmured. "Stay and keep me warm."

Obligingly she remained where she was, yet he could feel the tension in every part of her body.

He fingered a raven lock of her hair. "I'm still not certain what makes you so afraid to give yourself to me."

Her gaze lowered, focusing on his bare chest. "I told you. I never intend to succumb to hopeless passion the way my mother did."

"You never speak of your father," Kell observed evenly.

Her tone turned wary. "What is there to say?"

"I understand he wasn't your real father."

"Grandfather *told* you?" Dismay etched her beautiful features.

"He said he regretted forcing your mother to marry. I would like to hear about Kendrick. You must not have cared much for him."

Kell saw her blue eyes flash before she averted her gaze again. "I didn't care for him. And he never cared for me. He never let me forget that I was not his child."

"Was he cruel to you?"

She hesitated, but he could sense her pain simply in her silence. "Not in the physical sense," she finally whispered in a raw voice. "He never struck me. He just constantly reminded me of my illegitimacy. In public he claimed me as his own, but in private he called me his little bastard." The tremulous note in her voice held a touch of bitterness. "I suppose he ridiculed me simply to hurt my mother, because he was wounded by her sadness. She ignored him and hurt him with her continued pining, and he grew resentful."

Kell put a finger under her chin, compelling Raven to look at him. "So that was the true reason you wanted to marry your duke?"

"Largely." Her mouth twisted in a humorless, self-mocking smile, before she continued in a hoarse undertone. "A child of love, my mother always called me. But still I couldn't help feeling the shame of being conceived out of wedlock. Being titled would ensure my respectability, even if the question of my parentage ever became common knowledge."

Her voice was so low, he barely heard her admission. "Mama wanted that fear put to rest as well, but she was more concerned with my taking my rightful position in society. . . . To assuage her guilt, she said. For denying me my birthright." Raven's gaze took on an anguished, faraway look, as if she were lost in distressing memories. "I told her it didn't matter, but she insisted. I held her hand while she was dying, and she made me swear to wed a grand title. . . . But in the end, I couldn't keep my promise."

Tears burned in her blue eyes, and a shudder swept her body.

Kell wrapped his arms around her, drawing her close. A surge of hunger coursed through him at the intimate contact, yet mixed with his lust was a painful tenderness for her, a raw desire to protect and cherish. It wrenched his heart to realize how Raven's dreams had been shattered and to know that his own brother had been responsible. He had pretended not to care, but he did care . . . deeply.

"You weren't to blame for breaking your promise," he said quietly.

"No," she replied, the word a harsh murmur. "I had no control over that. But I can keep the vow I made to myself—never to make the same mistake my mother made, losing myself to a man and becoming so powerless. Never to let love destroy my life."

Drawing a slow breath, Kell spoke into her hair and lied. "You needn't worry about love developing between us. I told you I'm not interested in love." Pulling back, he raised himself on one elbow. "You have only to give me your lovely body."

Raven hesitated, torn. She wanted to surrender to the dark desire his words had stirred, wanted to give in to Kell. Yet she wasn't certain she could trust herself to make love to him and not hunger for more, for something even deeper than the closeness and comfort and warmth she already craved from him.

Involuntarily she reached up and touched her fingers to his sensual mouth, then higher, along his cheekbone and the scar she rarely noticed anymore, it seemed so much a part of him.

When she remained silent, Kell eased away from her, interrupting her roiling thoughts. She watched in surprise as he rose from the bed. He wore no nightshirt, only his drawers, and as usual the sight of his muscled build, sleek and elegant and superbly athletic, made her breath falter.

Going to the hearth, he built up the fire to a crackling blaze, then went into the adjoining dressing room. A moment later he returned with the black satin bag that contained the sponges.

"The decision is yours," he said, handing her the bag.

Rejoining her beneath the covers, he stretched out beside her, close but not touching. For a long moment he simply lay there, watching her. Waiting for her answer.

The room was warmer now, Raven realized. Or perhaps it was only she who was warmer. The heat in Kell's eyes was blazing enough to scorch her.

It grew hotter still when she murmured her hushed reply. "Perhaps just this once."

He smiled and pulled her into his arms, his mouth seeking hers.

"Kell . . ."

Tenderly he silenced her protest with a scorching

kiss. When she yielded with a needy whimper, his lips left hers to skim hotly against her throat, sending a wild surge of desire coursing through her.

"It's only sex," he whispered as he pressed her down into the pillows. "You know that, don't you?"

"Yes," Raven moaned in response, though not quite believing as she gave herself over to wanton abandon.

Chapter
Eighteen

The heavy snows eventually ceased, allowing their return to London at last. Kell resumed spending his nights in his own bedchamber and his days at his club, yet Raven was less grateful than she might have imagined. Without his company, her loneliness seemed magnified.

Moreover, although the new year had dawned bright with hope that the interminable war with Napoleon might soon be over, the winter was the coldest in local memory. So cold that even the Thames River itself began to freeze.

The absence of her closest friends from town didn't help, Raven knew. She had too much time on her hands to remember Kell and his lovemaking—the exquisite torment, the paralyzing pleasure—and the dangerous temptation he posed. During their intimate holiday interlude, he had probed her deepest emotions, exposed her greatest pain, and now she was left to deal with the aftermath, where her private yearnings battled her long-held fears.

Kell, too, was fighting his own battle. Business had dwindled significantly at the Golden Fleece, due both to the holidays and to the frigid weather, and he had little occupation to help drive thoughts of Raven from his mind or to make him forget her recent confession about her parentage.

She hadn't wanted to reveal so much about herself, Kell knew. Raven kept the emotions that hurt the most locked deep inside, as he did. But he'd heard the pain in her voice when she spoke of her illegitimacy, seen the grief in her eyes at breaking her promise to her mother—and he'd felt shaken by a profound tenderness.

He had tried not to let her concerns become important to him, but they had. And now he found himself wanting to make amends.

He could at least undo some of the damage his brother had wrought, Kell decided; he was wealthy enough to purchase a title for Raven. The Prince Regent's coffers were always in need of replenishing, since Parliament often refused his exorbitant requests for funds. And the Crown had been known to create new titles, regrant extinct ones, and recommend peerages in exchange for services rendered. Kell had little doubt he could be knighted or awarded a barony for the right price.

He asked Dare's opinion about the matter when the marquess returned to London at the end of January.

"No, it shouldn't be difficult for you to acquire a title," Dare responded with only a slight lift of an eyebrow. "Blessingham obtained his earldom by making Prinny a loan that was never expected to be repaid. If you like, I can put a discreet word in the Regent's ear. But I thought you disdained our snobbish aristocratic set."

Kell returned a wry smile. "I do. But Raven being able to attach 'Lady' before her name would set her mind at ease and let her fulfill the vow she made to her mother to wed a title."

Dare only nodded in approval, but the amused gleam in his eyes suggested incredulity that Kell would even consider such a step.

It amazed Kell as well. He had never aspired to join the ranks of society's upper crust, but now he was actually contemplating letting go of his anger for Raven's sake, relinquishing his self-imposed, admittedly lonely sentence as an outcast.

Indeed, his entire outlook on life had changed since wedding her. Before their marriage two months ago he would never have envisioned the lengths he would go to simply for the hope of seeing her smile.

By the first few days of February, the Thames had frozen to a solid surface, and Kell surprised both himself and Raven by inviting her to the impromptu fair on the ice that the papers were calling a Frost Fair. It was a sign of her restlessness that Raven accepted so readily, Kell suspected.

The scene between the London and Blackfriars Bridges did resemble a huge fair, with immense crowds milling on the frozen river, enjoying the spontaneous festivities. There were countless stalls and booths selling food and liquor and wares. Swings and merry-go-rounds. People dancing reels and playing skittles. And even printing presses turning out handbills and broadsides to commemorate the occasion.

Raven appeared delighted by the novelty, especially

the gaming, which included E.O., Rouge-et-Noir, and Wheels of Fortune.

"Are you certain you don't want to set up your own booth?" Raven laughingly demanded of Kell. "You could bring your hazard table here and make an outrageous profit, as these vendors appear to be doing."

"I think I will spare myself the trouble. The ice isn't likely to last, and I'd rather not run the risk of having my expensive hazard table sink to the bottom of the Thames."

They wandered about, munching on toasted cheese and hot chestnuts and gingerbread. Fascinated by the skaters, Raven made Kell pause to watch. Some of the performers appeared to be quite skilled, gliding gracefully across the ice like dancers, while others frolicked with amateurish glee, displaying clownish antics and clumsy pratfalls.

"I would never see anything like this in the West Indies," Raven murmured with delight.

In silent admiration Kell surveyed her heart-shaped face framed by glossy black tendrils. With her cheeks flushed rosy from the cold, her eyes bright with wonder, she looked more like an enchanting girl than a dazzling debutante.

"Do you miss your island?" he asked.

"Sometimes," she replied almost wistfully. "Certainly I miss the warmth. But my mother is gone, and without her there . . . And I've made a new life here."

"You might like to return there someday."

"Perhaps. England doesn't truly feel like home to me." She glanced up at him. "Do you consider England home?"

Kell reflected on the question thoughtfully. "Not really. I don't claim any place as home."

"Not even Ireland?"

"No. My happiest memories are of Ireland during my youth, but after my mother died . . ." He left the bitter thought unspoken. "When I returned as an adult, the magic was gone. And I found it difficult to earn a reliable livelihood at the hells there. Dublin isn't London."

"But now that your club is successful, would you want to go back?"

"I don't believe so. It took only a few months of living in city stews to realize that I'd developed an idealized view of the country from the stories my mother used to tell. And being half-English was a drawback. The Irish don't think any better of the English than the reverse."

"Would you ever want to visit the Caribbean?"

"Possibly." Kell smiled. "Just now your tales of hot sun and warm beaches sound infinitely appealing."

They spent another hour enjoying the Frost Fair before Raven started to shiver. When Kell insisted on returning her home, she thought it only polite to offer him a respite from the bitter cold by asking him to stay for tea.

They were ensconced in the drawing room by the fire, sipping hot tea, when he spied a set of foils lying on a side table—foils that belonged to him.

Raven flushed. "I didn't think you would mind my borrowing them."

"You've been practicing your fencing, then?"

"A little. But I'm not certain if I'm doing it correctly.

Dare offered to continue my lessons but he hasn't yet found the time."

She saw Kell's eyes narrow for an instant. "I'm perfectly capable of continuing your lessons," he observed, almost as if he were jealous.

"I didn't think you would wish to trouble yourself."

"I was only waiting for an invitation. Would you like a lesson now?"

Though surprised, Raven nodded. "Yes, indeed. Not only would I enjoy it, but I would do anything to get warm."

And so she found herself quite unexpectedly dancing across the drawing room, practicing the elements of thrust and parry and riposte with Kell.

It took only moments for Raven to realize her mistake. During their entire visit to the fair, she had been physically attuned to him . . . to his casual glances, to his nearness, to his slightest touch. But now her sexual awareness intensified.

Kell had removed his coat and waistcoat, and the fabric of his shirt stretched taut, revealing flowing muscles across his shoulders and arms. The sight so distracted her that she had to fight to recall any of the fencing skills he had taught her. And when she clumsily lunged against him and met the hardness of his thigh against her loins, the sensual shock of it scattered her thoughts so badly that she lowered her guard altogether.

Instantly she found herself disarmed, the buttoned point of his foil pressed against her throat.

Kell grinned, his bold, provocative look reminding her so much of her pirate that her breath faltered. Deliberately he backed her against the wall, his dark eyes gleaming in challenge. Her pulse took up an erratic rhythm when his rapier slid lower, brushing the swell of her bodice teasingly.

Then suddenly all teasing was gone. When their gazes locked, a sizzling tension leapt between them, the result of fierce need tightly leashed.

Kell breathed her name in a rough whisper and tossed aside his own foil. His eyes smoldering, he caught Raven to his chest, crushing her hard against him.

His kiss was carnal from the first, frankly sexual, his hard mouth bruising her with delicious force, his knee thrust between her thighs.

Raven whimpered. She hadn't intended to make love to him, but when his tongue ravished her mouth, her hesitation melted into liquid fire. She wanted him deep inside her, needed the heat of his savage passion.

It should have shocked her when he reached up and tore the buttons from her high-necked gown, baring the firm rise of her breasts to his hungry, demanding mouth, but she was too dazed to protest. The sensation of his rough suckling made her wet at once.

With stunning swiftness, she found herself on her back on the Aubusson carpet with Kell covering her, lapping at the straining silk of her breasts. She knew she should stop him, but the urgency was too strong, too immediate.

He shoved up her skirts and mounted her, his eyes glowing like embers, burning away the thin veneer of gentility. She arched as his plunging hotness penetrated her body, crying out in pleasure as he slid himself relentlessly within her.

He took her with a pirate's passion, and she responded with like fierceness, writhing beneath him as he thrust heavily into her again and again, his teeth bared. He was fire; he was heat and scorching flame that consumed her.

An explosion shot through her an instant later—erotic, incredibly intense—and carried him along. The harsh sounds that tore from his throat during their raw, frenzied mating matched her cries of delight as he pumped hotly into her, shuddering in racking tremors with his own burning need.

In the aftermath he sagged heavily in her arms. Her own strength shattered, Raven lay unmoving, loving the feel of his hard vital body pressed all along hers. Her fingers still clutched his hair, the ebony softness thick, sensual, alive, while his rapid breath teased the moist skin of her throat.

A deep sigh escaped her. She should deplore what she had done. She had given herself to Kell with abandon, without the slightest attempt to protect herself.

How could she have been so foolish? When she was with Kell, she shed any of the ladylike graces her mother had tried to instill in her. When he touched her, it was as if she became someone else, someone without shame or inhibitions. The rest of the world disappeared and desire alone infused her mind and body.

Raven squeezed her eyes shut, fighting a desperate urgency. A secret part of her thrilled at being wanted so fiercely by this man, at experiencing his wild, sweet mastery, while another, deeper part of her nearly despaired. He was everything her heart warned against.

Sweet heaven, she had to control herself. She

couldn't allow Kell to envelop her in emotional chaos. If she didn't take care, she could find herself at his mercy, reaching for love and getting nothing in return but pain.

And yet when he lifted his head, gazing down into her eyes with such warmth, her resistance fled.

"I intend to spend the night in your bed," he warned, his voice still hoarse with passion.

Raven nodded wordlessly, knowing she couldn't deny him.

Several hours later, Kell lay with Raven in the dark, examining the strangeness of his feelings. They had retired to her bed after dinner and resumed the passionate exertions they'd unexpectedly begun in the drawing room. But only after she'd fallen asleep with her back curled spoon fashion in the curve of his body did he recognize the unfamiliar warmth that was flowing through him like a warm current.

Happiness. He was feeling happiness for the first time since his childhood. All because of Raven.

His loneliness had vanished, while his house had taken on new life in her enchanting presence. Her uniqueness was amazing, Kell thought, breathing in the fragrance of her midnight hair. Sparring with her was more exhilarating than making love to other women, and making love to her was . . . incredible.

He didn't know how many lovers he'd had in his lifetime, but he knew that the way he'd felt with them was nothing compared to what he felt now. This sense of perfection. Of completeness. Raven made him feel joy, as if he would explode with it if she merely smiled at him.

He rubbed his knuckles softly against her bare arm, slowly savoring the silken texture of her skin. He hadn't meant to make love to her this afternoon, at least not with such violence. But hot need had welled up in him the instant he'd touched her—and fierce male triumph had flooded him when she'd responded so eagerly. Her soft moans of arousal had nearly driven him mad. Even now, after a night of lusty passion, he wanted to take her again.

He was caught in the heat of his own desires, he knew . . . and something more. *Is it love?*

The thought startled him. When an accusing image of Sean rose up to taunt him, he pushed the damning thought away. His loyalty to his brother had nothing to do with his feelings for Raven.

So what did he feel for her?

He wanted more than just a taste of Raven. He wanted to consume her, totally, absolutely, utterly. Desire for her burned like a fever. She was beautiful, tantalizing, everything he wanted in this world. But just as strong as physical desire was the need to be with her, to laugh and fight with her, to cradle her in his arms, to protect her, to make her happy, to know happiness with her. . . .

The want that rose up in him was so intense he had to shut his eyes.

Love. Was that the name for the overpowering feeling that was swamping him? The emotion he hadn't thought he needed?

Kell sucked in a ragged breath, recognizing the truth.

He loved her. The realization was frightening, exhilarating, unreal. He had lost the battle with himself.

Yet Raven was still fighting the battle. Even clasped against his heart, she still kept herself apart. She was too afraid of him. Afraid of giving herself, of losing herself, of loving.

Just then she stirred in her sleep, making him excruciatingly aware of her nakedness, of her ripe buttocks pressing against his loins. His longing was so sharp he had to clench his teeth. How could he still be this aroused after thoroughly sating himself?

Even as he swore a low oath, he gave in to his hunger. Shaping his palm to her feminine curves, he stroked her hip, then slid his hand around to her flat belly and lower . . . finding the warm, dewy cleft of her womanhood, plying her till he felt the sleek moisture that proclaimed her desire.

She still slept as, from behind, he slipped his arousal between her thighs; yet when he pushed himself into the yielding softness of her body, she stirred awake with a moan and pressed back against him eagerly.

Kell gave a rough sigh of pleasure and slid himself deeper into the hot, wet, incredibly tight clasp of her, his rhythm slow and tender, sheathing and drawing away until it became sweet, ecstatic torture for them both.

In only moments, though, the pleasure became too fierce to be borne. Kell shuddered, his tenderness giving way to savage demand. Rocking his hips, he drove her to a trembling climax before he found his own release, convulsing as his seed spurted from his body, filling her.

Holding her shaking body in the aftermath, he buried his face in her hair. He had met his match; he knew it without a doubt. But it remained to convince Raven of that.

Thus far their relationship had been purely carnal, based only on satisfying their mutual sexual needs. He had stirred her heart's hidden passion, he suspected, but if they were to have a true marriage, he would have to overcome Raven's fear of love. He would have to show her that loving him didn't mean losing herself.

As the final ripples of passion faded, she eased away and turned over in his arms, sleepily lifting her face to his. Her mouth was warm and soft, pliant and willing—and there was such sweetness in her kiss, it sent shock waves all the way to his heart. Gathering her close, Kell returned her kiss with tender fervor, treasuring Raven's gentle sigh of repletion when she curled her arm around his neck and nestled her head on his shoulder.

And as he lay there with her, wrapped in the night shadows of her hair, he made a silent vow. Someday they would be husband and wife in truth. If it took to the end of his days, he would convince Raven to let herself love him.

A welcome thaw put an end to the Frost Fair shortly after their visit, but that day proved to be a pivotal turning point in her marriage. To Raven's dismay, Kell began spending his nights in her bedchamber. He would come home late from his club and join her in bed, rousing her from sleep and stirring her to new heights of passionate abandon.

He shared her company during the days as well. She often found Kell still at the breakfast table, reading the morning papers, when she returned from her rides in the park. He provided her escort to the various social events she chose to attend. And occasionally he even invited her to join him at the club.

Raven found herself struggling desperately against her own awakened desires. Kell filled her with ecstasy and impossible longings, ruling her thoughts, waking or sleeping. She wanted to touch him a hundred times a day.

Even when she sought refuge in her fantasies, he foiled her. It had been so long since she had indulged in daydreams of her pirate lover that when she tried to conjure up his image, all she could visualize was Kell.

Her fantasy lover had become Kell in the flesh.

The realization that she was so vulnerable to him frightened her. But she had never before been subjected to a Kell bent on seduction, and she could summon little resistance to his determined charm. He seemed to be laying siege to her heart, tearing away the walls of her defenses, stone by stone.

Her defenses crumbled even more one day toward the end of February. They had just finished breakfasting when Kell asked her to join him in his study.

Upon inspecting the first document he handed her, Raven realized it was the deed to an estate. The second document was a copy of letters patent for a barony.

"My lady Frayne," Kell murmured, giving her a graceful bow.

She gazed at him in bewilderment. "I don't understand."

"We are now Baron and Baroness Frayne. You wanted to be wed to a gentleman of rank, and I managed to accommodate your wish."

"But . . . how?"

"It took less effort than I expected," Kell explained, his mouth curling cynically. "Dare was right. The Regent's coffers are so straitened that he leapt at my offer of financial aid. Subsequently I purchased an estate in the wilds of Northumberland, and now I have the title of baron to go with it."

Raven shook her head in amazement, still not quite believing. Kell was now Lord Frayne and she was his lady? His generous gesture must have cost him a fortune—and he had made the effort for her sake, even though he despised such things as rank and class distinctions and aristocratic privilege.

"The ton will undoubtedly fawn over us now," she said slowly, "but I know how much you dislike the trappings of society. You shouldn't be required to assume a title if you don't care to."

He shrugged. "It is only a term of address, as far as I'm concerned. It doesn't change who I am."

"I suppose it does not change who I am, either," Raven added, her tone thoughtful. "This does not make me a genuine lady. I will always be a bastard."

Raising an eyebrow, Kell surveyed her levelly. "Does it really matter a damn who your father was or wasn't?" When she didn't reply, he went on. "I regret that baroness is not as illustrious a title as duchess, but I hoped it might serve to satisfy your vow to your mother."

Raven flashed a tremulous smile. He was right, of course. The title itself wasn't as important as what it represented; she could indeed keep the promise she had made to her mother.

She felt her eyes burn with tears. "Kell . . . I don't know how to thank you. My mother would have cherished this."

His own smile was wry. "My mother would have been pleased as well. She was never one for retribution, but she would have enjoyed watching her son become a lord after all the slights she endured because of her modest origins. I wish she were alive to see it."

Raven heard the sorrow in his voice and realized it was a measure of how far they had come that Kell let her see his pain rather than try to conceal it from her.

Raven turned away to hide her dismay at another realization. She knew with frightening clarity that if she let herself, she could love Kell.

I can't fall in love with him, she murmured fiercely to herself. Loving Kell would be reckless, foolish, mad. He had made it abundantly clear he wanted nothing but her body. He wasn't the kind of man to surrender his heart in undying passion, especially to the woman he'd been compelled to offer his name in marriage.

Losing control of her own heart could be utterly disastrous. She could spend the rest of her life yearning for what she could never have.

And yet she very much feared he would leave her no choice.

Just then she felt his presence behind her. When Kell slid his arms around her and bent to nuzzle her nape, Raven tensed, calling on every ounce of willpower she possessed not to respond.

Fortunately she wasn't required to, for she heard a throat being cleared from the doorway. Feeling a surge of relief at the interruption, Raven turned to find the butler awaiting them, his gaze politely averted.

"Yes, Knowles?" Kell demanded without much patience.

Assuming an apologetic look, the servant handed him a folded slip of paper. "A message from Miss Walsh, sir."

Raven watched as Kell scanned the contents and saw his face cloud over with that same enigmatic mask he'd once worn.

"What is it?" she asked, not knowing whether to be alarmed.

"It seems my brother has returned to London," Kell said gravely, his dark eyes hooded as they met hers.

Chapter

Nineteen

Kell wished he could be pleased by his brother's return, but he couldn't summon any joy at the news. Instead, his most prominent emotion was guilt for shirking his duty.

For the past two months he'd tried to avoid thinking much of his brother. Even a fortnight ago when he'd received an alarming complaint from the horse farm in Ireland, he hadn't acted. According to the steward, Sean had whipped a mare until her coat ran with blood.

Kell knew he should have gone to Ireland then, but he'd been too wrapped up in pursuing his wife to spare time for his brother. The most he'd done was investigate a new doctor and inquire about uncommon treatments for someone of Sean's savage moods.

And Sean's mood would undoubtedly turn savage when Kell couldn't deny he had fallen for his wife. Certainly Sean would feel betrayed.

Kell had hoped they could discuss the matter in private, but his brother wasn't at the club, nor was he to be found at his lodgings.

Kell decided against traipsing all over London in

search of him, but he withdrew his invitation to Raven to join him at the club that evening. He wasn't going to hide, but he wanted Raven safely out of the way in case Sean's reaction was explosive.

Yet he couldn't shake the foreboding in his gut when the evening's gaming began.

He spent most of the night accepting congratulations, for word of his new title had gotten around. Regrettably, his brother had already gotten wind of it as well.

When Sean arrived near midnight, he was three sheets to the wind.

Kell intercepted him as he entered the hazard room. "Welcome back," he said, taking his brother's elbow to steady him.

Angrily Sean brushed off his assistance. "I hear you're a bleedin' lord now."

"Why don't you join me upstairs and we can discuss it?"

"Doan wanna discuss it!" His glaze bleary, he glanced around him. "Where is she?"

"Where is who?"

"That shhlut you made your wife. Hear sheesh leadin' you around by the nose."

"*Sean,* that is enough!"

Sean cast him a glance full of fury and pain. "Damn you, Kell. I warn' you what would happen."

Turning, he stumbled out. Kell followed him to the front door and watched as Sean climbed awkwardly into a waiting hackney.

Unable to shake his disquiet, Kell hailed another hackney and took the club's bruiser with him as a pre-

caution. Raven was at home alone, with only a few servants for protection.

He arrived in time to see Sean pounding on the
front door, yelling obscenities at the top of his lungs.
Kell leapt from the hired carriage just as lights appeared in several windows. An instant later the door
swung open to reveal O'Malley standing there.

Without warning Sean lunged at the groom. Unable
to dodge the hands that were intent on choking him,
the Irishman let fly a blow to the jaw that set Sean
reeling backward down the front steps.

After tumbling several revolutions, he landed facedown with a groan. When Kell reached him, he was
cursing violently again, but he brushed off any help
and struggled to sit up.

"I'll not be begging his pardon, m'lord," O'Malley
declared, flexing his fingers. "I would not let him harm
Miss Raven."

Kell glanced up, belatedly realizing he was the one
being addressed as "m'lord." Raven had come to the
door, he saw. She was holding a candle aloft and clutching the lapels of her wrapper closed with her other
hand, her hair a wild mane around her shoulders.

Climbing to his knees, Sean brandished his fists at
the groom. "You'll pay for that!" he growled, then
pointed at Raven. "And so will you!"

With a curse of his own, Kell helped his brother to
stand and escorted him forcibly to the first hackney.
He paid the jarvey double the usual fee to see that the
drunken gentleman got safely home and ordered his
own man, Belker, to watch over Sean until he could

call in the morning. The club's doorman was a former pugilist and could easily overpower Sean if need be.

When the carriage had driven off down the dark street, Kell dismissed the second hackney. Then he returned to the house where Raven awaited with her groom and a dozen other concerned servants. Kell sent them all back to bed, but O'Malley remained, the set of his massive shoulders belligerent.

"I had no course but to use my fives," the groom insisted, his gruff tone defensive.

"I agree," Kell said evenly.

"I'll not let him harm her."

"I should hope not. I'm grateful she has you for protection, Mr. O'Malley."

Giving Kell an assessing stare, the Irishman finally nodded.

Raven couldn't relinquish her own anger so readily, but she didn't wish to give vent to it in front of her groom. "I am grateful as well, O'Malley," she interjected. "Thank you. Why don't you return to bed now?"

With a tug of his forelock, he disappeared toward the back service stairs.

She gave her husband a blazing glare when they were alone. "Kell, you must do something. This cannot go on."

Kell's jaw tightened. "I know." Turning on his heel, he went into his study.

Almost trembling with rage, Raven followed. She shut the door carefully behind them and set down her candle before she threw it.

"What do you intend to do about Sean?" she demanded as Kell went straight to the brandy decanter and poured himself a glassful. "He is nothing but a dangerous bully."

Kell winced as if struck. Staring down at his liquor, he spoke in a low voice. "I had hoped Sean would have a chance to heal in Ireland, but spending time there doesn't seem to have helped him."

"No, it doesn't!" When he made no reply, Raven strove for control. "You don't mean to defend his behavior, do you? Even though he was beaten so horribly during his impressment, you cannot excuse his violence now."

"No," Kell said grimly, "I can't make excuses for him any longer. But Sean was fighting his demons long before his impressment."

"What difference does that make?"

A bitter smile touched Kell's lips. "Because I cannot excuse myself, either."

"What do you mean?"

"It isn't a pretty tale."

He tossed back a large swallow of brandy, then flung himself into a chair. Raven took a seat across from him, her hands clasped tightly together as she waited.

Kell was silent for a long moment before he spoke in a harsh murmur. "Sean wasn't always like this. My uncle is largely to blame for his suffering now. You once asked how I got my scar, and I told you I fought with my uncle William. But I didn't tell you why. For months while I was away at university, my uncle . . . sodomized my brother. Sean was only thirteen at the time."

She heard the revulsion and hatred that edged Kell's voice, and felt her own stomach churn with horror.

Sodomy was a serious crime, but to perpetrate it on a young, defenseless boy was abominable.

Raven swallowed hard, tasting bile in her throat. She'd always suspected Sean had a tormented past, but he was burdened with more pain, more desolation than she could imagine. And so was Kell, she had begun to realize.

He was staring down blindly at his glass, his face ravaged by grief. "Living with his shame has . . . twisted Sean. But I'm as much at fault as my uncle for the way he turned out. I left him alone with that bastard."

"Kell, you cannot blame yourself for what your uncle did."

"No?" The word was caustic as he sent her a fierce glance. "You should understand about vows, Raven. You made one to your mother. Well, I made a vow as well. I vowed to protect my brother. But I failed utterly. And I escaped unscathed while he suffered."

His voice dropped again to an anguished murmur. "Sean has never forgiven me for abandoning him . . . and I can never forgive myself."

Mutely Raven bit her lower lip. She could indeed understand Kell's dilemma more clearly. He felt a tremendous guilt because he'd escaped his uncle's perversions but hadn't protected his young brother. Most likely he had been doing penance all this time.

She wondered if Kell could ever let go of his guilt, but nonetheless, Raven knew her fear of his brother was justified. Sean had grown too dangerous. And she had to make Kell see it. He had to prevent Sean from becoming more destructive, even if compounding his brother's suffering would wound like a rapier.

"Kell, what happened to Sean is truly terrible," she said softly. "But that still doesn't excuse his violence. He can't be allowed to continue threatening people. And I'm afraid you are the only one who can control him."

"I know." His voice was a harsh whisper. He rubbed a hand roughly over his eyes. "I should have acted after he abducted you. But the choices were so grim—prison or a madhouse. I wasn't sure I could bear locking up my own brother in an asylum."

"You may have no choice now," she said quietly.

When Kell met her gaze, she could see the torment in his dark eyes. But he didn't refute her.

After a moment, he looked away. "I've arranged for Sean to go to a private house just outside London, to be treated by a doctor who specializes in disorders of the mind. If that doesn't work . . ." His tone turned bleak. "I will have to commit him to Bedlam."

The following morning Kell went to fetch his brother and escort him to his new dwelling in the country.

Hearing the plans for his incarceration, Sean grew white about the mouth and clenched his fists in cold fury, his expression clearly seething. But all he said was one word.

"Traitor."

Two nights later, however, Kell realized he had left the decision too late. He was at his club, playing host to a sizable crowd in the hazard room, when Timmons appeared and murmured in his ear.

"Mr. Lasseter . . . my lord . . . there is something you should see."

"My brother?" Kell asked, his heart giving a ragged skip. His first thought was that Sean had somehow fled the new doctor's care and come here to create worse trouble than his last drunken episode.

"No, not Mr. Sean."

The majordomo looked curiously pale, but Kell tamped down his alarm and followed the servant out to the corridor. Timmons held a handkerchief to his mouth and seemed to have trouble speaking.

"Well, what's amiss?" Kell demanded. "Spit it out, man."

"There is a man . . . in the rear alley. I fear . . . he is . . . dead."

"Dead?" Kell's stomach lurched. "Not my brother?"

"No . . . It appears to be your lady's groom, O'Malley."

Kell stopped breathing. Swiftly he made his way out to the alley behind the club. Several of his servants had gathered around a prone figure, and in the lantern light he could see the dead man was indeed Michael O'Malley. He was coatless, and a dark stain of blood covered his chest.

Kell knelt down. Sweet Christ, had Sean done this? He clenched his jaw in rigid denial, and yet who else would have committed such an atrocity—or even wished the groom ill? Sean had vowed revenge on the Irishman for striking him two nights ago and for being the cause of his impressment last summer.

There was no blood on the ground, Kell saw. The body evidently had been carried here to the alley. He bent forward, probing for wounds. He wouldn't put it past his brother to have deliberately picked a fight with Raven's groom—

Kell suddenly froze when his fingers found the tiny hole beneath the dead man's breast. O'Malley had been stabbed in the ribs with a blade of some kind. Very much like his uncle William's mortal wound.

Kell suddenly felt sick, dazed, while his throat burned.

"Sir?" Someone coughed deferentially.

He forced himself to look up while he tried to take in the enormity of what had happened.

"What shall we do with the body?"

He found it hard to speak. "Send . . . for the coffin-maker. . . . And notify the vicar. We will give him a decent burial." He would have to tell Raven—

Just them Emma Walsh appeared at his shoulder. "Kell," she began, but her quiet murmur turned to a gasp. "Oh, my God . . ."

Numbly Kell rose to his feet, pushing Emma back and shielding her shocked gaze from the dead man.

"Is that . . . ?"

"O'Malley," he returned grimly as he escorted her back inside. "What is it you wanted?"

She visibly shuddered and seemed to recollect what had brought her out to the alley. "Raven . . . she is here . . . and she seems distressed. I asked her to wait upstairs in your rooms."

"I'll go to her" was all he could manage to say.

Raven was pacing the floor of his study when he entered, her expression one of anxiety as she turned to him. "Kell, I am worried about O'Malley. He hasn't come home—in fact, I haven't seen him since our morning ride. This is so unlike him to disappear without a word."

"Raven . . . I'm sorry," he said, taking her by the shoulders.

"Sorry?"

"I have painful news. . . . O'Malley is dead."

She simply stared. "Not O'Malley. That's not possible. He cannot be *dead*."

"I just returned from examining his body. It was left in the alleyway behind the club."

She pressed a hand to her mouth, her eyes stark with anguish as she seemed to absorb what he'd said.

"*Noooo.*" Her cry of denial was a keening moan of pain. She took a step backward, her face twisted in torment.

Kell felt the same pain piercing him. Desperately wanting to comfort her, he tried to take her in his arms, but she wrenched herself away, refusing to be consoled. Instead she sank to the floor, her face buried in her hands. Her shoulders began to shake as muted sobs welled up in her and she gave vent to her grief.

She cried for a long while, while Kell watched helplessly until she began to quieten. Her body was still racked by convulsive shudders, but at least she didn't protest when he put a gentle hand on her shoulder. Immediately he picked her up and settled in a chair with Raven on his lap.

Even when he kissed her trembling mouth, though, she wouldn't look at him. Her cheeks were stained with tears, the dark crescent of her lashes squeezed tight against the horror. "I can't believe O'Malley is actually dead. He was like a father to me. He set me on my first horse and taught me to swim. . . . Oh, God, I can't bear it. . . ."

Fresh tears ran hotly down her cheeks as she hid her face in the curve of Kell's shoulder.

He encircled her with his arms, his voice soft against her hair. "I'm sorry," he breathed.

"It is my fault. He died protecting me."

Her grief made his eyes burn and his heart hurt. He held her more tightly, feeling an anguished tenderness for her—and a fierce, despairing anger at his brother.

It was a long moment before she drew a shuddering breath. "How . . . how was he killed?"

"A stab wound to the chest, I think."

He felt her stiffen before she drew back. "Emma said that was how your uncle was killed."

Kell flinched, hearing her put into words the dreaded conclusion he had already made. He'd assumed—prayed—all along that his uncle's killing was an accident, for Sean had claimed self-defense all those years ago. Now he wasn't so certain. The similarities between the two deaths were too close to be coincidence.

Raven was staring at him with dawning understanding, her tearstained cheeks pale. "You weren't the one who killed your uncle, were you? It was Sean."

Kell squeezed his eyes shut, unable to reply.

"You took the blame for him."

"I didn't want Sean to suffer further," he finally answered. "I was strong enough to withstand the rumors, the accusations, but Sean would have been broken."

"All this time . . . you have let people think you a murderer. But Sean is the *real* murderer."

"Raven—"

"No!" She pushed against Kell's chest, struggling to be free. When he released her, she leapt to her feet, looking heartbroken and outraged at the same time. "He will not get away with it! I swear I will hunt him down and see him punished!"

"I will see my brother punished," Kell said past the raw ache in his throat.

"How, Kell? How can I trust you to deal with him? You mean to protect him, just as you've always done."

Her chin rose as she fiercely dashed tears from her eyes. "Sean is a grown man, Kell! He is responsible for his own actions!"

Kell nodded, torn between love for his volatile younger brother and the necessity of facing the truth. It was hard to believe Sean could be so evil, that he had become a monster. Yet if he was indeed a killer, he was beyond saving.

And Raven was right. Sean couldn't be allowed to get away with murder.

Without answering, Kell rose to his feet and turned toward the door.

"Where are you going?" Raven demanded.

"To find Sean."

"I intend to go with you."

"No, I don't want you within a mile of him. I want you safe. I'll have Belker see you home." Kell's grim gaze met hers. "I promise you, I will deal with my brother."

Raven felt ravaged to the heart as she numbly climbed the front steps of Kell's house. When the butler admitted her with a polite greeting, she merely nodded. She would have to inform him and the other servants about O'Malley's death, but not now. She couldn't bring herself to talk about it.

She went up to her bedchamber to grieve alone. A fire burned low in the grate, and she sank into a chair, staring blindly at the flickering flames. She felt bruised, hollow inside.

God, if only this were a terrible nightmare. She would awaken at any moment. . . .

She felt tears slip down her cheeks as memories of O'Malley crowded into her mind. His strength and comfort had sustained her over the years, from the first moment her supposed father had repudiated her as a bastard. O'Malley had taught her about life, how to bear the pain and meet her fate with fortitude. . . .

The ashes of her grief filled her throat and choked her.

Bowing her head, she wept again wordlessly, her sobs muted gasps in the dark.

She had no notion of the passage of time, but it was probably no more than a handful of minutes later when she heard soft laughter behind her.

Raven froze, ice forming in her veins.

"I told you I would make you pay."

Her tears arrested, her heart pounding in her throat, she glanced over her shoulder. Sean stood at the dressing room door, a pistol trained on her chest.

"I wouldn't scream if I were you," he said mildly. "You wouldn't want to force me to use this on your other servants."

Her fingers dug into the arms of her chair. "What do you want?"

"Why, I mean to take you hostage, my dear. I have a carriage waiting on the next street." He gestured with the pistol toward the door. "We will leave by the front entrance, if you please."

She rose and turned to face her nemesis, casting him a glance full of scorn. "You expect me to meekly obey you?"

"Oh, I think you will. Otherwise I will kill anyone who interferes."

"You won't get away with this," Raven declared with scathing bravado. "Kell will stop you."

Sean's smile chilled her very blood. "Perhaps. I truly hope he tries. You see, I mean to make my dear brother pay as well, for choosing you over me."

Chapter
Twenty

She had never been so cold in her life, Raven thought as she sat huddled in the chair where Sean had kept her tied for the past hour. After driving through the night in a jolting, swaying coach, they'd arrived at a country estate that Sean said belonged to him. Immediately he had dismissed the caretakers with a brusque command and installed Raven in an unheated bedchamber, without giving her even her cloak for warmth.

At least he hadn't drugged her this time or rendered her unconscious, but her limbs were so numb, she could barely feel any sensation.

Sean had left her alone only once, to allow her to relieve herself, untying all but her hands and locking the door behind him. One look at the frozen landscape, however, made Raven reconsider attempting an escape, for snow was coming down in swirling gusts. Even if she somehow managed to elude Sean and flee the house, in these near-blizzard conditions she would likely freeze to death before she got half a mile.

And so she didn't fight him when Sean returned to retie her to the chair. And she kept her counsel as he stood watch at the window, her emotions swinging wildly between blazing fury and despair. When he deigned to give her an occasional glance, she tried not to meet his eyes, fearing that showing her outrage would only earn her more pain.

He would not balk at hurting her further, she had no doubt. Since their arrival, Sean had sunk into an icy calm devoid of any emotion whatever. His passionless detachment frightened her more than any ranting could have done. His eyes seemed soulless, almost dead.

She gave a start when he finally broke the silence. "Kell should not be too much longer," he murmured tonelessly, gazing out through the snow. "I left a trail even a blind man could follow."

It was the first time in nearly an hour he had spoken to her.

"What will you do when he arrives?" Raven ventured to ask.

He shot her a cool glance. "That is no concern of yours."

"You would not really harm him, would you? Your own brother?"

The sharp twist of his mouth sent a fresh chill through her. "How touching—you pretend to care for him. But I know your heart is made of ice."

"I do care what happens to him. He is my husband."

When Sean's eyes narrowed, she realized her mistake. Whatever her feelings for Kell, she shouldn't declare them for fear of provoking Sean further. "Kell doesn't care much for me, however," she murmured. "We have a marriage of convenience, nothing more."

"You lie." Crossing the room to her, he calmly struck

her across the face with his open palm, making her head snap back.

Raven stifled a cry of pain and clenched her teeth.

"Kell has been panting after you like a dog for a bitch. You seduced him, and he fell for it. He will pay for that."

His tone was so composed, he might have been remarking on the weather. Her stomach muscles knotted with dread.

She knew she shouldn't dare challenge Sean again, knew he would be impervious to pleas, but she couldn't help herself. "Please, Sean, whatever you are planning, Kell doesn't deserve to be hurt."

"He stole you from me."

Raven bit her tongue, recognizing that further argument was futile. Sean was so twisted by his tormented past, so filled with bitterness and hatred, that she truly questioned his sanity. Yet she couldn't allow Kell to walk blindly into a trap.

"What is it you want? Me? If so, then . . ." She swallowed hard. "You can have me."

His wintery smile lifted the hairs on the back of her neck. "Ah, but I no longer want you. Now be silent."

Sean turned back to the window. Another dozen minutes ticked by before he spoke again. "At last he comes."

His satisfied pronouncement filled Raven with alarm, and she flinched when Sean turned back to her.

With methodical efficiency, he released her from the chair but left her hands bound. She couldn't help but cry out when he jerked her savagely to her feet.

"Where . . . are you taking me?" Raven gasped as he ushered her forcefully to the door.

"You will see soon enough."

Kell cursed as he struggled through the drifts of snow in the rear of the Lasseter estate. He'd found the house empty but for four servants huddling in the kitchen. They'd been told to keep out of sight, but when asked, they pointed to the back exit, indicating the direction Sean had taken with his hostage.

Following the tracks, Kell bent against the razor-sharp wind, the capes of his greatcoat snapping. He could barely see in the swirling snow, yet he knew where Sean was headed. The gazebo had been chosen with a purpose, for that was where William's abuse had begun.

A sickening sense of inevitability buffeted Kell as he realized the past had come full circle.

In a few moments he could make out the delicate cupola roof and the lacy railings of the gazebo. The ornamental lake beside it was frozen over, while a stand of elms rose behind like ghostly sentinels, their bare limbs coated with ice crystals.

When he reached the gazebo, Kell felt the same ice freeze his veins. Two figures were seated on a bench, Sean holding a rapier at Raven's throat.

Kell's breathing ceased as he forced himself slowly to mount the snow-slicked steps. His heart pounded as if he'd run a great distance, while his gut churned with a tumult of emotions: fear for Raven. Hatred for the bastard who had destroyed his young brother's innocence. Anguish at what Sean would force him to do.

Sean meant to make him choose between the two of them, Kell knew. His brother and his wife. But he really had no choice.

Not wanting to incite his brother, Kell came to a halt and surveyed his wife. Her lips were blue and her body shook with cold, yet he couldn't tell if the expression in her eyes was pain or fear or both.

"Sean, let her go. Your quarrel is with me."

"Aye, it is with you, dear brother. You want to lock me away."

"You've hurt enough innocents. You can't be allowed to hurt anyone else."

"What of me? I was innocent when that bastard violated me."

Kell felt the familiar anguish rise up in him. "I know."

"You *know*?" The word was bitter. "You don't know a bloody thing, Kell. You can't understand what it was like to bear his touch, to have him pushing inside me. . . . He brought me here, did you know *that*? He would make me strip for him, and then he would mount me. . . . I puked at first. Once I cast up my guts all over him when he came in my mouth. He struck me so hard, he knocked me senseless. After that I learned to stomach his perversions. To conceal my shame. Even though I wanted to kill him."

Sean's mouth twisted in a sad smile. "I did kill him in the end. I made the bastard pay for what he did to me." His voice lowered, turning troubled. "I killed O'Malley, too, even though I didn't mean to. I couldn't stop myself."

A strangled sound of grief came from Raven's throat,

and Sean jerked her head back, pressing the blade harder against her skin.

Kell gritted his teeth till they ached. It was all he could do to refrain from leaping at his brother.

Sean's voice dropped even further, to a hoarse whisper. "I thought I wanted you to pay as well, Kell. You were my brother. You should have saved me from him. I hated you for that."

Kell felt the accusation like a knife thrust. Sean's resentment had festered all these years, and now, like some pestilent wound, was pouring forth. "Sean, you don't know how much I hated myself."

The younger man shook his head. "No, I was wrong. You could not have saved me. Not then," he whispered brokenly. "But you can now. You have to help me, Kell."

"Of course I will help you."

His green eyes turned desolate. "How? By having me thrown in prison?"

"I thought an asylum would be more humane."

Sean shook his head, his eyes bleak. "I cannot live the rest of my life locked away."

"I can't allow you to remain free to kill again."

"There is only one way to stop me, Kell. You know it." With his head Sean gestured toward the second rapier lying on the bench. "Do you recognize these? These are Uncle's dueling foils."

"You're asking me to duel with you? You have little skill with a rapier. I don't want to hurt you."

"You have no choice." Sean glanced down at his hostage. "If you don't want me to slit her throat, you will have to fight me, brother."

Kell hesitated, dread roiling inside him at what Sean was implying. But he couldn't allow Raven to be hurt any further. "Very well."

Sean bent down to retrieve the other foil, leaving the slightest opening for Kell to act.

Yet Raven moved before he could. Raising her bound hands, she struck Sean's shoulder, evidently hoping to throw him off balance. But all it did was earn her a vicious clout. Sean swung his arm and connected with her head, knocking her to the wooden floor.

Kell had started forward, filled with rage and fear, but he halted abruptly when he saw Sean holding the point of his foil at Raven's nape.

"Pick up your weapon," he ordered in a hoarse tone.

Kell's gaze riveted on his brother's blade, so perilously close to piercing Raven's flesh. "It doesn't have to be this way, Sean."

"You know it does. You have to end it." His mouth curved in a bleak smile. "You always tried to take care of me. Please . . . do it one last time. Pick up the rapier."

Grimly Kell complied, scooping up the foil. "*En garde*, then."

Sean raised his own weapon and moved forward.

From her painful position on the floor, Raven watched with her heart in her throat as the two brothers engaged in what could be mortal combat. From the first it was clear that Kell's skill was much greater than his brother's. Sean's movements were clumsy, slow, as if he were deliberately exposing his defenses. It was only moments before Kell caught his brother's blade and, with a powerful twist of his wrist, sent it flying across the gazebo.

The light in Sean's eyes was almost triumphant, Raven thought. He wanted to lose this fight, wanted to die, wanted Kell to kill him.

Just then Sean bent his head and lunged, charging at Kell like a maddened bull, clearly intending to impale himself on the sharp steel. Kell managed to jerk the point away at the last second, but Sean crashed into him, his momentum propelling Kell backward. They hit the wooden railing with a thud, and both of them tumbled over the edge, plummeting to the frozen ground below.

Raven gasped in alarm, realizing Sean could still win the battle. Struggling painfully to her feet, she stumbled to the rail. Even though it had been a short fall, both men seemed winded and dazed as they fought for possession of the rapier while rolling down the icy embankment toward the frozen lake, both grunting and gasping, their breaths puffs of steam in the frigid air.

Shaking with fear as well as cold, Raven strained futilely against her bonds. She wanted desperately to help Kell but had no idea how without proving a lethal distraction. She cried out when Sean clawed at his brother's face, nails raking blindly, but Kell twisted his head and eluded the vicious attack. Somehow he even managed to wrest the foil away, thank God.

Her gratitude came too soon. Sean swung a savage blow that connected with Kell's cheekbone. Then, rolling free, the younger man lunged to his feet and staggered across the snow-packed ice, heading toward the center of the small lake.

Kell went after him. He had nearly caught up to his brother when the ominous groan of cracking ice reached Raven's ears. Sean suddenly lurched forward as first one leg, then the other, broke through the frozen surface.

Raven clutched at the railing, her heart leaping in horror as he disappeared into the icy water.

"Sean!" Kell's cry was nearly whipped away by the gusting wind. Dropping to his knees, he crawled toward the jagged hole in the ice.

Sean's head appeared, his mouth wide with shock and gasping for air, his arms flailing. His fingers found purchase on the edge of the ice just as Kell stretched himself full length.

Raven's vision was hampered by the swirling snow, but she could see Kell straining to reach for his brother, urging Sean to take his proffered hand.

For a moment it looked as if he would succeed, but then Sean struck out fiercely, fighting the very man who was trying to save him.

"Sean!" Unwilling to give up, Kell tried again, clutching at his brother's shirt.

Resisting, Sean grabbed Kell's arm with both hands to fend him off. Raven drew a painful, gasping breath, knowing Sean could drag Kell under with him, drowning them both.

For the space of a dozen heartbeats, neither of them yielded. Raven bit her lip till it bled, but she could only watch in terror as the silent battle raged between the two brothers.

Kell's arm was submerged up to his shoulder, the

other braced against the ice when she saw Sean's mouth form the word, "Please . . ."

He was pleading for release, she realized.

His jaw clenched, Kell refused to let go, but then he gave a sudden jolt. The edge of the hole had broken off, upsetting his balance. With a jerk, Sean wrenched free. An instant later, he sank below the surface of the lethal water, vanishing from view.

Kell froze, staring in denial as Raven watched. When long moments passed with no sign of his brother, he squeezed his eyes shut in agony. The cry that tore from his throat was the keening of a wounded animal.

Raven gave a sob as well as another ominous crack sounded from the surface of the lake. The ice was fracturing beneath Kell's weight. Dear God, if he fell through, the frigid water would swallow him up the way it had his brother. . . .

Rasping Kell's name, she rushed across the gazebo and down the treacherous steps, nearly falling in her haste. Righting herself, she picked her way around structure, then slid down the embankment and started across the frozen lake.

"For God's sake, Raven, stay back! The surface could give way at any minute."

She halted in indecision. The ice might not bear their combined weight, and she could send them both plunging into the freezing depths. But if she did nothing, Kell stood little chance of survival.

From the corner of her eye, she glimpsed movement in the distance—the house servants, she realized. But they would never arrive in time to help. She had to try to save Kell on her own.

Kneeling on the surface the way Kell had done, she crawled forward, praying with every tentative inch that she wouldn't be too late, sobbing and cursing her bonds all the while.

"Dammit, Raven, you could die!"

She couldn't abandon Kell, though, even if it meant drowning with him. She loved him more than her own life.

His legs were closest to her, she saw through her blinding tears. She could see the soles of his boots a yard away.

"Kell . . . help me. . . ."

He uttered a grim curse, but stretched one leg out as far as he could. Her fingers were so raw and numb, she could barely grasp the toe of his boot, but somehow she managed to find purchase.

Not breathing, Raven pulled on his leg, trying to brace herself against the slick surface. It was nearly impossible; Kell barely budged an inch.

"Try again," he urged.

Stifling a sob, she pulled again, struggling with all her might. Her effort was more successful this time; he moved nearly half a foot.

With another desperate prayer, she threw every ounce of her strength into the task. Her progress seemed infinitely slow, but with her arms aching, her lungs straining, she managed inch by inch to draw Kell back from the treacherous edge and onto more solid ice.

An eternity later she felt grasping hands lifting them the final way to safety. The servants, Raven realized, exhaustion sapping the last of her will.

Kell had no more strength than she did. When he reached the bank, he collapsed to his knees, unable to go farther.

With a superhuman effort, Raven shrugged off the supporting hands and staggered to his side. Sinking in front of him, she clung to his neck as tightly as her bound hands would allow, the tears slipping down her face and turning to ice.

His arms came around her, and he held her without speaking, his face buried in her hair, his shoulders shaking.

He was weeping as well, she knew. Weeping for the brother he had been unable to save.

Chapter
Twenty-one

Raven paused at the library door, trying to summon the courage to enter. She'd seen nothing of Kell during the past two hours, and her disquiet only increased with each moment he avoided her.

He stood at the French windows now, his back to her, and stared out at the icy landscape. He'd changed his attire, and his impeccable chocolate coat and buff breeches gave no indication he had just fought a battle to the death.

Her own physical circumstances had improved as well. The servants had found her clothing that, while simple, was warm and dry. And her raw wrists had been bandaged. Yet no salve could ease the pain in her heart.

She felt drained, aching, filled with sorrow. Not for Sean, but for Kell. She found it hard to mourn Sean's death overmuch after his heinous acts. But she grieved for Kell.

He looked so remote, so unapproachable, so achingly alone.

As she watched him, Raven felt her eyes blur with tears. She had been so blind. She *loved* Kell.

It had stunned her to realize the truth. Shaken her to think he could have died without ever knowing how deeply she cared. Yet she couldn't tell him now. Kell wouldn't want to hear of her feelings, not when he was so devastated by his brother's death.

She might never be able to tell him and discover if he could possibly ever love her in return. Would Sean's death forever shadow their lives? His vengeful brother might have destroyed any hope of love between them.

As if sensing her presence, Kell glanced over his shoulder, surveying her bruised cheek, the abraded skin at her throat, her bandaged wrists. A shadow passed over his eyes. "Are you all right?"

"Yes," she lied, wanting to reassure him.

"I regret that I let him hurt you," he said, his voice low and raw.

I regret more that he hurt you, Raven thought. "Bruises heal, Kell. And you could not have known what he would do."

Kell locked his jaw, his expression one of sheer pain. "I promised to protect you. I promised to protect *him*."

She felt the despair in him, saw it in the bleakness of his eyes, before he turned back to the window.

Raven took a step toward him. She wanted desperately to hold him, to console him, but she wasn't sure where to begin.

"You tried your best, Kell," she said at last. "Sean didn't want to be saved. He . . . he wanted an end to his torment."

Kell made no response, but his silence was rife with anguish.

She moistened her dry lips. "You can't hold yourself

to blame. You couldn't be expected to sacrifice your life for your brother's."

"No?" he asked softly. He bowed his head.

Tears stinging her eyes, Raven looked down at her clasped hands. Her heart was breaking for him. His pain, his absolute aloneness, made her ache inside. His grief was a gaping, bleeding wound, one she couldn't heal.

Unbidden, she felt a fierce surge of renewed anger at William Lasseter. He had ravaged Kell's life almost as savagely as he had shattered Sean's.

Staunchly she swallowed the rawness in her throat and tried again. "Kell, there was nothing more you could have done."

"I could have done more to help him. I *should* have done more."

"He would not allow you to. Sean wanted to die, Kell. He gave you no choice."

"He did give me a choice." Kell's voice was no more than a whisper. "I chose you."

The edge of bitterness in his tone struck her like a blow. He blamed her for Sean's death? She couldn't refute the charge, certainly. Their marriage had indeed led to Sean's demise, at least indirectly. If she hadn't come between the two brothers, Sean would still be alive. If Kell had never wed her in the first place . . .

"Do you hate me?" she asked, the question dredged from her throat.

"No. Not you." His reply was so quiet, she wondered if she could believe him.

"I hate myself," he added. "I can't forgive myself."

"Kell . . ."

He held up a hand, as if he couldn't bear to listen to another word.

Kell was flaying himself with guilt, Raven knew. He wouldn't accept her comfort. She couldn't heal his hurt. Nor could she defend herself if he held her to blame for his brother's tragic end.

At least Kell wouldn't be charged with murder. There had been witnesses to Sean's death; a half a dozen servants could attest to the fight between the brothers. There was sure to be an investigation into Michael O'Malley's murder, though, and in all likelihood, Sean would be exposed as the groom's killer.

It was even possible the truth about their uncle's death would eventually come out. She doubted Kell would volunteer the information. He wouldn't reveal Sean's crimes to the world. He would continue letting everyone think him a murderer.

But now wasn't the time to argue with him over such remote possibilities.

His next words, however, filled her with dread. "I want you to go home, Raven. I will have my carriage return you to London."

Her hand stole to her stomach, pressing there, trying to quell the disquiet roiling inside her. "You won't come with me?"

"No. I can't."

"What will you do, then?"

"I need to find Sean's body . . . make arrangements for his burial. I suppose I will take him back to Ireland. Perhaps his soul can find peace there."

And will you *ever find peace?* Raven wanted to ask. "And after that . . . ?"

"I don't know."

Perhaps her dread was unfounded, she tried to tell herself. Possibly Kell only needed time to grieve for his brother. Time to deal with his own devils, his guilt and regret.

Or perhaps it was more ominous. He might be sending her away because he wanted nothing more to do with her. Despite his often brusque demeanor, Kell was a gallant man. He wouldn't tell her if he couldn't bear the sight of her.

Kell turned then and moved toward her. Raven held her breath, but he didn't pause. Without a word, without even a glance, he brushed past her and left the room.

She bent her head, trying not to cry. Perhaps Sean had won after all, even in death.

Raven shivered violently. She didn't think she would ever be warm again.

She returned to London alone, as Kell wished. The journey was almost as wretched as her last one, when she'd been at the mercy of a madman, but this time her misery was not physical. The pain and fear she'd experienced during the grueling hours of her abduction couldn't possibly compare to the torment in her heart now, for Raven couldn't shake the conviction that she had lost Kell.

When she arrived in London, it was to face a full-blown scandal. The murder of her groom, her own abduction, the death of her brother-in-law, her husband's apparent abandonment—none of that could be quietly swept under the carpet.

She had few allies to console her, either, for her closest friends were still away. Brynn had retired to the Wycliff family seat with Lucian for the final months of her confinement, although Lucian's work at the Foreign Office would require his frequent presence in London. Dare reportedly was following his rakish pursuits in the north.

Only Raven's aunt Catherine remained in town, and that outraged elderly lady washed her hands of her niece entirely in a scene that three months ago would have set Raven trembling with rage herself. Yet now she couldn't bring herself to care about her aunt's defection.

Emma called several times to offer sympathy and support, but the hostess had suddenly become remarkably busy due to the gaming hell's new notoriety. The Golden Fleece was now all the rage among the ton's fast set; everyone with any pretense to fashion wanted to be seen there.

Raven thought it best to avoid the gaming hell, for her presence would only stir the scandal further. Besides, the club would bring too many painful memories of Kell.

She'd been dismayed to realize that she loved him, that she had been blindly denying her feelings all this time. She had tried to keep him at a distance, to protect herself with indifference so she wouldn't be vulnerable to the terrible hurt love could offer. But she had failed miserably. And now, when she had finally understood her own heart, it might be too late.

She wanted desperately to believe that Kell had sent her away because he needed to be alone. That once he'd laid his brother's tormented soul to rest, his own could begin to heal. But when no word came from him, Raven began to realize she was willfully deceiving herself, that perhaps he truly couldn't forgive her for his brother's death.

At least she had another concern to distract her two days after her return, for her grandfather arrived in a show of support. The journey proved a severe strain on Lord Luttrell's health, as did his anxiety over her. Even though Raven baldly lied and assured him that she was perfectly fine, he continued to fret—voicing distress that she moped around the house all day yet understanding why she dared not show her face in public.

She couldn't bring herself to ride, either. O'Malley had always been her escort and protector on her early morning rides, and her one excursion to the park with a different groom made her grief all the more piercing. She made certain her horses were properly exercised, but other than periodically visiting O'Malley's grave, where he'd been buried in a quiet funeral service, she remained indoors.

A fortnight later Lord Luttrell was still fretting over her. He tried to persuade Raven to accompany him to East Sussex, but she wanted to remain in London in case Kell should return unexpectedly.

When her grandfather finally left, however, she was alone again. The days continued to crawl by and still she heard nothing from Kell. The house felt so empty without him. *She* felt so empty.

Her fantasy lover couldn't even comfort her, for she no longer wanted her pirate; she only wanted Kell.

The city began to thaw from the cruel winter, but

the chill in her soul wouldn't abate. She started a dozen letters to him, only to tear them all up. What could she possibly say?

Kell wouldn't want to hear of her love. He had wed her in the first place only to assuage his conscience, and to save his brother from her family's retribution. And now his brother was dead. His grief would undoubtedly overshadow any tender feelings he held for her.

Even if Kell eventually came to terms with his grief, even if he didn't hate her or blame her for her role in the tragedy, Sean's death might be too much for him to overcome, for he would forever associate his loss with her. She would always be a reminder of his guilt.

She wished Kell would write to her, wished he would give her some inkling of what he was thinking. She desperately wanted to end the dread and uncertainty gnawing at her. She didn't even know if he was all right, or if he had gone to Ireland as intended. He had shut her out of his life completely.

Spring had at last showed signs of emerging when Raven found the courage to ask Emma what she knew of Kell's plans.

Inviting the beautiful hostess to call on her, Raven forced herself to wait until tea had been served before blurting out the question that had been hounding her. "Have you by chance had any word from Kell?"

Emma lowered her gaze, looking almost embarrassed. "To be truthful, I have."

Raven felt a hollow ache in her chest. "Is he in Ireland?"

For a moment the hostess gave her a surprised look. "Yes, at his horse farm there. I thought you knew."

"No. He hasn't contacted me." She felt herself trembling and averted her gaze. "Do you know when he means to return to London?"

"Raven, I . . . I am not certain if he ever means to return. Kell has directed his solicitors to sell the club to me . . . or rather to Halford."

Raven stared, trying to absorb Emma's disturbing announcement. Kell didn't mean to return to London?

"The Duke of Halford?" she said finally.

Emma's mouth curved in a faint smile. "It does seem farfetched. But Halford is actually a very kind man," she said, echoing the same words Raven had once used to describe the duke. "He is purchasing the club for me."

Raven bit her lip to keep it from quivering.

"I am so sorry, Raven. I can only imagine that Kell wants to be rid of the Fleece because of the painful memories it holds for him."

"No, you shouldn't be sorry, Emma," she murmured. "You aren't to blame in the least if Kell . . ." She pressed her fingers to her eyes.

"Are you all right?"

Shaking herself, Raven raised her chin. "Yes, I'm splendid. Why don't you tell me about your plans for the club? You say Halford is funding its purchase? That must mean you and he are getting along famously."

Emma's smile was bashful this time, but she was clearly pleased with her relationship to the duke and by her prospects in the gaming world. Raven was happy for her, and yet she could scarcely keep her mind on the conversation, her heart was in such turmoil.

When Emma finally took her leave, Raven sat staring sightlessly at the floor. Kell didn't intend to return.

Had he even planned to tell her? If he cared for her at all, he would have disclosed something so crucial as his intentions to abandon his London life, not left it for her to discover secondhand. What more proof did she need that he didn't want her in his future?

She pressed a hand to her mouth to hold back a sob. He did blame her for what had happened to his brother after all. He clearly wanted nothing more to do with her. There was no hope for her.

Moments later, however, her emotions careened from despair to anger at her own stupidity. She'd done exactly what she vowed she would never do: follow in her mother's footsteps. She'd fallen hopelessly in love with a man whose heart she couldn't have—and brought herself more pain than she'd even thought possible.

Dashing away the burning tears, Raven leapt to her feet.

She would not be like her mother! She would not! Wasting her life, pining away for a man. She had to elude that terrible fate at all costs. She had to do something, *anything* to avert that future.

Feeling like a caged animal, she began to pace the room. She had to act. She couldn't remain here any longer, that much was becoming obvious. Everywhere she went, she was reminded of Kell. If she had any hope of forgetting him, of learning to live without him, she would have to break all ties with him. She would have to leave London.

But where in God's name could she go? Her grandfather would take her in, of course, but even at his country estate, she wouldn't be able to escape her memories of Kell—or her pain.

Perhaps she would do better to leave England altogether. Her life here was ruined anyway. She could go somewhere and start over. Somewhere warm, somewhere her heart would not be ravaged every moment of every day.

Somewhere without Kell.

Scalding tears filled her eyes again. Perhaps that would be best for Kell as well. If she left him, she would give him grounds to dissolve the marriage he had never wanted in the first place. He was wealthy enough to initiate the outrageously expensive proceedings for divorce. . . .

Her tears fell harder. She would no longer have claim to his name, then, or his title. And a divorced woman was even more scandalous than a bastard. But what difference did it make what the world thought of her if she couldn't have Kell?

Raven buried her face in her hands and wept.

Once she had resolved on a plan, Raven was almost desperate to implement it. She saw no reason to postpone her departure. And the sooner she left England, the sooner she could begin to forget Kell and get on with her life.

Her grandfather would not be happy with her decision, Raven knew. Yet she had already failed him by becoming embroiled in yet another scandal. She would simply have to make him understand that she couldn't bear to remain any longer.

Her destination would be the isle of Montserrat, where she had grown up. She would be most comfortable there, for she still had numerous friends and acquaintances in the British West Indies, and it would be warm there. She could purchase a small house overlooking the ocean and live quietly.

The largest barrier to her plan was that England was still engaged in a fierce conflict with America, which made sailing on the high seas perilous. When she made inquiries of the various commercial shipping companies about travel schedules, she was disheartened to learn there were no passenger ships scheduled to depart for the West Indies for several weeks.

Fortunately, Lucian returned to London just then. The earl owned a substantial merchant fleet, and when he realized she was completely serious about returning to the Caribbean, Lucian insisted on lending one of his armed ships for the journey.

With his guidance, Raven set her departure for the following week and then began putting her affairs in order, beginning with writing good-byes to her friends and relatives.

Her grandfather's reply came almost at once:

> *Your decision pains me greatly, my dearest girl, but I won't attempt to change your mind, for I know the difficulties you would face should you remain here as an outcast.*
>
> *I shall miss you more than I can say. Thank you for adding joy to my life these past months. For whatever it is worth, you have my blessing.*

She sent Dare's letter to his London home, asking that it be forwarded to him.

Her letter to Brynn was hand-delivered to the country by Lucian, and Brynn responded at once, saying that she would return to London to say farewell in person.

Raven called on her aunt, driven by common courtesy and the vague desire to make peace if she could. She expected to be refused, however, and was surprised when Lady Dalrymple actually received her.

"It is for the best," the elderly lady said, agreeing with Raven's decision to leave England. "You can no longer show your face in polite company, and you would only be miserable."

Raven bit back the retort on her lips—that her misery would have nothing to do with being repudiated by the elite society she'd always aspired to. That she realized how little their acceptance meant to her now. Instead she changed the subject, expressing concern over how her grandfather would deal with her absence.

Halford, much to her surprise, called on Raven when he heard the news. His manner toward her was far more congenial than in past interviews. He still hadn't completely forgiven her for jilting him, but Emma was providing him consolation.

"I can never wed her, given what I owe to my title, but she is a comfort to me," Halford said with unexpected cheerfulness. He regarded Raven with a wistful smile. "Strange how events have turned out."

"Yes, strange indeed," Raven murmured, preferring not to reflect on regrets or might-have-beens.

Her letter to Kell was the hardest to compose, and she saved it for last. In it, she expressed sorrow for his loss of his brother and regret for ever involving Kell in her life. And she clearly stated her wish for a divorce. She posted the letter two days before she was due to depart. By the time he received it in Ireland, Raven knew, she would have sailed.

Her final two days were spent packing and settling final details. Her maid, Nan, had chosen to accompany her to the Caribbean, so she would have companionship on the long voyage. Her biggest concern was for her horses, but Halford offered to take them into his most excellent stables so Raven could rest easy.

Otherwise she concentrated on keeping herself too busy to feel or dwell on the grief that was throbbing inside her like a wound.

It touched her that the Lasseter servants seemed as if they would genuinely miss her. And surprisingly, quite a number of her friends called on her to say farewell.

On Tuesday evening she dined with Brynn and Lucian at their London residence and returned to a quiet house. There was nothing more for her to do. The Wycliffs planned to see her off on her voyage tomorrow. Her trunks had already been conveyed to the docks, and she would board in the afternoon and sail with the evening tide.

She would have liked to say good-bye to Dare, but he was evidently still away from town, for she'd received no word from him.

She prepared for bed that night with an aching

heart. When she lay down to sleep, though, she forced herself to shut her eyes and ignore her tormenting thoughts of Kell.

On the morrow she would turn her back on England, where she had known such happiness and heartbreak. She would put the past behind her and embark on her new life. And she would do her damnedest to forget Kell Lasseter—if she only could.

He came to her that night, her fantasy lover. Naked, he stretched out beside her on the bed, his hand slowly sweeping her body, stroking, cupping her breast.

When she flinched at his touch, though, he rose above her, staring down with hot intensity. Questions filled his dark eyes, then pain as he realized the truth. He wasn't welcome.

She turned away without speaking.

"So this is good-bye?" he whispered, his voice hoarse. "You are sending me away?"

"I'm sorry."

His hand cradled her cheek, turning her face back to his. His fingertips brushed her lips with heartrending gentleness. "Your sorrow is not for me. You have no need of me any longer. You need him. You love him."

"Yes, heaven help me. I love him."

"But you cannot have him. Or his love."

"No." She lowered her head, meaning to bury her face against his hard chest, but gave a start as she met only empty air. He had faded away.

She squeezed her eyes shut. The longing inside her was like a knife blade, sharp, searing, unbearable. She could only hope that someday, in time, the pain would fade to a distant memory and become as illusionary as her imaginary lover.

Chapter
Twenty-two

"Are you certain this is what you really want?" Brynn asked as she said farewell to Raven at the dock.

Because of Brynn's advanced state of pregnancy, Lucian had not allowed his wife to board the ship, so the two women were saying their good-byes in the privacy of the Wycliff carriage.

No, I'm not certain, Raven wanted to answer. The closer she came to departing, the harder her stomach churned with misgivings. Was she making a mistake by leaving England?

"You don't think you should wait a while longer?" Brynn added quietly. "Wouldn't Kell wish to know of your plans?"

Raven shook her head. Her plans would matter little to him. There would be no point in delaying. She couldn't imagine that Kell would ever come to forgive her, that he could come to love her the way she did him. Nor could she bear to see the pain and accusation in his eyes. He blamed her for his brother's death, and that was just too enormous a barrier for love to overcome. And her leaving would make it easier for Kell to dissolve their marriage.

"It will be less painful this way for both of us," she said at last.

Brynn put her arms around Raven, hugging her close. "I shall miss you dreadfully."

"And I you," Raven replied, feeling the tears starting to come.

Determinedly she brushed them away and gathered her reticule. "You must promise to write me frequently, and to let me know at once when the baby is born, whether it is a son or a daughter."

With a serene smile, Brynn pressed her hand over her swelling abdomen. "It is a son; I have no doubt."

Forcibly swallowing a pang of envy for her friend's happiness, Raven stepped down from the carriage, where Lucian awaited her.

"Ready?" he asked, offering his arm.

"Yes," she lied.

He escorted her to the tall, three-masted schooner and assisted her on board. She had already toured the schooner under the captain's guidance, and Nan was below, unpacking their belongings in the two tiny cabins that would serve as their world for the six or more weeks of the ocean voyage.

Lucian turned her over to the captain, admonishing him to take good care of his precious cargo, then gave Raven a brotherly embrace.

She clung to Lucian a long moment, earning a searching look from his blue eyes when she stepped back. Thankfully he asked none of the probing questions his wife had asked, but merely kissed her cheek.

"Take care of yourself, sweetheart. And give my best

regards to Nick. You are likely to see him much sooner than I."

Raven managed a smile at the thought. Her half brother normally made his home in Virginia, but British troops had come threateningly close to his vicinity, so Nicholas had moved his family to one of the American islands of the Caribbean. She greatly looked forward to seeing him and his wife, Aurora, again. It was one of the few rays of light in her dark world these days.

"I will," she promised.

Going to the railing, she watched Lucian make his way off the ship and enter his waiting carriage. Her eyes blurred as she returned Brynn's farewell wave, while a piercing ache of emptiness filled her when her friends drove away. How desperately she would miss them! Yet there was little else about England she would miss, most certainly not the cold.

Shivering in the gusty March wind, Raven drew her cloak more tightly around her and stood overlooking the bustling docks, remembering her arrival last spring. She had come to England determined to fashion her future to her precise qualifications. But nothing had turned out the way she had planned. She had stupidly fallen in love against her will, with a man who couldn't love her in return.

And yet would she have changed her fate if she could? Would she rather have never met Kell? Never have known his touch? Never known the misery that was love? Despite the pain, she couldn't bring herself to wish she had never loved him.

"Lady Frayne," the captain said beside her, interrupting her disconsolate thoughts. "If you would be so kind as to go below now? We will get under way within the half hour."

Raven nodded and complied, not wanting to be underfoot of the crew, who were busy unfurling sails and untying lines.

She went belowdecks to her small cabin, and was grateful to find it warmed by a brazier. She took off her gloves and cloak and put them away, then had to brace herself against the shift and sway of the ship as it prepared to sail.

Fighting a surge of despair, Raven fetched the jeweled journal that had belonged to her mother and sat down on the bunk to read. Her gaze fell to a page well-worn from her mother's countless readings.

Love is both ecstasy and torment. Love fills me with a wild joy and an aching dread. . . .

Abruptly Raven shut the journal, unable to bear any more. For her, love was more torment than ecstasy.

She lay down on the bunk, curling her knees into her chest. An ache shuddered deep inside her. She understood love now. She understood so much better what her mother had faced. So much better what she truly wanted.

She had come to England to fulfill her mother's dream, but she realized now that she couldn't live someone else's dream. She couldn't live her life for anyone but herself. Her mother's dream wasn't hers.

Yet achieving her own goal of gaining a title had not provided her any more real fulfillment. She had been a fool to believe a title so important.

She'd thought it would take away the hurt and shame of her being a bastard, that it would make her good enough to join the society that had been denied her mother. In some ways, her whole life had been about proving that she was good enough. But she could no longer be ashamed of what she was: a child of love. Now that she truly knew what love was, she could only think of herself as blessed.

She could no longer deny a stronger yearning, either. She would have wanted Kell's child. But now there was no possibility of that.

Raven shut her eyes, feeling the tears start to fall. When, a moment later, she broke into sobs, she buried her face in the pillow to muffle the sound. She hadn't allowed herself to cry in so long. She hated watering pots. Her mother had spent so many nights sobbing into her pillow. . . .

The image of her mother crying over her lost love suddenly came to her, and Raven drew a sharp breath. Oh, God. Had she become exactly like her mother?

Brutally she bit back her tears. She *was* different from her mother. She wasn't a helpless victim, letting life act on her rather than meeting its challenges with defiance.

Yet what was she was doing by running away? Wasn't she acting the coward?

Raven swallowed hard, trying to staunch the flow of tears. O'Malley would have been ashamed of her for surrendering without a fight—and she was suddenly ashamed of herself. She couldn't deny the savage heartache that came with losing Kell, but she *could* choose how to deal with it.

Running away was not the answer.

It wasn't too late to change her mind about leaving,

either. And if she stayed? She could go in search of Kell. She could at least tell him she loved him.

It would be craven to slink away before she knew for certain what he truly felt for her. She could demand he tell her unequivocally, to her face, that he couldn't forgive her, that he would never come to love her, that he wanted her out of his life.

And if he said all those things? Fear curled in Raven's stomach at the possibility.

Then she would simply have to make him change his mind. She would have to fight to win his love. But first she would have to find him. She would tell the captain she couldn't sail—

Just then she felt a weight settle beside her.

Raven froze, certain she was imagining the hard arms that lifted her up and gathered her close against a warm male chest, the fervent lips that brushed her temple. . . .

"Raven . . . God, please, love . . . don't cry."

Kell. Her tears arresting completely, she stared up at him, searching the chiseled planes of his beloved face. Dear heaven, was her imagination playing dreadful tricks on her? Was he a fantasy?

Scarcely daring to breathe, she reached up to touch his scarred cheek, feeling the cruel ridge, the warm texture of his skin. He was truly real.

A startling joy spread through her, succeeded instantly by a sinking despair as she remembered their circumstances.

"What are you doing here?"

His mouth twisted in the semblance of a smile. "At the moment I am embracing you."

"No, I mean . . . why are you here?"

The intensity of his dark eyes never wavered. "Because I received word that my beautiful wife intended to desert me, and I desperately hoped to stop her."

She sat up on the narrow bunk, dashing absently at her tears.

Kell leaned back against the bulkhead, surveying her. "I was in Ireland, making plans to return to London, when Dare came to fetch me."

Her eyes widened. "Dare went all the way to Ireland to find you?"

"Yes . . . and barely in time, it seems. I rode like a madman to get here before you sailed."

For the first time she noticed Kell's mud-spattered clothing, the dark stubble on his chin, his bleary eyes.

A shadow touched his face. "I feared I might be too late. But if so, I would have followed you."

Raven squeezed her eyes shut, not knowing how to interpret his pronouncement. "I thought you hated me for making you lose your brother."

"Oh, God, I could never, ever hate you, Raven. Come here."

Reaching for her, Kell again drew her against his chest and rested his chin on the top of her head. "I needed to sort some things out in my mind. To try to come to terms with Sean's death."

Raven took a deep breath, afraid to hope. "And did you?"

Kell sighed. "As much as possible. Sean was a tormented soul, I know, but it tormented me that I couldn't help him. I see now that I was trying to punish myself for being unable to save him."

She was silent a moment, listening to the solid beat of his heart. Could she dare believe that Kell had come to terms with his grief and guilt? That he had been able to give up his burden of self-blame?

Raven could feel her own heart thudding as she searched for the right words. "Emma says that you have a fierce need to rescue anyone in distress, but I don't think you could have done anything to save Sean."

"I realize that now. If I had acted sooner, perhaps . . . But Sean was to blame for his own destructive actions." Kell tilted her face up to his, gazing deeply into her eyes. "I'm sorry for everything he did to you, Raven. I'm so sorry about O'Malley. . . ."

Raven felt an agonizing twist of pain at the remembrance. Her sorrow at O'Malley's death would always be with her, but she knew her friend wouldn't want her to spend her life grieving for him.

"I will never forget him," she said softly, her hand rising to her breast. "I will always keep his memory here, in my heart."

Kell covered her hand with his own, his expression as grave as she had ever seen it. "Do you think you could find a place in your heart for me as well, Raven? Please, tell me I'm not too late."

A thrill of hope ran through her. Hope and longing and joy. "No." Her throat constricting with relief, she managed a husky whisper. "You aren't too late."

His long lashes hooded his dark gaze. "And yet you planned to leave me. You intended to put an ocean's distance between us."

She refused to look away. "Because I couldn't bear to stay, believing you hated me. I thought my going would make it easier for you to seek a divorce."

"Is that what you want? A divorce?"

"No," she said emphatically. "Not at all. I only thought you would be happier without me as your wife."

His fingers clenched over hers. "I would sooner cut out my heart than lose you, Raven. I don't think I could bear to live without you. Not when I love you so much."

Her breath caught in her throat. "What did you say?"

"I said I love you."

Her gaze riveted on him. "You truly mean it?"

"Truly. I've loved you for a very long time." Kell cradled her face in his hands. "You made me love you, vixen. You turned my heart upside down and brought light into my life. How could I not love you?"

Elation swept through her, but she remained speechless.

"I should have told you before now," Kell murmured, gently exploring her face with his fingers, as a blind man might. "I didn't dare admit my feelings for fear of frightening you off. You'd told me numerous times you would never let yourself love anyone, and I couldn't see how to overcome your resistance. You married me only to escape the scandal. And I let Sean hurt you yet again. You lost O'Malley because of him. I didn't think you could forgive me for that, or that I deserved forgiveness."

"Kell, there is nothing to forgive. You couldn't be your brother's keeper."

"I know that now. Sean caused so much pain," he said quietly. "But in a way, I am grateful to him. He gave me you. If not for him, we never would have met, let alone married." Kell hesitated, his dark gaze holding her captive, his voice dropping to a hushed but fervent prayer. "When I learned you were leaving, I had to take the risk. I want ours to be a real marriage, Raven. I want you to be my wife in truth. I want to be your husband, your lover, the father of your children. Please say you will give me another chance."

The hunger in his eyes was soul-deep and made her yearn to reassure him. "Yes, Kell. Oh, yes."

His face eased, as if she had given him a reprieve from death. "I only wish . . . I hope to God that someday you can come to love me in return. I know how much you fear it—"

Raven reached up to touch his sensual lips, silencing him. "I already do love you, Kell. With all my heart."

Fire kindled in his eyes. He made a raw sound in his throat as he bent his head to kiss her. When his mouth covered hers in a wordless murmur of yearning, need, and hope, Raven clung to him, returning his kiss with the same fervor.

They were both breathing rapidly when he finally broke off. But he didn't release her. Instead he held her closer.

"God, how I have missed you," he whispered against her hair.

Raven sighed, pressing her face into his shoulder. "I never really expected to see you again. I didn't think you ever meant to return. Emma said you intended to relinquish the club to her."

"No, I was planning to come to London, even before Dare arrived. I hoped I could convince you to come away with me."

"Away?" His comment puzzled her. "Where would you want to go?"

"Somewhere—anywhere—that doesn't hold memories of my brother. In fact, the West Indies sounds like an ideal place. Would you mind very much if I accompanied you?"

She felt her heart fill with gladness. "I would like that above anything."

"You won't mind leaving England?"

"No. I don't want to remain here any longer."

"But what of your dream? I thought claiming your rightful place in society was crucial to you."

"Not any longer. I only just lately realized how little it all meant to me." She lifted her face to his. "I've come to understand so many truths these past few months, Kell. I thought fulfilling my mother's dream for me would bring me happiness, that gaining a title was what I wanted. But having your love is all that really matters to me. I would gladly be plain Mrs. Lasseter, if you will let me."

The fire burned hotter, but he raised an eyebrow. "And what of your fantasy lover?"

With her fingertips, she brushed the rough stubble shadowing Kell's jaw. He looked very much like the dangerous rebel he had once been; the lover of her dreams. "I haven't wanted that fantasy for a long time. All I want is you."

Kell pressed her palm to his cheek. "So then, we're agreed? We will start our marriage over in Montserrat. We will put the past behind us and begin anew."

"Yes, we're agreed."

His smile was blinding. He gave her a lingering kiss filled with promise and anticipation of the future to come. When he drew back, his eyes were dark with desire.

She shook her head. "I still think I might be imagining this. Are you sure you truly love me?"

"More sure than of anything in my entire life." His mouth curved in a tender smile. "I think I've loved you from the moment you first shot me."

Flushing, Raven shut her eyes. "Please, don't remind me."

Laughing again, Kell tightened his arms around her, reveling in the intense pleasure of holding her. He loved her more than his next breath. But he would have to prove it to her. To make her believe. He would have time to show her during the long voyage, though.

Tenderly he kissed the top of her head. "I know I've given you little reason to trust in my love before this, but I swear I will make it up to you."

"Will you tell me again?"

"I love you, my darling vixen. So much my heart hurts."

She smiled against his shoulder, shaken by the enormity of the emotion that surged through her. "I feel the same way."

"Then tell me." He tilted her face up to his. "I need to hear you say it."

"I love you, Kell." She declared it with abandon and joy as she twined her arms about his neck. "I love you, I love you, I love you," Raven murmured before she gave herself up to his passionate kiss.

Epilogue

Montserrat, British West Indies, July 1814

Raven caught her breath as Kell rose from the foaming surf, his magnificent nude body silhouetted against the aquamarine sea. He was so beautiful, he made her ache.

His gaze riveted on her, pinning her where she lay on the beach beneath a palm, and Raven smiled in secret joy. Her pirate lover had become Kell in the flesh; he had risen from the sea to claim her woman's heart, just as in her fantasies.

As she met his intense, soul-dark eyes, she felt her love swell for him until it was something painful. She wanted him as she wanted sunlight and air.

How perilously close she had come to missing his love! She had been so afraid of losing herself as her mother had, of being overwhelmed by the mind-numbing power of passion. But she had been wrong to fear it. Love was a vital part of life; passion was a joy. If anything, that was the primary lesson of the journal.

It was more than worth the risk of pain to find the kind of soul-shattering union she had found with Kell.

Without risk, she never would have known the ecstasy of true love. Indeed, the pain and sorrow in their past gave her present feelings for Kell even more depth and intensity.

And the things that had once seemed so important to her—wealth, possessions, titles, position—all of that counted for little if you were lonely, if you were not loved.

Kell had shown her that. She had tried to mold herself into what society expected of her, into something she was not, but he had liberated her from the false notions and oppressive strictures that had governed her life.

His passion had freed her imprisoned, lonely heart, and she could not have loved him more.

Raven watched with eager anticipation as he strode through the silver foam and across the crystalline sand to where she awaited. For a moment, he stood above her, vibrant, magnetic, intense, his hair very black against the golden light, his gaze heated, his engorged male flesh clearly proclaiming his desire. She had only to look at his virile, aroused body and she grew wet, her nipples tightening to aching peaks.

Kell understood exactly the effect he had on her, she knew. Desire crackled in the dark depths of his eyes as he knelt beside her on the blanket.

They often came here, their own private cove below their new home, to dive in the lagoon, search for sunken ships, or comb the beaches, hunting for buried pirate treasure.

"Did you have any luck?" she asked as he stretched his hard length against her.

"I have all the luck I need right here," he murmured, his voice husky. "You're the treasure I'd like to bury myself in."

His wet, sleekly muscled body was cool against her overheated skin, but his mouth was hot and moist as he bent to suckle her bare breast.

A whimper of pleasure sounded from deep in Raven's throat. Her skin felt acutely sensitive wherever he touched, and he touched her everywhere, his caresses dangerously, wildly sensual as they roamed over her body.

And then his mouth moved to that throbbing, most feminine part of her. Gasping, she arched against him and clutched at his hair. His lips felt hotter than the sun, the blistering heat searing her flesh. And his tongue . . . She felt it stroking, circling, sending ripples of pleasure through her aching flesh.

When she would have pulled him away, he caught her hands and held them at her sides. She gave a keening moan when his tongue stabbed deep into her, her hips writhing.

She withstood his primitive assault until she could bear no more. "Kell . . . Oh, God . . . please . . ."

He looked up, his eyes smoldering with barely leashed passion. His smile was knowing as he covered her body with his own. Parting her thighs wide, he slowly impaled her with his pulsing masculine flesh.

She was so aroused when he came into her that she nearly climaxed at once. With a sob, Raven rocked upward to receive him, needing him to fill her. His intense gaze burning into hers, he withdrew his slick shaft and sank forcefully into her again, thrusting completely home.

Raven nearly screamed with pleasure.

Desperate now, she wrapped her legs around his hips to hold him more tightly, meeting his powerful surges, her hunger matching his own as his mouth came down hard upon hers.

His kiss was wild and deep, his fierce intimacy driving her higher and higher toward the shattering peak.

Breathing in sobs of frantic need, Raven cleaved to him, their thundering heartbeats melding as their spirits soared. Kell not only took her, he claimed her, possessed her, enveloped her. The essence of him was fire, an irresistible fire that consumed her.

They came together, fused by the incredible heat, the delicious rapture. As their last shudders faded, Kell collapsed upon her, his gasping breath mingling with hers, their fierce hunger momentarily sated.

In the afterglow, a warm sea breeze blew across their heated bodies. Raven sighed in repletion as Kell gathered her in his arms. There had been a beautiful, animal passion to their coupling, yet it was the love between them that gave their joining such shattering bliss.

Her heart aching with love and tenderness, she reached up to cradle Kell's scarred cheek in her palm. She belonged to this man. She needed him as she needed her next heartbeat.

Long moments later, Raven found her thoughts stirring, drifting back over the months since their arrival.

The island of Montserrat had proven a good choice for them to settle. With such a large Irish population

here, Kell was welcomed rather than shunned for what
the English considered his inferior blood. And while
rumors of the scandals had followed them, the gentry
here was far more accepting than England's upper crust.
The title helped, of course. Baron and Baroness Frayne
were invited everywhere, and their invitations eagerly
sought in return.

They had bought a large house with a magnificent
view of the Caribbean, and it had begun to feel like
home. And Kell had filled the stables so that she could
ride to her heart's content.

Kell had not been able to forget his brother or the
role he'd played in Sean's death, but he was learning to
forgive himself. As for Michael O'Malley, Raven missed
him dreadfully. But they had erected a small memorial
for the Irishman on the grounds, and Raven took flowers there often.

She missed her other friends as well but was cheered
by the letters she'd begun to receive from both Brynn
and Emma and from her grandfather. Dare, they hadn't
heard from at all, possibly because he was too busy.

Raven had been astonished when Kell told her how
Dare had been occupying his time: he was hunting for
a traitor, a treacherous Englishman known as Caliban.
It was hard for her to imagine the charming, thoroughly wicked rake known as the Prince of Pleasure
immersing himself in espionage. But Dare reportedly
had become involved in the search for Caliban at Lucian's request. He'd interrupted his search to fetch Kell
in Ireland, and she could only be grateful to him for
helping Kell reach her in time for them to sail together.

The ocean voyage had been magical. They'd spent

the long hours not only making love and indulging in passionate delights but truly coming to know each other: their secrets, their hopes, their fears, their deepest emotions. Their love had seemed to grow each day.

Raven didn't think her cup of happiness could be much fuller.

She was not so certain about Kell, however. He loved her deeply, she had no doubt, but she worried that even love might not be enough to keep him content over the years. Already he seemed to be growing restless with a gentleman's life of leisure.

He needed something more, she knew. Just as Dare's new assignment had reportedly given him a purpose.

"Kell, I've been thinking . . ." she said finally.

"Mmmm?" The quiet murmur suggested he was nearly asleep.

"What would you say if I suggested you start a foundling home?"

Kell opened his eyes, suddenly awake. "For orphans?"

"Yes. There are numerous children in the West Indies who have lost their families. It's positively criminal the way they must forage for survival on the docks. Some are even forced into labor on board merchant ships."

Intrigued, he eased away from Raven's naked body and raised himself up on one elbow to stare down at her. "Do you mean start a home here on Montserrat?"

"Possibly, although one of the larger islands might be better, since there it would be easier to hire teachers and staff. . . . Antigua, perhaps."

He contemplated her for several moments, noting

how serious her blue eyes were. "You seem to have given this a good deal of consideration already."

"Well, I admit I'm concerned about you. Establishing a foundling home would give you an occupation. Without your gaming club to claim your time, you have often been at loose ends since coming here."

Kell couldn't help smiling at her. "Are you trying to be rid of me, my love?"

"No, not at all. I simply think you would be happier with a challenge to give you purpose. Rescuing creatures in distress is your dearest challenge. And you could do a great deal of good at the same time."

He regarded her in silent awe, wondering what he had done to deserve her. Perhaps it was indeed fate that she had wound up in his bed as a result of his brother's destructive machinations.

He gazed down at her, admiring her vivid beauty. A light breeze teased the ebony tresses spilling around her face in a glorious tangle.

"I would help you, of course," Raven added when he remained silent. "I don't know much about raising children, but I know how to manage a household. And it would be excellent practice for when we have our own children."

The thought warmed him. Not simply the prospect of having children with Raven, but that Raven had changed her mind so profoundly. She was adamant that no child of hers would endure the bitter experience she had suffered at the hands of her stepfather. It gladdened Kell that she wanted him as the father of her children, that she trusted him enough.

It amazed him that she had truly come to love him.

With tender solemnity, he drank in the sight of her, his eyes sweeping every tempting curve of her body. He had vowed to keep her heart safe always, and he renewed his vow silently as he bent to nuzzle her neck.

Raven was still trying to speak, however. "We could begin with boys at first, and then if that is successful, we could add a wing for girls. . . . We could even name the home after Sean, if you like—"

He made a sound of pleasure as he savored the salty taste of her ivory skin.

"Kell, are you listening to me?"

"Yes, vixen, I am listening avidly."

"So what do you think?"

"I think you are perfectly amazing."

"Kell, I am serious!"

"So am I, my darling. So am I." He cradled her face in his hands. "Have I told you lately how very much I love you?"

"Not in several hours."

"Well, then, allow me to remedy my lapse." His mouth found the rosy peak of her right breast.

"Kell, I think we should discuss our future—" She drew a sharp breath as his tongue laved her nipple.

"There will be time enough to discuss our future," he whispered huskily against her flesh. "Just now, however, I want to make love to my beautiful wife, so I'll thank you to stop arguing."

"I, argue?" Raven retorted with a laugh that became a sigh of rapture as she surrendered to her demanding husband's caresses.

Read on for a sneak peek at

Pleasure

the next breathtaking historical romance from
Nicole Jordan

Coming Spring 2003

London, March 1814

The cloying scents of orange peels and tallow from the footlights and torcheres seemed almost overpowering tonight, yet Julienne knew the normal stage accoutrements were not to blame for her feeling of faintness. An entirely different cause had set her senses spinning.

He was in the audience, watching her performance.

She found her knees shaking. Even the ogling bucks in the pit couldn't distract her from his relentless regard. He sat in one of the luxury boxes, his bright hair shimmering in the glow of theater's massive chandelier.

Dare North. The legendary lover who had stolen her heart and left her life reeling in the aftermath.

Under his intent scrutiny, Julienne had executed her leading role in the John Webster tragedy in a daze, barely able to remember her lines. Once she had even missed her cue, which had earned her a disapproving scowl from the theater's august manager, Richard Sheridan.

"I will *not* think of him," Julienne vowed futilely for

the hundredth time as she waited in the wings for her final entrance.

The Theatre Royal at Drury Lane was one of two premiere theaters in London, and tonight's house was completely full. Filled to overflowing, in fact, a distinction normally reserved for London's reigning thespian, the remarkable Edmund Kean. Yet Kean had reportedly "taken ill," a public fiction which concealed the truth that he was still recovering from a fierce bout of drunken brawling.

Julienne had been given top billing this evening—a splendid coup for a hitherto unknown actress from the provinces. She could not afford to squander this opportunity, or have her wits battered by memories she'd fought so hard to vanquish.

It had taken years to cleanse the ache for Dare from her soul, to conquer her yearning for him. She'd risked coming to London, knowing of his presence here, yet hoping to avoid him.

A foolish notion, she realized now. The Marquess of Wolverton—his present illustrious title—was one of the chief leaders of the Beau Monde, despite his scandalous reputation, or perhaps even because of it. He moved in London's most elite circles, as well as more disreputable ones. She could no more have avoided him than she could quell the painful memories that seeing him resurrected.

Another foolish notion, believing she could forget someone so unforgettable, or a passion so wondrous. She had loved Dare with a reckless hunger she'd never felt with any other man, before or since. But her love had proved her downfall.

Her eyes blurred as she remembered the last time she'd seen Dare. In a fleeting moment his regard had transformed from shock to desolation, from disillusionment to chilled contempt.

She had never had the chance to explain, to plead. Instead, he immediately had ended their betrothal with a highly public denunciation and walked out of her life. Leaving her devastated. Alone. Facing disaster.

A low hiss from the manager made Julienne realize she had missed another cue. Steeling herself, she swept out onto the stage to enact the final gory scenes of *The White Devil*.

It was a coveted role for any actress, playing a scheming Venetian courtesan, and she managed to make it through the dark tale of murder and vengeance with no more serious lapses. But she was grateful when her character's demise came at the end and the company could finally take their bows to shouts and whistles and sincere applause.

That the majority of the accolades were showered upon her surprised Julienne, considering her wretched performance. Plastering an alluring smile on her lips, however, she gracefully accepted the acclaim, executing a deep curtsey for the cheering crowd in the galleries, then the wilder throng in the pit, and finally the nobles and gentry in the boxes.

She was just rising when she made the mistake of glancing at the particular nobleman she'd tried so desperately all evening to ignore. Dare had moved to the front of his box to stand at the railing.

Julienne froze, caught in the hypnotizing power of his gaze; even at this distance, she could feel its searing impact. Her mouth parted in a sharp inhalation, while his curved in a faint smile, slow and lazy and provocatively rakish.

She saw his sensual lips move then, but with the rush of blood in her head making her senses swim, it took her a moment to realize he had spoken to her.

Without volition, she raised a hand, absently signalling for quiet. Slowly a hush went over the crowd, while countless heads swivelled in the direction of her fixed gaze.

Dare called her name again, this time loudly enough to be heard throughout the theater.

"Mademoiselle Laurent," he drawled, conversing as if they were completely alone. "Allow me to commend you on a most excellent performance."

Uncertain of what he planned, Julienne felt an unmistakable ripple of tension course through her, drawing her nerves taut.

"Th-Thank you, my lord," she replied, her voice unsteady.

"Is it true?" he asked.

"Is what true?"

Casually he lifted a hip onto the railing and lounged there, surveying her indolently. "That you intend to make your choice of protectors at the end of the Season?"

Bewildered, Julienne thought back frantically to the declaration she'd made last week, half in jest. She had been in the green room after a performance, surrounded by eager swains, all vying for her attention and urging her to accept their unwanted invitations. When one persistent coxcomb crudely pronounced his determination to have her in keeping, she hid her dismay and feigned a laugh, protesting that she couldn't possibly decide from among such delightful gentlemen just yet.

Her indecision was purely a defensive strategy. She had no intention of accepting any man's protection, but neither could she risk spurning her devotees, or alienating any of these wealthy theater patrons. She would have to tread a careful line, holding her courtiers enthralled while holding them off, maintaining their admiration without committing herself.

When pressed, she pledged to make her choice at the end of her acting engagement. Her unattainability had an added benefit, she shortly discovered. Being fought over by rich, titled admirers actually increased her value to the theater because it brought in more business.

That Lord Wolverton had learned of the episode, however, was a testament to the efficiency of London gossips, Julienne surmised.

Trying to regain her splintered composure, she uttered a polite response. "I fail to see how my intentions would concern you, my lord."

"I should like to declare myself as a candidate in the competition."

An audible ripple of surprise and interest emanated from the crowd.

To her shock then, Dare hoisted himself up to stand on the balcony railing. Julienne wasn't certain if the gasps she heard came from the audience or from her own throat. Both, she suspected. In all her days in the theater, she had never been more at a loss; her mind went blank, and she felt the particular panic that came from forgetting a crucial line.

Except that this time there were no scripted lines to learn. This was no play at all.

The crowd, however, was behaving as though it was merely a continuation of the earlier performance, maintaining an expectant hush. Julienne held her own silence, unable to guess what machinations Dare had planned.

Looking totally at ease in his precarious position, he leaned a shoulder against the column supporting one side of the box.

"I have made a wager regarding your choice, mademoiselle," he announced, enunciating clearly. "I've wagered that you will choose me."

The rowdy throng in the pit reacted with a chorus of titters and guffaws, while the rest waited with bated breath for her response.

"Have you indeed?" Julienne managed, stalling for time. "You have a very high opinion of yourself, it seems."

"An opinion that is warranted." His gaze slewed over the crowd. "Does anyone here doubt I can win the heart of this lovely Jewel?"

There were whoops and shouts from the riffraff in the pit and a spurt of clapping from the upper tiers. Dare sketched a debonair bow, acknowledging their approbation.

It was a dangerous maneuver, Julienne thought with alarm. If he were to fall from that height, he could severely injure himself. But then he had always been the most reckless man of her acquaintance. Reckless, daring, outrageous. He appeared totally unconcerned that he was making a spectacle of them both in front a multitude of gawking spectators.

And the audience obviously relished his bold tactics, responding with titillation and delight.

Gritting her teeth, Julienne moved along the stage, closer to his box, while trying to recruit her wits. He had cleverly trapped her with his public declaration. She had no intention of taking a lover, most certainly not the notorious rake who had shredded her heart, but she didn't dare refuse him outright, not without jeopardizing all she had worked for. Her livelihood depended on pleasing her audience.

Fortunately, she had performed for years, and she had a great deal of practice dealing with rakes and obstinate pursuers.

Making a belated recovery, Julienne placed her hands on her hips and eyed Dare up and down, looking him over critically as she might a horse at Tattersalls.

"Perhaps your inflated opinion is warranted after all," she agreed thoughtfully. "Your reputation certainly precedes you. The notorious Lord Wolverton—a thoroughly wicked rake, famed for his charm and address and his fondness for debauchery. The Prince of Pleasure, is that not the name I heard? Also known as the scourge of feminine hearts."

"Yet you have fast become the scourge of male hearts, *ma belle*."

"That was not my intention," she said, offering an alluring smile that contradicted her words. "But since you remark on it . . . I might venture to make a wager of my own," she declared, playing to the crowd. "I stand accused of willfully breaking gentlemen's hearts.

Well, in this instance, I shall endeavor to live up to the accusation. I wager that I can bring the Prince of Pleasure to his knees."

The roar of approval was almost deafening, punctuated by the thunder of stomping feet and howls of glee. It was several minutes before the theater quieted enough to allow the spectacle to continue.

Dare's own smile was devilish. "So you think you can break my heart?"

"I am certain of it."

"You are welcome to try." He gave another bow, holding her gaze riveted. "I look forward to the first engagement, my beautiful Jewel."